Second Time Around

Nate bragged on the ease of his conquests, unaware the roommate was eavesdropping.

Mandy Kearney, remembered Nathan Peters all too well. He was hot with a lean, muscular, farm boy physique, tawny brown hair wavy enough for a tousled look, like he just woke up, an aquiline nose above sculpted lips, and best of all, deep, sultry brown eyes that held the promise of paradise. Paradise with the hiss of a snake. Mandy had been down that road before and had no intention of traveling that path again.

Nate thought about the roommate, Mandy Kearney, a firebrand, exactly what he liked in a woman. She possessed a classic Irish beauty, flaming red hair, creamy white skin, freckles sprinkled across her pert nose like cinnamon on meringue, cheekbones with a natural blush, as if splashed with pink champagne, and blue eyes with the sparkle of faceted sapphires. Her mouth resembled her slender body; trim, toned, and . . . tart. But would Mandy Kearney go out to dinner with Nate? Not in this lifetime.

Starting Over

What do readers say?

I enjoyed the characters and locations in this book very much and hope for a sequel as they seem like "friends". I tried to take my time with the story to savor the experience. Thank you to the author. Look forward to more. *C. S.*

A tantalizing tease from start to finish, *Starting Over* had me wishing I was the main character - or at least young enough again to be! May I suggest a bottle of light wine and an afternoon at the beach with this book as your companion? Double the recommendation if you are vacationing in Seaside Oregon. *L. P.*

Other books by Paula Judith Johnson

Sweetbriar

Starting Over

Salsa of Salsa

The Thought of You
by Teresa & Wayne Brown

Second Time Around

Paula Judith Johnson

ISBN13: 978-0-9898715-2-5

Printed in the United States of America

Dedication

To three wonderful women of Clatsop County:
Nicole Williams (the *nice* Nicole), Monica Steele,
and Suzanne Johnson.

Acknowledgments

As always, I want to acknowledge my friend and editor, Vera Haddan. You help make me a better writer.

I would also like to express my appreciation to those who so graciously agreed to test read this work. Thank you to Ann Goldeen, Ruth Swenson, and my mother, Joan Johnson.

I appreciate the insight Suzanne Johnson and Monica Steele gave me to the inner workings of Clatsop County and Randi Post of Klickitat County for information regarding the federal Family Medical Leave Act.

My thanks to Mike McCormick for adjudicating my character's legal issue.

The author takes complete credit for errors, omissions, and embellishments to the information provided by the experts named above.

❧ Chapter 1 ❧

THE TWO BEDROOM CONDOMINIUM HAD ONLY ONE BATHROOM, SO
we shared.

"Stop whistling through your teeth," Justin growled. "It's
annoying as hell."

After rinsing off the last of the shaving cream, I towel dried
my face. "A bit grouchy this morning, are we?"

Leaning forward to flush the toilet, my brother grumbled,
"You would be, too."

"I get that Britney's southern sense of propriety won't allow
her to move in with you until after the wedding, Justin, but
since when does it preclude the two of you from having a
bounce on the bed?"

"Since you darkened the doorstep."

"It's not as if I don't know you have sex," I said, and crossed
the hall to the guest room to get dressed.

Justin followed. "It makes no difference, Nate. Until we're
married she won't step foot in a bedroom with me if someone
else is in the house."

"I still don't get it."

"She has her reasons and I respect them, even if it frustrates
the hell out of me."

"So, why don't you go to her place to play house?"

"Can't. Her roommate's there."

"Well, I'll start looking for another place to stay."

Justin had been surprised when I applied for the position of Assistant Finance Director of Clatsop County, Oregon. In fact, the whole family had been surprised since it corresponded to the position I'd held at Klickitat County. Although I loved the high desert farming community of Goldendale, Washington, a dispute over me using family leave to help out on Dad's farm during harvest season following his heart attack caused me to seek employment elsewhere. This marked the first day at my new job.

"Do you plan to stick around the area for long?" Justin asked.

"Sure. I wouldn't have taken a job here otherwise."

"I'm just saying what if something opens up around Goldendale."

"I'm not going back."

"You say that now."

Ignoring his comment, I slipped into my suit coat, turned, and asked, "How do I look?"

"Like my shithead baby brother playing dress up."

"You're envious because you've never looked this good." The comment was a long standing rib among the three of us brothers. We were all six foot-two, weighed within five pounds of each other, and had our mother's chocolate brown eyes. The only distinguishing feature among us was the color of our hair. Mine was dark blond, Justin's a russet brown, and our oldest brother, Mike, had hair as dark as mink.

I grabbed my empty briefcase and brushed by Justin to go to the kitchen.

"I'll give you six months before you adios back to Goldendale," he said, trailing behind me.

"I won't go back," I said, unexpectedly harsh.

"In that case, you might think about buying a house," he suggested. "The prices are hard to beat right now."

"I'll think about it." Opening the refrigerator, I grabbed an apple, flipped it in the air and caught it one-handed. "By the way, don't hold dinner, honey, I'll be late tonight."

"Up yours, sweetheart," he smirked. "Like I'd hold dinner for you."

We punched each other affectionately on the shoulder then I walked out to my truck.

"Give Brit and me a break tomorrow night," Justin called from the front porch of his condo. "Take her roommate out to dinner. A long dinner."

"Go back in the house, bro," I tossed back, hoping to get the last word. "You look ridiculous standing out here in your polka dot boxers."

Making the twenty minute drive to Astoria, I thought about the roommate, Mandy Kearney, a firebrand, exactly what I liked in a woman. She possessed a classic Irish beauty, flaming red hair, creamy white skin, freckles sprinkled across her pert nose like cinnamon on meringue, cheekbones with a natural blush, as if splashed with pink champagne, and blue eyes with the sparkle of faceted sapphires. Her mouth resembled her slender body; trim, toned, and . . . tart. Dinner was out of the question.

We'd met five weeks ago, shortly after Britney Thompson had initially rejected Justin's marriage proposal. Acting the besotted swain, he offered to help the two women move into a Gearhart beach cottage and asked me to assist with the heavy lifting.

After ribbing Justin about losing his touch with women, I bragged on the ease of my conquests, unaware the roommate was eavesdropping. Like a fool, I claimed I could entice her into bed within a week. Smug about my prowess with all things female, I chugged happily along the familiar tracks of flirtation and thought I was picking up speed when I barreled around a blind corner and suddenly derailed. Looking back, it seemed the entire weekend had slowly tumbled into a train wreck of magnificent proportions, with me tied hand and foot to the engineer's seat.

So, would Mandy Kearney go out to dinner with me? Not in this lifetime.

"Hey, boss," Nicole French said from the doorway of Mandy's office. "Nathan Peters, the new AFD, is here."

Of course he's here, you ditz, Mandy thought. Where else would he be?

"You should see him," Nicole continued. "He's hot—blisteringly hot."

"If you say so," Mandy muttered without looking up from her paperwork.

Eliciting no further response, Mandy's employee left.

Oh, he was hot all right, Mandy mused. With a lean, muscular, farm boy physique, tawny brown hair wavy enough for a tousled look, like he just woke up, and his aquiline nose above sculpted lips. Best of all, deep, sultry brown eyes that held the promise of paradise. Paradise with the hiss of a snake.

Mandy Kearney, the Deputy Assessor and Tax Collector of Clatsop County remembered Nathan Peters all too well. They met the day she and Britney moved from a Seaside apartment complex into the Gearhart cottage they now rented. Even though Mandy had sworn off men, she'd felt drawn in by the sensuous promise in Nathan's eyes when they shook hands. Her unexpected attraction to the man lured her up the stairs toward Britney's bedroom with the goal of asking the brothers if either wanted a soda or glass of cool water. In the hall, outside the room where the two men worked, her fascination dissipated when she overheard Nathan's bold brag that he could easily seduce her.

Mandy had been down that road before and she had no intention of traveling that path again. From now on, she sternly reminded herself, sexual encounters would be on *her* terms. *She* would decided who and when. *She* would be the one to walk away unscathed.

Slapping her pencil down on the papers scattered across her desk, Mandy rose and stomped to the window of her office. Above the rooftops of downtown Astoria black storm clouds scudded across the sky and mirrored exactly the disquiet of her thoughts.

Men were all alike. Not one could be trusted. She'd learned that the hard way. First by Tom, the man she married as a virgin bride, and then divorced six months later after he demanded she agree to an open marriage. Sam was no better. He'd been romantically relentless in his pursuit. But a few weeks after they became lovers he was harshly uncaring when he departed the north Oregon coast.

A tap on the door frame interrupted Mandy's thoughts.

***

FIRST DAYS WERE TEDIOUS. THEY ALWAYS STARTED WITH ENORMOUS amounts of new hire paperwork to fill out and the interminable human resources indoctrination, followed by endless rounds of staff introductions. With any luck, Ernie Gunderson, the Finance Director, would allow me to settle into my office around three this afternoon. The clock read eleven-thirty, and since leaving the H.R. Department, all I'd done was meet my small staff, which consisted of two accountants and a part-time administrative assistant.

"The set-up here is a little unusual," Ernie said as we descended a flight of stairs.

"Having the two departments you supervise on separate floors must be inconvenient," I commented.

"Not so much anymore," he replied as we came out onto the second floor. "When we first moved to this location it consisted of two buildings. To get from Budget and Finance to Assessment and Tax Collection you had to go down to the main floor, and then outside before coming back inside, and climbing the stairs up to the second floor."

"You've got to be kidding."

He pointed to an obvious seam in the carpet. "After a while they knocked out some walls and built connecting hallways between the buildings on all three floors."

We turned a corner, passed the elevator, and walked into a waiting area surrounded on three sides by counter space. Gesturing to the various areas, Ernie said, "Voting and recordings to the right, passports, marriage licenses, and cartography straight ahead, tax collection to the left."

Ushering me through a door on the left, Ernie said, "We'll go to lunch after you meet the Assessment and Tax Collection staff."

Even with the department organizational chart, I knew it would be at least a week before I remembered who was who in this department. We started with the administrative support and property management staff and moved through to the back where I met the Cartographer. We caught three of the five appraisers in their shared office before winding our way back around to the Tax Collector's office.

She stood with her back to us, gazing through her window at the troubled sky. My first impression was of a statuesque redhead in a tailored, royal blue dress. She had a delightfully trim ass above long, shapely legs. Overall, she was a nice piece of eye candy. But in the workplace, I thought, with an inner sigh, anything more would be asking for trouble.

After a gentle tap on the doorframe, Ernie said, "Nathan, I'd like you to meet the County Tax Collector, Amanda Kearney."

When she turned, I felt thrown off kilter.

"Hello, Nathan. Welcome to Clatsop County." She advanced with her hand out, which I found enough presence of mind to shake, but not to speak. "Surprise," she said.

"You two know each other?" Ernie asked.

"We met a few weeks ago," Mandy informed him.

Belatedly, I spoke up. "My brother is engaged to her housemate. We helped them with their move to Gearhart." *When Mandy said she didn't like me and sure as hell wouldn't ever toss the sheets with me.*

"But you didn't know Mandy worked here?" our boss asked.

"The subject didn't come up during the move," Mandy explained. "And we haven't seen each other since."

"Well, it's a small world, isn't it," Ernie commented, sounding pleased.

"Too damn small," I muttered inaudibly.

"You got that right," Mandy softly agreed.

◈ Chapter 2 ◈

LUNCH WITH ERNIE AND MANDY WAS ODDLY AGREEABLE. OUR table overlooked the Columbia River. While waiting for our meals we laughed at the antics of two seals frolicking in the water. The seals disappeared when a large, foreign freighter cruised by on its journey upriver.

After the waitress placed our orders in front of us, Ernie turned the conversation toward business. "I asked Mandy to join us today, Nathan, because your department works closely with hers, especially this time of year. She can be a valuable resource to you."

A nod was all the acknowledgement his statement required as I chewed a succulent piece of deep fried halibut.

"We're fortunate to have CPAs in both of your positions. That hasn't always been the case here in Clatsop County," he continued. "Mandy's work is exemplary, her crew is well trained, and she runs a tight ship. All in all, we're pleased to have her onboard."

"Thank you, Ernie," Mandy responded with a gleam of satisfaction in her eyes.

"I tell you this, Nathan, because things may be a little different here from what you were used to in Klickitat County."

"What sort of things?" I asked.

"One thing is the timber revenue we receive from the State," Mandy interjected.

"The County owns large tracts of timberland, more than is feasible for us to manage," our boss said, picking up the conversation again. "The management of that land was turned over to the State about eighty or ninety years ago."

"I see." Not at all sure I did.

"No offense, Nathan—" Mandy began.

"Call me Nate."

Surprised by the interruption, she sounded snide as she continued. "Once a quarter, *Nate*, the State remits the revenue from timber sales. We have one month from receipt of the funds to disburse them to the appropriate taxing districts."

"Okay," I said. "How hard can that be?"

Ernie laughed. "Not hard at all for you, Nate. Mandy's job, or that of her department, is to calculate the disbursements. You'll need to work closely with her to ensure everything is handled properly because some taxing districts, such as Jewel School, rely heavily on these funds."

Setting my fork aside, I made eye contact with Mandy and swiped a napkin across my lips. "I don't see a problem with that."

"Neither do I," was her smug reply.

"Good. With that settled, how about dessert?" Ernie suggested.

"No, thank you," Mandy and I declined simultaneously.

Disappointment momentarily clouded the Finance Director's face as he patted his soft belly. "Well, let's get back to work then."

As we walked out the door of the restaurant, I asked, "Any possibility I'll get settled into my office today?"

"Of course, but I want to introduce you to the rest of the department supervisors first. It shouldn't take more than an hour or so," Ernie stated before climbing into the car.

Ernie's hour turned out to be two and a half. Following a fifteen minute chat with the County Manager, we worked our way through the various departments until I'd met every department head, and what felt like half their staff. Before releasing me, my boss took the time to review the backlog of work, pointing out what required urgent attention.

After he left, and before knuckling down to work, I called a realty office hoping to schedule an appointment for six-thirty that evening. The receptionist said most of the sales people left by six, but after extracting my promise to be on time, she found one person willing to stay late.

By six-fifteen I'd made a passable dent in the "must do" list. However, to get caught up, I silently acknowledged the extra time I'd need to put in over the next few weeks.

The realtor, a woman in her mid fifties, was alone in her office when I arrived.

"Hello, I'm Kimberly Long," she said, with her hand extended in greeting. "I appreciate your promptness, Mr. Peters."

"Nate, please." We shook hands then sat on opposite sides of her desk.

"When you called, you mentioned you're new in town."

"That's right. Started working for the County this morning."

"Are you familiar with the area?" she asked.

"Not really. I've seen a little of Seaside and Gearhart but that's farther than I want to drive on a daily basis."

"In that case, you need to look at houses in the north part of the county. What price range are you considering?"

"Two—two and a quarter," I replied. "Unless you think I could find something decent for less."

"You should drive around and decide what area of Astoria or Warrenton you like. Price will depend on location, age, and how much work you're willing to put into a house."

Cringing a little at the thought of constant repairs, I shook my head. "I'm not interested in a house that needs major remodeling or heavy upkeep."

"We have a couple of condominiums available down by the water."

"Condos are too much like apartment living for my taste. If I buy, it'll be a house."

Kimberly dipped her head as she made a few notes. "Now, what about financing? Do you have anything lined up?"

"No, could you suggest a lender?"

"Of course." She flipped through some files in her desk drawer and pulled out a sheet of paper. "Here is a list of local banks, credit unions, and mortgage companies."

"Thank you. I'll get started contacting them tomorrow."

"There's not much point in looking at houses until you have a loan secured," Kimberly said.

"There won't be any trouble getting a loan," I assured her. "My credit is excellent. I have good cash flow and sufficient savings for closing costs, plus plenty of assets in retirement accounts."

"That's all good, Nate, but you said you started a new job today."

"Yes, as a CPA who's worked in the same field for over five years. The new job shouldn't be an issue."

Hedging, she said, "I need time to review inventory and schedule house tours. Thanksgiving is Thursday. It will be difficult scheduling anything before the weekend."

"Saturday morning works for me."

Kimberly smiled. "Shall we meet here about ten o'clock?"

"Sounds good." I rose, we shook hands, and I left.

⋘ Chapter 3 ⋙

THERE WASN'T ANY POINT TONIGHT IN FOLLOWING KIMBERLY'S suggestion of driving around, looking at neighborhoods, to see what I might like. It was pitch-black; the sun having set behind a cloud darkened sky ninety minutes ago. Besides, I wanted a cold beer, a snack, and some well-deserved relaxation before going to bed. Tomorrow promised another long day at work.

Britney's cream colored PT Cruiser, which I remembered from a few weeks back, was parked in front of Justin's condo when I arrived. Apparently, they'd taken advantage of my absence for a passionate interlude. Glancing at the dash clock, I hopped out of the truck. I figured they'd had plenty of time to finish a romp in the hay and wouldn't be surprised when I walked through the door.

The surprise was finding Justin, Britney, and *Mandy* grouped around the dining room table, elbow deep in wedding magazines, pictures of billowy white dresses, fancy tuxedoes, and page after page of lists detailing God knew what.

Tempted to flee, I glared at Mandy instead. "Don't tell me you're a wedding planner, too."

"No, she's my matron of honor," Britney said.

"What the hell is that?"

"She walks down the aisle in front of the bride," Justin informed me, sounding as if the question was the stupidest in the world.

"Then count me out," I stated, shifting a glowering gaze toward my brother.

"Come off it, Nate," he admonished without heat as he stood.

Britney gathered papers together in an orderly fashion and handed them to Mandy. "We've done enough tonight. Let's head home."

Silently, Mandy stacked the stuff from the table in a plastic crate sitting on the floor.

"I'll get your coats," Justin offered, walking into the living room. Coming back with two garments, he handed one to me before holding the other out for Britney.

Without a choice, other than plain rudeness, I held the firebrand's coat for her. From the sparks in her eyes as she slipped her arms into the sleeves, I wasn't sure she appreciated the gallantry.

"I'll take the crate to the car," she said.

"It's probably heavy," Justin speculated. "Let Nate get it."

Let Nate get it? No way in hell, I thought. But, box in hand; I trooped out to the car like an obedient child, the others trailing behind. When the car locks clicked open, Mandy raised the hatch, and I slid the crate inside.

"Let's get together for dinner at our place tomorrow night," Britney suggested. "We can pick up where we left off."

"Sounds good," Justin said as he drew his fiancée into his arms.

His goodnight kiss looked more like a prelude to lovemaking than closure to the evening. Mandy discreetly ducked into the car. I headed back indoors.

A pizza box sat on the kitchen counter. Inside was one lonely piece—Canadian bacon and pineapple. Not my favorite but it would suffice if accompanied by a cold beer. As expected, the fridge held most of a six pack. I snagged a bottle, unscrewed the cap, and took a long pull, appreciating my brother's taste for local microbrews. After quenching my thirst, a bite of pizza hit the spot.

The front door slammed and Justin stormed in. "What the hell was that about?"

Annoyance bit my butt. "You didn't tell me the firebrand was in on this."

"Who else did you expect Britney to ask? They live together, for crying out loud."

"She could have asked a sister or somebody she works with."

"She's an only child and works with just one other person— her boss, who happens to be a man."

"Fireworks go off when I'm in the same room with that redhead." I was heated now. "Why the hell did you ask me to be your best man when you knew she was going to be the honor guard?"

"Matron of honor."

"*Whatever.*"

"I asked you because you're my brother. Who else would I ask?"

"Mike, your other brother," I tossed back, refusing to be soothed.

Justin raked his fingers through his hair. "Mike's in Goldendale, in case you haven't noticed. You're here. Besides, I asked *you* because I want *you*. If I'd wanted Mike, I would have asked Mike. And if you ever tell him I said that, I'll kick your ass."

"Like you could kick my ass," I scoffed, feeling somewhat mollified. "Did you know she works at the County?"

"Mandy? Not until tonight. She mentioned it when she got here."

"Shit," I said. "It's bad enough I have to work with her. Now, I suppose, I have to socialize with her, too."

"It's only a wedding, for Christ's sake," big bro reminded me, opening the refrigerator and coming out with a beer. "It's not like you're dating."

That didn't deserve a response.

Justin took a swig from the bottle. Apparently deciding the argument won, he changed the subject. "How'd the house hunting go?"

That steamed me all over again. "If you want me gone, all you have to do is say so and I'll be out of here tonight."

"Settle down," he said, and hefted his haunch onto a bar stool. "I'm in no hurry for you to move out."

"Didn't sound that way."

"Stop being a jerk, Nate. I told you last week you could stay as long as necessary. That hasn't changed. I asked because I'm interested."

A long breath pushed its way out of my lungs as animosity drained away. "Instead of looking for a house to rent, I took your advice and spoke with a realtor about buying."

Crossing over to where I'd dropped my briefcase; I extracted a sheet of paper and handed it to Justin. "She gave me this list of local lenders. I thought maybe you could point me in the right direction."

He glanced at it and shrugged. "I went through my bank because they had my business loan. If I were you, I'd call around and ask about rates and fees."

"That's pretty much what I figured on doing."

"When you decide on a lender be sure to tell them about the situation with Klickitat County," he advised.

"Why?"

"Mortgage lenders like full disclosure. If the issues with your former employer grow into a full-blown lawsuit, they'll want to know."

"You think that'll cause a problem? Finding a house to buy takes a lot more time than finding a house to rent. Telling them about Klickitat might delay things even more."

"Don't worry about it. I said you could stay here as long as you needed," he reiterated.

"Thanks," I said, punching him lightly on the shoulder.

Pushing me away, Justin said, "Don't get all sappy on me."

Rattled by Nate's rudeness, Mandy was quiet during the short drive to Gearhart. She'd known he was Justin's best man; had presumed Nate knew she was Britney's attendant.

"Everything will work out," Britney said as she parked and turned off the engine.

"You say that with such confidence," Mandy returned.

"We still have time to look at wedding invitations tonight, if you're up to it," the bride-to-be suggested.

"Sure." Mandy pushed out of the car. Since all her roommate talked about anymore was the wedding, she asked, "Want me to get the crate?"

"Might as well. We'll need it for tomorrow night. Speaking of which, what should we do about dinner?" Britney held the front door open while Mandy lugged in the crate. "Get take-out or cook?"

"I don't want take-out two nights in a row," Mandy said, and placed the crate next to the couch. "I'll sauté chicken breasts in wine if you make a salad."

"Sounds good to me and Justin will love it," Britney agreed. She plunked a huge binder on the kitchen table. "The printer let me borrow his sample book of invitations. He's a friend of my boss."

"When do you need to take it back?"

"Not until Friday," Britney said. "We can pick out three or four styles and then let Justin make the final decision."

Mandy set two glasses of wine on the table. "Why not just pick out what you like?" Mandy suggested. "You know he'll go along with whatever you want."

Britney gave her friend a superior smile. "He'd relinquish the entire planning process to me, if I let him, but I'm not the only one getting married. I want him to remember that, and by involving him in every step, I drive that point home. You should remember that for when you get married."

"Sorry, Britney," Mandy said. "Been there, done that. Don't need to again."

✺ Chapter 4 ✺

AFTER THEIR LUNCH WITH ERNIE YESTERDAY, MANDY HAD ALMOST convinced herself she and Nathan Peters could work well together. That illusion dissolved with the first words out of his mouth last night at his brother's home. Forewarned is forearmed, she told herself when Nate walked into the room where Mandy was wrapping up a meeting with her staff.

"Good morning, Nate," she said in her best professional voice. "I believe you met everyone yesterday."

"Yes, I did," he acknowledged with a nod to the group. He shifted his gaze back to Mandy. "When you have a minute."

"We're done here," she said, dismissing her subordinates. Mandy turned and walked into her office, leaving the new Assistant Finance Director to follow if he chose.

He did. Closing the door, Nate leaned against it. "About last night . . ."

"Yes?" Mandy stood behind her desk with arms crossed protectively over her torso.

"Seeing you there caught me by surprise. I didn't mean anything by what I said."

She waited, not saying a word.

Annoyed by her silence, Nate pushed away from the door. "We need to work together in a spirit of cooperation. Both here and off the job. At least until after the wedding."

"And then?"

"We won't see each other," Nate said. "Off the job, I mean."

A knock on the door prevented Mandy from speaking her mind. "Come in," she said instead.

Nicole French, the Tax Technician, poked her head in. "Oh, you're still busy. I'll come back later."

"That's all right. Please come in," Mandy said. "You remember Nicole, don't you, Nate?"

"Sure." Seeing the interruption as a means of escape, he edged toward the door.

Mandy's voice stopped him. "Nathan, if you need anything else, contact Nicole. She can handle just about anything, and what she can't handle, she knows to pass along to me."

The dismissal was clear. Nate understood Mandy purported as little interaction as possible between them. Willing to accommodate her unspoken demand, he turned toward Nicole.

At a glance, he saw a woman of medium height, curvy but not plump, although her ankles revealed she carried weight in the extremities. He also noticed her stylish cap of soft black curls, well-defined black brows above wide-set eyes of a greenish hue, a ski-slope nose, and the sharp point of her chin. Nate's eyes flicked a second time to the beauty mark adorning the lower left corner of her red, lush-lipped mouth.

As Mandy watched, a gleam of male appreciation appeared in Nate's eyes and an engaging smile slowly graced his lips, while a provocative pout pursed Nicole's full mouth in an answering expression of awareness.

The redhead remembered the ease with which Nathan captured her regard when she first met him—before he bragged to his brother that he could bed her within a week. A frown creased her brow.

"I'll be in my office if you need me," Nate said without addressing either woman in particular.

"As a matter of fact, I do," Nicole responded.

Mandy's puckered brow deepened.

Nate gestured toward the door. "After you."

Within moments, Mandy was alone. And pissed. *Of all the unmitigated gall! All he has to do is apologize, but no, Nathan Peters is too pigheaded to do that.*

She paced in the too small office. *Who does he think he is, walking in and lecturing her on the spirit of cooperation! Well, he can cooperate all he wants with Nicole. She's probably his type anyway, never dating a man for more than a month or two. Nathan Peters shouldn't have any trouble getting her into his bed within a week. Of course, it's just as likely it'll be Nicole who gets him into the sack.*

Mandy flopped into her desk chair with a huff of bad humor. She picked up a pen and twiddled it angrily between her fingers. *The two of them are probably made for each other. It will serve him right if he falls for Nicole. It will be what he deserves.*

Dissatisfied with her ruminations, Mandy glanced at the clock. It was lunch time. Tossing her pen on the desk, she grabbed her purse, and marched out the door—chased by her thoughts. *Why does Nathan Peters have to be so damnably attractive?*

IGNORING NICOLE'S CHATTER, I FOLLOWED HER UP THE STAIRS TO the third floor, grinding my teeth the entire way. *Will it kill the firebrand to at least try to work together?* When Nicole stopped on the landing I bumped into her.

She gave me an odd look. "You weren't listening, were you?"

"Sorry, my mind was elsewhere," I said, and threw her an apologetic smile. "What were you saying?"

Nicole silently waited as I unlocked my office door, and then she walked to the small window overlooking the building's back courtyard. "I was saying you can see my desk from here."

I stepped up behind her. Across the way, at the second floor, was a large window.

"See? It's the one with the red sweater on the back of the chair."

"What do you know," I teased. "I can spy on you."

She looked over her shoulder; a seductive gleam lit her eyes. I took a step back, then another.

"It's lunchtime," she said in her sultry voice.

A glance at my watch confirmed the time. "So, it is."

"Care to join me?"

"Sorry, I have a prior commitment," I told her, and crossed to my desk to pick up a file folder. The appointment was with a lender. The lunch hour might be enough time to get the mortgage approval process started. Opening the door for Nicole, I said, "Perhaps another time."

She smiled as she passed by. "I'll hold you to it. Meanwhile, call me if you need anything."

"You can count on it," I said, knowing I'd need to accept her offer sooner or later.

❧ Chapter 5 ❧

THE NEXT EVENING, TWELVE HOURS AFTER LEAVING THAT MORNING, I was back where I started—parked in front of Justin's place. It was after seven. I was tired, hungry, and wanted a beer. Britney's PT Cruiser was nowhere in sight, which meant a night free of wedding plans. Good.

Justin greeted me by pushing a beer in my hand. "Tomorrow's Thanksgiving. I thought the County offices closed early today."

Before answering, I drank deep. "Yeah, at three o'clock."

"So, why are you late?" His eyes held a sportive light, as if he knew something he shouldn't.

As children, he got the same look on his face whenever he caught me in some boyish mischief. Then he'd torment me with the threat of tattling to our parents, although he never had.

"Or, should I ask?" His question was an insinuation.

As years before, I felt on guard. "What's that supposed to mean?"

"Thought maybe there was someone at work you couldn't resist."

Tipping beer into my mouth, I eyed my brother around the bottle, swallowed, and said, "If you're referring to Mandy, you're wrong."

"Not Mandy. She was here with Britney until an hour ago. I'm talking about someone else."

"You're still wrong," I said, and drained the bottle. "I adhere to one piece of advice you gave me years ago. I don't date women from work."

"It's good to hear you paid attention to something I said. But if you weren't with a woman, what kept you?"

"Work," was my terse reply as I started rummaging in the refrigerator, looking for something to eat.

"Work," Justin mimicked.

Finding a container of leftover soup, I dished some into a bowl and popped it into the microwave. "I was three weeks behind before I started the job. I needed some catch-up time. More gets accomplished when no one's around to interrupt."

The oven dinged. Armed with a spoon and paper towel, I sat at the dining table and shoveled in a mouthful. Around the food, I said, "I plan to go in tomorrow for a few hours. Get some more work done."

Justin sat down next to me. "In that case, go in early. We have dinner plans tomorrow."

"Really? Are Mom and Dad driving over from Goldendale?" I asked, perking up. "I thought I'd miss out on Mom's honey basted turkey. God, I can hardly wait."

"Hate to burst your bubble, bro," Justin said. "Brit and Mandy are cooking for us."

I scooped up the last bite of soup, got up from the table, and walked into the kitchen, saying, "Count me out."

"You're living in my home. You're going. End of story," Justin said with a note of determination in his voice.

After rinsing the bowl, I stuck it in the dishwasher. He had a point. I didn't really have a choice. "What time?"

"Show up at their place by one," he said. "I'm going over earlier."

"That doesn't give me much time to work," I argued.

"It will if you go in early," Justin countered.

"Shit," was my only reply.

AROUND ELEVEN O'CLOCK, JUSTIN SHOWED UP AT THE LITTLE cottage in Gearhart. Mandy tactfully stayed in the kitchen to give Britney a few minutes alone with her fiancé. Giggles in the living room suggested a game of grab ass was underway. The sounds stopped shortly before the couple sauntered into the kitchen.

Inhaling deeply of the tantalizing aromas, Justin sighed. "Something sure smells good. Anything I can do to help?"

Mandy set the turkey baster aside. "Nope, I think everything is under control." She replaced the lid on the roaster and closed the oven door.

"Look what Justin brought." Britney held up a magnum bottle in each hand. "Champagne." She gave him a smacking smooch on the cheek.

Mandy took the bottles and tucked them in the refrigerator before turning back to face her roommate. "I told you so," she taunted.

Britney remained silent.

Looking from one woman to the other, Justin asked, "What?"

"Mandy said Nate wouldn't come to dinner," Britney remarked.

"I said I doubted—"

"He's coming," Justin interrupted.

It was Britney's turn to tease, "Justin says Nathan is coming."

"I'll believe it when I see it," Mandy muttered.

"Why didn't he ride over with you?" Britney asked her fiancé.

"Nate wanted to clear some of the backlog at work," he said pointedly. "He went in early this morning."

Britney took Justin's arm. "I looked through the sample book of wedding cards and like four styles. Let's look at them so you can tell me which you like best. As soon as we decide on a location for the wedding we can order the invitations."

She led him back into the living room. The two lovebirds sat on the couch and propped the big binder on their laps. Their voices rose and fell as they weighed the pros and cons of card style, typeface, and wording for their invitations and announcements.

When Mandy was engaged to Tom, she and her mother handled all the wedding preparations. Looking back, his lack of involvement foretold of his whole attitude toward their marriage, Mandy realized.

She emptied a can of yams into a casserole dish, mixed in brown sugar, topped it with miniature marshmallows, and covered it with a lid. After warming it on the stove top, she planned to remove the lid and brown the melted marshmallows in the oven while the turkey rested before carving. She was peeling potatoes when Britney and Justin returned to the kitchen.

"Mandy, please explain to your housemate why her mom needs to attend the wedding," Justin instructed.

"I'm not getting in the middle of that debate," she replied.

The unwanted child of a shotgun marriage and, for years estranged from her promiscuous mother, Britney voiced another objection in an already overlong list. "She'd expect us to pay for her transportation and lodging."

Taking hold of his fiancée's knee length braid, Justin wrapped it around his forearm and pulled her into a coaxing kiss. "We pay for her transportation and lodging. She sees her only child marry Prince Charming, and then we send her on her way. What's wrong with that?"

Feeling her resolve weaken, Britney hedged, "We don't need to decide tonight."

"You're right," Justin conceded. He draped his arm over Britney's shoulder and smiled into her cobalt blue eyes. "So, other than turkey, what are you cooking for dinner tonight, gorgeous?"

Chortling, she slipped out from under his arm. "I suggest you bat those soulful brown eyes at Mandy. She did all the cooking."

"Not all of it," her friend said. "You made the fruit salad and promised to cook a cheese sauce to pour over the asparagus."

"Neither of which compares to the rest of this feast," Britney declared. "For all the good it did, I slaved over the stove for an hour this morning stirring a batch of homemade cranberry sauce."

Both women burst into laughter.

"What's so funny about that?" Justin asked, puzzled.

Britney opened the refrigerator door and pulled out a can of jellied cranberry sauce.

"After an hour of 'stirring constantly'," Mandy made quote signs with her fingers, "she re-read the directions."

"I used a sugar substitute to trim a few calories," Britney admitted. "Big mistake. The recipe needed real sugar to jell. I ended up throwing the whole thing out."

Justin's phone rang. After screening the number, he excused himself. Walking into the living room, he growled into the phone. "Where the hell are you? It's almost one."

"That's why I'm calling."

"It better be to say you're on your way."

"Cool down," Nate said, and sighed. "I got caught up and lost track of time. I'm heading out right now."

"So, you'll be here in . . . what . . . half an hour?"

"Yeah, maybe. If I don't get lost."

"Turn right at the Gearhart signal, head toward the ocean—"

"Yeah, yeah, I know." Grudgingly, Nate agreed, "Okay, I'll be about half an hour."

They clicked off and Justin headed back to the kitchen.

Mandy was basting the turkey again. "Will he be here soon?" she asked. "The bird's almost done."

"He'll be about half an hour. Is that okay?"

She shrugged. "Close enough, I suppose."

"You weren't planning to serve until two-thirty," Britney reminded her roommate, and received a cutting glance in response.

"By the way," Justin said. "If you ever want to get on Nate's good side, food is the way to go. He loves good cooking."

"So far, I haven't seen a good side to your brother," Mandy remarked. "Besides, if he has one, I'm not interested in getting on it."

❧ Chapter 6 ❧

AFTER LEAVING THE OFFICE, I REMEMBERED THE TRUCK WAS LOW on gas so I stopped at Fred Meyer's to fill up. The glass-faced, impulse-purchase product locker situated next to the attendant's booth usually contained snack food. Today it was filled with cellophane wrapped bouquets. One in particular caught my eye. Miniature sunflowers mixed with some type of autumn leaves, seasonal, in a cheery sort of way, and the perfect gift for my future sister-in-law.

Arriving thirty-five minutes late, I strode up the walkway, flowers in hand. Justin opened the front door before I knocked.

"You're late."

"I brought flowers."

"Kiss ass."

I grinned. "Food's involved."

He stepped back. The living room was empty and my stomach was rumbling. In anticipation of satisfying its hunger, I followed the rich scent of roasting fowl and pumpkin pie—my all-time favorite dessert—toward the kitchen.

My brother's fiancée stood at the stove, mashing potatoes, while Mandy, in tight jeans and turtleneck, set the table. Damp tendrils escaped her top knot of radiant hair and clung deliciously to her heat-flushed face. An image of her draped naked across the pristine tablecloth flashed across my mind and hunger of a different sort tightened in my loins.

"Everything sure looks good," I stated to announce my arrival.

Britney, having turned to greet me, snickered. "Don't you mean it smells good?"

Dragging my eyes from the firebrand, I went to give Britney a brotherly kiss on the cheek. "Justin is one lucky bastard to hook up with a woman who knows her way around the kitchen. Here's a gift for the cook," I said, and held out the bouquet.

She chuckled with a wicked sparkle in her eyes. "In that case, you'd better give those to Mandy. She did ninety percent of the cooking."

Silence stretched for one . . . two . . . three seconds.

"My mistake." Pivoting, I held out the flowers. "I guess these belong to you, Mandy."

"Thank you, Nathan," she replied politely without turning from her task. "Britney, do you mind putting them in water? There should be a vase in the cabinet above the refrigerator."

"He brought the flowers for you," Britney objected.

"You're taller and I can't reach that high."

Feeling my face flush, I growled, "I'll do it." Finding a tall, narrow glass on a short stem, I presumed it was the vase, filled it with water, then stripped the cellophane off the bouquet, and jammed it in. The fit was tight, bunching everything together.

"What are you doing?" Mandy grabbed the things out of my hands.

Justin snorted out a laugh. "Nate, you idiot, that's a champagne flute."

More heat washed up my neck and burned my ears.

"I'll get the vase," Britney offered, and rummaged in the cabinet. Finding it, she reached in and pulled it out. "It was clear in the back."

A nudge from Justin and I took the vase to fill with water.

Gently, Mandy edged the stems out of the flute. Transferring the flowers to the vase, she rearranged it all to her satisfaction, and placed the bouquet in the center of the table. Then she said, "We'll be ready to eat as soon as the turkey is carved."

As Justin wielded the knife, Nate stood, hands in pockets, spouting the occasional piece of unsolicited, and unheeded advice on how to whittle the bird, while Mandy and Britney loaded the table with assorted sweets, sours, and side dishes, both hot and cold.

"Make yourself useful," Justin told his brother. "There's champagne in the fridge that needs to be opened."

Happy to oblige, Nate retrieved a bottle and removed the foil and wire. Then, taking a dish towel from the counter, he wrapped it over the bottle and eased the cork out with barely a pop. The champagne flutes on the table were identical to the one from the flower incident. He filled them. Justin placed a platter of sliced turkey on the table, they all murmured a short grace of thanksgiving, and then passed serving dishes of food from hand to hand until the plates were heaped high.

"Mmm, this is delicious," Justin purred after the first bite of candied yams. "I think we should get this recipe for mom. What do you think, Nate?"

"It's too sweet for my taste. Besides, I like the way Mom does her sweet potato soufflé."

"I like the yams but sweet potato soufflé sounds good, too," Britney commented.

"You'll get a taste of it at Christmas," Justin promised, and then he took another bite of turkey. "This is great, Mandy."

"Not as good as Mom's," Nate said, receiving a kick under the table from his brother. "It tastes . . . different."

"I put rosemary leaves under the breast skin," Mandy said. "It adds a delicate flavor to the meat."

"It's okay, I guess." He smothered a piece of white meat in mashed potatoes and gravy before putting it in his mouth.

After a short, awkward silence, Britney said, "I'm thinking of asking Phil, my boss, to give me away. He's the only older man I know that I'm the least bit close to."

"You've been on your own since you graduated from high school," Mandy reminded her friend. "I don't think you need anyone to give you away."

"It is an antiquated custom," Nate noted. "But I like the symbolism of a woman being given into a man's care."

"You're kidding," Mandy sneered.

"No, I'm not," he replied. "In this day and age, a woman might not be dependent upon her father until that responsibility is transferred to her husband, but men today need the reminder that females are more emotionally fragile."

"What!" Mandy demanded in shrill voice. "I can't believe you said that."

"It's true," he insisted.

"Time out. Time out," Justin called, tapping the fingertips of his right hand on the palm of his left. "Britney and I will decide whether or not someone will give her away. So for now, end of discussion."

"That's fine by me," Nate said, and received a fire-filled glare from Mandy.

"Before we get off the subject completely," Britney threw in, "Time is getting short. We need to finalize a few things. Can we all get together after work on Tuesday?"

"Your place or mine?" Justin asked, hoping for another home cooked meal.

"Yours," Mandy and Britney chorused.

Nathan declined. "Count me out. I'm still buried at work and doubt I'd be much help anyway."

"We need you there, Nate," Britney urged.

He shrugged her off with one word, "Work."

"If Brit says we need you, then you need to show up," Justin asserted. "Helping with planning the event is part and parcel of being best man."

The brothers stared at each other, each wanting to make his point. It was an old routine between them.

When the women started to clear the table, Mandy asked, "Is everyone ready for pumpkin pie or should we wait?"

The mention of his favorite dessert distracted Nate. He broke eye contact first, conceding the silent argument to his brother. "Bring it on, I'm ready."

"My brother meant to say 'please'," Justin interjected. "So, I'll say it for both of us. Yes, please."

Pushing back from the table, Nate excused himself to go to the bathroom. When he came out, Justin was waiting for him in the hallway.

"You're being an ungrateful ass toward Mandy."

"I brought her flowers, didn't I?"

"Bull, you brought flowers intending to give them to Britney but outsmarted yourself by saying they were for the cook."

"Well, I probably would have enjoyed dinner more if Britney *had* been the cook."

"You're such a jerk," Justin declared. With a finger jab to Nate's shoulder, he added, "If you don't like the food you can leave any time."

Knocking his brother's hand away, Nate barked, "I didn't ask to come. As a matter of fact, I didn't want to come. I'm here because you pressured me into it."

Livid by what she overheard, Mandy flew out of the kitchen. "If you don't want to be here, you're free to leave at anytime, Nathan Peters. Just don't let the door smack you in the butt."

"Don't worry, I won't." He grabbed his coat and was gone before he finished shrugging into it. His absence left a silent vacuum.

Britney crept out of the kitchen, slung an arm over her friend's shoulder, and drew her close. "Think of it this way," she murmured. "You didn't want to get on his good side, anyway."

"Oh, God," Mandy cried. Tears glistening in her eyes, she ran into her bedroom and slammed the door.

❧ Chapter 7 ❧

MANDY ANTICIPATED NATHAN SHOWING UP AT HER OFFICE DOOR TO offer an apology for last night. But he didn't.

An apology she could accept in an offhand manner, as if it didn't matter. But it did.

She hated admitting she'd wanted to impress him, had wanted to hear words of praise flowing from his lips. His delectable lips.

The moment she heard the murmur of his voice last night as he entered the house, she felt a flush of steamy heat rise slowly from the pit of her belly until it burned in her face. Nathan Peters was too handsome for his own good—for *her* own good. She knew it was a mistake to want him. He was too much like Tom, her ex-husband; always on the prowl, always needing to cat around with a new woman.

Mandy couldn't trust Nate. Couldn't trust herself not to fall in love again, as she almost had with Sam Samuelson, the Harley riding banker, who rode off into the sunset to take a new job, deserting her three weeks after she gave herself to him.

"Hey, boss, it's almost quitting time," Nicole said from the open doorway. She held up a file folder. "I'll take this week's tax compilation up to Nate before leaving."

"Thanks, have a nice weekend."

"Sure thing. See you Monday."

With a last sigh of discontent, Mandy cleared her desk, grabbed her coat, and headed home.

TIRED OF WAITING FOR THE ASSISTANT FINANCE DIRECTOR TO SEEK her out, Nicole sauntered into his office at two minutes to five. She expected to see him slumped in front of his computer, hard at work. Instead, he was beside his desk, counting pushups.

Mm-mm, she thought, licking her over full lips, I do like men with nice pecs.

She must have hummed out loud because Nate broke count at thirty-seven and rose from the floor.

"Good evening, Nicole," he said with an easy smile.

"Good evening, yourself," she tossed back, and held out the file folder. "Here's the compilation of this week's property tax receipts."

"Thanks. You saved me a trip downstairs." He took the file and pitched it onto his desk. Then he pulled on his suit coat and buttoned it.

She recognized the hint but didn't plan to be put off so easily. "Did you have a nice Thanksgiving?"

His eyes sharpened with a pinched look around the edges. "What's it to you?"

The question startled and offended her. "Nothing. It's just what people say." She spun on her heel to leave. "Forget I asked."

"Wait."

She stopped but refused to turn around.

"Sorry, I didn't mean to jump down your throat," Nate said. He rubbed a hand on the back of his neck and a rueful smile touched his lips. "I had a crappy Thanksgiving but it would take a beer to tell you about it."

She faced him and gave a one-shoulder shrug. "I have time and sympathetic ears. We'll find beer down the street."

Deciding there wasn't anything on his desk that couldn't wait an hour, or even two, Nate agreed, "Lead the way."

Pleased, she said, "I need to get my coat."

"Where are we going?"

"The Supper Club is close. It's over on Twelfth between Commercial and Duane, north side of the street."

"Okay, meet you there in ten minutes."

"THIS IS AN INTERESTING LAYOUT," I COMMENTED AFTER ENTERING the restaurant. A balcony in the northeast quarter overlooked the main floor.

"Let's go up there," Nicole suggested, pointing with her chin. "It isn't as crowded."

A waitress followed us up the stairs, and as we sat across from each other, placed menus we wouldn't need on the table at our elbows. "Would you like something to drink to start your evening?"

"A local microbrew on tap," I said. "Preferably dark."

"Pale ale for me," Nicole stated.

We each leaned back in our chairs, getting comfortable at the end of a long day.

Sometime between leaving the office and arriving at The Supper Club, it had occurred to me that Nicole worked for Mandy. It was probably a bad idea to complain to one about the other. "Have you worked at the County long?" I asked to avoid the topic of yesterday's dinner.

"Over eight years now but it took me a while to find my niche," Nicole explained. "I was in the sheriff's department until about four years ago."

The waitress delivered our beers. She must have noticed we hadn't touched the menus. "Do you need a few more minutes?" she asked.

"Yes, please," Nicole said, surprising me with her response.

"So, you must have started in the tax department before Mandy."

"That's right." She gave me a curious look before continuing. "Just between you and me, if I had known it was up to me to train my own boss, I would have applied for the position myself."

Treading cautiously, I said, "Everyone in a new job needs someone to show them the ropes."

She sipped her beer with a considering look on her face. "That's true, but she's had the job for three years." Leaning toward me, Nicole whispered, "Not a week goes by that I don't find mistakes."

"Ernie seems satisfied with her work." I was careful to keep a neutral tone of voice.

Seemingly resigned, Nicole sat back and drank. "I approached him about it once but he didn't listen. Mandy is a CPA and I'm not." Nicole shrugged. "It's easy enough to make corrections when necessary."

"Maybe you should talk to Ernie again."

"No," she said, emphatically. "Mandy is his fair haired child and I'm not. I won't jeopardize my job by constantly complaining."

As inequitable as it was, I saw her point. Fairness rarely came into play when a person was forced to resign. That was a lesson I'd learned at Klickitat County.

"You were going to tell me why you had a rotten Thanksgiving," Nicole prompted.

Dragging my thoughts back, I looked at our almost empty glasses. "As I recall, we need a beer for the telling of that tale. Let's order dinner and I'll divulge everything over another round." As I signaled downstairs for the waitress, Nicole looked at her watch.

"Someplace you need to be?"

"I need to pick up my son from day care, but I have some time yet."

"Oh, I didn't know you had children."

"A son," she reiterated. "He's five and quite a handful."

"Are you married?"

"No, divorced. It's been over three years now."

"I'm sorry to hear that. Not that you're divorced," I clarified. "But that you're raising a son by yourself. That can't be easy."

"It's not," she said.

The waitress took our orders, and over a fresh beer, I started my story. "The worst part about yesterday was missing out on dessert."

❧ Chapter 8 ❧

NICOLE'S UNEASINESS, OVER BEING FORTY-FIVE MINUTES LATE, ratcheted up to agitation when she saw the day care center was closed. Tacked to the door was a sealed envelope bearing her name. With anxious fingers, she ripped it open and read the note. It said Dr. French, her ex-husband, had picked Tyler up at six-thirty-five. Angrily, Nicole wadded up the paper and hurled it to the ground. Then she stomped to her car and slammed inside.

The phone in her purse made a chirping sound, signifying a message. She didn't need to look to know who'd left it, but pressed the voicemail button anyway. She listened to her ex-husband's voice. "Nicole, it's Alan. I have Tyler. Call me."

She punched his speed dial button.

"Where the hell are you?" he answered—curt, as always.

"At the day care center, where I expected to find my son," she snapped back.

"Tyler is *our* son, in case you forgot. The way you obviously forgot the day care center closes at six."

"In case you forgot, Alan, this is the busiest time of year at work, which is where I was."

"That's strange, Nicole, because Janet from the day care center told me she tried calling you three times. If you were at work, why didn't you answer your phone?" he demanded.

"I wasn't at my desk, that's why," she said, her tone precise and clipped, as if explaining to an imbecile. "I was in a meeting," she lied. Dinner with Nathan Peters wasn't exactly a meeting.

"Come off it. What meeting is so damned important you can't take two minutes to call the center and let them know you'll be late?"

"Stop it, Alan!" she bawled. "It's been a long week and I'm tired. Where are you? I want to get Tyler and go home."

Her loss of control satisfied his sense of outrage. "He's eating dinner. I'll make sure he's bathed and in pajamas when I bring him by. But don't think I'm doing you any favors, because once he's in bed you and I are going to have a long talk."

He clicked off before Nicole could object.

AFTER TUCKING TYLER INTO BED, ALAN FRENCH READ HIM A SHORT story from the current issue of *Highlights*, then kissed his forehead, and turned out the light. It was a ritual Alan never pursued before the divorce, and now one he wasn't able to enjoy often enough.

Descending the stairs, his heels clicked on the dark mahogany of the hardwood risers that gleamed underfoot. The risers matched the rich smoothness of the custom made handrail. The curving staircase was only one of the extravagances his ex-wife had insisted upon when they'd built the house.

She was in the kitchen, a room Alan hated. Ultra-modern in style, the bright overhead lights reflected off the stainless steel surfaces of the stove, double ovens, dishwasher, wine chest, and commercial refrigerator. Walking into the room, he felt an ache in the back of his eyes from the glare.

Known for her on again-off again diets, Nicole stood at the counter, pouring beer into a frosted mug. On the rare occasions Alan imbibed, he drank beer straight from of the bottle. Standing across the counter from his ex-wife, he fired the first salvo in a familiar dialogue meant to put her on the defensive. "You wouldn't need to diet so often if you cut out the beer."

"I like beer. Besides, I deserve one after a day like today." She took a sip.

"Switch to Lite, it doesn't have so many calories."

"How many times do I have to tell you, I don't like Lite beer? It's all pee and no flavor."

"How many have you had?"

"Don't start on me, Alan. I was at work—"

"Where you were isn't the issue."

"Then what is?" she snapped.

"Not picking Tyler up from day care."

"Next time, I'll call."

He raised hands to hips. "There won't be a next time, Nicole." She opened her mouth to protest, but he cut her off. "They said to make other arrangements."

"They can't—"

"Yes, they can."

Her chin came up belligerently. "I'll need a few days—"

"I've already taken care of it," he informed her. "Tyler can go to Tiny Tots."

"You bastard! You did this on purpose."

Alan's live-in girlfriend used to work at Tyler's day care center. It was where they'd met. A few months ago, with Alan's financial backing, she opened Tiny Tots Day Care.

"You have no one but yourself to blame, Nicole. The day care has regular hours of operation, which you habitually abused."

Angered by the accuracy of her ex-husband's accusation, she slammed her beer mug on the quartz counter. "I will not—"

"On nights you work late, or go out for a beer with someone," he sneered, "Jodi can take Tyler home and he can spend the night with us."

"I don't want my son at a second rate day care center run by your bimbo slut," she hollered.

"Watch your mouth," he warned quietly. "Jodi isn't a bimbo or a slut. She's an intelligent, devoted woman. We're getting married in April."

The announcement stunned Nicole. Her eyes darted around the kitchen as she absorbed the implication of Alan's forthcoming marriage. "Don't get the idea of Tyler calling her mommy. *I'm* his mother—"

"That's not all," Alan declared, interrupting her building tirade. "I received a late notice from the bank—again."

"So what?" she blustered.

"You seem to forget my name is still on the mortgage. When the loan goes thirty days past due, it reflects on my credit as well as yours."

"It's not thirty days past due."

"Not yet, but if that happens," he warned, "I'll take you to court and force a sale of this house."

"Property taxes were due last week—"

"If you can't pay the mortgage and keep the taxes current now, while I'm paying you two grand a month in alimony, how do you expect to afford this monstrosity of a house fifteen months down the road when the alimony stops?"

"Don't threaten me, Alan. You can't get out from under your obligation to me so easily. It's expensive raising a child. I'll take you back to court and get the child support raised," she asserted.

"Like hell you will," he scoffed. "You get fifteen hundred a month in child support. There's not a judge in Clatsop County who will increase that amount."

"There's college to consider—"

"I already agreed to pay one hundred percent of Tyler's college expenses. It's in black and white in the divorce decree, or did you forget?"

She had. But she'd find another way to make him pay. She had to, because if the house sold, the divorce decree stipulated he was entitled to most of the equity. She wouldn't give him the satisfaction of wresting the house from her.

"You should have thought about how you were going to hang on to your fancy Victorian replica before you started screwing around behind my back."

Fury, as hot and molten as the lava in Mount St. Helens, spewed into her brain. "Get out! Get out before I call the cops and have you thrown out!" she screeched.

"I didn't know you still had friends on the police force," he taunted her. "Not after Jackson dumped you and patched things up with his wife." Seeing he'd hit his mark, Alan turned and strode to the front entry.

Speechless with rage, Nicole flew after him.

Throwing her a disgusted look, which stopped her headlong flight, Alan opened the door and walked out.

Racing forward, Nicole slammed it, rattling the stained glass window above the frame. A whimpering noise sounded behind her. Turning, she saw Tyler crouched on the stair, sucking his thumb.

❧ Chapter 9 ❧

SATURDAY MORNING I TOURED TWO HOUSES WITH KIMBERLY LONG, the realtor. Neither interested me so we returned to her office and browsed the listings. She made phone calls to listing agents and homeowners but was unsuccessful in scheduling any appointments before Monday. Apparently, everyone was either out of town or entertaining guests over an extended holiday weekend.

After agreeing to meet around five-thirty Monday evening to continue the search, I swung by the office and put in a couple of hours. It was late afternoon when I drove back toward Seaside.

Wanting to give Justin and his girl a few more hours without the third wheel, I decided to take in a movie. The theater was small and cramped, with seats too close to the big screen for easy viewing of the military thriller's explosive scenes. All in all, the most enjoyable part was the salty, buttered popcorn.

Sunday was all-day-men-only football with beer and pizza. Britney and her sidekick were in Portland on a wedding planning foray. Topping off the near perfect day, I pocketed sixty bucks from Justin after all three of my teams tromped his. Life didn't get much better.

Monday was hectic, as usual for this time of year; however, the extra hours I put in last week shrank the pile of backlogged work. At lunchtime, intending to eat at my desk while crunching a few more numbers, I left to pick up a sandwich and soft drink. In the vestibule on the way out, I ran into Mandy. We exchanged a few polite words, mostly about work. Thinking to ask her about yesterday's trip to Portland, she said I'd see the results tomorrow evening, but I wasn't really paying attention.

A few minutes past five as I was preparing to leave, Nicole walked into my office. "It was a madhouse today," she grumbled. "I'm ready for a tall, cold one. How about you?"

"Sorry, not tonight. I have an appointment. Maybe tomorrow," I replied absently, shrugging into my overcoat. After I picked up my briefcase, she preceded me out of the small office, and I locked the door.

"I'll hold you to it, Nate," she said as we headed to the stairs.

"You will, huh?"

"Sure, because sharing a beer after work builds rapport and opens the door for increased on-the-job cooperation," she declared with the sparkle of humor in her eyes.

"In that case, how can I refuse?"

"You can't," she said, and we parted company.

I drove to the realty office where I learned one house on our list had sold earlier in the day. That left three to tour this evening. The color scheme of the first didn't suit my taste and I wasn't interested in buying a house only to change it. The second dwelling was to my liking but the large yard would require hiring regular maintenance service, an expense I didn't want. The last residence was the nicest of the three but at the high end of my price range. Kimberly was unfazed that I wanted to look at more properties before placing an offer.

In mid afternoon the next day, for the first time since taking the job at Clatsop County, I felt I had a handle on the work flowing my way. I wasn't completely caught up but the seeds of success were firmly planted and taking root. A celebration was in order so I dropped to the floor beside my desk and pumped out fifty pushups. With fresh oxygen racing through my bloodstream, I rose, feeling refreshed.

From the corner of my eye, I caught movement through the small office window. There, across the way on the second floor, Mandy stood in the crowded tax office, conversing with Nicole. A file folder passed from hand to hand between the two women and then Mandy walked away, heading in the direction of her office. Nicole sat at her desk; glanced at her watch, then raised the receiver of her phone. A moment later, mine buzzed.

Reaching across the desk, I answered.

"You promised to have a beer with me after work. I'm ready if you are," she said.

Checking the time, I replied, "It's only quarter after four."

There was a pause before she said in a quiet voice, "I need to blow a little steam. I was hoping you'd lend an ear."

I couldn't very well refuse after she'd listened to my complaints last Friday. "I have a few things to wrap up but it shouldn't take long. We can meet at that place we went to last week."

"Okay, I'll see you about five-fifteen."

We sat at the same table as before, on the balcony, overlooking the main floor of the restaurant. In addition to beer, Nicole asked for a nacho appetizer for us to share.

"You won't believe what happened today," Nicole began as soon as the waitress departed with our orders.

"Then tell me so I don't have to guess."

She hesitated before saying, "This is between just the two of us, right? You won't say anything to anyone else."

I sat back as our beers arrived. "The nachos will be a few more minutes," the waitress informed us and left.

After we both took a sip, I said, "If it's something I can keep between us, I will. But as the Assistant Finance Director, I have a responsibility to the County."

"Oh, it's nothing, really." She paused, and then blurted, "It's Mandy. It's always Mandy. If not for her, I'd love my job."

The waitress climbed the stairs and approached our table with a heaping plate of hot beans, crisp tortilla chips, salsa, guacamole, and sour cream. "Here you go, eat it while it's hot." We both dug in.

"Have you heard about the holiday party?" Nicole asked.

It was a deliberate change of subject, which suited me fine. The less Nicole said about her boss, the better it was for everyone involved.

"I've been keeping my nose to the grindstone instead of my ear to the ground," I wisecracked in response to her question. By the expression on her face, I knew my joke fell flat. "In all seriousness, I'm too busy at work to pay attention to anything but the most pressing matters."

"The party is on a Friday this year, after work. No one wants to party after working all day."

As far as I was concerned, work related holiday parties were something to endure rather than enjoy. Wanting an excuse to remain silent, I selected another chip, dipped it in guacamole, popped it into my mouth, and chewed.

"This year I'll barely have time to pick up Tyler from day care, drive home and change clothes, then hope the babysitter arrives on time."

"When's the party?"

"December tenth."

"That's almost two weeks. Don't you know someone who can pick your son up from day care and let him spend the night? What about his dad? Is he in the picture?"

She sat back in a pout. "Another sore spot," she said.

My cell phone rang. I checked caller ID. It was Justin so I answered. The sentence he spat out was short and sour. Then he hung up.

"Crap, I forgot," I said, tucking the phone away. "I gotta go. My brother's getting married."

"Now?"

"No, in January, but they're in the middle of planning everything and expect me to help. I'm best man," I explained. Rising from the table, I tossed down a ten dollar bill. "Oh, and get this—Mandy is the matron of honor."

"Mandy? Mandy Kearney?!"

"Yeah. See you later." I hurried down the stairs and out to my car.

"WE NEED TO DECIDE ON THE COLOR AND STYLE OF YOUR DRESS tonight," Britney commented as she gave a final stir to the spaghetti sauce she'd started in the crock pot that morning.

Mandy was aware of her friend's former career in fashion design and was awed by Britney's ability to create stylish clothes. "I still can't believe you're sewing your own wedding gown."

"With any luck," Britney said, holding crossed fingers in the air, "finishing touches go on tomorrow night."

"That soon?"

"I'll tell you a secret," Britney gloated with a wickedly pleased gleam in her blue eyes. "Do you remember the black crepe evening gown with the narrow rhinestone straps and trim around the bodice and hem?"

"The one you made in August to take to New York?"

A few months ago, before Justin proposed marriage, Britney had considered returning to The Big Apple to resume her previous profession.

"Justin's eyes almost popped out of his head when he saw me in that dress." Britney sighed with the memory of Justin pulling a Rhett Butler and carrying her up the stairs to the bedroom of her old apartment. "It's very simple yet elegant. I used the same pattern for the white bridal gown and added a silver-gray lace bolero jacket. I thought it might remind him of our first time together."

"Oh, Britney," Mandy breathed, and hugged her friend. "It sounds beautiful. When do I get to see it?"

"As soon as it's finished. I'll throw a salad together if you set the table."

Mandy went to the cupboard to gather plates and utensils for three. "I doubt Nate will come," she said.

Britney stopped pulling vegetables from the refrigerator and turned toward her housemate. "Of course, he's coming. Why wouldn't he?"

The frown on Mandy's face gave a sour tilt to her lips. "He's seeing someone."

"Since when?"

"Last Friday. They had dinner together."

"How do you know?"

Mandy coughed out a harsh laugh. "She works for me and made a point of telling me yesterday. Ironically, I introduced them and told Nate to contact her if he needed anything. I meant work related."

"Boy, he moves fast," Britney commented, and went back to gathering items for the salad.

"Too damn fast," Mandy muttered.

"I had the impression you weren't interested in Nate."

"I'm not!" Her response was quick and forceful.

Two sharp raps on the front door interrupted the conversation.

"That's Justin," Britney all but sang. She set the vegetables on the counter and headed to the front of the house.

After a not-so-quick kiss, she disentangled herself from his arms. "Mandy doesn't think Nate's coming tonight," she said.

Justin pulled his phone out of his pocket and speed dialed his brother. "Get your ass over to Britney's house, pronto," he commanded, and then disconnected.

❧ Chapter 10 ❧

WALKING INTO THE KITCHEN, JUSTIN WENT TO THE FRIDGE FOR A beer.

Mandy raised a brow as she watched him. "Make yourself at home."

"Thanks, I will," he said, tipping the bottle toward her in salute.

Britney nudged Mandy and handed her a glass of wine. "Should we hold dinner?"

"No, he's late and I'm hungry," Nate's disloyal, older brother said. "I say we eat now."

"I agree." Mandy took a fourth place setting from the cupboard while Britney put the pot of spaghetti on a hot pad in the middle of the table.

After donning hot mitts, Mandy pulled a foil wrapped loaf of garlic bread from the oven. "Since you're so familiar with our refrigerator, Justin," she quipped, "you can get the salad and bring it over."

They were almost finished eating when Nate arrived. "I see you started without me," he said, taking the only vacant chair at the table.

"Serves you right," Justin verbally jabbed at his brother.

Undaunted, Nate filled his plate with spaghetti, plopped a serving of dressed salad on top, covered it all with Parmesan cheese, and started to mix it up. There was total silence around the table. Glancing up, he saw Mandy's astonished gaze locked on his plate.

"What? Haven't you ever seen anyone eat spaghetti before?"

"Not like that," she murmured.

"He's done that since he was a kid," Justin informed them. "Rather disgusting, isn't it?"

"It all ends up in the same place," Nate said.

"Yeah, but we don't have to look at it when it's in our stomachs," Justin argued.

"You always were squeamish." Looking at the women, Nate continued, "He refuses to let anyone put ketchup on their eggs at breakfast."

"Oh, please," Mandy said, getting up from the table and starting to clear it.

Britney pulled a portable dishwasher out of the pantry. One woman rinsed while the other loaded.

A couple minutes later, Nate took his empty plate and silverware to the sink. Handing them to Mandy, he said, "Thanks for dinner. It was great."

She gave him a pitying smile. "Britney cooked tonight."

"In that case," he said, grabbing his future sister-in-law around the waist and dipping her low, he gave her a smacking kiss on the mouth.

"Hey!" Justin objected. "Get your hands—and your lips—off my woman."

Standing again, Nate chortled, "Wow! Dinner was great and so are you. How about seconds?" He reached for her again.

Britney laughed and slapped at him playfully. "Be good, Nate."

"I can't be good—I'm great. In fact, I'm past great. I'm beyond your wildest dreams."

"You're full of bullshit," his brother growled. "Now can we get this show on the road?"

Britney spread photos of flower arrangements and bouquets on the table and set swatches of various colored material next to the pictures. "We'll use the same material for the groomsmen's cummerbunds as we use for Mandy's dress."

"I'm not wearing a cummerbund," Nate said.

"Yes, you are," Justin countered.

"You're the groom. You should wear a cummerbund. I'm only the best man. I don't need one."

"You're right about one thing, Nate. I'm the groom so what I say goes. If the bride wants you to wear a cummerbund, you're wearing one."

Nate gave Britney a sad puppy dog look. "Do I have to?"

"Please," she asked, without asking at all.

He huffed out a breath. "For you, I will."

"Thank you," she said, and turned back toward Justin. Pointing to three groupings of photos, she asked, "Which flower arrangement do you like best?"

He glanced at Nate, who shrugged, indicating it was Justin's problem to figure out. "We grew up on a vegetable farm not a flower farm," he said, feeling out of his element. "I like roses."

"All the arrangements have roses," his fiancée pointed out. "Which color do you like best?"

He shrugged. "The pink, I guess."

Britney picked up a swatch of hot pink material. "Then we'll use this for Mandy's dress and the cummerbunds."

"I'm not wearing a pink cummerbund," Nate stated with no room for argument.

"It's not pink. It's fuchsia," Britney clarified.

"It's pink," he insisted.

"Think of it as salmon," Justin threw in. "Men can wear salmon."

"It's not pink and it's not salmon. It's fuchsia," Britney repeated.

Nate looked at Mandy. "With that fiery red hair, you won't look good in pink."

Her mood matching the material, Britney snapped, "It is not pink."

"I don't care what you call it," the best man barked. "She'll look like sh—" Feeling Justin's kick under the table, Nate modified his choice of words. "It won't look good on her." To prove his point, he took the swatch from Britney and held it next to Mandy's hair.

Mandy grabbed it out of his hand. "I'm not wearing it in my hair, you idiot. It's for my dress."

"Actually, he's right," Britney admitted. "Remember, we planned for you to wear a small head covering in matching tulle. Hold it up again."

Reluctantly, Mandy did. The colors clashed.

"There's a lot of green in the bouquets. Green looks good on redheads," Justin said helpfully.

"Green is for grass and trees," Britney blithely discarded his suggestion. "Not for bridesmaid's dresses or cummerbunds."

After a momentary silence, Nate said, "Not green—blue. The blue of her eyes." He pick up the swatch of royal blue that lay next to another group of photos and held it next to Mandy's face. She started to pull away but Nate took hold of her shoulder with his free hand.

His touch felt warm and soothing through the fabric of her blouse.

"It makes your eyes come alive," he murmured, staring into them.

Mesmerized, Mandy stared back. Under his scrutiny, her breath caught. Nervously, her tongue peeked out as she moistened her lips.

Nate's glance dropped to her mouth and he wondered for the umpteenth time what she tasted like. As if in anticipation of finding out, his heart thumped against his ribcage.

"Yes, the blue is perfect," Britney said. "But it won't go with the pink roses." She scooted a group of pictures closer to Justin. "Are yellow roses and delphiniums okay with you?"

He took her hand and kissed each finger, one by one. "Choose whatever flowers you want, Brit. I'll have eyes for only you."

And I'll have eyes for only Mandy. The thought burst full blown into Nate's mind. "Well, if we're done, I'm out of here," he said in a near panic as he pushed back from the table.

"Not quite," Britney said. "Take off your shirt. I need to measure you for the cummerbund."

A devilish grin spread across his face and he winked at her. "I'd oblige, but with my brother sitting right across from me, there's no way I'm undressing in front of you. You can measure him, if you haven't already. He and I are the same size." Walking out of the kitchen, Nate said, "See you around."

✍ Chapter 11 ❧

THE PHONE BUZZED, IT WAS AN INSIDE LINE. "NATE PETERS," I answered.

"It's almost lunch time," Nicole announced. "Are you eating in or out today?"

Kimberly Long had scheduled two more houses for me to look at that evening so I'd planned to work through lunch and leave a little early. "In today."

"I'm going out for a sandwich. Would you like me to bring anything back for you?" she asked.

"No, I'm good. But thanks for offering." After disconnecting, I turned my attention back to the task at hand.

Twenty minutes later, Nicole walked into my office carrying a take-out bag. "No point in both of us eating alone," she said. I didn't agree, but before I voiced that opinion, she pulled a small Styrofoam box from her bag. "They had pumpkin pie so I got you a piece."

The thoughtful gesture required I resign myself to the inevitable lunchtime schmoozing. "You didn't happen to get a fork with that, did you?"

She continued to empty the bag, placing an individual-sized bag of chips, a paper wrapped sandwich, and napkins on the desk. Reaching back inside, she came out with a plastic fork, which she presented to me with a Cheshire cat grin.

"Thank you," I said, smiling back.

Nicole made herself at home across the desk from me and opened her bag of chips. "How did the wedding plans go last night?" she asked.

Dipping into the pie, I shrugged. "Okay, I guess. Personally, I think it would be a lot easier if the women planned everything then told us guys when and where to show up."

"It's a female conspiracy," she confided with a laugh. "We put you through wedding purgatory in preparation for marriage hell."

I didn't much care for her dismal perspective of weddings and marriage. "On the positive side, I helped prevent a color catastrophe."

"How's that?"

"I mentioned, didn't I, that your boss is the maid of honor?"

Nicole nodded and bit into her sandwich.

"Britney, that's the bride, laid out pictures of different flower arrangements and asked Justin, my brother, which he liked best. He chose pink roses." Taking another bite of pie, I savored the creamy flavor for a moment before continuing. "Britney whipped out a sample of a god awful hot pink material. She called it 'fuchsia,' as if that made any difference. It was still hot pink. She said she'd use it for Mandy's dress." And the cummerbunds, but I refused to mention that.

"You talked her out of it?"

"Fortunately, for Mandy, yes. They're going with royal blue instead, to match her eyes."

A startled look flashed across Nicole's face for a brief second then she sipped through the straw of her soda cup. Abruptly changing the subject, she asked, "Are you taking a date to the holiday party?"

Her question caught me off guard. "I haven't thought about it one way or the other. When is it, again?"

"December tenth, a week from Friday."

"I don't know anyone well enough to take to a job related event. I'll go stag."

"I don't have a date, either," Nicole said, then jumped when the phone beside her buzzed.

I grabbed the receiver, freeing myself from responding to her unveiled hint. "Nate Peters."

"It's Mandy." Her voice had a creamy texture, like the pumpkin pie I'd just eaten. "You ran off so fast last night, Britney forgot to tell you about the schedule for Saturday."

I didn't have a clue what she was talking about but my plans for Saturday began and ended with house hunting.

"Did Justin mention it to you?" Mandy asked.

"No, not a thing." Which was typical of my brother, I thought, as the prickle of irritation heated my neck.

"We'll meet for breakfast. Afterward, we have appointments at some of the hotels to look at banquet rooms for the ceremony and reception."

"You don't need me for that."

All silkiness gone, her reply was crisp. "I'm just the messenger. If you don't want to join us, take it up with Justin." She hung up without saying goodbye.

"You're a little hot under the collar," Nicole observed after I replaced the phone receiver.

I looked at her, trying to remember why she was at my desk. She slurped her soda and it all came back. "It's nothing."

"The Starving Artists craft fair is at the Event Center this weekend," she said, shifting the subject again. "It's a good event if you're looking for unique or unusual gifts for the holidays. I'm going. Do you want to come along?"

"Sorry, I was just informed I have other commitments," I grumbled.

"More wedding plans?" she asked with a sympathetic look.

Nodding a confirmation, I mumbled, "You nailed it."

"It can't possibly take the whole weekend."

I didn't want to go with her so I grimaced. "No telling how long things will take once Mandy starts putting in her two cents worth."

Nicole's empathetic expression vanished at the mention of her boss' name. "You and Mandy must spend a lot of time together. Due to the wedding and all."

I shrugged. It really wasn't any of her business.

✦ Chapter 12 ✦

JUSTIN WAS HOME ALONE WHEN I WALKED IN THE FRONT DOOR Friday evening. He had papers strewn across the dining table and a yellow legal pad filled with notes. "Get comfortable and grab a beer," he said. "We need to talk about the situation with Klickitat County."

He was referring, of course, to whether or not the County had violated the Federal Family Medical Leave Act when they denied my use of sick leave for the time I took off following our father's heart attack. Some of the wages had been withheld from my last two paychecks, and unless I won a claim against Klickitat County, I'd be required to repay the balance. It amounted to a few thousand dollars. In defending the integrity of my professional reputation, Justin was like an avenging angel with the Sword of Justice raised high. Settled in a new job with its corresponding responsibilities, I, on the other hand, resembled an ostrich with his head in the sand, preferring to ignore the issue altogether.

As if girding my loins for battle, I exchanged suit and tie for jeans and sweatshirt. Prepared to wrestle with the legal issues, I returned to the main living area and leaned against the counter separating the kitchen from the dining area where my brother sat at the table.

"You have a choice," Justin said. "The safest route is to file a law suit. We go to court and eventually win."

"How long is 'eventually'?" It seemed the pertinent point.

"About eighteen months."

I didn't like the thought of an unsettled legal matter hanging over my head for that long. "What are the other options?"

"One, you can turn tail and run." He smirked. "That's like admitting you tried to pull a fast one."

"I didn't."

"I know and that's why we won't even consider taking that route. The last option is arbitration, but it involves some risk."

"How so?"

"There are a number of reasons." Preparing to elucidate, he held up his hand with the index finger raised. "First, if we go to court and don't like the outcome, we can appeal."

I nodded.

"Not so with arbitration. Whatever the mediator decides is final. No appeal."

"Can the decision be arbitrary?" I asked, and then thought the question sounded foolish. From the look on his face, Justin did, too.

"It will be within the letter of the law," he explained. "But as you know, the law has a lot of gray areas. That's where arbitration gets a little dicey. Gray areas become a matter of opinion—the arbiter's opinion. If you had spent all your time away from work caring for Dad it would be an open and shut case in your favor. Unfortunately, you were seen helping out at Mom's vegetable stand on more than one occasion."

I decided it was time to crack open a beer and took two from the fridge. Sitting at the table, I placed one in front of Justin. "What do you think the chances are his opinion will side with me?"

"You have a good case," he said, before raising his bottle and drinking.

"There's a big 'but' behind that statement, isn't there?" I asked, knowing his thought process.

"A couple of big 'buts'." Raising his hand again, first one finger and then another went up as he said, "The cost and the arbitrator."

Waiting for him to continue, I sipped from my bottle of brew.

"Arbitration can be expensive," he said.

"How much?"

"In your case, I'm guessing between eight and twelve thousand, but it could be more."

"Jesus, Justin!" I exclaimed. "That's—"

"I know," he said, cutting me off. "But court costs and attorney's fees—if I was charging you, which I'm not—could cost at least that."

"That'll put a serious dent in my savings unless I dip into my retirement account, which I don't want to do."

"Klickitat has to pay half," he informed me. "And if you can't pay your half, they have to foot the whole bill."

"I can do half," I admitted, reluctantly. "But it'll mean putting off the purchase of a house for awhile."

"If you go with arbitration, we'll figure out a way for you to buy a house," my brother assured me.

"You just want me out of here."

"There's no big rush." He gave me a shit eating grin. "And after the wedding it won't make any difference. Brit and I will be on our honeymoon."

"Okay." Getting back to the issue at hand, I asked, "So, how long does arbitration take?"

"That depends on how long it takes for both parties to agree on a mediator. Klickitat will try for someone who has previously decided in their favor. We want someone who has decided against them."

"So both sides haggle until we can agree on someone," I said in understanding.

"Exactly. Then it depends on the arbitrator's schedule. All told, it could take four to six months."

"That sounds better than a year and a half."

Justin tipped his head and looked at me as if I were a simpleton. "Only if the arbiter decides in your favor."

"So . . . are you saying I should file a lawsuit?"

"That's up to you. Your ex-employer is pushing for arbitration. They know that even if they lose, it'll be less expensive than a court battle and the possible appeals."

"How long do I have to decide?"

"Either way, I'd like to get the ball rolling by the first of the week."

I blew out a long breath. "I'll let you know before Monday."

"Good." Justin gathered up his papers to stuff in his briefcase. "What have you got going tomorrow afternoon?"

"That depends on how long it takes you and Britney to decide on the wedding venue."

Justin shrugged. "One place is as good as another as far as I'm concerned, but I'm not Britney. She has a long list of questions to ask at each hotel."

"Why am I not surprised?"

"I'll make a deal with you," he said.

I hated bargaining with my brother, the lawyer, because I usually came out on the short end.

"I'll make sure we get everything wrapped up and cut you loose by lunchtime—if you take Mandy with you tomorrow afternoon."

Shaking my head, I declined his suggestion. "No can do, bro. The realtor told me about a few open houses scheduled for tomorrow. Going through them will save me a lot of house hunting time."

"Come on, Nate. Britney and I need some time alone together."

"I'm not taking Mandy with me, but I'll agree to make myself scarce until after dinner. That should give you plenty of time to put the make on your fiancée."

"You just don't get it, do you? Once Britney and Mandy get going on wedding plans, I can't separate them. It's like they're joined at the hip. I'm asking you, man to man," he practically pleaded, "take Mandy with you."

It was pathetic to see my ex-playboy brother brought so low, but I was adamant. "You're asking too much."

"You're living in my home," he reminded me. "You owe me."

I hated when he had a valid point.

SATURDAY MORNING DAWNED UNDER AN ICY BLUE SKY WITH temperatures to match. The small tourist town Justin called home boasted numerous wedding venues within walking distance of downtown, so the four of us met at the Pig 'N Pancake for breakfast. While eating, we reviewed Britney's, thankfully short, list of hotels and the not-so-short list of questions she wanted to ask.

She had scheduled appointments an hour apart. At each location, we were promptly met by an event coordinator. Throughout the ordeal, that's how I thought of it, Justin and I mostly stood around while Britney and Mandy interacted with the various hotel representatives. While walking from one location to another, bundled up against the chill, we listened to their discussion about what appealed and what didn't, grunting appropriately when needed. At the last hotel, I quietly reminded Justin about the open houses I wanted to see in Astoria.

He leaned close, and whispered in my ear, "You owe me."

Annoyed, I nudged him away. He nudged me right back and mouthed the words again.

"Thank you for your time," Britney said as she shook hands with the last event coordinator. "I'll call on Monday and let you know one way or the other."

"I look forward to hearing from you," he replied, and then continued to chat with her as he led us back to the main lobby.

"Let's have lunch," Britney suggested as she slipped her arms into the coat Justin held. I was about to decline when we walked outside, and she added, "I'm in the mood for a bowl of Norma's World Famous clam chowder." She stamped her feet and hugged herself in the freezing north wind. Justin put his arm around her and pulled her close. They headed east.

I looked at Mandy as she pulled on her gloves and meticulously smoothed the snug fitting fabric over each finger. Her actions looked damned erotic, and watching her, I felt a pleasant tingle in my groin.

Satisfied, she looked up and smiled. "Clam chowder sounds yummy."

Not trusting myself to speak, I nodded. Jamming my ungloved hands in my pockets, I hurried after the lovebirds.

"Hey, wait," Mandy called, rushing to catch up. "Where's the fire?"

In my balls. It had been too long since I'd made love to a woman. "I don't know where we're going and don't want to lose sight of Britney and Justin."

"We're going to Norma's."

"Who is Norma?"

She chuckled. "Not who—where. Norma's is a restaurant."

Like I was supposed to know that.

We turned the corner and there it was. My brother opened the door for his girl and then held it for us.

The place was busy even though it was not quite the lunch hour. Within minutes we were led to a booth overlooking the street. Justin slid in next to Britney, leaving me to share with Mandy.

Sitting beside each other, we both started to shed our coats at the same time. Our shoulders bumped, separated, and came together again as we shrugged opposite arms out of the sleeves. Glancing at each other apologetically, our eyes held. I smiled, slow and easy, feeling a comfortable amity.

As if to protect herself from me, the firebrand scooted over toward the window and dropped her purse on the padded seat between us.

"At one time," Justin said, having removed his coat, "I swore I'd never set foot in here again."

"Why not?" Mandy asked. "The food here is great."

Justin gave Britney a sidelong glance.

She laughed. "A night I'll never forget." Her smile, as she looked at my brother, was full of sweet intimacy.

"I should swear you to secrecy."

Britney patted Justin's hand. "Don't worry, I'll never tell that you—"

He covered her mouth with his in a quick, hard kiss.

"This should be good," I said, in anticipation of a story my brother didn't want told.

"Sorry, Nate," Britney said, leaning her head on her fiancé's shoulder. "I'll never tell."

The server came and we gave our orders. Soon four big bowls of steaming clam chowder arrived along with a basket of fragrant garlic bread. The rich scent warmed my insides. We all dug in as if starving.

After a few minutes, Britney said, "We need to go over these notes this afternoon and make a decision."

Justin gave me a meaningful look as his foot nudged mine under the table.

"I need to head over to Astoria," I hedged, and looked at my watch. "Right away, as a matter of fact."

"You're not working again, are you?" Mandy asked. "I thought you were pretty much caught up."

"He's looking at houses," Justin threw in. "Something to buy."

"Wow, you've only been here two weeks and you're already buying a house," Mandy remarked.

"I'm only looking at this point."

The light of inspiration rose in my brother's eyes. "Just this morning Nate was saying he wished Mom or our sister-in-law, Becky, was in town to give him a woman's perspective on the houses."

Refusing to play along, I dug a ten dollar bill out my wallet and tossed it on the table. "I need to get going."

"Mandy could give you a woman's perspective," Britney suggested.

Whose side was she on, I thought as I rose from the table. Stupid question, I answered myself when Justin put his arm around Britney's shoulders and squeezed.

"You know, I haven't thought about buying a house," Mandy said. "I planned on moving back into an apartment after the wedding but buying might make more sense."

"There you go, Nate." My horny brother almost gloated as he spoke the words. "You can get a woman's perspective and Mandy can dip her toe in the house buying pool at the same time."

The firebrand looked up at me with enthusiasm, as bright as the summer sun, shining in her face. "My car's not too far from here."

Dangling my keys in front of her face, I countered, "Neither is my truck."

⊰ Chapter 13 ⊱

"I THOUGHT YOU WANTED A WOMAN'S PERSPECTIVE," MANDY pouted as she hoisted herself into the truck.

Her delectable backside was the only perspective I cared about at the moment.

"I'll pity the poor woman you marry if you buy that house."

As she turned to reach for the seatbelt, I slammed the door and felt a flicker of satisfaction at the surprise on her face. Rounding the hood, I climbed into the driver's seat. "Since I don't have any immediate plans to get married," I told her, "I think it makes more sense to buy what appeals to me than to worry about the likes and dislikes of a woman I haven't even met."

Ignoring my comment, Mandy referred to the list I'd handed her when we'd first started out. "There's only one left. It's in the Alderbrook area."

"Where's that?"

"The east side. Probably the best way to get there is through downtown." She sat back and sighed. "I never really thought about it before, but renting is easy compared to this."

"How's that?" I started the engine and pulled away from the curb.

"With renting you move in, and if you decide you don't like it, you move out. There's no real commitment." Her voice sounded wistfully sad. "Have you ever owned before?" she asked.

"No, Justin suggested it. He said property values were still depressed and it was a good time to buy, so I started looking."

As we turned the corner onto Commercial, the light at Ninth Street changed to red. We coasted to a stop.

Mandy sat up straight and pointed to our left. "Oh, look! The Starving Artists Bazaar is at the Event Center this weekend."

I glanced in the direction she indicated. "Yeah, I heard about it. What is it, anyway?"

The light changed; I drove and Mandy sat back. "Local artists of every kind get together to sell their wares. Paintings, photography, jewelry, pottery, hand woven baskets, you name it. Sometimes they even have an author or two. We have to stop there after we look at this last house."

"No, we don't," I snorted.

"Sure, you'll love it."

"How do you know?"

"I just know," she said confidently.

Alderbrook was a section of town by the river, two blocks deep and almost half a mile long. The house we sought was situated next to the Columbia. The second story windows sparkled, as if they were laughing eyes, and a wide, covered deck stretched across the front, like a sassy smile on the recent facelift of the older clapboard.

"It's enchanting," Mandy murmured as she slid out of the truck.

"I'm the one looking to buy," I reminded her.

"I'm just saying I like the exterior."

"Yeah, me too," I agreed, hoping the inside pleased me as much.

The frigid east wind gusted along the exposed canyon of the avenue. Taking hold of Mandy's elbow, I led her up the gravel walkway. As we mounted the three broad wooden steps leading to the veranda, the front door opened and a young couple came out.

"I don't know, Cody," the obviously pregnant woman whispered. "It's a little out of our price range?"

The man glared at me, as though it was my fault, and drew the woman out of the doorway to let us pass. Their backs were toward me so I lingered a moment and heard his response. "I really like this house, honey, and—"

Mandy grabbed my arm and pulled me across the threshold. "You were eavesdropping," she accused in a hushed voice.

"Yes, I was."

"Good afternoon, please come in." A man handed each of us a flyer with a color photo of the house and all its vital statistics, so I presumed he was the realtor. "Feel free to look around."

"Thank you," Mandy said, taking the initiative.

I gave her a sidelong look, which she missed because she was studying the brochure.

"I'll be right here if you have any questions," the man continued.

"Thank you," Mandy said again.

We wandered through an archway to the right and came into a living room that ran the width of the house. To our immediate right, in the southwest corner of the room, a Franklin stove offered a much appreciated warm welcome against the afternoon chill. Most of the east wall was taken up with a glassed in breakfront, which might double as a home office, I thought.

Next to me, Mandy gasped and reached out a hand to grasp my arm. "Look," she breathed.

One glance and I understood her breathlessness. The entire north end of the room was an expansive bay window, reaching from the top of a room-wide window seat all the way to the ten foot high ceiling. A breathtaking view across the Columbia River to the hills of Washington was partially obstructed by an ocean freighter, which was moored close enough to see rust stains on its hull.

"With a view like this, I don't care what the rest of the house looks like," I stated. "I want it."

"Don't you think you should at least look?" Mandy asked.

"Why? I doubt I'd ever move from this spot."

"Well, for one thing," she said, referring to the paper in her hand, "The brochure says there is a gas sauna."

"What?"

"Right here." She pointed to the page.

Forgetting I had a flyer of my own, I took hers and read the detailed description of the house. Sure enough, there it was in black and white, a four foot by six foot cedar lined gas sauna. "This I gotta see."

We made a quick walk through the rest of the house. In front was a convenience kitchen with a breakfast nook. Facing the river was a small formal dining room and a family room, or den, both with floor to ceiling windows overlooking the river. On the south side of the central hallway were two smaller bedrooms with a full bath in between. Toward the back was the master bedroom, complete with the expansive windows I'd come to expect, and surprisingly, two large walk-in closets. The master bath was unremarkable except for the double sinks and the frosted glass door with the word *SAUNA* stenciled in black italics across the face.

Pulling the door open, we both ducked inside. The floor was ceramic tile with a drain in the middle. The low ceiling and all the walls, with the exception of the glass door, were tongue-in-groove red cedar with an open slatted cedar bench along the back wall.

"This house is too good to be true," I murmured.

"Yeah, makes you wonder what's wrong with it. Why is it on the market?" Mandy asked.

I looked down at her. For a moment, I wondered if this would be the only time I'd have Mandy in a sauna. Not that I'd *had* her, but still. "I don't know. Let's go ask."

We passed another couple in the hall as we made our way back to the realtor. "Thank you for coming," he commented as we approached.

"We have a question," Mandy said before I could.

"Yes?"

"We wondered why this house is for sale," she continued.

"I don't know what you mean."

"She means," I said, taking over. "With all the amenities, why would a person sell?"

He leaned his shoulder against the wall. "The owner bought the house with the intention of doing some cosmetic work and turning it for a tidy profit. Unfortunately, he bought at the top of the market. When the bottom fell out, he decided to keep the house and did a total makeover. It turned out real nice."

"So why is he selling?" I asked again.

The realtor sighed and stood up straight. "The owner worked construction. A lot of people worked construction, for that matter. When the recession hit, most found another type of work or moved away. Not this guy. I guess things finally caught up with him financially. The bank foreclosed last year."

"If the bank foreclosed last year, why is it still on the market?" Mandy asked.

"I have no idea. Maybe it's taken this long for the dust to settle," he speculated. "All I know is that it came on the market last week."

"Okay," I said. "I want to make an offer."

"Do you have a realtor?"

"Yes, Kimberly Long."

"You should talk to her. She can draw up the papers."

I pulled my phone out and hit Kimberly's speed dial number.

"I should warn you though," the realtor said as Kimberly's phone rang. "The bank's not dickering. They want full price."

"I don't have a problem with that." Voice mail picked up. "Kimberly, it's Nate Peters," I said, leaving a message. "I want to make an offer on a house. I'm in Astoria. Please call me as soon as possible."

When I clicked off, Mandy nudged my elbow. "Maybe we have time to go to the Starving Artists Bazaar."

Looking at her like she was crazy, I said, "I'm trying to buy a house."

"You can't buy it until your realtor calls back. We might as well do something while we wait."

My phone rang, relieving me of arguing with her. "Nate Peters," I answered, turning away from Mandy and the salesman. "Hi, Kimberly. Thanks for calling back so quickly. I found a house."

"I gathered that from your message. Do you have a listing number?" she asked.

I looked at the flyer in my hand. The number was at the top. "Yeah."

"Bring it with you. I can meet you at my office at four-thirty today."

"Okay, great. See you then." I looked at my watch. It was almost three. Enough time to take Mandy home before meeting Kimberly. "Come on, let's go."

❧ Chapter 14 ❧

Buckling her seat belt, Mandy asked, "What time are we meeting your realtor?"

"We aren't," Nate informed her. "You're going home."

"You can't take me home yet."

"Sure I can." He started the engine and made a three point turnaround in the street.

"No, you can't. We have to go to the Starving Artists Bazaar."

"No, we don't."

"Yes, we do," she asserted, planting her butt more firmly in the seat. "It's fun. You'll enjoy it."

Nate glanced briefly in her direction. "We don't have time."

"What time is your appointment?"

"There's enough time to take you home."

"Which means, if you don't take me home, we have time to go through the Starving Artists Bazaar," she pointed out.

"I'm taking you home."

"Aarrgh," she growled. "You are not taking me home, Nathan Peters."

"Yes, I am."

"I promised Britney to give her an afternoon of private time with Justin."

Glaring at her, Nate sneered. "No, you didn't. You came with me because my brother fed you a line of crap about me wanting a woman's perspective."

"Get real. I didn't believe that for a minute," she scoffed. "I came along as a courtesy to my friend. And I don't want to go home until I'm sure I won't intrude on them."

"They're at Justin's place."

"You don't know that," she argued. "If you remember, I gave Britney my keys so she could drive my car home. They might have stayed at the house instead of going to the condo."

Damn, Nate hated being out maneuvered but couldn't think of a good argument.

Mandy took his silence as agreement. "Turn here," she instructed. "There's a parking lot next to the Judge Boyington Building."

Within minutes, they walked into the bazaar at the Astoria Event Center and immediately split up, each looking for what attracted their personal interests.

Later, while flipping through a crate of colorful eight by ten inch, matted photographs, Nate's elbow was bumped. Twice. Unconsciously, he took a half step to his left to give the other attendee more room, and then his elbow was bumped again. Annoyed, he looked to his right and saw Nicole French. Her face sported a wide grin.

"Hi, Nate. I see you escaped the wedding plans hell."

Shrugging a shoulder, he said, "It wasn't that bad. Besides, my brother knew I had things to do today."

"Like meeting me at the Starving Artists Bazaar?" she asked, slipping her arm through his.

Extricating himself from her grasp, Nate picked up a black and white shot of the Astoria Column sharing the night sky with a full moon, and asked, "What do you think of this photo?"

Nicole inched closer, crowding him. With people on the other side hedging him in, Nate felt trapped.

"I like it." She took the photo and held it at arm's length to study the detail. Then she flashed an enticing smile. "It looks dreamy and . . . romantic. Are you dreamy and romantic?"

Nate considered himself anything but dreamy. However, when the situation and the woman called for it, he knew how to be romantic. Now was not the situation, nor was Nicole the woman. Jostled again, someone stepped up to join them.

"Wow, what a great picture," Mandy exclaimed, taking the photo from Nicole's hand. "If you're not going to buy it, I am."

"Excuse me, ladies, but I saw it first," Nate said, reaching for it. His hand brushed Mandy's and an electric shock passed between them. He felt her tremble. Their eyes met and lingered.

Seeing the exchange, Nicole frowned.

Reluctantly, Nate turned away and pulled out his wallet.

Mandy tapped her watch to remind him of the time and noticed her fingers still quivered from his touch. "You better hurry up or we'll be late."

"Late for what?" Nicole asked, her scowl deepening.

"We've been house hunting," her boss said.

"Together?" The word burst out.

"I've been house hunting," Nate tossed over his shoulder as he handed the photographer behind the table payment for the purchase. Turning back toward the women, he jerked his head in Mandy's direction. "She's just along for the ride."

"I see," Nicole said through stiff lips.

"Not really, but we don't have time to explain," he told her. With the photo in one hand, Nate pressed his other on the small of Mandy's back and maneuvered her toward the exit.

"You need to get that framed," she said as they crossed Commercial Street.

"You don't say."

"It'll look great in a plain, black frame."

"I was thinking chrome."

"Won't chrome detract from the photo?" she asked as Nate unlocked the passenger door.

He decided the best entertainment of the afternoon was watching the swing of Mandy's hips as she climbed into his truck. He considered the wisdom of finding other occasions to be entertained in the future.

"Well, won't it?" she asked once more, when he was behind the wheel.

Nate looked at her. The fading light of late afternoon cast her face in shadow. He was tempted to reach out and touch her, pull her into his arms for a slow, sensual kiss, and then take her home and make love to her.

"Nate?"

"Hmm?"

"A chrome frame would be lost against an eggshell colored wall."

The bubble of his fantasy popped. With a shudder, he realized how long it had been since he'd had sex.

"The photo needs—in fact, demands—a simple, black frame," Mandy insisted. "I'll go with you to make sure it gets done right."

Nate faced forward and turned the ignition key. "You're not going anywhere with me." He put the truck in gear, checked his mirrors, and backed out.

Offended by his sudden change of demeanor, Mandy frowned. "Right now, I'm going with you to your realtor's office."

"Where you will wait in the truck until I'm finished."

"I'm not waiting in the truck," she objected.

"Yes, you are."

"Nate, it's December. It's cold. I'm not waiting in the truck."

She had a point, but . . . "I won't be that long."

"The heck you won't. You're making an offer on a house. That takes time. I'm not waiting in the truck."

"You don't understand," Nate reasoned. "I don't share personal financial information with others."

She turned to face him. "You're not applying for a loan. You're making an offer on a house. I was with you, remember? I read the flyer and know how much the house costs." She saw his jaw muscle ripple. "Besides, the man said the bank won't negotiate so I already know whatever it is you want kept private. I promise, I won't tell a soul."

The muscle in his jaw twitched again. Everything she said was beside the point. "I'll take you to a coffee shop."

"I don't want coffee."

"So order a piece of pie and have a cup of tea."

"Aarrgh," she growled for the second time that day. "I refuse to sit in a coffee shop, all by myself, for who knows how long. I'd be bored out of my mind within five minutes."

"Read a magazine or something."

As Mandy's agitation rose, so did her voice. "I'm not going to sit in a coffee shop. I'm not going to read a magazine or something. You'd probably get so caught up in the process you'd forget all about me. No way. I'm going to the realty office with you, and that's final."

"All right!" Nate shouted. "You win!" He pounded the steering wheel with the palm of his hand. "But this is the last time you're going anywhere with me. Do you hear me? *The last damn time!*"

❧ Chapter 15 ❧

THE WOMAN DROVE ME CRAZY. TAGGING ALONG WHERE SHE WASN'T wanted, dragging me to an artist's bazaar I didn't want to attend, forcing me to take her with me to the realtor's office. It was all too much.

A sniffling noise sounded beside me. I refused to look. If I didn't look, it would stop. *Please, God, make it stop.* The sound came again, a little louder. Hazarding a brief glance in Mandy's direction confirmed my worst fear. She was crying.

"Please, don't," I groaned, regretting the loss of my temper.

"Take me home," Mandy wailed. "I want to go home."

With a fast look in the mirrors, I safely whipped the truck to the side of the road and ignored the blare of a horn as the car behind drove past.

"Mandy, don't, *please.*" I felt the urge to scoop her up and let her cry on my shoulder but didn't know if I should touch her or not. "Please, Mandy. I didn't mean to yell at you."

"Yes, you did." She hunched down in the seat and sobbed.

Tentatively, I placed my hand on her quaking shoulder. She didn't pull away so I gentled her with a feather-light sweep down her back, letting my hand rest at her waist. She quieted and sniffled again.

Reaching into my back pocket, I came out with a clean hanky and handed it to her. She dried her cheeks, dabbed at her eyes, and then blew her nose. "You can take me home now," she said with hushed solemnity.

"There isn't time," I soothed in a soft voice.

"Then I'll stay in the truck until you're done."

The woman was contrary, plain and simple. "It's too cold for you to sit in the truck," I reminded her. "We'll get this done and then I'll take you home."

She wouldn't look at me but nodded her consent.

Shifting in the seat, I realized I'd driven a good mile past the realty office. After waiting for a break in traffic, I made a U-turn in the middle of the street.

A few minutes later, we walked into Kimberly's office together. While conducting business in a glassed-in room, I watched Mandy sitting in the waiting area, flipping through a magazine and sipping the cup of tea the realtor had offered.

When the buyer's portion of the purchase agreement was completed, Kimberly informed me she would present my offer Monday morning to the bank currently owning the property. She said it might take a couple days to hear back from them, promising to call as soon as she did.

WEDNESDAY, ABOUT MID AFTERNOON, NATE RECEIVED THE LONG awaited phone call from Kimberly. The news wasn't good.

"I'm sorry. The bank received four offers on the house. Yours came in second."

"What you do you mean? You called first thing Monday morning, didn't you?" Nate felt his temper straining against his usually placid composure.

"Yes, but they knew the property was hot and accepted offers through the close of business Monday. They took their sweet time reviewing them, which is why I haven't called before now."

"Why did mine come in second? I offered full price."

"I know, but someone else offered more. How much, I don't know."

"How can someone offer more than the asking price?"

"Potential buyers can offer anything they want. Before the real estate bubble broke I saw properties sell within a day of going on the market, sometimes for twenty or thirty thousand more than the asking price," Kimberly informed him.

"Damn it!" Nate ground out. "I really wanted that house."

Sympathizing with her client, she served up a ray of hope. "All is not lost. They accepted your offer on a contingency basis."

"What does that mean?"

"It means that if the other sale falls through, you're first in line."

"What are the chances of that happening?" The flat tone of his voice expressed his doubt and disappointment.

"It's a possibility," she said. "The person I spoke with told me that, unlike you, the first choice buyers haven't secured a loan yet. If for any reason they don't qualify, the house is all yours."

Nate sighed, unwilling to let the slim possibility excite him. "How long until we know?"

"That depends on the strength of their qualifications and where they apply for the loan. If they use a local lender we'll probably know within a week or two. If they apply online, it might take a little longer. If they need a government loan," she snorted softly, "it could take a month to six weeks."

"Is there any way to find out?"

"Not really. Everything is confidential. I probably wouldn't know this much except the bank wants to secure a backup buyer in case this one doesn't qualify."

Nate already had the mental discomfort of the unsettled situation with his former employer and wasn't sure he wanted additional uncertainty.

His hesitation prompted Kimberly to say, "If you don't want to wait you can pass on the contingency and look for something else."

"Damn it," he said again, but with less force. His mind searched for options and found none. "I really want that house, if at all possible."

"Then I'll tell the bank you agree to the contingency," Kimberly said. "You need to sign some papers. What time can you come in?"

"After work, say about five-fifteen."

"Sounds good. I'll have everything ready."

"Okay, thanks," Nate said, and hung up the phone.

***

DRIVING SOUTH ON HIGHWAY 101, MANDY WAS HALFWAY HOME from work, on the narrow stretch of raised roadbed that ran past the exit to Glenwood Village. Without warning, the car in front of her made a suicidal left turn. Horns blared. The car at the head of a long line of oncoming traffic swerved to avoid a collision, and hit the southbound guardrail, bounced off, and careened in Mandy's direction. Instinctively, she braked hard and turned the wheel to miss the other vehicle. The metal-to-metal screech of her front fender grinding along the guardrail sounded like fingernails scraping down a chalkboard. Simultaneously—violently—with stunning force, the airbag slammed into Mandy's torso. Time, stretching fluidly, expanded the few brief seconds into long, agonizing minutes—hours—of disorienting terror. Finally, the jarring rock of her car came to a complete standstill.

Dazed, Mandy looked up at a man tapping on her window. His lips were moving. She heard words but could make no sense of them. He knocked on the window again, and slowly, her mind cleared.

"Unlock your door," he instructed in a loud voice.

With quivering fingers, she reached over and flipped the switch.

The man pulled the door open and crouched by her side. "Are you all right?"

"I think so." Her voice trembled. Mentally, she took a quick survey. "Nothing hurts. Yeah, I'm okay."

"Then let's get you out of there." The Good Samaritan reached in and disengaged her seatbelt. Then he stood and held out his hands.

She grasped the offered support, swinging her legs out as he pulled her up and out. Mandy's knees buckled and she plopped back into the driver's seat. "I think maybe I should just sit here a few minutes."

Hunkered down on his knees in front of her, he asked, "Do you want an ambulance?"

"No, I'm okay, just shaken up a little."

Sirens sounded in the distance.

"That's probably the police," he commented, looking north toward Warrenton. He stood and walked to the front of

Mandy's car. A minute later he came back. "The police can call you a tow truck."

"Huh?"

"You probably can't drive the car until repairs are made."

Mandy felt like weeping. She had only four payments left on the car loan. "Is it totaled?"

"I doubt it, but you'll need a new fender," the man said.

"Oh."

The sirens faded and were replaced by the pulsing flash of the overhead police lights.

IT WAS AFTER SEVEN BEFORE I TRUDGED THROUGH MY BROTHER'S front door wanting nothing more than a cold beer and some hot food. Instead, I found Justin in his spare bedroom, *my* bedroom, packing clothes into a garment bag. At second glance, I realized he was packing *my* clothes into *my* garment bag.

"What the hell are you doing?" I demanded.

"Packing your bags, bro." As I stood watching in disbelief, he kept working, tugging meticulously to straighten the fabric of my shirts so they wouldn't wrinkle. "Don't worry, it's only 'til the weekend or maybe the first of the week. You can come back to watch the game on Sunday."

Releasing my briefcase, it thumped to the floor. My self control followed. "I don't know what the hell's going on, but I've had one hell of a day. On top of everything else, I was stuck for the better part of an hour on that narrow damn stretch of highway this side of Warrenton while they cleaned up after an accident. I don't need any more crap tonight."

Justin paused in his task and glared at me. "Mandy was *in* that accident."

The rusty knife of his words sliced through my anger. "My God, is she okay? I saw a car get hauled up the embankment. It was a wreck."

"She's okay, shaken up pretty bad but not hurt. I can't say the same for her car, though." He zipped the garment bag closed. "Her right front fender clipped the guardrail. Thank God it held or she would have sailed down into the slough."

"Jesus, that's at least a thirty foot drop."

He opened my small duffle and tossed in a few pair of boxers and some sox.

Coming back to the moment, I asked him again, "What the hell are you doing?"

Justin stopped and raised his hands to his hips. His brown eyes, hot as a tar pot, glared at me again. "I'm doing you the favor of packing your bags."

"Why?" I asked, still tired and now confused.

He drew a deep breath and blew it out. "Mandy's going to need a ride to work until her car's repaired. Britney and I thought it would be easier for you to stay at their place."

"No way." I backed out of the bedroom and headed for the kitchen. The way things were going, I needed something stronger than beer.

"Come on, Nate, it makes sense," Justin argued, chasing after me like a yapping dog nipping at my heels. "She needs transportation for a few days and you work at the same place."

"That doesn't mean I have to live with her," I stated as I twisted the cap off a beer.

My brother took it from my hand, tipped it to his mouth, and swallowed deep. "Staying at her place will save you the hassle of driving over there morning and night to pick her up and drop her off. That's at least a half hour, twice a day."

"That's bullshit," I said.

"No, it's not. Besides, Britney agreed to stay with me until Mandy's car is fixed," he informed me with a face splitting grin. "So you really don't have a choice in the matter."

❧ Chapter 16 ❧

THE CRASH VICTIM WAS IN BED WHEN I ARRIVED.

"Whether she knows it or not," Britney told me quietly, "Mandy is going to feel that accident all over tomorrow. I insisted she take a nighttime pain pill and suggest you let her sleep until six-thirty in the morning. If you wake up and get your shower before that, you'll have time to fix her breakfast."

Considering what the firebrand had been through, I didn't argue. "Does she know about the new sleeping arrangements?" My voice was as hushed as Britney's.

"Yes. She wasn't particularly happy about it but agreed that it made sense. By the way, we have eggs and cheese in the refrigerator or there's granola if you don't cook.

"I know how to prepare a hot breakfast." Continuing to whisper, I asked, "What about coffee? I don't recall seeing a coffee maker in your kitchen."

"I converted Mandy into a tea drinker. There's both caffeinated and herbal in the cupboard above the stove."

I'd make a point of stopping at one of the numerous coffee huts on the way to work.

"I put fresh sheets on my bed and clean towels are on the wicker stand-up rack in the bathroom. There's not much room in the little mirrored cabinet," she added, rather sheepishly. "Sorry, but we're women and it's full of our cosmetics."

"Don't worry about it. I usually keep shaving gear and stuff in my ditty bag when I travel. It's easier that way."

"Okay, then, I'll leave you to it," she said, and picked up her suitcase.

I gave her a brotherly kiss on the cheek before opening the front door for her. Then I reached for the remote control, and keeping the volume low, made myself at home.

The next morning, Mandy grumbled a little about the late rise-and-shine call but bit back her words when told a cheese omelet would be served for breakfast. She took a shower hot enough to billow fragrant steam into the hallway. I reflected on that for a few seconds before deciding the bathroom door was left open out of habit, not as an invitation. Still, the thought was there.

Mandy moved with stiff precision as she climbed into my truck for the drive to work. The fresh scent of her shower filled the cab. When we stopped at a well known coffee drive through, I learned that contrary to Britney's belief, the sexy redhead beside me wasn't a true convert to tea. She ordered a hot mocha and greedily sipped from the cardboard cup for the remainder of the trip to work.

Oregon's Astoria is built on a hill. Except for two blocks downtown, most structures are on different levels from one side to the other. Turning from Eighth Street onto Exchange, I coasted to the curb in front of the County office building. "Why don't you get out here so you don't have to climb the stairs in back," I suggested.

"Thanks, I will," Mandy said, and gingerly slid out of the truck.

I drove around to the back lot. Other vehicles followed me in and one parked beside mine. Nicole stepped out of it. We hadn't seen each other since our encounter at the bazaar and the blaze in her eyes told me it wasn't accidental. Her icy, tight-lipped smile confirmed my impression.

"Dropping Mandy off in front won't fool anyone," Nicole said.

"What are you talking about?" I asked.

"Did you spend the night with her or are the two of you carpooling?" she asked with dripping sarcasm.

"As a matter of fact, for the next few days, we are," I said. We headed toward the office building. "Mandy was in an accident last night. Her car is in for repairs."

"How convenient."

"Actually it's not but that's beside the point. Until she gets her car back, I'm her chauffer."

Nicole crossed her arms. "What about the office party tomorrow night?"

"What about it?" I asked, starting to sound like a parrot.

"I thought we were going together."

Not likely, I thought, and bit my tongue as I held the door open. She stomped into the building and I followed. "Look, Nicole," I said with an appeasing smile. "There's no time for explanations right now. Let's have lunch and I'll tell you about this ridiculous predicament."

She punched the elevator button, still looking disgruntled. "Okay, but if I don't like what I hear, you're buying."

"I'll buy regardless," I assured her, figuring a meal was a small price to pay for maintaining congenial work relations.

The elevator bell dinged, she stepped in. I hung back because I preferred to take the stairs. As the elevator door closed, it dawned on me that Nicole hadn't asked if her boss had been injured in the accident.

BACK AT HER DESK AFTER LUNCH, NICOLE RUMINATED ON THE situation. According to Nate, he'd been forced into the role of cabby by his older brother. Although the explanation sounded reasonable, even comic from the way Nate told it, she wondered why he wasn't put out about it. Maybe escorting Mandy to the office party didn't bother him, at least not at the moment. But by tomorrow night, Nicole thought, he'd regret it. She would make sure of that because she had wanted Nathan Peters to take her to the party. She wanted to invite him into her home for a night cap afterward and let one thing lead to another. That wouldn't be possible with Mandy in the picture.

In fact, a lot of things weren't possible because of her boss—like the promotion Nicole wanted, or rather needed. As long as Mandy was the Deputy Assessor/Tax Collector, Nicole was stuck in the position of Tax Technician. There was nowhere else for her to go without a degree in Management. After meeting the available Dr. French, and getting pregnant, the Business Management degree Nicole had been working toward hadn't been as important as planning their hurry-up destination wedding in Cancun. Now, even if by some miracle Nicole received a raise to the highest end of the pay scale for her current position, it would be insufficient to maintain her house payments once her alimony ended.

Damn. Without a promotion, her only alternative was to find a second source of income. One sure way to do that, Nicole knew, was to marry another above-average wage earner. Except, she didn't want to get married, she liked her single lifestyle. Damn, damn, and double damn. It felt like being squeezed between the proverbial rock and hard place.

Of course, if the man was good looking and had a nice set of pecs, marriage might be okay—at least for a few years. After all, Nicole reminded herself, marriage wasn't a forever kind of thing.

"I ACHE ALL OVER FROM THE ACCIDENT," MANDY TOLD ME AS WE arrived back in Gearhart that evening.

Putting the truck in park, I turned off the engine. "You should see a doctor."

"I don't need a doctor," she said, but her slow movements getting out of the truck belied her assertion. "Doctors prescribe pain medicines but my system doesn't tolerate them. Pain meds knock me out and I'm down for the count. It took me forever to wake up in the shower this morning after taking an over-the-counter medication last night."

"I'm not talking about a medical doctor," I clarified as we walked toward the house. "You hurt because your body sustained a massive jolt. The bones of your ribcage or shoulders might be out of whack. A chiropractor can fix that."

"You're kidding?" she asked, unlocking the door.

"No, that's what chiropractors do." I looked at my watch. "It might not be too late to call one and schedule an appointment for tomorrow."

"I don't know." Mandy sounded like she wanted to be convinced.

"Tell you what," I suggested. "Take a couple aspirin and I'll find a chiropractor for you. Trust me, a chiropractor will fix you up."

"I'll tell you what," Mandy countered. "You schedule an appointment, but if I feel better tomorrow, I reserve the right to cancel it."

"Fair enough."

The next morning Mandy could hardly move, and even after taking three aspirins, required my help getting into the truck for the drive to work. We went through the whole process again when it was time to drop her off at Astoria Chiropractic for her ten-thirty appointment.

Shortly before lunchtime, she showed up at my office door. "Hey, Nate, thanks for suggesting the chiropractor."

"Feel better?"

"Amazingly so." Mandy wiggled her trim, little body around to prove her point. "She told me to take it easy for a few days and scheduled a follow-up appointment for Monday, just in case I need it."

"Good," I said, and then frowned. "How did you get back here? I thought you were going to call me to pick you up."

"Another patient was nice enough to give me a lift."

"I would have gone to get you."

"I know, but you're doing enough as it is." After a moment, she added, "In case I haven't told you, I do appreciate everything."

"What are friends for?"

"Are we? Friends, I mean?" She looked unsure. And maybe she was after our rough start.

Giving a nonchalant shrug, I smiled. "Sure we are, Mandy."

Her blush delighted me.

ALTHOUGH I HAD PLANNED TO STAY IN THE OFFICE AND WORK UNTIL the party, Mandy insisted she needed a shower and change of clothes. Why did that surprise me? Since we had to drive back to Gearhart, I decided to shave and change out of my suit and tie. Justin hadn't packed many clothes for me but I found a pair of heavy brown corduroy slacks and a russet pullover that went okay with an open-collared, button-down dress shirt. There was also my favorite pair of cordovan loafers.

I wanted a beer but decided it was best to forgo that pleasure until party time. Instead, I perused the music selection, ignoring all the country western and country rock, presuming those were Britney's preferences. What remained gave me an unexpected insight into my date's musical tastes.

Eerrrt ... replay that! *Mandy is* not *my date!*

A faint rustling sounded behind me and I turned. *God! I wish she was.*

Wearing a form-fitting, long sleeved dress that came to mid thigh, it looked much shorter due to the fancy stilts adorning her feet. Whoever said redheads couldn't wear red had never seen Mandy in this particular shade. The fabric was shot through with gold metallic thread. When she moved, she glittered.

"I'm ready if you are," she said, and picked up her purse.

Oh, I'm ready all right. But I doubt we're ready for the same things.

Using public monies to finance employee recreation would be malfeasance, so the no-host cocktails and dinner holiday celebration at The Supper Club included individual tabs for the attendees.

Mandy and I separated shortly after arriving. She headed upstairs to join a gaggle of women while I remained below with the men.

For a short time, a group of us talked shop before the conversation shifted to football, a universal language. Periodically, whooping laughter drifted down from the female aerie. We paid it scant attention. The Seattle Seahawks were enjoying a phenomenal season, racking up win after win, and debate of possible Super Bowl contenders ensued. Soon though, wives and girlfriends claimed their armchair coaches and led them to various tables for dinner.

I considered asking Mandy and Nicole to join me but the sounds emanating from above left me unsure if I was brave enough to venture up there to find them.

Screaming laughter had everyone's eyes tilting toward the balcony. A waiter hurried down the stairs and walked directly to me.

"Excuse me, sir," he said in a stage whisper. "Did you arrive with the redhead wearing a red dress?"

My senses went on full alert. "Is there a problem?"

"She's had too much to drink, sir."

"That's impossible." Checking my watch, I said, "We haven't even been here forty-five minutes."

"All I know is she's wasted and in no condition to . . . someone should take her home," he advised.

"Does she have a tab?" I asked.

"Yes."

Pulling out my wallet, I handed him a ten. "Will this cover it?"

"I'll check," he said, and scurried away.

Another burst of laughter came from overhead as I made a beeline for the stairs. Gathering what fortitude I could, I began the climb. At the top, a group of women perched around a table, cawing in merriment. I, however, failed to find what amused. Then I saw Mandy, her elbow on the table with her head propped precariously on her hand. She hiccupped, dislodging her elbow and, in turn, her head. Laughter pealed again. Mandy weaved drunkenly before managing to resume her prior position. As I strode forward, she hiccupped again and the entire, humiliating process repeated itself.

Scowling at Nicole, who sat beside her boss, I leaned down and hissed, "What the hell is going on here?"

"Looks like our fearless leader can't hold her banana . . ." she guffawed in glee and the others followed suit. "Her banana daiquiri," Nicole finished with a snickering snort.

"Hi, Nathan," Mandy chimed in and sat up a little straighter. "Are you here for me, hot stuff?" she asked.

The women around the table howled.

"Yes, Mandy, I'm taking you home," I murmured. "Come on, let's get up."

She hiccupped again. "Not sure I can."

"You can," I said, stepping behind her and slipping my hands under her elbows. She came up readily enough but leaned heavily against me. I wasn't sure how we'd get down the stairs and out to my truck. She made it easy for me by passing out.

As I lifted her into my arms, my furious glance swept around the table. In the sudden silence, all eyes except Nicole's dropped in shame. For a moment I thought hers held hard satisfaction before they melted with soft sympathy. "Should I get Ernie to help?"

As if Mandy wanted our boss to see her in this condition. "No, I can manage," I ground out between clenched teeth. I hefted the little firebrand onto my shoulder in a fireman's carry and tucked her shirt under my forearm.

At the base of the stairs, the waiter stood, hesitantly holding out a couple dollars in change.

"Keep it," I said tersely, and kept walking through the suddenly quiet restaurant.

Mandy slept all the way home but came to a little when I picked her up to carry her into the house. As I eased her down to the bed, she put her arms around my neck and purred seductively.

Ignoring the suggestive sound, I coaxed her pragmatically, "Come on, sweetheart, let's get you into bed."

"You come, too."

The words invoked an uncharacteristic tremble in my knees. "Not tonight, Mandy," I murmured.

"You want me. I know you do," she slurred. "I heard you tell Justin."

That had happened six weeks ago, on the day we'd met. Before we started working together. Long before I had a chance to get to know her as a person.

"Come on, Nate," she wheedled, and locked her lips to mine. She teased my lips, so I obligingly tangled our tongues together. There was nothing drunk about the sweetness of her kiss, unless it was how it made me feel.

She hummed that seductive purr again, shooting fire straight to my loins. As I deepened our kiss, her hands fell away from my shoulders and Mandy went limp in my arms. She had passed out again.

"Shit," I said.

Not knowing what else to do, I removed her shoes, dress and stockings. Pulling the covers up to her chin, I placed a solicitous kiss on her forehead and hoped to hell Mandy wouldn't remember any of this in the morning.

∝ Chapter 17 ∾

I TRIED TO TELL MYSELF COWARDLINESS WASN'T THE REASON I LEFT
before Mandy woke, nor was it because she kissed me. It was
out of consideration for her feelings and not wanting to share
her embarrassment about last night.

Six-thirty normally wasn't too early to return to my brother's
place, except his lovely fiancée was warming his sheets on this
blustery, overcast day.

A leisurely trip to Astoria for breakfast and a light flirtation
with the waitress diverted my thoughts from Mandy's kiss,
from the feel of her in my arms.

After leaving the restaurant, I felt at loose ends and decided
to cruise around to familiarize myself with the town. On Eighth
Street, past the century old courthouse where Justin spent
some of his time, and one block up, across the street from
where I worked, was Flavel House Museum. I'd heard the
aging Victorian-era mansion had been built by a rich sea
captain. Shifting the truck into second gear, I crept up the
steep incline to the top of the hill, turned left onto Niagara, and
then a minute later, wound my way up Coxcomb Drive to the
Astor Column. I studied the exterior of the spire, which
illustrated in pictorial splendor, the history of the region, and
then counted the one hundred sixty-four treads of the
Column's interior spiral staircase as I climbed to the lookout
deck at the top. The view of the Columbia River and Youngs
Bay was worth every step of the ascent.

Soon after, heading back toward the heart of town, I drove down the narrow curves that spilled out onto Fifteenth Street. Two blocks later, the road was permanently closed to all but pedestrian traffic due to the abrupt degree of inclination. Bounding down the hill on Sixteenth Street, I passed older homes that were interspersed with apartment buildings and businesses, all of a similar age. A little farther on, near the base of the hill, was a venerable old structure with white columns and a balcony built for giving speeches. In a bygone era it had been City Hall; it now housed the Heritage Museum.

My wandering drive eventually took me past a uniquely modern building on the riverfront. A huge windowed section at the front, containing the life-sized diorama of a Coast Guard cutter battling its way up a nearly vertical wave, drew my attention, but I didn't stop.

Minutes later, I parked in front of the house I coveted. Wind buffeted the truck; I sat and indulged my imagination. Fantasizing about puttering around the yard and fishing off the small dock that jutted into the water at the back of the house brought to mind Mandy's face, glowing in pure delight, as she gazed at the moored freighter out the big bay window of the living room. From there my mind naturally drifted to thoughts of Mandy's arms twined around my neck, her firm lips pressed to mine, and the sweet taste of bananas on her tongue.

Raindrops splattered on the windshield and washed away my reverie. The house wasn't mine. Neither was Mandy. She was my co-worker, and therefore, off limits, I reminded myself sternly.

Dissatisfied about the situation with the house and perturbed by recurring thoughts of last night's kiss, I worked the gearshift and headed back toward Justin's place and the reality of my life.

The savory scent of stew seduced my olfactory system when I walked in the door of my brother's condo. He was sitting at the counter between the kitchen and the dining room eating lunch.

"Smells good. Is there any more?" I asked.

"In the fridge," he said around a mouthful. "Leftovers from last night. Brit made it."

Scooping a healthy portion into a bowl, I said, "You don't deserve her. She should marry me instead of you."

"Sorry, buddy, I saw her first."

I put the bowl in the microwave and inserted a slice of bread in the toaster.

"By the way," Justin said as he finished eating and rounded the counter with his dirty dishes. "We settled on a mediator yesterday."

My stomach fell to the floor. "Why didn't you tell me?" I asked.

"I'm telling you now." He rinsed his bowl and put it in the dishwasher.

The toast popped and the oven dinged. "So, what now?"

"Now, we wait for a hearing date to be set."

He acted calm, but to me it felt as if my entire future hung in the balance. "How long will that take?"

"I'll probably hear back next week."

"Next week," I said, the words stumbling over my lips.

"Yeah, next week," he repeated. Then he punched me on the shoulder in typical brotherly fashion. "Don't forget your stew is in the oven," he said, and walked out of the kitchen.

LIGHTLY TAPPING ON THE BEDROOM DOOR, BRITNEY CALLED OUT, "Mandy? Are you in there?"

Although her house mate was not a crack-of-dawn riser on weekends, she was usually up by eight or a little after. It was now past ten. Britney had arrived home a few minutes before, expecting to find both Mandy and Nate eating a late breakfast. Instead, there was no sign her future brother-in-law had ever been there and Mandy's bedroom door was closed, which it never was once she was up.

Britney knocked on the door again, louder this time, and heard a groan. Opening the door a crack, she looked inside. Mandy was in bed, on her back, with one arm thrown over her eyes. "That must have been some party."

"Go 'way," Mandy groaned.

"Sorry, girl, but we're supposed to pick up your car before noon, remember? It's almost ten-thirty."

Mandy made a pitiful mewling sound and then rolled out of bed.

Britney gasped. "You're wearing your bra and panties!"

Plopping back down on the bed in a sitting position, Mandy dropped her head into her hands. "My brain feels like it's smothered in molasses."

"How much did you drink last night?"

"Not much," Mandy moaned.

Once before Britney had seen Mandy in this condition, it was the morning after the redhead was dumped by her banker/biker boyfriend last summer. That morning, before they'd moved in together, Britney had found three empty wine bottles in Mandy's kitchen sink. "How much is not much?" she asked.

"A glass of wine and a banana daiquiri, but I didn't finish the daiquiri. Anyway, I don't think I did. God, I feel drugged.

Frowning with concern, Britney inched toward the door. "I'll fix you a cup of caffeinated tea. That should help wake you up."

"I want to shower first."

"Okay, you shower and I'll fix breakfast. Then, on the drive over to pick up your car, you're going to tell me about last night."

A nod of Mandy's head caused her to moan again. "I'll tell you what I can remember." She stood, a little shakily, and shuffled off to the bathroom.

On the drive to Warrenton, Britney commented, "You still look half dead."

"I took a hot shower and rinsed in tepid water," Mandy told her. "It helped, as did the caffeine, but I still feel sluggish."

"What happened last night?"

"I don't really know. I felt fine when we got to the restaurant and I ordered a glass of wine. While waiting for it, I checked the place out. You know how these things go, the guys huddled in one group and the girls in another."

"Go on."

The women were in the balcony section so I went up to join them. They were sharing pitchers of banana daiquiris. I didn't have any at first because I had the wine. The wife of one of the appraisers, Brandon Kohl, had a baby a couple of months ago. It's their first, a cute little towheaded boy. She was showing me pictures," Mandy said, and seemed to run out of steam.

"Then what happened?"

"I was flipping through the pictures on her iPad, and without looking, reached for my wineglass. When I took a sip, it was a banana daiquiri."

"Had you finished your wine?"

"I guess so. Anyway, the daiquiri tasted okay so I thought what the heck. That's when things starting getting fuzzy."

"You must have had more than one," Britney reasoned.

"No, I didn't," Mandy said adamantly. "That much I know. What little I had hit me hard and fast. I remember pushing the glass away, probably too hard because it slid on the table and bumped into Nicole's glass."

"Who's Nicole?"

"She works for me and is a real pain in the butt, but she's also the sister of a higher up. Therefore, I'm stuck with her."

"That's nepotism," Britney said as if it left a bad taste in her mouth.

"Which is beside the point since he didn't hire her and exercises no direct supervision. Nicole is separated by two levels of management, so in theory, the relationship doesn't make a difference," Mandy explained with a long, drawn out breath.

"Tell me the rest."

"Some of the women went downstairs . . . to eat, I guess. There were, maybe, five or six of us left. They were laughing their heads off and I could barely hold mine up. That's about all I remember."

Britney pulled into the auto body lot and parked. "Don't you remember going home?" she asked as she turned off the engine.

"Nope, not a thing." Mandy paused. "Well, maybe something else but I hope that was just a dream or a nightmare or anything except what I think might have happened."

"What?"

"I might have come on to Nate."

❧ Chapter 18 ❧

A NOTE ON MANDY'S DESK MONDAY MORNING DIRECTED HER TO appear in Ernie Gunderson's office as soon as she arrived. Occasionally, she received directives from her boss, normally with an indication of the topic he wished to discuss. This note gave no such hint. Nervous jitters danced in her stomach as she crossed the few yards to his office.

His door, usually closed, stood open. "Shut it, please," he said, not unkindly, when she entered. He gestured to a chair across from his desk. "Sit down, Mandy."

She did as instructed.

"In all the years I've worked here," he began, sitting forward, "I've never seen one of my employees in the condition you were in Friday night."

Shame burned in Mandy's cheeks.

"I'd like an explanation," he said.

"I d-don't have one," Mandy stammered. "I don't know what happened."

"I see."

"No, not really," she said. "What I mean is, I don't know *why* what happened . . . happened."

"Then, why don't you tell me what you remember."

Taking a deep breath to calm her nerves, she trembled. "When I arrived, I ordered a glass of wine. After a few sips, I went upstairs. There were pitchers of banana daiquiris on the table. Two when I got there but more were brought up. I don't normally drink hard liquor, Ernie."

"Did you Friday night?"

She nodded and twisted her hands in her lap. "I was looking at the baby pictures Brandon Kohl's wife had on her iPad. Someone switched my wine for a daiquiri. I only took a few sips."

"Then how do you explain—"

"I can't," she said with a pained face.

Ernie sat back in his chair. "Perhaps you are unable to ingest hard liquor," he suggested.

"I've had hard liquor before without getting drunk." Edging to the front of her chair, Mandy said in a rush, "Ernie, I think I was drugged."

He sat, unmoving, as if contemplating Mandy's words. Then, with quiet solemnity, inquired, "Who would do a thing like that?"

"I have my suspicions, but would rather not say," she whispered.

After a few seconds of silence, he asked, "Who gave you the daiquiri?"

"I don't know." His skeptical expression prompted her to add, "Honest, Ernie, I'd tell you if I knew for sure."

"I suggest you speculate."

Anxiety burned in Mandy's stomach. "If I name someone and I'm wrong . . ."

"Mandy, Nate Peters hauled you out of that restaurant in full view of everyone from your department and his. You were slumped over his shoulder like a hundred pound sack of potatoes."

Hiding her face in her hands at the disgraceful description, Mandy fought against tears of humiliation.

"Unfortunately," Ernie continued, "the condition you were in Friday night was brought to the attention of the Powers-That-Be. Everyone from the County Manager to the Commissioners wants an explanation."

Shocked, Mandy dropped her hands and stared at her boss. The situation was worse, much worse, than she had anticipated.

"If I tell them you were stinking drunk, they may ask for your resignation."

"I wasn't drunk," Mandy insisted, desperately trying to keep control of her voice as well as her emotions.

"If I tell them you suspect you were drugged, I'll have to provide them with a name. I won't have a choice in the matter and neither will you."

"What if I think it was Nicole?" The words barely made it past her lips.

Ernie's mouth pressed into a flat line. He knew who Nicole was related to—everyone working at the County knew. Growling, he asked, "Was it?"

"I don't know, not for sure."

"You expect me to go to the County Manager and all the Commissioners and accuse Nicole French of drugging you? *Nicole French?*"

With a defeated sigh, Mandy slumped in her chair. "No, Ernie, I don't expect you to tell anyone that I suspect she drugged me. Without proof, that would be defamation of character. Nicole could, and probably would, sue me."

"Then what do you suggest I do?" he asked, throwing the burden squarely on Mandy's shoulders.

She stood, and wringing her hands, paced in front of her boss' desk as she gave the matter some thought. "I was in that accident a couple of days before the party. You could say I'd taken a pain pill and didn't realize the effect it would have when mixed with alcohol."

"Is that what happened?"

"No. I don't like taking pain meds."

"You want me to lie for you?"

"Oh, God," Mandy cried, and sank back into her chair. She struggled to hold back her tears. "I swear to you, Ernie, I didn't take any pain pills and I didn't get 'stinking' drunk. I was drugged!"

Blowing out a breath that puffed his cheeks, Ernie rose. "I'll do my best to cover your ass this time, Mandy, but never again. And I don't want any more unfounded accusations against Nicole French, you hear me?"

"Yes, sir."

"Very good. I'll let you know if there are any ramifications from Friday night. Other than that, get back to work and keep your nose clean."

"Yes, sir," Mandy repeated, and cautious as a cat, crept out his door.

"Well, good morning," Nicole sang out before Mandy reached the sanctuary of her office. "How are you today?"

"I'm fine."

"Bet you weren't Saturday morning. Boy, you really tied one on Friday night."

Mandy looked directly into her subordinate's face. "I didn't tie anything on Friday night, Nicole."

"Is that so?" She followed Mandy into her office. "Nate called while you were in with Ernie."

Other than her boss, Nate was the one person she dreaded seeing most. It wasn't only the humiliation of him toting her out of the restaurant; it was the uncertainty about what had transpired afterward in her bedroom. "What did he want?"

"I don't know. He said he'd leave you a voice mail."

Mandy checked her watch. "I have another chiropractic appointment. I'll be back around quarter to ten."

"You're leaving now?"

"Yes, do you have a problem with that?" Mandy snipped.

Leaning against the doorframe, Nicole crossed her arms and shook her head. "No, I just thought you'd want to check your voicemail first."

"I'll check it when I get back," Mandy said, slipping into her coat. "Have you finished the tax disbursement calculations for last week?"

"Yeah, I took the spreadsheet to Nate late Friday afternoon."

"Good, then I'll see you when I get back."

It was a relief to leave the office. Even though no one but Nicole had uttered a word, the silence was telling. Instead of the usual Monday morning greetings and chatter about the weekend, heads were lowered as everyone diligently worked at their desks, but Mandy felt their sidelong glances.

The short drive to Astoria Chiropractic took no time at all, which made her early for the appointment. She was greeted by the receptionist and sat in the rocking chair by the small, gas Franklin stove.

Right behind her entered a man who looked to be in his mid to late thirties, wearing a well-cut suit and conservative tie. He gave his name as Joe Hernandez and asked if he could be worked in between patients. Mandy couldn't help but overhear that his complaint was due to a car accident the previous week. When told it would probably be a half hour, he said he was willing to wait. There was stiffness to his movements as he took a seat in the chair next to Mandy. He smiled in a painful manner.

"I was in a car accident last week, too," she said.

"On the road out by Glenwood Village?" he asked.

"Wednesday, after work? Yes."

He shrugged his shoulders in acknowledgement and then winced. "Sounds like the same one. I swerved to avoid an imbecile who turned in front of me without signaling or anything. Damn near plowed head-on into another car."

"That was me," Mandy blurted. "I ended up sideswiping the guardrail."

"Yeah, I bounced off the same guardrail before missing you and jumping back into my own lane. I couldn't stop though, and sailed off the side of the road."

"Ouch!" she exclaimed. "That must be a twenty foot drop."

He nodded. "All of that, if not more." He held out his hand. "I'm Joe Hernandez, by the way."

"Mandy Kearney," she reciprocated as she slipped her hand in his for a quick shake.

"You okay?" he asked.

"I am now but the day after the accident I could hardly move. A friend insisted I see a chiropractor and I'm glad I did. She really fixed me up. I came back today as a just-in-case."

"I should have come in last week, too, but . . ." he shrugged and winced again.

"Better late than never," Mandy offered.

The doctor walked in the reception room with the patient she'd been helping. "Schedule a follow up for two weeks," she told the receptionist. Then, to her patient, said, "If you have any pain, ice it and call me."

"I will."

The doctor turned toward Mandy. "How are you feeling today?"

"Hardly a twinge," she replied, and followed the chiropractor into the treatment room.

Fifteen minutes later, when Mandy came out, another patient had joined Joe Hernandez in the waiting room. Before taking the other patient back, the doctor told Joe he would be next.

As Mandy waited to schedule another appointment, he came to stand beside her. She faced him and smiled. "Nice meeting you, Joe. Have a good day."

"I will if you have lunch with me."

His request caught Mandy off guard but she liked the friendly interest she saw in his dark blue eyes. Other than that feature, Joe Hernandez had a handsomely dark complexion and a porcelain-white smile. Although less than average height, he was still inches taller than Mandy.

She looked at her watch to buy time. "Mondays are always busy."

"Tomorrow, then."

Her eyes met his. On impulse, she said, "I'm not sure of my schedule but we can exchange business cards." She dug one out of her purse and handed it to him, taking his in exchange.

His smile widened. "Until tomorrow, I hope."

Afterward, driving back to work, Mandy couldn't help but feel the promise of his words.

⚜ Chapter 19 ⚜

IT WAS AFTER TEN, MORE THAN AN HOUR SINCE I'D LEFT MANDY A voicemail asking her to call me. She wasn't still in Ernie's office, I knew, because he'd called me at nine-thirty. After telling him what little I could about Friday night he had wanted my opinion as to whether or not Mandy had a drinking or prescription drug problem. Surprisingly, our boss seemed disgruntled when told I thought not.

However, her employment troubles, if in fact any existed, were not my concern. At least, that's what I told myself. I'd called Mandy to discuss a significant error in her tax disbursement calculation. It was only by chance that I'd found the mistake and it made me question the possibility that others may have slipped past without notice. There was no excuse for the miscalculation and waiting to hear back from her delayed my work, which annoyed me.

Then it occurred to me that if Mandy remembered trying to seduce me, she might be embarrassed. Even if she didn't recall our kiss, she probably wondered why she woke up Saturday morning wearing only her sexy red bra and panties. That, no doubt, would lead to other questions about her disrobing. Mandy was avoiding me, I realized, and that irritated the hell out of me.

Deciding to put an end to the situation, I gathered up both the old and revised spreadsheets then headed downstairs to her office. She was working at her computer when I stormed through the door. I closed it with a distinct click to draw her attention.

She glanced up and saw me. "Hi, Nate," she said as a blush rose in her cheeks.

"You didn't return my call."

"Not yet."

"What part of 'call me as soon as you get this message' didn't you understand?"

She turned to face directly toward me. "Obviously, your call was more urgent than I realized. How can I help you?"

I tossed the spreadsheets onto her desk. "You can start by explaining why you instructed me to disburse twenty-one thousand, three hundred, and fifty-six dollars more than we collected in tax revenue last week."

"What?!"

"These are your figures aren't they?" I demanded, tapping the sheet of miscalculations.

She snatched the page from beneath my finger and quickly perused the numbers. "This isn't right."

"You're telling me."

"Where did you get this?" she wanted to know as she swung back around to her computer and clicked a few keys to bring up her program.

"Nicole gave it to me Friday afternoon."

With the fingers of her left hand scanning down the column on the page, her right hand correspondingly browsed down the numbers on the monitor. Everything matched. "This isn't right," Mandy reiterated.

"Is there an echo in here?" I asked, and crossed my arms.

"Cut the sarcasm," she snapped, glaring at me over her shoulder. "There has to be an explanation."

"There is. You screwed up."

What had been the becoming pink of embarrassment darkened to the unattractive flush of anger. "I did not! These aren't my figures."

"Don't you password protect your work?"

"Yes, I do."

"Then they're your numbers."

"No, they aren't," she yelled, whipping around to face me.

"Then whose the hell are they?" I yelled right back.

Mandy turned toward her monitor and sat staring at the screen. Moments later, she muttered, "Nicole did this. She changed them."

"Come off it, woman," I spat. "It's bad enough you screwed up, you don't have to make it worse by blaming your staff."

She swiveled around in her chair, blue sparks flying from her eyes. "These aren't my figures, damn it!" Mandy growled with her back teeth set.

"If you password protect your work, how do you explain those numbers?"

"Nicole must know my password. It's possible," she insisted, seeing the skeptical gleam in my eyes. "She's seen me type it in often enough she must have memorized the key strokes."

"You expect me to believe that?"

"I expect you to believe my calculations were correct. Since Nicole gave you this spreadsheet, she must be responsible."

"Jesus," I said, scathingly. "You are a piece of work."

"What's that suppose to mean?"

With a shake of my head, I left without replying.

IN LATE AFTERNOON THE REVISED SPREADSHEET I'D PREPARED AND left on Mandy's desk was returned to me by one of her assistant staff. Mandy's initial in the lower right corner was the only indication she agreed with my calculations. Processing the disbursements to the various taxing districts kept me tied to my desk until after six. It was small consolation that the firebrand was probably stuck in her office double checking every page of the spreadsheets since tax day a month ago. The only bright spot on the horizon was that from now until next November, property tax disbursement took place on a quarterly basis.

On the drive back to Seaside, I encountered gusty rain, heavy traffic, and every slow poke in the county. It's no wonder I walked into Justin's home tired and ill-tempered.

Before I had time to shed my overcoat he called out from the dining room. "Hey, bro, guess what came in today?"

"Give him a chance to walk in the door," I heard Britney say from around the corner in the kitchen.

To my way of thinking, Justin, who didn't appreciate food the way I did, didn't deserve to marry a woman who cooked.

"Take a look," Justin said, hurrying into the entryway and shoving a card under my nose.

"Do you mind?" I grumbled, and knocked his hand away.

"Yeah, I mind," he claimed. "Would it kill you to look?"

"Would it kill you to wait until I get my coat off?" I countered.

"Probably," he said with a self-mocking tilt to his mouth.

I took my sweet time just to see if I could rile him but Justin was in too good a mood. "Okay," I said, and held out my hand. "Let's see what you've got."

"Wedding invitations," was his succinct reply as he passed the card to me. "And announcements."

I read the deckle-edged, cream colored card. A knot formed in my throat. Here was my brother, a formerly confirmed bachelor, so damned happy about getting married, while I was acting like a perfect ass. Despite my cranky mood, I gave him a grin I didn't feel and handed the card back. "I guess this means she hasn't come to her senses yet."

"No, and I'm not giving her a chance to back out. Tomorrow night we're having an envelope addressing party. You, me, Brit, and Mandy."

The smile slid off my face. "You don't need me for that."

"Sure we do. You wouldn't believe how many envelopes there are to address. Not just the invitations. There are announcements, too. No point in dragging this thing out."

"My handwriting sucks."

"Somebody's got to lick the envelopes and slap on the stamps."

"Justin," Britney said, coming out from around the counter and slipping her arms around his waist. "Let Nate change his clothes before you dump all this on him." She kissed his cheek and then looked at me. "Do you want a beer or wine with dinner?"

"Beer."

"We'll serve as soon as you change."

The perfect fricking end to the perfect fricking day, I grumbled in the privacy of my room. Ripping off my suit jacket, I resisted the childish urge to fling it into a heap on the bed, and instead, carefully draped it over a hanger.

There was a valid reason for avoiding romantic involvement with co-workers. It prevented off-the-job discord from developing into contention at work. The current situation, however, was a case of professional conflict spilling over into my personal life, without the benefits afforded by a sexual relationship.

How the hell long had it been since I'd enjoyed an amorous evening with a woman? Too damn long. Maybe that was why I still felt tied in knots from the steamy, wet kiss Mandy laid on me the other night. In a twisted sort of way, it was a good thing she passed out; otherwise, we would have awakened together and spent the weekend getting to know each other in the biblical sense. Just the thought of a weekend romp with the redhead caused an ache in my groin.

But none of these musings had relevance at the moment. The issue at hand was that Justin and Britney deserved cooperation between their two wedding attendants. As best man, whether or not I believed Mandy's excuse about the incorrect figures on the spreadsheet, I owed it to my brother to make it up with the firebrand. That meant giving her an apology.

With a double dose of determination, I sucked it up the next morning and headed for Mandy's office. She wasn't in.

Nicole was. "Mandy said she and Mr. Gunderson had an appointment with the County Manager."

"What about?" I asked, not liking the smugness on the tax technician's face.

"How should I know?" she replied with a shrug that was a little too nonchalant.

I bumped shoulders with her and murmured confidentially, "Come on, Nicole. You know more about what goes on around here than you let on."

"Maybe I do. But that doesn't mean I'm a blabbermouth."

"I would never accuse you of that."

She looked around to ensure no one was listening and dropped her voice to an intriguing whisper. "I thought it had to do with the holiday party. You know, being carried out dead drunk and all," she sneered. "But since you're here and not with them, I'm probably wrong."

"For some reason, I trust your instincts," I said, stepping back. "I need to talk with Mandy this morning. Will you give her a message to call me when she gets back?"

"Sure."

She looked prepared to say more but I didn't give her the chance. "Good. I'll be in my office," I said, and walked away.

WITH GRUDGING SUPPORT FROM ERNIE GUNDERSON, MANDY convinced the County Manager that the unfortunate incident at the holiday party resulted from a combination of over-the-counter pain medication, a glass of wine, and a partial banana daiquiri. Shocked by his suggestion she submit to alcohol and drug treatment, she somehow persuaded the two men it wasn't necessary. Her job was secure, for now at least, but her personnel record was forever blemished.

Returning to her office, resentment and rage burned like a stoked furnace in Mandy's chest.

"How'd your little tête-à-tête with the higher ups go?" Nicole inquired from the doorway with a barely concealed smirk.

Mandy was tempted to cram her subordinate's sneering words back down her throat but refused to give her the satisfaction of knowing how truly bad it was. She smiled sweetly. "Some conversations are best savored privately."

"Oh." The word popped out of Nicole's mouth and her eyes fluttered in surprise. "I thought—"

Silence.

"Yes?" Mandy prompted.

"Nothing," her subordinate said.

"Is there anything else?"

Remembering the piece of scratch paper in her hand that was the excuse for standing in her boss' office, Nicole handed it over, "Nate wants you to call him."

The smile on Mandy's face felt brittle. Without glancing at the note, she wadded it up and tossed it in her trash can. "Close the door on your way out."

A huff escaped from overfull lips but Nicole left, shutting the door with a thud.

It seemed a small triumph, getting the last word in, but a triumph nonetheless.

***

Twenty minutes after leaving her boss' office, Nicole buzzed Nate. "By any chance, has Mandy called you?" she whispered when he picked up.

"Not yet."

"Don't be surprised if she doesn't."

"I can barely hear you. Can you speak up?"

"No," she said a little more stridently. "I have to talk to you, but not here at the office."

"What do you suggest?" His voice sounded a bit wary.

"Meet me for lunch." A door in the direction of Mandy's office opened. Nicole furtively glanced over her shoulder, confirming her boss was headed her way. "Noon at The Supper Club sounds good to me," she said in a normal voice, and hung up the receiver.

"Am I interrupting?" Mandy asked with a hint of sarcasm.

"Not really. That was Nate. He asked me to lunch." Seeing Mandy's lips flatten into a straight line, she asked, "Care to join us?" knowing the invitation would be declined.

"Sorry, I already have lunch plans."

"Maybe next time," Nicole offered, as if she and Nate ate lunch together frequently.

For all Mandy knew, they did. Changing the subject, she said, "Nate told me there was a significant error on the last spreadsheet you gave him."

"So?"

"After I completed it did you make any changes before you printed it out for him?"

"How could I do that?" Nicole asked snidely. "You password protected the damn thing, as if you don't trust me."

"Password protecting my work has nothing to do with trust. It has everything to do with making sure it doesn't get changed inadvertently when someone else in the department needs to look at the file."

"The only time I pull up that particular file," Nicole informed her boss, "is when I print it out for Nate."

"That's what I wanted to know," Mandy said, and marched back to her office.

Nicole's revelation about Nate asking her to lunch had caught Mandy flat-footed. She'd been unaware the two were seeing each other socially. That explained Nate's behavior in her office yesterday. He didn't like hearing accusations against the woman. "Well, the hell with you, Nathan Peters," Mandy hissed through her teeth.

She rummaged in her purse and came out with the business card of Joe Hernandez. He worked for a local car dealership. Before she could think of a reason to change her mind, Mandy punched in his number on the keypad of her phone.

"Joe Hernandez," he answered.

"Hi, Joe, this is Mandy Kearney. We met yesterday—"

"At the chiropractor's office."

"Yes."

"Are you free for lunch?"

"Yes, that's why I called."

BALCONY DINING APPARENTLY APPEALED TO NICOLE. SHE SAT AT the same table she had occupied at Friday's party. I didn't like the subliminal reminder.

"You're late," she harped in a chastising manner.

"Better late than never," I cajoled, taking the chair across from her.

In response to an old Willie Nelson tune, Nicole dug in her purse. "I have to take this call," she said as she stood, and walked away from the table.

A waitress climbed the stairs and handed me a menu. "Separate checks?" she asked.

I nodded.

Rushing back to the table, Nicole ordered her lunch. "I'll have the shrimp salad with honey-mustard dressing and garlic toast."

"Shroom and Swiss burger for me," I said, handing the menu back.

Her phone tucked away, Nicole said, "I wish you had come earlier. There's not much time left."

My watch read quarter after twelve, plenty of time, by my way of thinking. I leaned my crossed arms on the table. "What did you have to tell me you couldn't say in the office?"

She leaned in close. "It's about Mandy." Her words came out in a stage whisper, which I thought was odd since we were the only two in the balcony.

"What about her?" I asked, sitting back.

"Well, first of all, she wouldn't tell me anything about the meeting she and Gunderson had with the County Manager."

"Ernie Gunderson?" I clarified, noticing Nicole had dropped the mister from in front of his name. "Mandy's and my boss?"

"Yes." She almost hissed the word.

"Why would Mandy have told you about the meeting?"

"If it had to do with the department, it only makes sense she would have told me."

I could think of lots of departmental issues a manager wouldn't share with the staff, but kept my thoughts to myself by giving Nicole a non-committal shrug.

The waitress delivered our meals and efficiently cracked pepper over Nicole's salad. "Can I get you anything else?" At a shake of our heads, she departed.

After taking a bite, Nicole continued, "So, if it didn't have to do with the department, it must have been about the party."

The burger was more enjoyable than the conversation. "I really don't think any of this is your concern."

She huffed and stabbed at her salad. "Did Mandy ever call you?"

"That's not your concern either."

"I only ask because Mandy wadded up the message I gave her and threw it away."

The longer I stared at Nicole without speaking or eating, the more her smug expression slipped.

A few too many seconds passed before she defended herself. "I had to tell you or else you would think I didn't give her your message."

"Did you—give Mandy the message?"

"Yes, and she threw it away." Nicole insisted, and then dabbed her mouth with the napkin. "She has it in for me, you know."

"No, I didn't know," I said, and took a bite out of my burger.

"She accused me of altering the last spreadsheet I gave you." Nicole leaned across the table toward me. "Mandy password protects all her work. It's like she's paranoid or something."

"I don't know what to say," I told her, pushing my plate aside. "There's an apparent conflict between you and your boss."

"There is," she pouted. "I thought if I talked to you, we could do something about it."

Feeling sorry for her, I said, "I'm not the appropriate person for this. If you can't resolve your differences with Mandy, you should talk to Ernie or someone in the Human Resources Department."

"It's not just me," she said earnestly. "Mandy's got it in for you, too."

The burger didn't sit well in my stomach. "In what way?

"I don't think the errors on that spreadsheet were mistakes. I think Mandy made them deliberately, hoping you wouldn't notice. Then, if you had paid out the wrong amounts to the taxing districts, a corrected spreadsheet would have miraculously turned up, leaving you hip deep in dog doo-doo."

Her reasoning had an awful sense of logic to it but I didn't want to believe it of Mandy. "That's a serious allegation," I said somberly.

"At this point, I don't have enough evidence to make an allegation," Nicole backpedaled. "What I said is more of a supposition."

I thought about that a moment. "Okay, then. We'll keep this strictly between us for the time being. After all, forewarned is forearmed."

Nicole's relief was palpable, giving credence to her concerns.

"I have to get back to work," she said. Gathering up her coat and purse, she dashed off.

When I paid the bill, both lunches were on the tab.

❧ Chapter 20 ❧

THE DISTINCTIVE RINGTONE SIGNALED A CALL FROM JUSTIN'S mother. He balanced the pizza box on his left arm and wrestled open the connecting door from the garage to the living area of his condo, and then retrieved the phone from his right coat pocket. "Hi, Mom. What's up?"

"I haven't heard from you or Nate in over a week," June Peters stated matter-of-factly. She rarely fretted over her children, after all, they were grown men, but Christmas was fast approaching and she wanted all her chicks home in the proverbial henhouse for the holidays. "I thought I'd better call and make sure the two of you still graced the face of the earth."

Juggling food and phone, Justin managed to slide the pizza box into the wall oven. "Yes, Mom, we're both alive and kicking," he assured her as he tapped the temperature control to warm. "Nate's been up to his eyeballs in the new job."

"That may be his excuse for not calling his mother but what's yours?"

"Well, let's see . . . how about a full case load at work and planning a wedding?"

"I'll buy the full case load but not the wedding," she said. "Women plan weddings. Men just show up for the food."

Justin laughed. "That would be so true in my case, Mom, except Britney refuses to do all the heavy lifting for this shindig. She insists I be involved every step of the way." He opened the refrigerator and pulled out a beer.

"All right, Mr. Wedding Planner, how's the project coming along?"

"Tonight the four of us are getting together to address envelopes for the invitations and announcements."

"And who, precisely, are the four of you?" she queried.

"Britney, her matron of honor, Nate and me."

"Good Lord," June exclaimed. "No one can read Nate's handwriting."

"Don't worry," Justin said, after taking a sip of his beer. "All he's going to do is lick the envelopes." He heard his mother sigh. "Okay, Mom, what's the real reason for your call?"

June, a math teacher at Goldendale High, was easier to comprehend than the subject matter she taught.

"Neither you nor Nate has said one word about coming home for Christmas. Your father and I are hoping both of you will come."

"I can't speak for Nate—"

"I not asking you to."

"And I haven't discussed the holidays with Britney, yet. We've had other things on our minds, like planning a wedding."

"Christmas is less than two weeks away."

"I know, Mom."

"Your father and I would like to meet the bride *before* the wedding."

"I know that, too."

"We want you to bring Britney home for the holidays."

Justin rolled his eyes. "You're starting to sound like a greeting card." He heard another sound, like a long suffering sigh.

"Just bring her home, dear."

"Yes, Mother."

"Is that a snickering 'yes, Mother'?"

"No, Mother," Justin chuckled. "I promise to bring her home."

"Thank you, dear." Having accomplished her goal, June said, "We'll talk again soon. I love you."

"Love you, too, Mom. Bye."

A few minutes later, Britney arrived "Sorry I'm late," she said, shedding her coat. "I remembered we needed stamps—"

Pulling his fiancée into his arms, Justin interrupted her with a long, steamy kiss.

When he released her, she breathlessly finished, "So, I stopped at the post office."

"Good thinking. I got a pizza. It's in the oven to keep warm."

"If I eat much more fast food before the wedding, I'll outgrow my dress."

"I'll throw a tossed salad together if you want that instead of pizza," Justin offered.

"You would do that for me?" Britney asked in a little girl voice as she twined her arms around his neck and nibbled on his mouth.

He tried to take control of the teasing kiss but she wiggled free. "I'll have a salad and one small slice of pizza."

Justin moved into the kitchen and started pulling produce from the fridge. "My mom called a few minutes ago," he said.

Britney hoisted herself onto a bar stool to watch as he washed and sliced the vegetables. "How're your folks doing? Is your dad okay?"

"Yeah, everyone's fine. Mom asked me to bring you home for Christmas."

"Oh," Britney said, somewhat surprised. "I've been living and breathing the wedding and haven't even thought about the holidays."

"That's what I told her or words to that affect, anyway."

"We should have waited until spring to get married. There's too much going on this time of year."

"There's no way I would have waited until spring. Not with you living in Gearhart instead of here. The invitations go out tomorrow, period."

"So, what do we do?" she asked, not arguing.

He dried his hands and came around the counter to take her hands in his. "Christmas is a three day weekend. I suggest we pack up all your notes, all the magazines and whatever else you have, and take it with us. My mom and sister-in-law will get a kick out of putting in their two cents."

"But what about Mandy?"

"What about her?"

Stepping off the stool, Britney crossed to the refrigerator and rummaged around for a soft drink. "Her family is in California and she's not flying home. If I go with you, she'll be all alone."

"Not a problem," he said with a shrug. "She can come, too."

"You can't just invite a stranger to your parent's home," Britney objected.

"Sure, I can. We did it all the time growing up. Mom and Dad never blinked an eye when two, or sometimes even three, extra kids showed up at the dinner table."

"Are you sure?"

Before she realized what he was doing, Justin pulled out his phone and speed dialed his mother. When she answered, he asked, "Mind if we bring the matron of honor with us for Christmas?" A second later, he said, "That's what I thought. Talk later. Bye." He disconnected.

"I take it she said to bring Mandy."

"You got it. By the way," he said, returning to the kitchen, "speaking of mothers . . ."

"Which we weren't."

"We need to make a decision about your mom."

Britney climbed back up onto the barstool. "If we don't invite her, I'll never hear the end of it, will I?"

"We can always go to Tennessee for our honeymoon"

"We'll send an invitation," she readily agreed. "But whether or not she comes and how she gets here should be entirely up to her."

"It won't kill us to pay her way."

An uncharacteristic bitterness tinged Britney's voice. "I've been a burden to my mother since before I was born. Why should I make it easy for her to come to my wedding?"

Drying his hands again, Justin came around the counter, drew his fiancée close to his heart, and murmured into her ear, "Because she gave you life. Because it is my wedding, too. Take your pick."

Britney sighed in capitulation. "I'll call her tomorrow."

"That's my girl," he said, and kissed her.

The doorbell rang.

"I'll answer it, you finish the salad," Britney said, sliding off the stool.

"Here I am," Mandy announced as she sailed in the door.

"Is Nate on his way?"

Mandy ripped off her gloves and jammed them in her coat pocket. "I have no idea, nor do I care. I haven't seen him since yesterday and next month would be too soon to see him again."

"I take it you two are on the outs."

"You have to be on the ins before you can be on the outs," Mandy quipped.

At that moment, Nate pushed through the front door. He glared at Mandy as he peeled off his overcoat.

Britney decided now was not the time to mention a Christmas trip to Goldendale. "Justin bought pizza and is making a salad," she said instead, slipping her arm through Mandy's and leading her into the dining area.

"I had Mexican food for lunch and I'm still stuffed."

"I make a killer salad," Justin told her.

"In that case, I'll force down a bite or two. How are you this evening?"

"Good. Yourself?"

"Never been better," Mandy replied. Lunch with the attentive Joe Hernandez had improved her outlook.

"Are we ready to get this show on the road?" Nate inquired. He had changed into jeans and a sweatshirt.

"As soon as we eat," his older brother said. "Pizza's in the oven. Why don't you get it out?"

With every bite he took during dinner, Nate cast dark glances toward Mandy, which she gamely ignored. She chatted about the delicious food she'd eaten earlier in the day but omitted mention of her handsome luncheon companion. Soon, with dinner finished, the dishes were cleared. The men rinsed and stacked tableware in the dishwasher while the women wiped the crumbs from the table and organized the work.

They had previously determined that Britney and Mandy had the most legible handwriting, so addressing the envelopes fell to them. Justin stuffed the double envelopes, and then Nate licked the flaps and ensured a good seal before adding the stamps.

The work proceeded smoothly until Mandy, needing more space, started to gather up the piles of completed cards.

"What are you doing?" Nate demanded of her.

"I'm making more room at the table."

"You're making a mess of things, is what you're doing," he countered, grabbing the cards out of Mandy's hands.

"No, I'm not," she argued, and collected more cards from the table.

"Damn it, woman! I had them organized."

"What's to organize?" she challenged.

"The invitations and announcements," he sneered, standing up and scrambling to take them all away from Mandy. "The invitations get mailed tomorrow but the announcements won't go out until after the wedding."

"I know that."

"I won't let you sabotage this wedding the way you're trying to sabotage my career.

"What the hell are you talking about?" she erupted.

"Hold it! Hold it! Hold it!" Justin yelled, jumping out of his chair with both hands raised, palms out, as if stopping traffic. In the sudden silence, he implored, "What the hell is the matter with you two? You sound like a couple of squabbling kindergarteners."

"I was keeping the invitations and announcements separated so they didn't get mixed up," Nate explained in frustration.

Recovering from her momentary shock, Britney said in as soothing a voice as she could muster, "Nathan, it's all right. Mandy's addressing the invitations and I'm doing the announcements."

Firming his loosely held temper, Nate conjured up a civil tongue when he asked, "What does that have to do with anything?"

Mandy snatched two envelopes off the table and stuck them in his face. He pushed her hands away. Not to be thwarted, she taunted him. "Any moron can see the difference." She held up the evidence with a smug smile. "Our handwriting is completely different."

It was painfully obvious to Nate, now that he looked. With a hard set to his jaw, he scooped up all the envelopes and held them out to Mandy.

She refused to accept them. "You owe me an apology."

"Mandy, please," Britney pleaded.

"Nate," Justin said with a furious gleam in his eyes.

"What?" The younger brother snapped.

"Apologize to Mandy. And to Britney for upsetting her."

"That's all right, Justin," Britney murmured.

"No, it's not. My brother owes both of you an apology. As a matter of fact, he owes one to all of us."

"Fine, I apologize."

As quick as lightning, Justin was out of his chair and grabbed the front of Nate's sweatshirt with both hands. "I can still whip your ass, asshole."

"Just try it," Nathan growled, breaking his brother's hold and raising his fist.

"Stop it! Just stop it, both of you!" Mandy wailed. Covering her face with her hands, she burst into tears.

From their father, the Peters boys had learned at an early age to fear a woman's tears. The spectacle froze them in mid-swing.

Britney's eyes shot both men with bullets of accusation, as if to say, "Now see what you've done."

Nate was the first to move. He rounded the table and knelt before his weeping co-worker. "I'm sorry," he murmured, this time sincerely, and laid a hand on her quaking shoulder. "Mandy, I'm sorry," he repeated.

"Leave me alone," she sniffled.

"I said I'm sorry."

She raised mascara smudged eyes. "I haven't tried to sabotage your career," Mandy professed quietly.

Sitting back on his heels, Nate searched her eyes, but was unable to determine the truth of her words. He blew out a breath. "I'm sorry I said that."

Mandy nodded, "I am, too."

Unsure of her meaning, Nate decided not to ask. Rising, he offered his right hand, expecting Mandy to shake. Instead, she placed her left hand in his. A rippling surge, like sparkling stardust, flowed between them. Their eyes locked in recognition of the sensation.

With a jolt, Mandy sprang to her feet. "I'll be back in a minute," she told the group, and hurried off to the bathroom.

Her departure left Nate feeling odd, as if buffeted by stormy winds.

"We're almost done," Britney commented, resuming where she left off.

Justin settled back in his chair. Changing the subject, he asked his soon-to-be-bride, "Can you get off work about three on Friday?"

For a moment, she mentally reviewed her schedule. "Off hand, I can't think of any reason why not, but I'll need to clear it with Phil. Why do you ask?"

"We need to get our marriage license."

"God, I forgot all about that."

"Good thing I'm a lawyer. We get paid for remembering all the little legal details. Don't worry," he gave her a lecherous grin, "I'll let you trade service for service."

"Excuse me, am I in the way here?" Nate asked, dragging his eyes back from the direction Mandy had gone.

"No, so you might as well sit down," his brother instructed.

Taking his seat, Nate again looked toward the hallway. "What about Mandy?"

"She's okay," Britney said. "She just needs a little time."

The door to the bathroom opened and the redhead came back. Her face was washed clean of makeup, her eyes were puffy, and her nose red.

She's beautiful, Nate thought.

"Since marriage licenses are issued at the County, we should make it a celebration and all go out to dinner Friday night," Justin suggested. "We could go to the Mexican restaurant where Mandy had lunch today."

"I can't," she said. "I have a date."

"What do you mean you have a date?" Nate challenged.

Mandy looked directly at him. In a clear, concise voice, she said, "I mean, I have a date. As in a dinner date. As in a man, a very nice man, I might add, asked me to dinner, and I agreed. That kind of date."

"You'll have to break it," he ordered, like he was in charge.

"I'm not breaking my date."

"I've had to change my schedule to accommodate every stage of planning for this wedding. I think it's only fair for you to do the same."

"Getting a marriage license isn't part of 'planning for this wedding'," Mandy argued, making quotation marks with her fingers. "Besides, I've only just met Joe, I can't very well break our first date."

"What do you mean you just met him? Where did you meet him?" Nate fired the staccato questions like rounds from a machine gun. "You probably don't know anything about him."

"I don't believe this!" Mandy yelled. "I met him yesterday. At the chiropractor's office. He sells cars. And none of that is your business."

"*Please!*" Britney said, rising from her chair. "Stop bickering."

"Tell her to change her plans," Nate demanded.

"That's it," Mandy stated. "I'm not taking any more of this. I'm leaving." She stormed away from the table, threw her coat over her shoulders, grabbed her purse, and fled out the door.

In the shocked silence, no one moved. And then, slowly, methodically, Britney began clearing the table.

"What are you doing?" Justin calmly asked.

"Packing everything up."

"We're not done."

Continuing to stuff both the completed and blank invitations and announcements into her white organizer crate, Britney said, "We're close enough that Mandy and I can finish this at home."

Justin swung a frowning glare in his brother's direction. "This is all your fault."

Still confused by his feelings of outrage over Mandy's date, Nate pushed up from the table. "Seems any more, everything is my fault." Without another word, he slammed out the front door.

❧ Chapter 21 ❧

THE POUNDING PULSE IN MY EYE SOCKETS BEAT IN DULL synchronization with the torturous tattoo in my temples. I rolled onto my back, groaned, and then slowly crawled out of bed.

A steaming hot shower, followed by a bone chilling rinse, cleansed the sludge from my brain but did little to alleviate the hangover. On a work day, hair of the dog wasn't an option, so I dry swallowed three aspirin with little hope of significant relief.

During my first year in college, after a wretchedly wild weekend, I'd determined the thrill of drinking hard liquor wasn't worth the pain of recovery. I hadn't touched it since— until last night.

Boilermakers—straight shots of whiskey with beer chasers— I had sucked up three before the bartender told me to slow it down. I did and amused myself by putting the make on her. Spacing my high octane alcohol consumption judiciously, it looked for a while as if I might score before the night was over. My anticipation of soaring to the heights with the sexy, raven-haired bartender was cruelly shot down when she told me, at closing time, that the brunette cocktail waitress in the ass-hugging mini was her life partner. Damn.

She made up for it, though, and drove me home in my car while her soul mate followed in theirs.

Dressed, and trying to make the most of the morning, I joined my brother in the kitchen. His cold shouldered silence and icy glare shouted his disapproval of me better than any words. The devil-may-care smile I attempted to paste on my face felt more like a wince. My insouciant façade eroded further when my jittery stomach rebelled with the first sip of coffee. I set the mug aside and opted for a slice of dry toast.

Witnessing my discomfort, Justin merrily finished his breakfast and swilled another cup of coffee before he spoke. "You lit out of here so fast last night I didn't have a chance to tell you . . ."

He paused for another sip of coffee, forcing me to ask, "What?"

"We set a date for your arbitration hearing."

The bottom fell out of my already queasy stomach. Without conscious thought, I slumped into a chair at the dining room table. "When is it?"

"February tenth."

"Where?"

"Goldendale, where else?"

Not having a clue, I shrugged.

From there the rain soaked day picked up steam on its downhill plunge. Since I'd over slept, my foot was heavy on the gas pedal, resulting in a Christmas tree show of lights flashing in my rearview mirror. The police officer was unsympathetic when told I'd never had a traffic violation. As he wrote up the speeding ticket, he implied it was probably long overdue. At that point, deciding silence was golden; I kept thoughts about his ancestry to myself.

I'd barely settled into the morning's work when Ernie dropped by my office. "Nate, there's a conference in Mt. Hood next month I want you to attend," he said, handing me a flyer.

Glancing down the session titles, I saw most topics dealt with property tax issues. "Wouldn't Mandy be a better candidate for this conference?" I asked.

"Oh, she's going. I want you to attend, also."

With my brain still spongy from last night's whiskey, I failed to understand his reasoning. "Why?"

My boss looked at me curiously. "To start building your network," he told me. "Assessors and tax collectors from all over Oregon will be there."

"Of course," I said, belatedly catching up.

"I'm sure you'll find the subject matter of at least a few of the sessions interesting," he added.

"I'm sure I will." The brochure felt heavy in my hand as I scanned it again.

"Separate travel isn't in the budget so get together with Mandy to work out the details."

A sudden vision of sharing a room with the firebrand burned in my brain. "Ah, I'm not sure that's a good idea."

"If the two of you decide to drive in separate vehicles instead of carpooling, only one of you will receive mileage reimbursement," he said. "I repeat, get together with Mandy to work out the details. I've already booked your room. It's on a different floor from hers due to the late registration."

Carpool. Rooms on separate floors. Get a grip. "I'll call Mandy right now, while it's fresh in my mind." *If I still have one.*

"Yeah, you do that," Ernie said with another strange glance in my direction, making me wonder how much of my thoughts I'd uttered out loud. "Are you all right?"

"No, I'm fine. I mean . . . I have a lot on my mind right now." Rubbing my aching eyes with gentle fingertips, I said, "Which reminds me, I need to take a few days off in February. The ninth, tenth and eleventh, to be exact."

Ernie reached over and swung the door shut, the click of the latch reverberated like a gunshot in my throbbing brain. "You have a problem, Nate? Something you want to discuss?"

"No." One thing I definitely did not want to discuss with my current boss was the arbitration with my former employer.

"You've been here less than a month. You're not thinking of leaving, are you?"

"No. *No.* Nothing like that," I was quick to assure him. "I have a few loose ends that need tying up back in Goldendale. Legal issues."

Crossing his arms, Ernie scrutinized me closely. "What kind of legal issues?"

"It's nothing. I mean, it's something, obviously, because it requires my attention." I closed my eyes, managing to suppress a moan as the hole I dug grew deeper. *Damn! Why couldn't I keep my mouth shut?* "What I mean is . . . it's a matter I'd rather not discuss."

"Just so long as it's not anything that will jeopardize your employment here," he said, seemingly displeased.

"No, absolutely not." *Shut up, you idiot.* "I'll chalk it up to vacation. The time off, I mean."

"You don't have to do that," Ernie offered, suddenly more affable. "With all the hours you put in, you'll probably have more than three days of comp time by February."

"I don't want to use comp time. At least not for this," I hurried to say. Using compensatory time would be too similar to the issue that required arbitration. "I'll just use vacation."

"I don't know why you want to use vacation when you can use comp time," Ernie said, shaking his head. Then, as he opened the door, added, "It's up to you. Use vacation if you want."

After he was gone, I leaned back and blew out a hefty breath of relief, swearing I'd never—ever—drink hard liquor again.

Another sigh and I was ready to resume work. Realizing the conference flyer was still in my hand, I huffed out another breath. No time like the present, I thought grumpily, and leaned forward to pick up the phone.

Mandy's voicemail answered. Wasn't the woman ever at her desk, I wondered, and said, "It's Nate. Call me." Hanging up, it registered that the message was too curt, but I decided not to make it worse by leaving another.

If not for the hangover haze that smogged my brain it would have taken half the time to complete the boring and mundane tasks that consumed the entire morning. It was nearing one o'clock when the ants gnawing on the lining of my stomach reminded me that breakfast had consisted of only a partial piece of dry toast. Rain battered against my small office window, discouraging me from summoning up the energy to battle it.

Staring through the rivulet streaked pane, I saw Mandy in the second floor office across the courtyard strip off her raincoat and head back toward her office. I gave her a minute to settle at her desk and then dialed her extension. Voicemail picked up.

"Mandy, it's Nate. Call me as soon as you listen to this message," I growled. Back at the window, I watched the office across the way for ten minutes by the clock. With the lunch hour over, employees returned to their desks, resumed their duties, and continued to serve the fine citizens of Clatsop County who had braved the weather to show up at the counter. Mandy did not return my call.

HOW MANY VOICEMAILS WOULD THE JACKASS LEAVE, MANDY ASKED herself, before he got the message that she had no intention of returning his calls? If Nate wanted to apologize for his unreasonable request that she break Friday night's date, he could, by God, do it in person.

The answer was two. It took only two unreturned voicemails before the donkey's backside came galloping into her office to beg an apology for his stubborn demand. Niggling at the edges of Mandy's smug satisfaction over winning the trite battle of wills was awareness that the mulish man, standing straddle-legged, with hands on hips, looked as if he'd been trampled in a stampede of wild horses. His dark almond hair, typically combed neatly in place, was an unruly mess, his brown eyes, usually as soft as warm chocolate, were streaked an irritated red, and the normally attractive golden skin of his face held an unbecoming flush.

Her cantankerous co-worker's words tore Mandy from her unintended inspection. "What?"

"I said," Nate reiterated obstinately, "My truck has four-wheel drive and snow tires. Besides, I have more experience operating a motor vehicle in winter weather than you possibly could, coming from California and all."

"And what, exactly, does that have to do with anything?" Mandy demanded, confused by a conversation that had nothing to do with an apology.

Nate threw his hands in the air and barked, "Haven't you listened to a word I said?"

Mandy crossed her small office and closed her door. Then she stood toe to toe with her adversary, glaring into his face.

"All right, Nate. You now have my undivided attention. What is this all about?"

He leaned down until they were nose to nose. "Our illustrious boss," he growled, "decided I should attend the winter conference with you next month. The travel budget is tight. He wants us to carpool. I'm driving. Got it?"

Searching his bloodshot eyes, Mandy saw more than she cared to acknowledge. Beyond his anger, she perceived a bone deep weariness. And, perhaps, loneliness of the type brought on by betrayal—something she knew all too well. "I don't mind if you drive," she said agreeably.

Something in his eyes shifted. His anger seemed to evaporate. He leaned back so he was no longer towering over her. "Okay. I'm glad that's settled. Now, about Friday ni—"

"No."

Nate's hands went back to rest on his hips. "You don't even know what I was going to say."

"You were going to demand—again—that I change my plans."

"And will you?"

"No."

His lips flattened into a straight line. "Fine," he snapped. Turning, Nate threw open the door and came face to face with Nicole.

"Hi, Nate."

"Hi," he said, and brushed past her. Then he turned. "Nicole, you have anything on for Friday night?"

"No," she said, and smiled.

"How about dinner?" He had the satisfaction of seeing Mandy's jaw drop.

"Sure." Nicole's smile blossomed into a grin. "What time?"

"Right after work. I'll pick you up at your desk."

Mandy's teeth clicked as her mouth snapped shut.

❧ Chapter 22 ❧

WITH MARRIAGE LICENSE IN HAND, JUSTIN AND BRITNEY CLIMBED one flight of stairs from the second floor to the third and found Nathan in the process of clearing his desk for the day.

Holding hands with his bride-to-be, Justin waved the legal paper in a grand flourish, and declared, "Mission accomplish. Let's celebrate."

"I'm ready," Nate said as he shut down his computer. "All I have to do is collect my date."

"Did Mandy change her mind about coming?" Britney asked.

"Nope. I asked someone else." Nate ushered the couple out of his office, then closed and locked the door. "Nicole French. She works in the tax office."

"You're kidding," Justin said. "Since when do you date coworkers?"

Nate shrugged with a grimace. "I don't, as you well know."

"Didn't you just say—?"

"Yes, but it's not really a date," Nate explained in a stage whisper as his gaze swung furtively around the office. The only person he saw was the payroll specialist, bundled up against the weather, leaving her cubicle.

"I'm the last one out, except for you, boss," she said in passing. "Have a good weekend."

"You, too. See you Monday," he replied.

Once she was out of earshot, Nate stood huddled with his brother and future sister-in-law. Keeping his voice low, he said, "I didn't mean to ask her out. It just happened."

"Dinner dates don't 'just happen,' Nate," his lawyer pointed out in a similarly hushed voice.

"Well, this one did. Believe me, if I could undo it, I would."

"What happened?" Britney wanted to know.

"Didn't Mandy tell you?" he asked.

"No, should she have?"

"I'm surprised she didn't, that's all. She wouldn't break her date with the car salesman—"

"Not this again," Britney huffed her annoyance.

"Well, she wouldn't," Nate insisted, defensively. "It pissed me off and when Nicole showed up suddenly, I blurted out the invitation without thinking. It's not really a date."

"Sounds like a date to me," Justin commented.

"Well, it isn't."

"Hi, everyone," Nicole sang out as she entered the third floor vestibule. Walking up to join the group, she slipped her arm through Nate's. "I'm Nicole French—Nathan's date."

PREPARING TO LEAVE THE RESTAURANT TWO HOURS LATER, NATE held Nicole's coat while she slid her arms into the sleeves. Britney had gone to the restroom and Justin was paying the tab. Turning, Nicole faced her date as she pulled on knitted gloves. She stepped closer, crowding his space. "Want to come up to the house for a nightcap?

"It's been a long day," he hedged, not wanting to refuse her outright.

She gave him a pouty look. "At least drive me home."

His brows drew together. "Where's your car?"

"It's at home. I didn't drive to work this morning."

"You walked? In this weather?"

"No, silly," she giggled. "My next door neighbor gave me a lift. Since we had a date, I didn't see any point in driving."

Returning from the restroom and slipping into the coat Justin held for her, Britney said, "It was nice meeting you, Nicole."

"I enjoyed meeting the two of you, also," she reciprocated, sending a sly glance toward her escort. "There's a good chance we'll see more of each other."

Nate's eyes met those of his brother, whose left brow rose in an I-told-you-so arch. "We'd better get going, Brit," Justin said. He took her hand and they stepped out into the lashing rain.

Nicole drew her coat's hood over her head before taking Nate's arm in a two handed hug. "Shall we brave the storm?"

They rushed to Nate's truck. He unlocked the passenger door and hurried around the front without helping her to climb inside.

"Whew! What a storm. Are you sure you don't want a nightcap?" she asked, renewing her offer. "I guarantee it'll keep you warm—all night long."

After firing up the engine, Nate turned on the heater, cranked the blower to high, and pulled away from the curb. The holiday festive streets were almost deserted due to the storm. "Nicole, about tonight," he began.

She unhooked her seatbelt and slid into the middle of the bench seat. "What about it?" she murmured, and placed a hand high on his thigh.

He whipped into an empty parking space and abruptly stopped the truck. With both hands on the steering wheel and staring out the windshield, he said, "Nicole, tonight was not a date."

"Of course it was," she crooned, close to his ear. "We had drinks and dinner. Now you're taking me home. That sounds like a date to me." Her teeth nipped his ear.

He turned and took her by the shoulders, gently pushing her away. "Tonight was supposed to be the four of us from the wedding party. You know—bride, groom, matron of honor, and best man. Mandy had other plans and wouldn't change them," he explained. "To keep from being the odd man out in a threesome I needed a date and asked you."

"There, you see. You just called it a date," Nicole reasoned, smiling, as yet unperturbed. "I don't usually ask men in for a nightcap on a first date but we've known each other for a while. Don't worry. I know how to be discreet." She leaned in to kiss him.

Nate pulled away. "I don't get involved with coworkers."

A sullen line formed between her brows. "It's a little late to play that card. Tonight may have been our first official date but we've had a number of lunches and dinners together. The way I see it, we're already involved."

"Sorry, but all those other times were just between two coworkers. That's all. One thing was not leading to the other."

Nicole's chin came up as she pushed herself away. Angrily, she strapped herself back into the passenger side seatbelt, and then crossed her arms over her chest. "Take me home."

"Please, don't make an issue out of this. I want us to be friends."

She turned her head and glared at him. "Okay, we're friends," she snapped. "Now take me home."

Nate blew out a breath and put the truck in gear. He figured it was best to let her have the last word. She'd cool off over the weekend and everything would be fine by Monday.

SATURDAY MORNING, SHORTLY AFTER EATING BREAKFAST, JUSTIN left, saying he and Britney had plans for the day. I called Kimberly Long, hoping she had news about the house I wanted to buy. The realtor said it was too soon to know whether or not the government loan for the other buyers had gone through. She told me it could take up to another three weeks before we knew for sure. She wished me happy holidays before hanging up, which brought to mind that I'd had no time to shop for Christmas.

A look outside indicated the weather was better than the past few days. After finishing the coffee Justin had brewed, I shrugged into my coat and headed out. Starting in downtown Seaside, I browsed the shops lining Broadway, the main east/west street, and found great stuff for my oldest brother, his wife and their kids.

Working my way north to the outlet mall, I bought the perfect gift for Mom. Dad's gift was always difficult. A hard working, organic farmer, he tended to buy what he needed when he needed it. What he didn't need, he didn't particularly want. Although, he did still have the singing fish plaques the three of us boys had bought him ages ago.

As I tucked the latest purchase in the waffled chrome carryall installed in the bed of the truck, I glimpsed the flash of vibrant red hair across the parking lot and heard a musical peal of laughter I recognized as Mandy's. The reason for her gaiety was obvious. A swarthy, dark haired man, wearing a ridiculous set of felt antlers on his head, pranced around her like a comical imitation reindeer. Two questions popped into my mind simultaneously. *Was that her date from last night? Had they spent the night together?*

Thrusting the thoughts from my mind, I told myself with grim resolve that I didn't care if Mandy spent her nights with any number of men. But it was a lie.

Hurriedly, I turned my back on the gleeful pair, hopped into the truck, and once on the road again, drove north. Focused on forgetting Mandy with her probable date, I passed by the box stores and shopping mall in Warrenton without realizing it. After crossing the bridge into Astoria, I stopped for lunch at a Kentucky Fried Colonel. Afterward, determined to complete my gift list, I continued my holiday shopping foray in downtown Astoria.

Trudging in and out of the stores lining Commercial Street, I picked up odd little White Elephant gifts for my boss and immediate subordinates, deliberately ignoring my lateral counterpart in the Assessment and Taxation Department. For Justin and Britney, I wanted a "his and hers" something but didn't know exactly what. When I'd almost given up hope, the perfect gifts presented themselves in the last store I entered. With only my father's name remaining on the list in my pocket, I reversed my earlier direction and steered the truck south. There were a couple of places I wanted to try on the way out of town. In the first, I lucked out and purchased dad's gift, knowing he would like that it was useful as well as stylish.

Satisfied with completing the shopping expedition before the weak, winter light faded altogether, I thought of food. Calling Justin, I asked, "You home yet?"

"Yeah, where are you?"

"Been Christmas shopping. I'm headed back now. Want me to pick up something to eat?"

"No, the girls are cooking. I'm heading over there in a few minutes."

"Oh," I said, feeling a little put out. "Guess I'll see you when you get home."

"Or you could show up for dinner," he suggested.

"I wasn't invited."

"What do you want? A written invitation?"

"No, but what if Mandy's new boyfriend is there?"

"What if he is?" Justin asked, sounding puzzled. "You don't even like her."

"I never said that."

"You don't have to. Whenever the two of you are in the same room you practically crawl down each other's throats."

"We do not," I objected.

After a brief pause, he said, "Sounds like you've got the hots for Mandy."

Justin was yanking my chain, and I knew it, but it rankled just the same. "Yeah, it's been so long since I've had a woman," I said, snidely. "Even Mandy looks good."

Laughter assailed my ear. "Want me to set you up?"

"Thanks, but no thanks," I growled. "I do quite well on my own."

"Doesn't sound like it to me. So," he said before I could respond, "you coming to dinner? We need to tie up a few loose ends for the wedding—about Brit's mother, to be precise. I could use your support."

"What is it with Britney and her mother?"

"Bad history. Long story. You coming?"

"Yeah," I exhaled. "I'll see you in about half an hour."

After disconnecting, I blew out another breath. Yeah, I was hot for Mandy, all right. Problem was, I didn't know what the hell to do about it.

❧ Chapter 23 ❧

Putting the last touches on a salad, Britney covered the bowl with a damp paper towel and slid it into the refrigerator. The front door opened and her housemate sailed in. "You're back early. I didn't expect you for another forty-five minutes."

"The movie was boring. We didn't see any point in staying to the end," Mandy said, moving to the sink to wash her hands. "Where's Justin?"

"He dropped me off and went home to change." Britney chuckled. "I shouldn't laugh. It wasn't funny, not really. But it was, in a way."

"What happened?" Mandy filled a pot with water, salted it, and poured a dab of oil on top. Then she placed the pot on the stove and turned the burner to high.

"We went down to the docks in Astoria to look at the sea lions. God, they're huge and make one heck of a racket with their barking."

"I know. I've been down there."

"There were dozens of them lying on those floating walkways. It's hard to believe those critters are vicious. They look like lazy blobs of blubber."

"As I recall, there are signs posted warning people not to get too close?" Mandy said.

"Yeah, we saw them. Not that Justin paid any attention."

The water started boiling so Mandy stirred in a package of egg noodles. "What happened?" she asked again.

"There was this one sea lion, smaller than the rest. Maybe he was an adolescent, I don't know for sure. Anyway, he slid up onto the walkway, barked as if he was proud of himself, and then slid back into the water. We watched him do this three or four times before Justin decided he wanted a video. He took his phone out and crept as close as he thought safe."

Enthralled with the story, Mandy forgot about the noodles until the pot boiled over. Quickly, she turned the burner down and stirred the pot. Once it was at a simmer, she turned back to Britney. "Nothing happened, did it?"

"Well, Justin's okay, if that's what you mean, but something did happen." Britney took a carton of coconut milk from the fridge and nudged Mandy away from the stove. "I'll make the cheese sauce, you open a couple cans of tuna."

As Mandy moved to comply, Britney resumed her story. "Justin hunkered down, ready to capture that silly sea lion on video. It was almost as if the animal knew. He slid up onto the walkway and scooted directly toward Justin, barking the whole way. The love of my life screamed, I swear to God, he *screamed* and scrambled to hightail it out of the way." Britney held her stomach and laughed. "His shoe caught on something, and for a moment, he damn near went ass over tea kettle into the water."

"You're kidding!"

"I kid you not. It was the funniest damn thing I've ever seen. Or heard, for that matter. Of course, he tore his pants and had to go home to change."

The doorbell rang.

"That's probably Justin. Here," Britney said, and handed the wooden spoon she was using to Mandy. "You stir the cheese sauce and I'll get the door."

"Good evening, gorgeous," I greeted Britney, and planted a brotherly kiss on her cheek. "At last, I have you alone."

"No such luck, honey. Your brother, my fiancé, will be here any minute and Mandy's in the kitchen."

"Mandy, huh?"

"Yes, Mandy. You know, my roomie."

"Is she alone or did she bring her new boyfriend home with her?"

A quizzical look flashed in Britney's blue eyes and she blessed me with a smile. "I don't know if Joe is her boyfriend, per se. They've only gone out a couple of times."

Inhaling deeply and blowing out a breath, I said, "Sometimes that's all it takes."

"If you want to know for sure," Britney whispered, leaning in close. "You'd better go directly to the source." She wrapped her arm through mine and led me toward the kitchen. "Look what the cat dragged in."

Mandy glanced in our direction before turning back to stir something in a small pan. "The cat can drag it back out," I heard her mutter under her breath.

"How'd the hot date go last night?" I asked, feeling belligerent.

She looked at me again, this time with a jaundiced eye. "I should ask you that question."

Let her wonder for a while, I thought, and gave her a shit-eating grin.

Her eyes widened. "Couldn't you have at least waited until the second date?" she demanded, contemptuously.

Goading her, I asked, "Is that what you do?"

"What I do is none of your damn business."

"Back at ya, baby."

The doorbell rang.

"I'll get it," Britney sang out. She turned and raced away.

"You're not the first man Nicole has taken home on the first date," Mandy informed me.

"But I might be the first who doesn't ask her out for a second."

"Why not? Didn't she live up to your expectations?"

I laughed. "Mandy, I'm not in the habit of dating co-workers."

"Well, then, it's a good thing you didn't wait until the second date," she huffed, before I had a chance to tell her I'd refused Nicole's offer of a nightcap.

I stepped forward, backing Mandy up against the stove. Staring into her eyes, I said in a quiet, yet firm voice, "I have never slept with a co-worker."

She stared back at me, as if mesmerized.

Then I leaned close and whispered in her ear, "But for you, sweetheart, I'd make an exception."

Mandy gasped and pushed me away. "What makes you think I want you?"

I gave her that grin again. "Don't you remember? The night of the office party?"

A telltale flush started at her neckline and rose to her hairline.

"Ah, you do remember." Slipping my arms around her, I drew her against the length of me and leaned down until our mouths almost met—almost. Her peppermint scented breath caressed my lips. Her eyelids fluttered shut. The boiling blood in my veins rushed south.

"How long 'til dinner?"

Mandy and I jumped apart.

My brother stood in the kitchen doorway with a smirk on his face. "How long 'til dinner?" he repeated.

"About forty-five minutes," Britney said, brushing past him as she came into the room. "Someone set the table while I get the casserole ready to put in the oven."

Mandy moved to comply and I helped by getting out of the way. Making himself at home, Justin snagged two brews from the fridge, and then he and I made ourselves scarce. In the living room, he showed me a phone video of a sea lion. I laughed at the end when the bark of the sliding animal was drowned out by a masculine shout and the screen abruptly wobbled, showing sky, and water, and then a close up of the dock timbers before ending.

Almost an hour later we were called back to the kitchen. In the center of the lace covered table a scrumptious casserole, with a mouthwatering vapor rising from it, sat on a hot pad. Britney placed a bowl of salad next to it and set the serving tongs on top. Seeing Mandy apply a cork screw to the top of a wine bottle, I obligingly moved to help.

"I can do it," she said.

"I didn't say you couldn't," I countered, and bumped her hip with mine.

Relinquishing the bottle, she moved aside but not away. As the cork released with a soft pop, Mandy reached for the bottle. Her fingers brushed against mine causing her to jump, as if singed. I smiled and gave her a wink. The rose blush that colored her cheeks pleased me immensely.

Dinner started out pleasant enough with discussion of Justin's sea lion escapade. He wanted to delete the last part of the video before posting it on Facebook, but the girls convinced him it was the best part.

Toward the end of the meal, he asked Britney about her mother. She set her fork down with a long suffering sigh.

"I talked to her again after you dropped me off this afternoon. She finally agreed to come."

My brother smiled. "Great."

"You might not think so after you hear the details."

"Now what?" he asked, the smile fading from his face.

"This is obviously an ongoing discussion," I said. "Don't keep Mandy and me in the dark. What's the deal with your mom?"

"She doesn't want to come to the wedding," Mandy threw in, having more information about the situation than me.

"Why not?"

"At first it was because of the short notice," Britney explained. "As if five and a half weeks isn't enough. And then it was the expense." She almost spat the word.

"Come on, honey," Justin murmured, placing his hand over her balled up fist.

She huffed. "I told her we would pay for everything—the round trip flight, all her meals, the hotel. She balked at that. Said she wouldn't come if her daughter—her only child—didn't have the decency to welcome her own mother into her home for the time she was here."

"You don't have room," I said.

"That's what I told her. But you'd have to know my mother to understand. Good southern hospitality demands I welcome her into my home, she told me." Britney snorted. "As if she'd know southern hospitality if it slapped her in the face."

"What are we going to do?" Mandy asked. "This house is too small—"

"Don't worry," Britney assured her friend. "I promised to create a one-of-a-kind, mother-of-the-bride gown for her. Designer wear from the top of her head to the tips of her toes. She wasn't able to refuse that."

Patting her hand, Justin's voice soothed. "Everything will work out."

"You haven't heard the last of it," she told him.

I sensed we were all holding our breath, waiting, as if a live grenade sat in the middle of the table.

"Since my mother is unable to stay with family, she insists on as short a visit as possible."

Justin raised his hand and scratched the back of his head, a sure sign of agitation.

"She flies into Portland the day before the wedding," Britney informed us. "And back out the day after."

I watched my brother take a cautious breath. "That's not so bad, is it?"

The bride-to-be looked at him appalled. "I'm making her dress, Justin. It needs to be fitted and I can't do that until she gets here. I'll be sewing half the night!" Her voice rose in near hysteria. "I'll look haggard for my own wedding."

"No you won't, honey. I promise."

Tears spurted from Britney's eyes. Justin pulled her onto his lap and held her close. "We'll find someone to help," he crooned, stroking her hair. "Hush, baby, hush."

"That's not all," she wailed. "My mother doesn't drive. Someone has to pick her up from the airport and take her back."

"Don't worry, honey. Nate can pick her up and take her back."

"Wait a minute," I objected. "That's a two hour drive—one way."

"So what?" Justin growled at me.

"So, I have a job. I can't pick her up on Friday. I work on Friday. I'll take her back to the airport on Sunday. Mandy can pick her up on Friday."

"Thanks a lot," Mandy complained. "You make it sound as if I sit on my hands all day. I work, too, you know."

"Yeah, but you've worked there longer than me. You probably have all kinds of time you can take off. I don't."

That shut her up—at least for a while.

❧ Chapter 24 ❧

UNFORTUNATELY, MY BROTHER WASN'T THROUGH TALKING.

"Nate, I forgot to tell you—Britney and I are driving to Mom and Dad's after work on Wednesday."

"I thought the three of us were driving over together. I work half a day on Thursday, or did you forget?"

"We didn't forget but the folks are anxious to meet my bride," Justin said, smiling at his betrothed as he lifted her hand and kissed it. "It's a slow week, so Brit's boss agreed to her taking Thursday off."

What could I say to that?

"You and Mandy can drive over together," he continued.

My head swung around to face the woman in question. "You're going, too?"

She dropped her eyes and shrugged. "Maybe, I haven't made up my mind, yet."

"Of course, you're going," Britney interjected. "My best friend is not spending Christmas alone."

I glared at Justin.

His shoulder lifted and fell. "You know Mom and Dad. They love a houseful, especially during the holidays."

And what could I say to that? It was true.

Turning back toward Mandy, I said, "We can leave straight from work."

"I want to change into something casual before leaving."

"Take a change of clothes to work with you," I suggested. "That's what I plan to do."

"Why go to all that trouble? We get off work at noon. That gives us plenty of time to come home before leaving."

"If we leave from work," I reasoned, "we can head east and cross over into Washington at Longview—"

"What about my car?" she wanted to know.

"It can stay in the parking lot at work until we get back."

"I don't want to leave my car in an unattended parking lot over a long weekend," she objected. "Besides, that would require us to come back through Astoria on the return trip. We'll get home faster taking the Sunset Highway."

"Six of one, half dozen of the other," I commented.

"There'll be more traffic coming home Sunday night," Mandy argued. "It makes more sense to have the shorter drive coming back. I'll pack my bags Wednesday night so they're ready to go. While you go home to change, I'll fix us lunch—"

"Damn it, Mandy," I snapped with more volume than intended. "If we do it your way, we won't get out of Gearhart and through Seaside until mid afternoon. By then we could be half way to Goldendale. We'll leave from Astoria."

She crossed her arms. "I'm not leaving my car at work, period."

"Time out, guys," Justin barked as he jumped up, making the sign with his hands. "I swear to God, I'm going to start charging to referee your shouting matches."

Ignoring the interruption, I insisted, "It won't hurt to leave a vehicle—"

"Then leave your truck and we'll take my car."

"I have four-wheel drive and snow tires."

"I'm not leaving my car—"

"Stop it!" Justin yelled. In the sudden silence, he growled his instructions. "Mandy, Thursday morning you drive to my place and park your car in the garage. Take everything you need— suitcase, change of clothes, whatever. There's plenty of room in the cab of Nate's truck for all your stuff. After work," he continued as his glance swept between us, "the two of you leave straight from Astoria. Mandy's car won't be left unattended and you can take the Sunset to come home. Got it?"

Mandy and I looked at each other. I hoped my face didn't show as much chagrin as hers.

"Fine by me," she said in a huffy tone.

"Seven o'clock, sharp," I stated, to clarify the time.

"Why so early?" she countered.

"So we have time to transfer your stuff into my truck."

"That won't take more than two minutes."

"It'll take longer than that. I don't want to be late for work."

"Seven-fifteen will get us to work on time."

Britney reached across the table and gripped her friend's wrist to gain her attention. "Mandy, for heaven's sake, the two of you are quibbling over fifteen minutes. Just humor the man."

"Fine," she hissed, pushing up from the table. "But you'd better be ready when I get there."

"Men don't keep women waiting," I said with a pitying smirk. "It's the other way around."

She made a snarling sound I'd never heard from a woman before, but instead of raking me with her claws as I half expected, she stomped out of the room. A moment later, a door down the hall slammed, shaking the small cottage.

Not in the habit of provoking women, I realized riling Mandy felt sexy as hell.

ARRIVING AT SEVEN ON THE NOSE AND FINDING JUSTIN'S GARAGE door open, Mandy drove her car into the small space and parked. After slinging her purse strap over her head and one shoulder, she removed an overnight bag and small toiletries case from the trunk, along with a plastic grocery bag containing the set of casual clothes she'd change into before starting their drive. She carried her collection to the truck parked at the curb and stowed everything behind the passenger seat. Seeing Nate's bag on the floor behind the driver's seat, she presumed he was ready to go, so she climbed in and buckled up. Then she waited. And waited. As she contemplated marching through the open garage and into the condo to drag him out, her phone rang. Caller ID indicated it was Nate.

"Hello," she sang, giving the second syllable two notes.

"It's five after seven. Where the hell are you?"

"The same place I've been for the past five minutes. I'm sitting in your truck, waiting for you."

There was a short pause, and then the front door opened and Nathan peered out. Mandy waved.

"You could have let me know you were here," he said into the phone as he stepped back inside and closed the door.

"You said to be here at seven, so I was here at seven. I saw your bag behind the seat and presumed you'd come back out any moment." Mandy saw the garage door lower.

"I didn't hear you arrive. I must have been brushing my teeth when you got here. I'll be right there."

Without another word, the connection ended, and a few seconds later, Nate trotted out the front. He opened the cab door and handed a travel cup to Mandy before sliding in. "I thought you might like a cup of coffee."

"For me?"

"Yeah. I would have offered it in the kitchen if you hadn't been late."

"I wasn't late," she said defensively.

Nate looked over as he started the engine. "I'm kidding," he said, the humor gleaming in his eyes.

"You're in a good mood this morning," she commented, and took a sip. "Mmm, this is good."

"Thanks."

They drove in silence for a few minutes, and then she asked, "What should we do about lunch?"

"I thought we'd stop at a fast food place in Longview. Eat on the way."

"I s'pose." She took another sip. "They have a pizza place in Clatskanie. Or, for that matter, we could pick one up on our way out of Astoria. After all, it will be lunch time."

Nate glanced over and easily capitulated, "Call it in ahead of time so it's ready."

"Okay." Mandy settled back in the seat and finished her coffee. "What are your parents like?"

He glanced over again and shrugged. "My folks grew up at the tail end of the hippie movement. They wanted to leave the big city—Seattle, in their case. Get back to nature—flower children and all that Earth Mother stuff."

"Yeah, we had a few of those where I grew up."

"Mom and Dad are good people. Caring. Involved in the community. I admire them."

Satisfied, Mandy nodded her head and fell silent.

"What about you?" Nathan asked.

"What do you mean?"

"Where did you grow up? Not around here or you wouldn't be alone for Christmas."

It was Mandy's turn to shrug. "I grew up in Mendocino, California. Wine country. My mother's parents owned a small vineyard and winery. They sold out after Grams had a stroke. Dad still works there. He would have been happy to continue it as a family operation but Mom, having been raised there, was tired of it. Now she runs the wine festival—almost single handedly, to hear her tell it."

"You miss them?"

Mandy shrugged again. "Sometimes, but I couldn't stay. Not after my divorce."

"What happened?"

"I don't want to talk about it," Mandy stated as Nate turned into the County lot.

He parked and turned off the engine. "Come on, you can't leave me hanging like that."

"Sure I can," she countered, and hopped out the truck.

EARLIER IN THE WEEK, NICOLE HAD TOLD NATE THAT HER SON WAS spending the long holiday weekend with her ex-husband, and then had invited Nate to a turkey-with-all-the-trimmings dinner on Christmas Eve. She explained the get-together was for singles only, keeping to herself the fact that he, Nathan Peters, was the sole invitee. He declined, however, explaining he was leaving straight from work to join his family in Goldendale.

Thursday morning, before entering the County office building, Nicole couldn't resist peeking through the windows of Nate's truck. In addition to the worn duffle lying on the floor behind the driver's seat, her snooping revealed a matched set of floral overnight bags, definitely not the type of travel cases she envisioned the masculine Nathan Peters owning.

Except when it suited her, Nicole made a point of leaving the office promptly at five. Today her curiosity caused her to linger. Uncharacteristically, she chatted with coworkers for a few minutes until they bid her "Merry Christmas" and left.

She straightened her desk and took time to freshen her lipstick before donning her coat and gloves. As Nicole ran out of reasons to delay, Mandy hurried out of her office wearing jeans and a turtleneck sweater. She carried a plastic grocery bag, which looked as if it contained the business clothes she had worn that morning.

"Merry Christmas. Have a good weekend," Mandy hailed as she rushed past.

"Yeah, same to you," Nicole replied, and hastened to follow. Seeing Nate waiting in the vestibule, she ducked back behind the door, leaving it open a crack to facilitate eavesdropping.

"Ready to go?" she heard him ask.

"Yeah." The voice belonged to Mandy.

"Did you call in the pizza order?"

"Yes." There was a pause, as if she needed to check her watch. "It should be ready by the time we get there."

The sound of the outer door closing prompted Nicole to follow. She saw Nate open the passenger door of his truck for Mandy. And damned if he didn't put his hands on her butt to boost her inside!

✥ Chapter 25 ✥

THE JOURNEY TO GOLDENDALE WAS UNEVENTFUL. AND DULL, AS far as Mandy was concerned. After stopping for the pizza, they took Highway 30 out of Astoria, crossed the bridge into Washington at Longview to pick up I-5, and then hopped back into Oregon at Vancouver-Portland for the drive up the Columbia River gorge on I-84, the only practical route.

Rain fell, heavily at times, as they traveled east. To pass the time, Nate teased Mandy with a verbal travelogue of all he would not stop for them to see. In fact, as they sped past the turnoff to the scenic Multanomah Falls, his foot remained planted on the gas pedal, as if rooted in place.

The precipitation turned to snow as they made the climb after crossing the river one last time at Biggs, and Mandy didn't mind missing a stop at the Stone Henge replica or the side trip to Mary Hill Museum. The roads, previously graveled to give traction in icy conditions, had not yet felt the blade of a snowplow. The laden sky obscured the sun and brought early twilight to the late afternoon. Swirling white flakes fell heavy and thick. Nate shifted into four-wheel drive.

The spiraling snow shrouded the slowly turning arms of the hundreds of ghostly windmills that haunted the landscape. They drove past hills and broad expansive plains covered with white fluffy down. In places, the rough bulge of volcanic rock protruded through the snow like the blackened knuckles of frostbitten hands.

"Is it much farther?" Mandy asked with a note of anxiety in her voice.

"No, not far at all. We should be there within fifteen minutes." With a quick glance, Nate saw the apprehension on her face and noticed her hands were clenched in her lap. "Don't worry, all of us boys learned to drive in snow before our parents allowed us to get driver's licenses. I'll get you there safely."

"I'm not worried, not really," she lied. "It's just I've never driven through a snow storm before."

"This isn't a storm."

"It didn't snow where I grew up," Mandy reminded him. "And the only time I saw it snow in Astoria was following an ice storm. They closed everything down for the day. That night the snow stopped, and by morning, and the roads were plowed and sanded."

Nate reached over and squeezed her knotted hands. "Don't worry. I'm an old hand at this and we're almost there."

She gave him a weak smile in return.

They continued in silence until Nate turned off the highway onto what felt, to Mandy, like a gravel track. She turned in her seat but saw nothing through the back window to indicate a reason for their change of direction. "Do you know where we are?" she asked.

"I do. Another two miles up this road and we'll be there."

"How did you know to turn?"

Nate coughed out a laugh. "I've lived here all my life."

"But everything is covered in snow. How did you know this was a road instead of a field?"

He realized she was serious. "I saw the corner markers."

Again, Mandy turned in her seat and searched for a sign through the back window.

"I don't know how they do it where you come from, but here we have a lot of volcanic rock. Farmers and ranchers clear it from their fields. I guess it just makes sense to use it to mark property lines."

"I don't understand," she said, facing forward again.

"A lot of people construct a waist or shoulder high cage out of split rails or posts and wire. Then they fill the cage with the stones they clear from their fields," Nate explained. "There were two such markers on either side of the turn onto this road."

"That's how you knew?"

"That and the spindly oak tree back there."

Slowly, they drove past an old farm house on the left.

"Oh, look," Mandy exclaimed, and pointed. "They're building a snowman."

Nate stopped and honked his horn. The man and two children turned and waved. The smaller child, a girl with long brown braids flopping with each leaping step, jogged toward them, followed more slowly by the man and boy.

Nate buzzed down his window as they drew near.

"Uncle Nate. Uncle Nate." The young girl called out from the other side of a split rail fence.

"Whatcha' doing, Ruthie?" he called back.

"We're building a snowman. Who's that with you?"

"Her name is Mandy. Come on up to Gramma and Grampa's and you can meet her."

The girl hopped up and down like she was on a pogo stick and clapped her mittened hands. "Can we, Daddy? Can we?" she begged as the tall man walked up.

He placed a hand on her shoulder, stilling her antics. "Sorry, sweetheart," he told her.

The boy, standing on the other side of his father complained, "We can't go until dinner time."

"Mom and Becky are baking today," the man said. "We've been warned to stay away."

Nate turned to Mandy. "Want to help build a snowman?"

"I thought we were going to your parents house," she said, surprised by the suggestion.

"We'll get there eventually," he said, turning off the engine. "Come on, I'll introduce you to my oldest brother and his kids."

"We can't just get out of the truck here," she objected. "You're parked in the middle of the road."

"Do you see any traffic?"

"No," Mandy hesitantly admitted.

Nate buzzed up his window. "Then let's go," he said, opening the truck door.

Mandy climbed out the passenger side, somewhat reluctantly. She rounded the front of the truck and saw Nate throw first one leg and then the other over the low fence. He turned and held out a hand to assist her across.

"Mandy, meet Mike and his kids, Robbie and Ruth. He's twelve and she's nine."

"I'm thirteen now, Uncle Nate. Remember?"

"And I'm ten," Ruthie added.

"Right," Nate said. "Well, meet Mandy Kearney. She's going to be Britney's matron of honor at the wedding."

Politely, the two children extended their hands to shake. "Nice to meet you, Ms. Kearney." They said the words in unison.

"Nice to meet you, too, Robbie, Ruthie," she replied. "You may call me Mandy, if you like."

"Mandy," they parroted.

"How do you do, Mandy?" Mike stuck out his hand.

"Fine, thank you."

"Race you to the snowman," Nate challenged as he sprinted off. His niece and nephew took off after him.

"What about you? Want to race?" Mike asked.

"Not particularly," Mandy said, looking down. "I'm wearing athletic shoes, not boots."

The children's father grinned. "I guess that makes you the rotten egg," he chortled as he turned, and loped after the others.

THE SWEET SCENTS OF RUM AND PIE SPICES CARESSED MANDY'S nostrils as she descended the stairs. The aromas were not as strong this morning as they had been last evening when she'd entered the kitchen through the back door with Nate. Still, Mandy was reminded of the organized chaos she encountered when she first met Nate's mother, June, and sister-in-law, Becky.

June was dousing fruitcakes with rum at one end of the counter, Becky was cutting out sugar dough in various holiday shapes at the opposite end, and Britney was decorating a batch of recently cooled cookies at a large oak table cluttered with numerous pies, both pumpkin and fruit filled, a variety of cookies, including oatmeal, chocolate chip, and peanut butter, along with homemade fudge and nut brittle.

"Hi," Britney said, grinning as she continued to squeeze white icing trim onto a pink frosted Santa.

Becky waggled the fingers of her flour covered hand.

June took one look at Mandy's soaked sneakers and wet gloves, wiped her hands on her flowered apron, and threw her youngest son a scolding glance. "What were you thinking, Nate, dragging her out to build snowmen dressed like this?"

They had called before leaving Mike and the kids with three wise men, Joseph, Mary, and a baby Jesus. "Mike said we had to stay away during the baking frenzy."

"Ha!" Becky scoffed. "Mike was supposed to keep the kids occupied so they wouldn't be underfoot all day."

"You were supposed to bring your guest home," June admonished. "Not let her catch her death of cold."

"I'm fine, really," Mandy interjected.

"You'll be fine after you've had a hot shower," June stated in her take-charge way. "Come, I'll show you to your room. You're sharing with Britney. I hope you don't mind."

"Not at all."

"You, young man," June turned, and pointed a finger at Nate, "are bunking with your brother."

With a resigned sigh, he said, "I already had that figured out, Mom."

June led Mandy upstairs, explaining the layout of the house as they went. She finished by saying, "The boys were always bringing their friends home to spend the weekend, so we put two sets of bunk beds in each room. When it was just the three of them, they all shared one room. The rest of the time it was like musical beds around here. We never knew who was sleeping where."

Mandy set her bags in the designated room and grabbed a change of clothes before following her hostess down the hall to the bath.

"If you prefer a soak to a shower, I have some scented bath oil," June offered.

"A shower is fine," Mandy assured her.

Stepping into the bathroom, the older woman opened a cabinet door. "Towels and wash cloths are in here. Use whatever you need. You bring your wet clothes down when you're done and I'll wash them."

"You don't have to do that," Mandy objected.

"I might not have to, but I will."

"Thank you."

"You're welcome." June surprised Mandy with a quick hug. "We're so glad you came. Nate hasn't brought a girl home to meet us since he graduated from high school."

Momentarily speechless, Mandy stuttered, "Ah . . . ah . . . I'm Britney's friend."

"I know, dear."

The teasing sparkle that had been in June's eyes when she'd assumed Mandy was Nate's girlfriend had made her feel odd. She still felt a little off balance this morning. It was as if they were sharing a secret joke. Only she wasn't privy to the secret and had the uncomfortable feeling the joke was on her.

Entering the kitchen, Mandy was overwhelmed by what appeared to be boisterous mayhem. Everyone, including Mike's family, was there and all of them seemed to be talking at the same time. Only June and Becky weren't seated at the breakfast table, now cleared of all pies, cookies, and candy. June was busy flipping pancakes on an oblong electric fry pan and Becky was stirring a vegetable and egg mixture in the largest skillet Mandy had ever seen.

Suddenly, Nate catapulted himself out of his chair and rushed to her side. Drawing her over to the group at the table, he announced, "Sleeping Beauty has arrived. That means we can eat." He pulled a chair out. "Have a seat, your highness."

"Leave the girl alone," Bob Peters told his son. "I believe she did you and Justin a courtesy by waiting until last to use the bathroom."

"While you're up, Nate, pour the orange juice," his mother instructed as she added a stack of pancakes to a plate already full of them. She then tucked the plate back into the oven next to an equally full plate of crisp bacon. "We'll be ready to serve in less than five minutes."

"Is it always like this?" Mandy muttered in awe under her breath.

"I thought you grew up in an agricultural family," Nate spoke right next to her ear.

She pulled away and he placed a glass of orange juice next to her plate.

"Never like this."

He grinned. "Awesome, isn't it?" Picking up another glass, he poured juice into it and set it in front of Mike, then continued on to the next person.

"Are the hot pads on the table?" June raised her voice to be heard above the crowd.

"I'll get them," Ruthie all but hollered as she jumped up and raced to a drawer next to the stove where she snatched up a handful of colorful crocheted squares. Coming back, she placed them side by side in the middle of the table.

With hot mitts protecting her hands, June brought the platters of pancakes and bacon to the table as Becky scooped the scrambled eggs into a large serving bowl. Soon everyone was seated and blessed quiet descended on the group.

"Good food. Good meat. By God, let's eat," Robbie prayed irreverently.

"Robbie!" Becky censured her son.

"Dad says it."

"Don't sass your mother," Bob Peters told his namesake. "Say a proper grace."

Robbie tried again. "Dear Lord, bless this food and all who gather here in Your name. Amen."

"Amens," chorused around the table as hands reached for serving dishes. Food was quickly passed as conversation, at a much more civilized volume, resumed.

Mandy discovered the marathon baking of the day before was a contribution from the combined Peters' households to the holiday social at the community center. Bob, June, and Mike's family planned to leave early to help set up.

Bob and Mike went out to their four-wheel drive rigs to warm up the engines and interiors. When they returned, Becky herded her children out the back door.

Justin helped his mother into her coat, and as she pulled on her gloves, she asked, "How long until we can expect you?"

Nate and Justin exchanged glances.

"Ah . . . we don't plan on going," Justin said.

"Of course you'll come. How else can I show off my future daughter-in-law?"

"We can't, Mom," Nate put in. At her frown of consternation, he added, "You know certain parties will be there."

"And I'll be damned, excuse my French, if those 'certain parties' will keep my boys and their women from enjoying a little Christmas cheer."

Mandy, assuming the 'certain parties' were ex-lovers of the 'boys' in question, put in her two cents worth, "I'm sure Britney can handle any potentially awkward situation and I don't have a dog in this fight."

"Butt out, Mandy," Nate snapped.

In a gentler tone, Justin said, "It's not personal, Mandy. It's business."

June's mouth flattened into a straight line. "Not going makes you look culpable."

"Mom, on the advice of my attorney, I am not to discuss the situation or talk to the parties involved," Nate calmly explained.

"And you know that will be the hottest topic of conversation if either of us show our faces," Justin said in support of their decision.

"What's this all about?" Mandy ventured to ask.

"None of your business," Nate said in an offhand manner.

"It might be my business if the situation, whatever it is, affects your job at Clatsop County," Mandy snipped back.

Nate glowered in irritation.

"It's doubtful the issue or its outcome will have any influence on his current position," Justin placated.

"It has to do with your last job, doesn't it?" Mandy guessed.

Looking ready to grind glass with his back molars, Nathan snapped, "Now see what you've done, Mom?"

"Careful, Nate," Justin warned. "That's our mother you're talking to."

The younger man jammed his fists into his pants pockets. "Sorry," he muttered.

"I am, too, dear," June said as she stepped up to her son and kissed his cheek. "It'll all work out. I just wish it didn't have to cast a pall on our time together."

"I know. Things will be better next year."

"Next year," June said with forced enthusiasm, and an apologetic smile toward Britney, "I'll have at least one new daughter-in-law to introduce around."

Understanding the veiled hint, Nathan chuckled and returned his mother's kiss. Then he whispered in her ear, "Don't hold your breath, Mom."

❧ Chapter 26 ❧

FOR A MOMENT, NO ONE SPOKE AFTER THE DOOR CLOSED BEHIND June, then Britney asked, "How long did it take to build the snow Nativity yesterday?"

Mandy looked at Nate, who shrugged. "I'm not sure," she said. "A couple of hours, I guess. Maybe a little longer."

"You thinking about building one?" Justin asked his fiancée.

"Can you think of anything else to do on a snowy Christmas Eve?" she responded. The suggestive sparkle in Justin's eyes caused her to blush.

"I have an errand to run," Nate said, and left the kitchen to go upstairs. He rummaged around in his old bureau, found what he was looking for, and slipped it into his coat pocket before heading back downstairs.

"Mind if I go with you?" Mandy asked as Nathan entered the kitchen.

"Yeah, Nate, take Mandy with you," Justin backed up her request.

Britney made a strangled sound and gave Justin's shoulder a smack with the back of her hand.

Nate barked out a laugh. "Sorry to disappoint everyone but this is something I need to do by myself." He opened the back door and turned to face the group seated at the table. "By the way, Britney, you'll have to get over your embarrassment if you are going to survive in this family," he said before leaving.

Three hours later, satisfied with the results of his trip into town, Nate returned to find Mandy putting the finishing touches on three pathetically crooked snowmen.

"Are you working on the wise men or their camels?" he asked, coming up beside her.

She sighed. "If you have to ask I might as well give up." She tried realigning the topmost lump of snow on her current figure, which only made it more lopsided.

Nate looked around, and then asked, "Why are you out here by yourself? Where're Justin and Britney?"

"They went in the house."

"What for?"

"What do you think?" Mandy said in a snide tone of voice.

"How long ago?"

"About an hour, I suppose." She slapped more snow onto the misshaped head of the figurine.

"And you've been out here by yourself the whole time?"

Mandy stopped her ineffectual efforts at creating a recognizable snowman. "No way on earth am I going to risk interrupting whatever it is they're doing in the house."

Humor sparkled in Nate's eyes. "I think we both know what they're doing." He gathered up a handful of snow. "But what makes you think going in the house to warm up will interrupt them?"

"I'm not taking any chances."

"Know what I think?" Nate asked, and then answered his own question as he stepped away from Mandy. "I think it's time for a snowball fight." He lobbed his missile right at Mandy's chest, where it hit with a plop and broke apart.

"Very funny," she said, scooping up a handful.

Nate was forming another round of ammunition when Mandy's projectile hit him in the shoulder. "Oh, you're good," he laughed, firing another shot.

She sidestepped but wasn't fast enough to keep from getting hit. She gave a squealing laugh as the powdery cold sprinkled down her collar. Ducking behind the snow sculptures, Mandy toppled them to create a low wall of protection. Quickly scrunching snow into two more rounds, she pitched them at her adversary. One hit, the other flew wide of its mark.

By this time, Nate had four hastily made balls tucked into the crook of his arm. While on the run, he threw them in rapid succession and made a flying leap into Mandy's snow fort. Screaming, she tried scooting away but he grabbed one of her ankles and scrambled up her body. Flipping her onto her back, he trapped her wrists and held them above her head. "Gotcha."

They panted from their exertions, the fog of their breaths mixing in the frosty afternoon air. Slowly, their laughter faded as first Nate and then Mandy became aware of their warm bodies pressed together from breast to groin. Slowly, Nate dipped his head and their lips met as gently as the falling snow.

With the force of a fastball, snow smacked Nate between the shoulder blades.

"It's about time you got back," Justin called from the other side of the snow fort wall.

Reluctantly, Nate released Mandy's wrists and sat up. The cold seeped through his jeans and cooled his ardor.

"Where were you, anyway?" Justin asked.

"I had something that needed doing," Nate replied, standing up and reaching a hand down to assist Mandy to her feet.

"Like what?" The question sounded accusatory.

Exasperated by his brother's interrogation as much as by the interruption of a very pleasant kiss, Nate responded sharply. "Like none of your business."

The two men stared at each other until Nate blew out his breath and gave his brother the assurance he wanted. "Don't worry, I didn't do anything stupid." Then, with a sideways glance toward Mandy, he added, "At least, not yet."

FOLLOWING A LATE, LIGHT DINNER OF CHESTNUT SOUP AND Waldorf salad, the entire Peters' clan and their two female guests trouped out the kitchen door and drove caravan-style to a Christmas Eve candlelight service. Ruthie fell asleep toward the end and, as they left, was carried to the truck by her father. Robbie shuffled tiredly along behind.

"I bet the kids sleep in tomorrow," Britney said from beside the children's mother.

"Not likely. They're farm kids and used to getting up before the crack of dawn," Becky enlightened her husband's future sister-in-law. "And tomorrow, I guess I should say today, is Christmas. They'll be clamoring to open presents long before I'm ready to get up."

"That's how it was for me growing up," Mandy agreed.

"Not me," Britney said. "My mother never allowed me to get up before she was out of bed. She rarely rose before ten, except on school days."

"You're kidding," Becky and Mandy chorused.

"Nope. You'd think I'd be a bed slug, too, but from as far back as I can remember, I've awakened early."

"You'll fit right into this family then," Becky assured her. "Now give me a hug goodbye."

"Won't we see you tomorrow? I mean, later today?" Britney asked, sharing an embrace.

"That depends on how early you want to get up. My parents retired last year and moved to Spokane. We'll stop by for a few minutes right after breakfast to exchange gifts, and then we need to hit the road."

"If I don't see you before you go, have a Merry Christmas," Mandy said.

"You, too." Becky hugged Mandy. "It was nice meeting you."

"Same here. Have a safe trip."

June and Bob walked up and another round of hugs ensued, and then the men exchanged handshakes.

After Mike and his family drove off, Nate rubbed his gloved hands together. "Let's go home and open presents," he suggested.

"Let's go home and go to bed," his mother countered. "Your dad needs his rest."

"Ever since my heart attack, your mother says that whenever she wants sex," Bob said with a wink, and sidestepped to dodge June's elbow.

"That's enough of that kind of talk," June chided. "Now, let's go home. I'm tired."

It was a little after seven when hooting laughter woke Mandy. The room was cold and she snuggled deeper under the quilt, pulling it over her ears. When the noise from below grew louder, she assumed Mike and Becky's kids were opening their presents and resigned herself to getting up.

Throwing back the covers and simultaneously reaching for her robe, Mandy jammed her feet into the slippers that lay on the floor by the bed. Then she sleepily trudged into the bathroom. A half hour later, showered, dressed, and holding two small gifts, Mandy stood looking into a room strewn with torn wrapping paper. Sitting in their overstuffed chairs and surrounded by their recently opened gifts, June and Bob were in their bathrobes, and Bob incongruously wore a spanking new straw cowboy hat above the grin on his face. Nate, Justin, and Britney, also in bedclothes, sat on the floor by the tree. There was no sign at all of Mike's family.

"Hey, you missed all the fun," Nate said, spying her in the doorway.

"I hope not," she replied, and stepped into the room.

"Careful where you put your feet," June cautioned. "There's no telling what's under all the wrapping paper."

Sliding her feet along the hardwood floor to scoot Christmas wrap out of her way, Mandy crossed to June and handed her a present. "It's more of a hostess gift than something specifically for Christmas," she said.

"How thoughtful." June tore off the paper to reveal a battery operated clock in a small, brass replica port light. "It's darling. Thank you."

"Thank you for sharing your family Christmas with me," Mandy said in return. Then, she joined the group around the tree, and sitting, handed the other gift to Britney. "Merry Christmas."

Britney removed the bow and ribbon before painstakingly releasing the scotch tape securing the paper. Inside the small jewelers box was a gold lapel pin with the word *Bride* in tiny script letters. "Oh, Mandy, it's beautiful," Britney cried, and pulled her friend into a tight hug. "Thank you."

"I'd suggest you put it on but you're wearing a bathrobe," Mandy said.

"I'll put it on as soon as I dress." Britney handed the box to Justin for safekeeping and rummaged through the scattered paper to come up with a colorfully wrapped present, which she handed to Mandy. "Merry Christmas to you, too."

Mandy, as fastidious as Britney had been, opened the gift and revealed an emerald green, watered silk dress. Sewn inside the collar was a label, *Original Designs by Britney*. "Oh, it's gorgeous! Thank you." Standing, Mandy held the dress in front of herself for all to see. "Thank you," she said again.

"Okay, everyone, how about you clean up this mess while I cook breakfast," June suggested.

Nate held up his hand. "We're not done, yet." He pulled a present out from beneath the tree. "Merry Christmas, Mandy," he said, holding it up.

Resuming her seat on the floor, she seemed reluctant to take it, but did. "I'm sorry, Nate," she murmured. "I didn't think—." Shaking her head, Mandy tried to give it back. "I can't accept it. I don't have anything for you."

"I didn't give it to you expecting something in return. It was something I had lying around that I thought you'd like."

"Don't look a gift horse in the mouth," Bob told her. "Open your present like a good girl."

With a nervous little chuckle, she did as instructed. The black box inside was embossed in gold. *Cross*. "No one has a *Cross* pen and pencil set just lying around," she said.

"Nathan does," Justin tossed in. "He received three as graduation gifts from various women he dated in college."

"Shut up, Justin," the younger man snarled.

"I can't, really," Mandy insisted, holding the box out to Nate.

"Open it, Mandy, and then tell me you can't accept it."

With trembling fingers, she lifted the lid. The slender gold cylinders were etched with her name. *Amanda*. She gasped with pleasure and looked at Nate. "I don't know what to say. Thank you."

"Let's see," Justin said, leaning over to look. He whistled under this breath. "That must have cost a pretty penny, etching her whole name instead of only her initials."

"I couldn't decide on AK for Amanda Kearney or MK for Mandy Kearney," Nate told her.

"Either would have been fine." She traced the etched letters with her fingertip.

"Yeah, well . . . your initials will probably change when you get married. I figured this way it wouldn't make any difference."

"I guess not. Thank you."

"Are we done now?" June asked as she stood. "If so, I'll start breakfast."

"Oh, let me," Mandy said, jumping to her feet. "I can cook breakfast while the rest of you shower and dress."

June patted her arm. "The minute we met, I knew I liked you."

✥ Chapter 27 ✥

FOR A WHILE, AFTER THE LONG CHRISTMAS WEEKEND, RELATIONS between Mandy and me improved, both on and off the job. Neither of us mentioned the unintended kiss in the snow but at odd, idle moments I found myself pondering what that kiss may have become except for a snowball in the back interrupting us.

Monday, shortly after lunch, Nicole stopped by my office, her previous angst seemingly forgotten, and asked me to go out with her on New Year's Eve. When I reminded her I didn't date coworkers, she claimed the invitation was just a friendly gesture and not intended as a date. I declined anyway and she left in a huff.

I spent the rest of the short work week tying up loose year-end details and preparing for the fiscal year budgeting process scheduled to begin next month.

With Friday a holiday and my brother's wedding only three weeks away, the four of us got together for a marathon session of double checking each aspect of the event and every invitation response card. By dinner time, all of us were ready to call it a day. Justin suggested we order a pizza but the women objected. It was New Year's Eve, they said, and as good an excuse as any for a night on the town.

It was just my luck that close to midnight we ran into Nicole. She was alone. Odd, I thought, for her to be in Seaside instead of closer to home. She walked up to our table but the music was too loud for conversation, which was fine by me. I didn't care to hear her thoughts about me being in a foursome with Mandy. Trying to make the best of the situation, I asked Nicole to dance.

We jostled our way to the dance floor as a hip jarring tune ended and the musicians announced they'd play an old Beatles song before taking their break. The melody was slow. I would've preferred to hold Mandy in my arms as Nicole and I swayed to the sensuous rhythm. Catching a glimpse of the firebrand edging her way to the dance floor with a buff surfer-type, I thought there was definitely something in the way she moved.

The song ended and the lights dimmed as the countdown to the New Year started. There was no chance for me to step away from Nicole. She tightened her arms around my neck, calling out the diminishing numbers in my ear. As the crowd yelled "Happy New Year" at the tops of their lungs and *Auld Lang Syne* began, she pressed her lips to mine, her mouth open and wet. Her pelvis rubbed against me as she flicked her tongue into my mouth. With the crowd pressing close around us, it was impossible to escape from her embrace. As the lights came up and people started to move off the dance floor, I reached behind my neck, grabbed her wrists, and broke her hold.

It surprised me to find Mandy standing next to us with shock plain on her expressive face. Not saying a word, she turned and fled back to our table.

As I started after her, Nicole grabbed my arm. "Let her go. I'll take you home."

I had no doubt as to whose home she referred. "Sorry," I said, and hurried after Mandy.

"I'm ready to leave," she told Justin and Britney, who were still seated. Then, snatching her purse from the back of her chair, Mandy slung it over her shoulder.

I grasped her arm and she jerked it away.

"You can stay and enjoy yourself," she said. "I'm sure Nicole will give you a ride."

Catching her double entendre, I said, "I'm sure she would but I'm not interested."

"That's not how it looked to me."

"Looks can be deceiving."

Mandy barked out a scoffing sound.

"What difference does it make to you?" I demanded. "As I recall, you have a boyfriend."

"I don't have a boyfriend," she claimed.

"What happened? Did your caustic attitude toward men scare him off?"

She seemed to flinch before saying, "For your information, when I got back from Goldendale, Joe called and told me he had been separated from his wife for a time but they had reconciled over Christmas—for their children's sake."

"Are we going or what?" Justin asked.

"We're going," I said, and took Mandy's arm again. This time she didn't pull away. She also didn't look at me on the drive back to Justin's. Nor did she say goodnight when Britney dropped us off.

LATE MONDAY MORNING, AFTER COMPLETING A MEMO EXPLAINING the new calculations for assigning indirect costs to each department and detailing changes in various budget categories, I distributed preliminary budget packets to the department managers' inboxes. I then started work on month end property tax disbursements. Things weren't adding up the way I expected and I put a call into Mandy but her voicemail picked up. Instead of leaving a message, I dialed another extension.

"Nicole French speaking."

"It's Nate. Is Mandy in her office?"

"She's in a meeting."

I waited a moment before realizing that was all the information Nicole intended to give me. "Will she be long?"

"I have no idea."

Her frosty attitude came through loud and clear. "I don't want to leave her a voicemail in case she doesn't check it before going to lunch. Give her a message for me, will you?"

"I'm not her secretary."

Squelching my exasperation, I stated, "I know you're not but I'd appreciate a little cooperation."

"Fine," she said in huffy agreement.

"I need her to double check the month end property tax calculations and get back to me ASAP so I can make the disbursements this afternoon. I'll be in my office through lunch."

"I'll give her your message when I see her."

"Thanks."

By two-thirty that afternoon I hadn't heard back from Mandy. I gathered up the spreadsheets and marched downstairs. Seeing Nicole, I veered over to her desk. "Did you give Mandy my message?"

"You asked me to, didn't you?"

It wasn't a straight answer to my question but close enough. I marched back to Mandy's office. "How much longer on those figures?" I asked from the doorway.

"What figures?"

"The figures I asked you to double check before lunch?"

"I don't know what you're talking about."

"Since you were in a meeting, I asked Nicole to give you a message—"

"I never got it."

Sidestepping her comment, I said, "I need the property tax calculations double checked."

"Why?" There was a defensive belligerence in that single word.

"Because, I think you're numbers are wrong."

"I suggest you do your job and let me do mine. The numbers are correct," Mandy declared.

"How do you know if you haven't double checked them?"

"Oh, give me those sheets," she demanded, and grabbed the printouts from my hand. As she compared the numbers to the ones on the computer monitor her face turned first pink and then as red as her fiery hair. "Where did you get these?"

"From my inbox, where I presume you left them."

"This isn't correct."

I raised my eyebrow but refrained from saying, "Duh!" The thought transmitted itself anyway.

"These aren't the spreadsheets I put in your box."

"They were the only ones there and those are your initials, aren't they?" I asked, pointing to the blue squiggles in the bottom corners of the pages.

Raising the sheets to her eyes, Mandy peered closely at the markings on each page. "They look like my initials," she admitted softly.

"There you have it," I said.

She looked me square in the eyes and waved the pages in my face, saying forcefully, "These are not the spreadsheets I put in your box."

"Then why are your initials on them?"

"I don't know," she replied quietly. "But I have my suspicions."

"Don't give me that crap, Mandy." I said softly. "Just admit you made a mistake and let's move on."

Without another word, she turned back to her computer, tapped a few keys and printed out a new set of spreadsheets. She initialed each page and held them out to me.

"Thank you." Taking them from her hand, I left.

Tuesday morning when I arrived at work, Mandy stood outside my office door. "We need to talk about this," she said, indicating the budget packet she held in her hand.

"Not much to talk about," I commented as I unlocked the door. "But come in and have a seat anyway." As a precaution against the possibility of raised voices, I closed the door behind us.

Opening the manila envelope, Mandy slid the papers out. On top was the explanatory memo. "I disagree with the indirect cost factor you've assigned to my department," she began.

"Take it up with Ernie. He approved the changes."

"I wasn't even consulted."

"Neither were the other department heads," I told her. "This came down from above."

That stopped her cold. Her shoulders drooped. "Why do they do that?"

I shrugged, knowing she didn't expect an answer. "Anything else?"

"Yes," Mandy said, straightening her spine. "Your January thirty-first deadline is two weeks earlier than usual."

"So I've been told—by at least half the other managers. I'll tell you the same thing I told them—live with it."

"But I have the quarterly timber revenue to calculate this month," Mandy pointed out. "Unlike your arbitrary time frame, the timber disbursements have a mandated deadline. I have no choice but to get the calculations done."

"If I grant you an extension it will force me to grant extensions to everyone else who asks. That or be accused of favoritism," I explained.

"I can't meet this deadline. We have the Mt. Hood Conference to attend. I'll lose the better part of three days because of that." she argued.

"I guess you better plan on burning a little midnight oil."

"Have you forgotten about the wedding?" she asked, her voice starting to rise. "It's in two and a half weeks. I've committed every evening to helping Britney. Plus, I'm taking vacation days on the Thursday and Friday preceding the wedding. How in the hell am I supposed to meet your stupid, arbitrary, unrealistic deadline?" She shouted the last words in obvious frustration.

"Okay, I see your point," I said, with both hands held up, palms out. "Quite frankly, I wasn't thinking about the wedding."

"So, I can have until the middle of February, as usual?"

"No, I can't do that. Another commitment will take me away from the office for a few days in February. I need the worksheets back before then. I can give you until Friday, February fourth," I offered.

"Make it Monday the seventh and I'll get it done, one way or another, with no complaints," she countered.

I couldn't help laughing. "Fine, you have until the seventh but this has to been kept completely quiet. No one knows except you and me."

"Deal," she said, and held out her hand.

We shook and afterward, I wondered if that was the date she'd been shooting for all along.

৶ Chapter 28 ৶

W<small>EDNESDAY AFTERNOON</small>, M<small>ANDY AND</small> I <small>LEFT WORK EARLY TO MAKE</small> the three hour drive to Mt. Hood. On the first leg of the trip we discussed various conference session topics. Due to the differences in our jobs, we would attend different meetings. By the time we crossed the coastal mountains and headed into Portland it was too dark for her to read the brochure. Setting it aside, we talked about a few work issues before moving on to a discussion of Justin and Britney's wedding. Soon, that subject was exhausted and silence fell between us. Mandy fiddled with the CD player and discovered my musical tastes reflected her own. For a while, we listed to the soaring voices of *Il Divo*.

Perhaps it was the anonymity afforded by the darkness in the truck's cab or maybe the rich emotion of the music's swelling crescendos, but for whatever reason, Mandy decided to confide in me.

"My marriage lasted less than a year." She spoke softly, almost as if to herself. "Six months, to be precise."

Not knowing what to say, I kept quiet.

"I mean, we broke up after only six months. The divorce took longer, but it was all over in less than a year."

"Why are you telling me this?" I asked, keeping my voice low.

"I disliked your brother before ever meeting him," she said. "He was a blatant womanizer."

"He isn't like that now."

"Was," she said, and sighed. "Britney told me Justin was the way he was because a woman broke his heart while he was in college."

"That's right. He took it hard."

"What about you, Nate?" she asked, looking at me. "Did a woman break your heart?"

I debated how to respond and decided the truth couldn't hurt. "No, I've never felt strongly enough about anyone to get my heart broken."

Mandy lapsed into silence again. After a while, she said, "I'd never had sex before getting married. It took a long time to get over my husband's infidelity. Then last summer I met someone else. He lived in the same apartment complex as Britney and me."

She didn't continue, so I prompted, "What happened?"

"Sam acted nice, romantic even. It took six weeks for him to convince me to make love with him. Then, after three short weeks of intimacy, he walked out on me. Not for other women —like Tom—but Sam was cruel, just the same." She paused. "I thought I was better prepared the second time around, but I wasn't."

I glanced over but couldn't make out the features of Mandy's face. "I'm sorry." It was inadequate but what else was there to say?

"I was disappointed when Joe told me he was married. He seemed nice."

"Maybe he is, Mandy."

"Yeah, maybe. He didn't tell me why he and his wife separated, only that they got back together."

Reaching over, I clasped her hand. "You just haven't hooked up with the right man, yet."

"I've come to the conclusion there isn't a right man. Not for me."

"Don't say that."

She turned her head to look at me again. "I'm serious, Nate. I won't chance another broken heart. Until some fairy godmother waves her magic wand and turns planet Earth into the perfect world, I'm staying emotionally unattached."

"How do you plan to do that?"

Before she answered, the GPS informed us the exit we wanted was ahead one-quarter mile.

"You hungry?" I asked. "We can eat dinner before checking in, if you want."

"No, I prefer to check in first," she said in a rush, as if abashed by our previous conversation. "I want to get settled. I'll order room service."

"Look, Mandy," I said, pulling into the rotunda "You don't need to be embarrassed."

"I'm not. I want to get a good night's sleep so I can be fresh for tomorrow's meetings."

"You're sure?"

"Absolutely,"

Parking the truck, I left it at that.

UPDATED TAX LAW WAS PRESENTED AND EXPLAINED AT THE morning meeting Mandy attended. She sat next to a man from a county in the south central part of the State. Karl Williams was his name. They had briefly met at a previous conference but hadn't conversed past introductory hellos.

Today, they chatted during the twenty minute break, and when the meeting let out shortly before noon, Mandy accepted his congenial invitation to join him for lunch. Not only could they compare differences between the inner workings of their county offices, she thought, it gave her a good excuse to avoid eating with Nate.

She had no idea what possessed her last night to share the secrets of her love life failures. Perhaps it was the still vivid memory of seeing him kiss Nicole at the stroke of midnight. It had made her feel like the charmed step-daughter fading back into the unwanted girl, Cinderella.

Her salad was mostly consumed when Mandy saw Nate enter the banquet room reserved for the Oregon State employees' luncheon. He was in a late arriving group of five men and one woman. Glancing around the room, he saw Mandy, and raised his hand. She waved in return, but not as if beckoning him to join her and Karl, who sat alone at their table for six. The petite woman standing next to Nate touched his arm in a too familiar manner and spoke to him. He dipped his head closer to hers, perhaps to better hear her words, and laughed. In the crowded room, their conversation held a peculiar intimate quality that Mandy found oddly disturbing. One of the men nudged Nate and the group took their places at the only unoccupied table.

"Mandy?" Karl said, as if repeating himself.

Pulling her attention back to her luncheon partner, she smiled, "Yes?"

"I asked which session you planned to attend this afternoon."

"Let me look." She took the conference brochure from her purse and referred to it. "There's only one that interests me." One she knew Nate wouldn't attend. "It's concerning property assessment."

"What do you know, that's the one I plan to attend."

Mandy returned his smile. "Good, we can sit together again."

During the afternoon break, Karl asked Mandy to have dinner with him, suggesting they meet in the lobby bar for a drink before their meal. She agreed.

FOLLOWING THE AFTERNOON SESSION, NATE RETURNED TO HIS room and changed clothes before going downstairs to the bar where he joined Ted and George, two of the men he'd met earlier that day. Unlike his associates who were imbibing in cocktails, Nate ordered an on-tap microbrew.

They were talking shop when he saw Mandy standing just inside the door to the bar. She was in a cute little lime green outfit, the blouse tucked into a skirt abbreviated well above her knees, and sandaled heels that accented the feminine curve of her long legs. It was not the type of casual clothes he'd expected her to wear after hours at a business conference.

Nate waved to gain her attention but she never looked in his direction.

"You know her?" Ted, a guy about Nate's age, asked?

"Yeah, she's the Deputy Assessor/Tax Collector at Clatsop County," he replied.

The man on his right, George, was older by at least two decades. Casting an appreciative eye at the lovely redhead, he asked, "When did they start making tax collectors look like that?"

"They don't where I live," Ted said. "God, she's hot."

Nate chuckled, "I call her the firebrand. Not to her face, of course."

"The firebrand. I like that because she sure as hell torched a fire in me. I don't suppose you'd introduce us?" Ted asked. "If you're not playing with fire, I mean."

Frowning into his beer, Nate said, "Sorry, but I think a couple of jerks from her past doused her flames."

"Looks to me as if someone was able to fan the embers," George commented. "Unfortunately, it's another jerk."

Nate looked up. With a hand on the small of Mandy's back, a man guided her to a table on the other side of the room. It was the same man he'd seen her with at lunch.

"What makes him a jerk?" Ted asked. "Other than he's with Ms. Hottie Pants and I'm not."

Curiosity kept Nate from uttering a word but he frowned at Ted to indicate his displeasure.

"We used to work together," the older man said. "When it comes to county business, Karl Williams knows his stuff. But he can't keep his pants zipped."

The grunt from the back of Nate's throat sounded as if it was caused by a fist slamming into his belly.

"He has the nicest wife," George continued, tipping his chin to indicate the man sitting with Mandy. "He had an affair with a coworker while his wife was pregnant. It caused a bit of a stink at the office. Word got back to his better half and she threatened divorce. To patch things up, Karl ended the affair and took a job in another county. It was a big step down for him."

"I see Karl is up to his old tricks," a soft, feminine voice said.

It was the woman who had monopolized his attention during lunch. He couldn't remember her name but recalled she worked with George.

She smiled at Nate and sat next to him. "I talked to the sleaze ball a little while ago," she told the table at large. "His wife is pregnant again. Fortunately, this time it's not twins."

Just then, Mandy and her companion stood, but instead of walking into the adjacent restaurant, they turned toward the lobby elevators.

Nate belted back the last of his beer and declined George's suggestion of another round.

The woman with the unmemorable name looked at Nate. "If you're going into dinner, mind if I join you?"

Normally, Nate would have been the one to offer dinner, and a whole lot more, to the eye-catching female seated beside him. Tonight, he found himself saying, "Sorry, I have another commitment."

Momentarily, an irritated line appeared between two meticulously drawn brows before disappearing again. Ms. No Name turned a sultry smile on Ted. "I'm starving, how about you?"

"I don't mind being second choice," he said, standing. "Lead the way."

As Nate made a beeline to the elevators, he hoped his unsuspecting coworker hadn't followed the married s.o.b. to his room. Outside Mandy's door, hand raised and ready to knock, Nate hesitated. Perhaps Mandy knew the s.o.b. was married. Maybe she didn't care. A short fling with a married man was one way to remain emotionally uninvolved. On the other hand, Nate found it hard to believe she intended to do to another woman what had been done to her.

Damn it! He walked away. Mandy didn't need a babysitter and he sure as hell wasn't her keeper. She was well over the age of majority and thoroughly capable of making adult decisions on how to live her life.

But damn it! She was the best friend of his brother's fiancée. She was more than that—Britney claimed Mandy was like a sister. That damn near made her family. Close enough, anyway.

Nate turned back. If she didn't want his interference she could tell him to mind his own business. Hell, she could throw him out, for all he cared, but he'd be damned if he'd let that married s.o.b. take advantage of her.

After knocking on the door, Nate waited a couple of seconds before he knocked again—pounded was more like it. "Mandy, are you in there?" he called out. "If you're in there, open the door."

The heavy metal door flew open and she stepped out, pulling it behind her. "What do you want?" she demanded. Her hair was in disarray, her rumpled blouse no longer neatly tucked into her skirt.

"Who's in there with you?"

"That's none of your damned business."

"I'm making it my business," Nate said, and pushed past her into the room.

The s.o.b. lounged on the bed in shirt, trousers, and sox, as if he had the right. Quickly, he scrambled to his feet. "What the hell do you want?"

"Hi, Karl," Nate said in a deceptively pleasant voice, but with a smirk on his mouth and ice in his eyes. "How's the wife and kids? I understand she's expecting again. What is this, number three?"

"What are you talking about?" Mandy questioned, tugging on Nate's sleeve.

"Didn't your friend tell you? He's married with children."

She looked at Karl. "Is that true?"

"More or less. We have an open marriage."

"That's not how I heard it," Nate interjected. "I heard your wife damn near divorced you the last time she was pregnant."

"Who the hell are you?" Karl wanted to know.

"It makes no difference who he is," Mandy declared. "I have no respect for or interest in philanderers. Get out."

"Don't forget your Wingtips," Nate threw in for good measure.

Glaring at the two of them, Karl picked up his shoes and slammed the door on his way out.

"Do you think a business conference is the best place to pick up a quick lay?" Nate asked, sarcasm evident in his voice.

"What I do away from the office, after working hours, is nobody's business but mine."

"If you're with a married man, I should think it's his wife's business, too."

"I didn't know Karl was married, but I suppose I should have been suspicious since he seemed nice." Mandy's statement of self-defense took a belligerent turn. "Next time I'll remember to hook up with an egotistical jerk like you."

"You could do worse," Nate sneered. "Oh, excuse me, you did do worse."

Mandy's eyes narrowed. "Yes," she hissed softly. "I guess I did. So, I'll just have to make do." Without taking her eyes from his, she started to unbutton her blouse.

Hot blood surged through his veins as he watched one button after another release its hold. Every nerve ending in his body tingled and his manhood throbbed. He waited until her fingers touched the bottom button before saying, "I have a hard and fast rule. I don't date coworkers."

"We're not dating." Mandy's words flowed out of her mouth like warm molasses. "I'm talking about one night of no-strings sex. Tomorrow we'll both forget it ever happened. "

"Believe me, baby, one night with me and you won't *ever* forget it."

Mandy snorted. "Oh, yeah? Watch me." The last button came undone.

So did Nate. In one swift motion, he grasped the hem of his turtleneck with both hands, pulled it off over his head, and tossed it aside. The movements flexed every muscle in his well-defined chest. Seeing the sparkle of appreciation in Mandy's eyes, his lips curled into a devilish grin.

Without a word, he took hold of her wrists and drew her toward him. They stood bare inches apart. The scent of woman, sultry and seductive, tantalized his senses. He reached up and tenderly traced her collar bones with his fingers, then slipped his hands beneath her blouse and slid the garment from her shoulders, letting it float off her arms onto the floor.

Only then did Nate's eyes drop from hers. His gaze caressed the creamy smoothness of her skin and saw pink nipples crinkle into tight rosebuds under the sheer fabric of her bra. His heart pounded in his chest.

"You're beautiful," he whispered, before dipping his head and finding her mouth with his. They meshed perfectly, as if two separate parts became whole.

Her lips tasted like summer sunshine. A moan formed deep in Nate's throat. It escaped when his tongue delved into the warm, lush cavern of her mouth.

Delicately, almost hesitantly, Mandy's hands came up to rest on his torso. Instinctively, seductively, her fingers nestled in the crisp hair of his chest.

Nate felt on fire, scorched by her touch. He wanted more. Much more. He wanted to feel all of her, the brush of her skin against his, the press of his flesh into hers.

Reaching around, he undid the clasp of Mandy's bra, drew it off and let it fall to the floor between them. "You're beautiful," he repeated, having no other words left in his vocabulary.

His large, strong hands gently caressed her high, firm breasts. He captured the catch of her breath in his mouth, kissed her fervently, probing with his tongue. Their lips parted. His trailed, hot and avid, across her jaw, down her neck, and nipped at the sensitive juncture of her shoulder.

She moaned and stepped closer until the tips of her breasts, like small, eager knots, grazed his skin.

Holding her close, his hands glided down her bare back, smoothed over cloth covered buttocks, pulled her up, and nuzzled the solid ridge of his sex against her softness.

She gave a low sob of need and came alive in his arms, arcing into him. He bent his head and took a rigid nipple into his mouth, alternately sucking hard and then soothing with his tongue. His hands found the fastening of her skirt, unzipped it, and pushed it to the floor. Sliding his hand under the elastic of her panties, he felt the moist heat of her desire. He dropped to his knees and, through the sheer silk of her panties, raked his teeth on the mound of her womanhood.

She cried out and gripped his shoulders but did not push him away. He eased her back and down onto the bed. Then he removed her panties, confirming she was a natural redhead, and took her into his mouth. Within moments she cried out in climax.

Hurriedly now, Nate released himself from the confines of his pants, and still kneeling between her thighs, buried himself in the lushness of Mandy's moist, hot body.

He felt as if the woman lying on the bed was all he'd ever desire. He drove into her, repeatedly, insane with need. He found her breasts with hand and mouth. Long, strong legs clasped around his hips. He felt her climax again and followed her over the edge.

❧ Chapter 29 ❧

THE BEDSIDE PHONE BUZZED LOUDLY, ABRUPTLY AWAKENING Mandy from a deep lethargic slumber. She stretched somnolently across the cold expanse of bed, lifted and then immediately replaced the receiver to stop the rude sounding noise. Flopping back onto the pillows, she threw her arm over her eyes, reluctant to give up the amnesia of sleep.

Sharply, the phone rang again. Buzz, buzz, buzz. She slapped her hand on the receiver, held it to her ear, and unwilling to release her mind from its soporific state, mumbled something unintelligible.

"Don't blame me if you oversleep," Nate said.

Like the California Santana winds remembered from her youth, hot and restless images of last night's sexcapades with Nathan Peters blew through Mandy's consciousness.

"You have forty-five minutes before today's sessions begin," Nate continued. "Don't be late."

Before she could respond, the call ended. Slowly, Mandy replaced the receiver.

Last night and Nate Peters. A leisurely smile formed on Mandy's lips. Definitely a night to remember. The edges of her mouth turned down and she groaned. Definitely a night to forget! And forget it she would.

She threw back the covers and rolled out of bed. Nate's intention was clear. So was hers. No office dalliance for him.

No-strings sex for her. He had what he wanted. She had what she wanted. So why was that so damned aggravating?

IT WAS SILENT ON THE LONG DRIVE HOME—EXCEPT FOR THE occasional kittenish sound Mandy made in her sleep. The lengthy bouts of slow, sultry sex following that first feverish burst of lust, and too few hours of sleep, obviously fatigued the firebrand. I, on the other hand, feeling sexually replete, was energized.

I glanced at her snoozing on the other side of the truck. After her confession in the shadowy confines of the cab during the drive to Mt. Hood, I found her lack of sexual inhibitions both surprising and gratifying—as was her apparent sophistication.

Unsure of what to expect from her on the morning after, I took the easy way out, and shortly before dawn, left her sleeping in the wide hotel bed. By neither word nor action during our brief encounters today did Mandy allude to the intimacies of last night. Only the rosy blush that colored her cheeks when our eyes first met betrayed her memory of our time together.

After one night of shared ecstasy, both Mandy and I were able to walk away unscathed emotionally. She got what she wanted. I got what I wanted. So why, I asked myself, did I feel seeds of discontent sprouting in my gut?

THE WEEKEND WAS UNEVENTFUL WITH THE WOMEN OFF DOING whatever women do. The only thing of a wedding nature to occupy my time Saturday was to finalize a few details for Justin's bachelor party. At his insistence the event would be small and pitifully sedate. The men-only Sunday offered football playoffs on TV, and with Super Bowl only four weeks away, lengthy analysis and discussions by the commentators. Although my brother wouldn't admit it, I secretly believed he had taken Super Bowl Sunday into account when setting the wedding date. Considering they would return from their honeymoon just two days before the annual event, the timing was too close to think otherwise.

Late Monday afternoon my realtor called. "Nate, are you still interested in buying that house down by the river?" she asked.

"Are you kidding?" I blurted. "Of course, I am."

"I heard from the bank a few minutes ago," Kimberly said. "If you recall, the offer they accepted was for five thousand dollars over the asking price."

"Yeah, I remember. It irked the hell out of me."

"Yes, well . . . I guess the buyers didn't realize the government lending agency expected them to come up with the extra cash. They don't have it and the conditions of the loan won't allow them to borrow it."

"Does that mean the bank has accepted my offer?"

"At this point, they only want to confirm whether or not you're still interested."

"Damn right I am," I assured her.

"Okay, that's what I needed to know. I'll call them, relay the information, and get back to you as soon as I hear anything."

"Thanks, Kimberly."

"Don't thank me until it's a done deal."

"Okay, I won't, but . . . thanks anyway."

The possibility of getting that house was too intoxicating to keep to myself and at the same time too uncertain to share. Unable to sit still, I walked to the little window overlooking the building's back entrance. Across the courtyard, and through the big second floor window, I saw Nicole serving a customer at the counter.

Last week she gave me the cold shoulder and confirmed my suspicion she was miffed at me for leaving with Mandy on New Year's Eve. It was to prevent petty situations like this that I avoided office entanglements. I supposed it was up to me to mend fences and hoped enough time had passed for Nicole to get over her pique.

When she finished with her customer, I picked up the phone and punched in her extension.

"Nicole French," she answered.

"Nate here," I said in return. "How about lunch tomorrow?" The long pause before she spoke told me her nose was still out of joint.

"I don't know. Work is really piling up on my desk," she whined.

"I'll buy," I said, to sweeten the pot.

Nicole sighed deeply, as if imposed upon. "I suppose, but it will cost you for leaving me the way you did."

She made it sound like I'd walked out in the middle of a date. "I left with the people in my group," I reminded her.

"You could have left with me," she countered in a hushed voice.

Putting a little firmness in my tone, I said, "No, Nicole. I could not have left with you. I was in a party that included my brother and his fiancée."

"Fine, have it your way," she relented. "Lunch is still going to cost you."

"You're worth it," I said. To my way of thinking, lunch wasn't near as expensive as conflict and ill-feelings in the work place.

WITHIN SECONDS OF WALKING IN THE FRONT DOOR OF JUSTIN'S condo, my phone rang. Caller ID indicated it was Kimberly. Sending up a silent prayer, I answered. "Please tell me you have good news."

"I do if we can get earnest money into escrow before close of business tomorrow."

"I'll bring you a check on my lunch hour. How soon can I move in?"

"You were smart enough to get pre-approved for a loan, so unless something unforeseen comes up, I think escrow can close within thirty days," the realtor told me.

"Can I move in before closing?"

"No, I'm sorry. The bank wants to unload this property as soon as possible. If you moved in and the deal fell through it would delay putting the house back on the market. They won't take that chance."

"Nothing will happen," I assured her. "I want the house and I'll move heaven and earth to get it."

"Sorry," she said again. "You can have the keys as soon as title transfers, not before."

"All right." Refusing to let one small disappointment mar the thrill I felt, I said, "I'll be in your office by twelve-fifteen tomorrow, checkbook in hand."

"You get the house?" Justin asked, having overheard my end of the conversation.

As if the ear-to-ear grin on my face wasn't answer enough, I said, "Yes—hot damn!"

"When does the escrow close?"

Too happy to give his question any thought, I teased, "What's the matter, bro? You anxious to get rid of me?"

Justin raked the fingers of one hand through his hair. To me, his brother, it was a recognizable gesture of agitation. "Not exactly," he said.

The smile slid from my face. "Well, what is it, exactly."

"Nothing. I'm glad you're getting the house you wanted."

"Which means what? That I've imposed on your hospitality for too long?"

"No, you're my brother."

"But my being here is a pain in the butt."

"I didn't say that."

"You don't have to, Justin. I can take a hint."

"I wasn't hinting, damn it!" he swore in a raised voice, raking both hands over his head. "You can stay as long as you need— as long as you want. Hell, for all I care, you can move in permanently!"

We stood stiffly, glaring at each other, hands fisted. Justin's phone rang. He snapped it off his belt and answered. The fight drained from his eyes, replaced by a softness that told me the caller was Britney. He turned away and walked into the kitchen as he spoke.

Watching him, I knew what I had to do. When he hung up, I said, "I've overstayed my welcome. I'll find an apartment or motel room or something tomorrow and move out."

"Like hell you will," he replied. "There's no point in throwing your money away. With paying your half of the arbitration costs, you need to hold on to every penny you own to close the escrow. Besides, in less than two weeks, Brit and I will be in Hawaii enjoying a sun baked honeymoon."

He had a point, one I'd be foolish to argue over. But, I decided right then to be out of his home before the two lovebirds returned from Hawaii."

A WEEK AND A HALF LEFT UNTIL THE WEDDING, BUT ONLY FIVE work days, Mandy figured, since she was taking next Thursday and Friday as vacation. How on Earth would she meet all her deadlines? Timber revenue calculations needed to be finished within the next two weeks for funding to be completed by month end. If she could get it done before the wedding, she might be able to slap together the department budget by her extended deadline.

Ha! Who was she kidding? She'd be hard pressed to get it all done without taking the two days off. She should tell Nate she needed more time.

Her mind drifted, as it had a tendency to do lately, when she thought about *him*—Nate—Nathan Peters. When she remembered—NO. She wouldn't think about *that*. She'd eradicate it from her memory, the way he obviously had.

She hadn't seen him, not once, since they'd returned from Mt. Hood. They barely spoke on the drive home. Of course, she slept most of the way; she was tired after all the—NO. Don't even go there, Mandy told herself with a stern, mental wag of her finger. He owed her nothing, not even a phone call. That's how no-strings sex worked.

The next time their paths met, probably at the wedding rehearsal, she'd act as if *it* had never happened. She'd date other men. He'd date other women—

"Guess what?" Nicole said from the doorway, breaking into Mandy's line of reasoning. "Nate's buying a house. It has a sauna," she almost sang.

It took a moment to wrap her mind around the words and then Mandy said, "He made a contingency offer last month but nothing's definite."

The tax technician flaunted a know-it-all smirk on her face. "Oh, yes it is. Nate was going to take me to lunch yesterday but had to reschedule until today because yesterday during his lunch hour he had to meet with his realtor to give her a check for the earnest money."

"Wait a minute, you've totally confused me." Knowing she would be sorry for asking, Mandy did anyway. "Please start at the beginning."

A gleeful sparkle lit Nicole's eyes. "Monday afternoon, Nate called and offered to buy me lunch on Tuesday. But then, Tuesday morning, he called again to reschedule our date."

A knife of disappointment stabbed at Mandy's heart. It was foolish to feel betrayed, she knew, because her night with Nate came with no strings. She breathed deep and slow to keep her pain from showing.

Nicole continued, "Apparently, there was a house Nate wanted to buy but someone else offered on it first."

"That's right," Mandy acknowledged. "Nate put in a contingency offer but it was iffy at best."

"He said his realtor called Monday night and told him the house was his if he still wanted it. That's why Nate had to change our date."

"Your lunch date," Mandy clarified.

"Yeah, whatever," Nicole said. "A date's a date, as far as I'm concerned. Anyway, yesterday on his lunch hour, Nate took a check for the earnest money to his realtor. He told me all about it when he bought me lunch today."

"I see."

"I thought you would." Nicole turned to leave but over her shoulder she delivered the coup de grace. "I plan to be the first person he invites over for sauna sex. Nice, long, *hot* sauna sex."

❧ Chapter 30 ❧

WITH NO FURTHER GROUP WEDDING PLANNING SESSIONS scheduled, a week passed without any direct communication between Mandy and Nate. They had no chance encounter in the office foyer or even a business related phone call. It was as if each was as reluctant as the other to test the waters of their professional association after the intimacies they'd shared.

At least, Mandy preferred to think that rather than admit to deliberately avoiding Nathan Peters. She'd see him this weekend; there was no getting around it. Their joint involvement in a wedding made it inevitable.

Saturday, Mandy was in the clear. She'd be busy preparing for that night's bridal shower. Britney's future in-laws were driving over from Goldendale. She felt superior knowing that while a group of men made fools of themselves at Justin's bachelor party, a houseful of women would bond over cake, champagne punch, and presents.

Sunday brunch was another matter. There was no getting out of it.

Mandy's phone buzzed. It was Nicole.

"Guess what?" the tax technician asked. Without waiting for a response, she excitedly rushed ahead. "Nate hired a topless bartender for his brother's bachelor party."

"Topless!" *You wanted no strings.* The cold voice of self-rebuke withered Mandy's knee jerk indignation. "You'd get more work done," she snapped, "if you gossiped less."

Ignoring the sharp reprimand, Nicole taunted in a husky voice, "Don't you want to know who the bartender is?"

The question ensnared Mandy's curiosity. "I'm afraid to ask."

"My cousin, Rashell. She called to tell me she's been hired for a private gig. When I found out whose shindig it was, I promised her a crab and champagne lunch Sunday in exchange for all the smutty details of their lecherous little affair." Nicole chuckled provocatively. "Care to join us?"

The offer slithered passed Mandy's defenses and was as inviting as a blood red apple. Britney had arranged for the two of them to meet with the entire Peters' family at the Pig 'N Pancake Restaurant before the out-of-towners made their trek back home. Justin, his parents, older brother, sister-in-law, and Nate—presuming he survived the bachelor festivities he was in charge of hosting. "No, I'm already committed to brunch."

"With Nate?" Nicole demanded.

The curt question handed control of the conversation to Mandy. She let silence drift over the phone line like smoke in a breeze, before saying, "Yes, with Nate." No need to mention everyone else. "Now, enough of this nonsense. Get back to work."

FOLLOWING JUSTIN'S INSTRUCTIONS, I PICKED UP THE WEDDING rings from the jeweler after work on Friday and delivered them to his office where he locked them away for safekeeping until the big day. My brother was usually an easygoing guy, but if his recent testiness was any indication, the strain of anticipation was beginning to take its toll.

"Remember," he reminded me for the umpteenth time as he closed the safe. "It's your job, as best man, to make sure we pick up the rings before the ceremony."

"Will do."

"It's important," Justin stressed, looking me in the eye. "We can't forget the rings. It would ruin everything."

"Don't worry, bro," I assured him with easy confidence. "I'll remember."

Looking doubtful, Justin hoisted his hands to his hips. "Maybe you should put a reminder alarm on your phone."

I already had—two, as a matter of fact, just to make sure.

When I didn't jump to do as he suggested, my brother pulled out his phone and proceeded to push buttons. "I'll put the reminder on my phone."

"I'll remember the rings," I said, calmly.

"The way you remembered my autographed Garth Brooks album cover at Billy Prescott's house?"

"For Christ's sake," I blurted, taken completely off guard. "What the hell does that have to do with anything?"

"I trusted you to bring it home and you forgot it."

"I was ten years old, for crying out loud. I went back to get it the next day."

"And it was gone."

"How was I supposed to know his jerk-off older brother would hawk it for ten bucks?"

"The point is," Justin emphasized, "you forgot it."

I coughed out what passed for a laugh. "I'm not ten anymore, Justin. I'm twenty-eight, almost twenty-nine. I won't forget your wedding rings."

His brown eyes stared aggressively into mine. I stared right back. Abruptly, he released the tension from his shoulders and laughed. "Yeah, that's right, but you'll always be my baby brother." Then he slapped me on the shoulder and we headed for the door. "So, tell me about tomorrow's party."

He was fishing for secrets I refused to divulge. "Hey, I'm your best man, remember? Trust me to know how to organize a bachelor party."

I'd rented the community room at the condominium complex for the event and spent most of Saturday afternoon getting things ready. Dozens of centerfolds from various men's magazines were taped to the walls around the room, a large screen TV and video equipment was set up for the two soft porn movies I'd rented, and as instructed by the hired bartender, the bar was stocked with all the essentials. Justin knew about the movies and figured they were inevitable at a stag party, but the topless bartender would come as a surprise.

Finding her hadn't been difficult. All it had required were a few pleasant stops after work at Astoria's popular topless watering hole. The woman I hired was the prettiest of the pack with bold breasts and plump nipples. In that respect, she reminded me of Mandy.

I hadn't seen the firebrand since returning from Mt. Hood and wanted to chalk it up to a full work schedule, for both of us. But, in all honesty, I knew that was only an excuse. Mandy was keeping her distance. For the first couple of days that had been fine by me. I needed the space to put things right in my head. But things weren't right. Not in my head and not in my heart.

That thought stopped me cold. I realized the sprout of discontent I'd felt a week ago had silently grown like a noxious weed and was now deeply rooted and spilling seed.

I wanted to see Mandy, to kiss her, to stroke my hands over her soft, silky body, to feel her writhing and bucking under me, to hear the faint little whimper in the back of her throat evolve into an elated cry of ecstasy as she climaxed. I wanted to make love with her—again, and again. Not for just one night—one night wasn't nearly enough. I wanted—

"Hello," a voice called out.

Turning, I saw Rashell, the topless bartender—only she wasn't topless at the moment. She was all decked out in black from her stylish down-filled jacket to her skin-tight turtleneck sweater, ass-hugging jeans, and high-heeled boots. It didn't take much in the way of imagination to visualize her in a skimpy black leather getup, complete with a satin ribboned cat o' nine tails.

"I'm early," she said, with a knowing smile. "Can I help with anything?"

"Not really," I replied, pulling my thoughts away from a rocky precipice. "I'm pretty much done setting up. Just waiting for the food to arrive."

Rashell nodded, and walking farther into the room, glanced around at the decorations. "I can call a couple friends, if you want—dancers—to liven up the party. I know you said you didn't want strippers, but it's not too late to change your mind."

"If it was up to me, I'd go for it," I said. "My brother turned over a new leaf when he got engaged. He agreed to a bachelor party but only if I kept it sedate. You're my only concession to female flesh, in the flesh, so to speak."

Once again, Rashell nodded. "Okay. In that case, I'll check out the bar. Make sure everything is set up the way I want."

"Be my guest." I gestured to the corner area, which was stocked with a keg and assorted liquors, mixers, a few lemons and limes ready for slicing, one jar each of green olives and pearl onions, a bag of red plastic beer cups and another of clear plastic cocktail cups, swizzle sticks in the shape of naked women, and an array of drink napkins, each sporting a different sketch of some very imaginative sexual positions.

She made a quick inventory of everything, and when finished, murmured her approval.

The caterers arrived. I showed them the tables set aside for the buffet and got out of their way while they carted in the food.

As soon as they were gone, Rashell looked at the feminine gold watch on her wrist and said, "Guess it's about time for me to get ready. I left a few things in the car. I'll get them and change."

Pointing to a little alcove at the back of the room, I said, "The restrooms are back there."

"I gathered as much," she commented with an amused smile, before leaving to get her things.

While she was gone, I double checked the video equipment and paused the DVD on a full frontal close up of an obviously natural blond, satisfied it would set the mood for the festivities to come.

Rashell returned, carrying a tote over her shoulder, and ducked into one of the two small restrooms. Circling the room, I pulled the shades. It wouldn't do for young kids and teenagers living in the condominium complex to walk by and inadvertently look in the windows. With a last visual sweep of the room I saw the cardboard sign I'd made identifying the event as the *Justin Peters' Bachelor Party* and took it outside to slide in the sign holder next to the entrance door.

When I returned, Rashell stood next to the bar, as bold as can be. She'd pulled her midnight hair back into one of those fancy braids women liked, which exposed the delicate curve of her shoulder. Wispy tendrils graced her neck, begging to be swept aside by a pair of lips. A bright red pendant drew my eyes to the level of her breasts, as lovely as I recalled. Her nipples looked invitingly rouged, tempting me to brush them with my thumbs to find out. Resisting, I continued my inspection. Rashell wore a red ruffled thong-like affair that barely covered her woman's mound and curved up to the top of her slender hips like the wings of the letter V. Her shapely legs were as naked as her torso. Red sandals, with three inch stiletto heels, adorned her feet and exposed the red nail polish on her toes.

A spinning motion of my upheld index finger instructed Rashell to turn and give me a view of her backside. For a moment, I thought I'd died and gone to heaven. She was well proportioned—almost as perfectly as Mandy. The unexpected thought drew a frown to my forehead.

"Is something wrong?" Rashell asked. Looking over her shoulder, trying to see what I saw, she stretched in a hip twisting arch that lent an appealing tilt to her bottom. But my enjoyment of Rashell's endowments was spoiled by my thoughts of Mandy.

A wolf whistle sounded from the entrance way. "Why the frown?" asked a middle aged man I'd never met before. "Most men grin from ear to ear when presented with a view like that."

"And a fine view it is," I answered back, forcing a smile to my face, and extending my hand. "Nate Peters, Justin's brother."

"Phil Carey," he said. We shook hands. "Britney asked me to give her away at the wedding."

"Then you must be her boss."

"I prefer to say we work together."

"Phil, I'm Rashell," the bartender said as she stepped behind the bar. "Can I get you something to drink?"

"A beer will be fine. Thank you."

More people began arriving, and before long, the room was full of Justin's local friends and better known business associates, all of the male variety. Not wanting the locals to think me a blockhead who didn't know how to organize a decently decedent bachelor party, I had intentionally scheduled the guests to arrive before the honoree. When Dad, Mike, and Justin walked in and saw the deliciously disrobed bartender, the latter threw me a look so cutting, I thought it capable of slicing me in two.

Ignoring his bloodthirsty glare, I whistled to garner everyone's attention. Mike thoughtfully muted the movie, but in deference to the occasion, left the DVD playing. I raised my glass and toasted the bridegroom. Others followed suit and Justin graciously joined in the festivities.

"I hope your mother doesn't hear about this," Dad said, sidling up.

"No one's forcing you to look, Dad," I reminded him with a grin.

"I wouldn't be human if I didn't look."

"Me either," Mike said as he came to stand on my other side. "But if Becky finds out, I'll be relegated to the barn for I don't know how long."

"Neither one will find out unless one of us spills the beans," I asserted. "I, for one, don't plan to tell a soul. This is our little secret."

"Sounds good to me," Dad agreed. Then he headed back to the bar, ostensibly to get another beer.

"It's a good thing we're going home tomorrow," Mike commented.

"Why?"

"Less chance of word getting back to Mom and Becky."

"You worry too much," I smirked. "There's not a chance in hell of them finding out."

❧ Chapter 31 ❧

AFTER THE LAST OF THE BRIDAL SHOWER GUESTS LEFT, MANDY poured wine for June and Becky Peters, Britney and herself, serving them in the living room.

"Were you surprised?" June asked.

"Completely," Britney responded fervently. "I thought we'd just sit around and talk about wedding plans while the men had fun at Justin's bachelor party. I never expected a bridal shower."

"I wanted to surprise you," Mandy said.

"How on earth did you know to invite all those women?" Britney asked. "Most of them I only know from work."

"I called your boss," Mandy confided. "After explaining what I wanted to do, Phil told me to get together with his wife. I couldn't have pulled this off without Karen's help. She knew which of the female clients of his firm would want invitations."

"Just look at this," Britney said, indicating the gifts scattered around the room. "Remind me to send Karen a bouquet of flowers tomorrow as a thank you for her thoughtfulness."

"I beat you to it," Mandy informed her friend. "Karen received a lovely bouquet of mixed flowers this morning. Since I asked for her help, I thought the gesture should come from me."

"Britney, will we meet your mom at the rehearsal dinner Thursday night?" June asked.

"No," Britney said, a little too forcefully.

"Unfortunately," Mandy interjected, "Britney's mother isn't arriving until Friday. She has a mid morning ETA at Portland airport. I'll pick her up, and with any luck, have her here by early afternoon."

"That's cutting it kind of close, isn't it?" Becky commented. "Didn't she want to come early and help with last minute preparations?"

The fleeting grimace that crossed Britney's face was more expressive than words.

"Britney has me for that," Mandy said emphatically.

"With you travelling to and from the airport most of Friday," June pointed out, "it's a good thing Becky and I will be here."

"Yes," Mandy agreed, with a cheerful smile. "By the way, do either of you know how to sew."

"We both do. June insisted I learn before she let me marry Mike, like it was some sort of pre-requisite," Becky joked. "While Mike was away at agricultural college, she taught me everything."

"Hardly that," June put in, and looked at her future daughter-in-law. "Compared to you, we barely know the essentials."

"Don't let her kid you," Becky argued. "June might not know as much about tailoring as you, Britney, but she knows a lot more than the average seamstress."

"What Britney isn't saying," Mandy piped up. "Is that she won't be able to fit her mother's dress until she arrives, which doesn't leave a lot of time to finish sewing it. I don't know anything about sewing, so I'm no help at all."

"Count me out," Becky said. "I'd be scared to death of botching something."

"I'm more than happy to help," June enthused, with her eyes sparkling mischievously. "As long as you promise to teach your redheaded friend here how to sew. She should know more than just the basic use and operation of a straight pin."

Looking relieved, Britney raised her right hand, as if giving an oath on a bible. "I swear I'll do anything in exchange for your help, June. I'll lock Mandy in the sewing room and feed her only bread and water until she learns."

"Hey, don't I have anything to say about this?"

"No," both June and Britney chimed together.

"If you're going to be that way about it," Mandy said, picking up a sheet a paper from the table beside her chair, "I probably shouldn't give you this."

"What is it?" Britney asked.

"The guest list."

"Why would I want that? I know who all was here."

"As you opened your gifts, I jotted each one down next to the giver's name to make it easy for you to send thank you notes. Without this list you'll need to sift through the presents and hope each one has a card with it."

Britney tossed her long braid over her shoulder, leaned forward, and snatched the paper out of Mandy's hand. "That was very thoughtful of you. I'll return the favor someday."

"An easy promise to keep, considering I don't plan to remarry."

"How can you say that?" June chided. "Not only would refusing to marry deny a fine man—someone like my youngest son—of a wonderful wife, you'd deprive a nice woman—such as myself—of a lovely daughter-in-law."

In the process of taking the last sip from her wineglass, Mandy gasped, causing her to inhale the liquid. With a choking cough, she sputtered, "You're not implying I should marry Nate, are you?"

"Why not? He's responsible, has a good paying job, and is as handsome as sin. If you ask me, he's a fine young man."

"No offense, but I have a feeling Nate isn't ready to settle down."

"Most men aren't," June countered, "until the right woman takes them in hand. Mike was lucky. Becky took him to task early in life. Poor Justin suffered through years of heartbreak before Britney came along to straighten him out."

Wide eyed, Mandy stared at the older woman. "The first time I saw Justin, he was sitting in a Jacuzzi with a half naked blond. I wouldn't call that suffering."

June sighed. "It's not uncommon for a man to hide a broken heart by cavorting with loose women. Nate always idolized Justin and showed a tendency to emulate his wild ways. But Justin has settled down now, which means I can stop worrying about Nate."

Mandy laughed so hard tears ran out of her eyes. "Oh, June, don't stop worrying yet," the redhead gasped when she caught her breath. "If tonight is any indication, Nate is nowhere near ready to settle down."

"What do you mean?" Britney asked, knowing her fiancé's brother had organized everything for Justin's bachelor party.

"Nothing. Forget I said anything."

"Mandy, if you know something I don't about Justin's party, then as my friend, I think you should tell me."

"Yes, Mandy, tell us," Becky instructed. "After all, both my husband and June's are there. We deserve to know whatever it is you don't want to tell Britney."

Trapped, Mandy squirmed in her chair and looked at her roommate. "I wasn't going to mention it. I didn't want to upset you."

"You know how I feel about friends keeping secrets," Britney said, referring to the breakup of her first engagement by a woman who'd called herself a friend.

"I heard a rumor, that's all. I don't know if it's true," Mandy hedged.

"Oh, you must have heard about the titty flicks," June pooh-poohed. "We know about that. Men will be men, after all."

Looking a little relieved, Mandy said, "Then you know about the bartender."

Frowns furrowed three female brows as June, Becky, and Britney exchanged glances.

"You don't know about the bartender," Mandy concluded in a mutter, as she again shifted about in her chair.

Britney crossed her arms. "Perhaps you'd better tell us."

Mandy stood. "Before I say a word, I think we need another drink." She escaped into the kitchen, and a minute later, returned with a fresh bottle of wine. Silently, each woman held out her glass for a refill. When Mandy resumed her seat, she took a big gulp from her glass.

"We're waiting," Britney needlessly reminded her.

"One of my coworkers called me yesterday afternoon. She said her cousin sometimes tends bar at private parties. Apparently, Nate hired this gal for . . . he hired her to go topless."

"Topless!" Becky shrieked, jumping up. "Wait 'til I get my hands on—"

Smacking her wineglass down on the table, June exclaimed, "My husband and sons know how I feel about things like that. They'd better have a damn good explanation—"

"They do, June," Britney said, with a sour smile on her face. "You said it a moment ago. Men will be men. The question is, will they admit to it?"

"What do you mean?" Becky demanded.

Britney drew in a deep breath to give herself time to gather her thoughts. Then she looked at Mandy. "I know Justin told Nate to keep things low key, so I will give my fiancé the benefit of the doubt. Let's presume, girls," she said, including the others in her glance, "that Nate took it upon himself to add to the entertainment value of tonight's event without disclosing his intention to anyone. If that is the case, our men are innocent of collusion."

"That's no excuse," June stated adamantly.

"I'm not excusing them, but it's not like those three men could just walk out. It is Justin's bachelor party, after all."

"So what? Are we supposed to pretend we didn't find out?" Becky asked, angrily.

"I think the soon-to-be newest member of our family has a shrewd mind," June commented. "Tell us your thoughts."

"If Nate did hire a topless bartender, as rumored," Britney waved a conceding hand toward Mandy. "Do you think Bob or Mike will mention it when they get back to your rooms tonight?"

"Not likely," Becky huffed, crossing her arms. "But if Mike's been ogling a nice set of knockers all evening, he'll be horny as hell and expect to get some." She blushed when she realized what she'd said in front of her mother-in-law.

June chuckled. "Don't be embarrassed, sweetie. Since I have two grandchildren, I presume you and Mike get it on once in a while."

"Well, he's not getting any tonight or anytime in the foreseeable future," Becky announced.

"Don't cut off your nose to spite your face," her mother-in-law advised. "For the most part, it's all water under the bridge now, anyway."

"Except for the disclosures," Britney said. "Not knowing in advance and not having the option of walking out of the party doesn't negate the need for a good, soul-cleansing confession."

"I couldn't agree more and I'll get one out of Mike if I have to —" With a sideways glance at June, Becky closed her mouth and pressed her lips together.

"We're all meeting for brunch tomorrow," Britney reminded everyone. "I think it would be fitting to not say a word until we have a chance to spring it on all of them at the same time."

"In order to do that," June pointed out, "Becky and I will have to act as if we don't have a clue."

"I admit it will be easier for me than for the two of you. I won't see Justin until tomorrow. But it sure will be fun watching them squirm."

Becky and June exchanged glances and slowly smiled. "I like the way she thinks," Becky said.

❧ Chapter 32 ❧

Two o'clock in the morning the party was finally winding down. Most of the attendees were gone. Only two or three diehards remained, and even they took the hint when my brother joined their group and thanked them, once again, for coming.

The party would have wrapped up long ago, shortly after the second movie ended, if someone hadn't slipped a music CD into the built-in sound system and encouraged Rashell to dance. She was happy to oblige and earned a few hundred dollars in tips for her efforts. She'd even offered to give the guest of honor a free lap dance, which Justin declined amid the noise of whistles and good natured ribbing from his friends.

As soon as the door closed behind the last of the guests, Dad, Mike and Justin shrugged into their coats.

"Thanks for coming, Dad," I said, giving him a hug. Over his shoulder, I added, "You, too, Mike."

"Great party," Dad commented, as we broke apart. His eyes slid to the bar, where Rashell was straightening things up. "Wouldn't have missed it for the world."

"Well worth the drive," Mike pitched in. He pulled me into a bear hug and heartily slapped my back while I pounded his in return.

Justin broke up the heartwarming moment of sibling bonding when he barked, "Pig 'N Pancake. Eleven o'clock. Don't forget."

"How could I forget?" I asked. "We planned to drive over together."

"We talked about it," he replied, and then tipped his chin toward the bar. Rashell had her luscious backside to us. "I wanted to remind you in case your plans changed."

I wouldn't admit it to my brother, was surprised to admit it to myself, even though Rashell looked utterly delectable, both front and back, I wasn't interested. For the past week—hell, longer than that, if truth be told—the redheaded firebrand had grabbed my attention and hadn't let loose. The trouble was, for the first time in my life, I didn't have any idea if there was a reciprocal attraction. In the past eight days, since returning from Mt. Hood, I'd neither seen her, nor heard her voice. Mandy was avoiding me, and the only conclusion I could make was that the avoidance was by choice. She didn't want to see me or talk to me. She wasn't interested.

"Remember, eleven o'clock," Justin, standing in the open door, called to me. "Don't be late."

"Don't nag," I replied as my brothers and father filed out.

"Your father's cute," Rashell said from across the room.

"My father's married."

"He's still cute, as in funny," she clarified. "He must know every joke that's ever been told about farmers and their daughters."

"Yeah, they're his specialty." I wandered across the room toward the bartender. "You can get dressed, you know."

She looked up from what she was doing. "I know, but I'm almost done."

"You don't have to do that. Pack everything away, I mean."

"I don't mind helping. Besides, when you're done here, I'm hoping you'll give me a lift home."

A feeling of being played came over me. I asked, "Where's your car?"

"In the shop, getting the tranny repaired. As she continued to work, Rashell gave me a wide grin. "The tips tonight will help a lot. Thanks for the job."

Unsure if I should believe her explanation, I asked another question. "How'd you get here?"

My cousin brought me. She said to call her when I was done, but neither of us expected me to work so late. You don't mind taking me home, do you?"

"Where do you live?"

"Not too far from here. That's the other reason I hate to call my cousin. She lives in Astoria . . . and she has a young child. I don't want her to have to wake him up and pack him into the car just to come get me."

There really was no choice in the matter. Take her home or be an asshole. "Yeah, I'll take you home," I said, and started circling the room to remove the centerfold decorations. "The boxes I used to bring stuff in are in the storage closet across from the restrooms. We need to pack everything out to my truck before leaving."

"Not a problem," she said, heading for the closet door.

Less than an hour later, Rashell, garbed all in black once more, gave me directions as we drove through the Glenwood Village mobile home park.

"That's it," she said, pointing to an older double-wide. "It's not fancy, but the price was right. I was able to pay cash from a small inheritance." The place looked well maintained. "Plus, the monthly space rent is about a quarter of what I'd pay if I'd bought a house."

"I guess you can't beat that."

"I don't spend that much time here, anyway. When I'm not working at my regular job or doing an occasional private party, like tonight, I try to cram in a college course or two," Rashell said as I stopped the truck in her empty driveway.

"I didn't know the college offered advance degrees in—"

"Don't be a jerk, Nate," she interrupted before I could prove myself to be exactly that. "I'm twenty-eight and smart enough to know my looks won't hold up forever. I want a good job with decent pay and benefits before my tits hang down to my waist."

"God, Rashell." We sat for a minute in silence, and then I asked, "What are you taking . . . in college?"

"Computer sciences." She shrugged. "I'd like to design computer games. That's probably not realistic, but if not that, I hope to find a job with a company that develops computer programs."

Seeing the midnight haired woman in a new light, I said, "Either is a worthy goal. I wish you luck."

"Thanks." She grabbed hold of the door handle but sat without opening it. Then she turned back to face me, saying nothing. Her teeth worked her lower lip, as if she was debating a thought with herself. Finally, she said the words I expected. "Care to spend the night?"

She was a nice woman and I didn't want to hurt her feelings but I wasn't interested. She picked up on my hesitation.

"Don't get me wrong, Nate. I rarely make the offer and I don't take money." She paused. "Just in case you thought that maybe I did."

I reached across the seat and traced the back of my fingers down her cheek. "I appreciate the offer, Rashell, really I do. At another time in my life, I'd take you up on it, but not now. The timings all wrong. Sorry."

"No biggie," she said, opening the door. She hopped out, and then turned back. "Thanks for the ride home. See you around."

NATE AND JUSTIN, RIDING TOGETHER, PARKED ACROSS THE STREET from the Pig 'N Pancake Restaurant at ten to eleven. They were the last to arrive. In boy-girl fashion, Bob and June, Mike and Becky, Mandy and Britney, occupied a large, round table to the left of the entrance. Justin sat between his fiancée and sister-in-law, leaving Nate the chair between their mother and Mandy. For a few minutes they all concentrated on the menus, and then placed their orders.

As soon as the waitress left, Bob said, "You must have had one heck of a bridal shower, Britney. June, who's usually a light sleeper, didn't twitch an eyelash when I got in." He reached over and squeezed her knee. "Did you, honey?"

His wife smiled, a little too sweetly, and made a point of removing his hand from her thigh. "I know exactly when you got in bed and what you had in mind."

"Mother, please," Nate said, squirming uncomfortably. "There are some things best left unsaid in front of your sons."

Looking his way, she raised an eyebrow. "And how, may I ask, do you think our three sons came into existence?"

Nate rubbed his earlobe, still looking ill at ease. "Everyone at the table knows how, but that doesn't mean we want to contemplate it before breakfast—during or after breakfast, either, for that matter."

The waitress arrived with their orders and the conversation died a natural death.

As the first bites slid into hungry mouths, Becky asked, "Did everyone have a good time at your bachelor party, Justin?"

He grunted, swallowed, and took a hurried sip of coffee as his eyes furtively touched on those of the other men at the table. "Yeah, I guess so."

His sister-in-law raised both her eyebrows inquiringly. "It was almost two-thirty before Mike returned to our room. Did all your guests stay so late?"

Another quick glance told Justin his father and brothers were fascinated by the food on their plates. He was on his own. "Yeah, for the most part everyone stuck around."

"It makes one wonder," she said.

Mike's eyes slid toward his wife. Not wanting to ask, but knowing she expected the question, he voiced it. "Wonder about what?"

"About what kept you out so late. Both you and Bob make a habit of early to bed, early to rise. There must have been *something* about the party last night to keep you both out so late."

Nate's groan was audible.

"I can't imagine what it could be," Britney said, playing along. She looked her fiancé in the eye as she spoke the next words. "Justin assured me it would only be a bunch of guys eating, drinking, and ribbing him for giving up the swinging single life. Maybe a light skin flick or two. Nothing that sounded all that entertaining. Nothing as interesting as—"

"Don't say it," Justin interrupted. "It's obvious you know."

This time it was Britney's eyebrows that rose. "Know what?"

"I swear I didn't know anything about it. It was all Nate's doing."

"Throw me to the lions, why don't you?" the youngest brother said, setting down his fork.

"Why not?" Mike asked. "It was your idea and you're the only one of us who doesn't have to answer to a woman."

"He has a point, Nate," their father said. He looked at his wife. "Should I get down on my knees and make a public spectacle of myself or will you accept my apology with my butt planted in this chair?"

"Either way, it's going to cost you," June said, with her nose in the air.

"I figured as much," Bob grumbled, and took his wife's hand. "June, you know you're the only woman I'll ever want, but I wouldn't be a man if I didn't look when the opportunity presented itself."

"You call that an apology?" Becky scoffed. She looked at her husband. "You'd better do better than that."

Without a word, Mike slid out of his chair and onto his knees. "Becky, darlin', I swear her tits aren't near as pretty as yours."

Laughter erupted at a nearby table. "You're digging yourself in deeper," a round faced man said. "Take it from me, you guys will be better off promising them a trip to Paris or someplace like that."

"Paris," Becky sighed reverently. "I've always wanted to go."

Mike groaned and crawled back into his chair. "Did you put him up to that?"

"I've never seen the man before in my life," his wife assured him haughtily. "But a trip to Paris will go a long way toward forgiveness."

Poking a finger in the air at his youngest brother, Mike said, "You're paying for it."

"No way," Nate objected. "It's your marriage and your wife. You pay for it."

"There's one thing that I don't get," Justin broke in. "How did the three of you find out?"

June and Becky and Britney all looked at Mandy. She smiled weakly and shrugged. "A woman at work told me," she explained to the others around the table. Then she looked Nate straight in the eye. "Nicole French."

"How the hell did she know?" he demanded.

"Your topless bartender is Nicole's cousin."

"Oh, give me a break," he groaned, rubbing his brow.

"You're buying two airline tickets to Paris," Mike insisted.

"Make that four," June said, emphatically.

❧ Chapter 33 ❧

THERE IS A REASON I BECAME A CPA—NUMBERS ARE LOGICAL AND unemotional. When a mistake is made, numbers don't get their feelings hurt, they don't yell or pout, they don't question your value as a human being, or the origins of your birth. Numbers don't hold grudges and mistakes are relatively easy to correct. The same can't be said about people.

Dad, Mike, and Justin blamed me for the chastisements they received. After they swore solemn promises to their better halves, they were welcomed back into the good graces of their women.

Mom, Becky, and Britney were slower to forgive my poor judgment—their verbiage, not mine—in hiring a topless bartender for Justin's last brouhaha as a single man. It took a personally embarrassing amount of humility on my part to get me off the financial hook for airline tickets to Paris. Mom and Becky still insisted Dad and Mike take them, but not at my expense. All in all, I'd weathered the Sunday storm with barely a tattered sail.

By late Monday afternoon, black thunder clouds again darkened the horizon. It was nearly closing time when Mandy walked into my office, calmly closed the door, and stood before my desk. Blue fire flashed like lightning from her eyes.

"You lied," she snapped, her outburst sounding like a thunderclap. "You, both your brothers, your father—all of you lied."

Anger vibrated from her, stimulating in its intensity. I silently cursed myself as being a sick bastard for the sudden arousal I felt. Thankful for the concealing desk between us, I leaned forward and rested my forearms on its cluttered surface. "Have a seat, Mandy, and tell me what's on your mind." As if I couldn't guess. One, and only one, recent occasion tied the four of us men together.

The storm rolled in, fast and furious. Mandy slapped her hands on my desk top and leaned in until we were nose to nose. "That woman you hired did more than bare her breasts and tend bar. *She danced.*"

Somehow, keeping my cool, I said, "You must be referring to Rashell."

Mandy straightened and crossed her arms. "Oh, the floozy has a name."

Unable to help myself, I laughed, a full-bellied guffaw. "The floozy? You sound like the wronged woman in an old-time movie. A corny movie, at that."

Her face heated, reddened, turned blotchy. I knew I was in trouble. Blood fled from my nether region, releasing me from the need to hide. "Listen, Mandy," I said, standing and coming out from behind my desk. "I hired . . ." an inner voice told me not to say Rashell's name again, ". . . her to tend bar—nothing else. I don't know who talked her into dancing. Maybe one of the guests."

"Don't lie to me, Nathan Peters!"

"I'm not—I swear." Raising my hands, I reached toward Mandy.

"Don't touch me!"

Quickly, I pulled my hands back until they touched my shoulders. "I swear I was using the restroom when it all came down. The second movie was ending when I went in. Someone put on music and I heard a few catcalls through the door. When I came out, she was dancing."

"A fact all of you conveniently failed to mention yesterday."

My hands dropped to my hips. "We're not stupid."

The disparaging look she gave me said otherwise. "I wish I didn't know. If I didn't know, I wouldn't have to tell Britney."

"You'll do everyone a favor," I said, "Britney included, if you forget you ever found out."

Mandy's shoulders slumped as the gale blew itself out. "I don't have a choice in the matter. Britney trusts me. If I don't tell her—"

"I'll tell her." The words burst from my mouth without conscious thought. Realizing what I said left me feeling trapped. I held my breath.

"Everything?" she asked. "Even about the lap dancing."

Shit! The tattling had to have come from Nicole, and as far as I was concerned, she had a lot of explaining to do. "A few guys paid her for lap dances. None of us participated in that. Not Dad, or Mike, or Justin. Not even me. *None of us*," I reiterated.

"Maybe not at the party," Mandy said, as her arms crossed again. "But what about afterward, when you took her home?"

My eyes sharpened until they were almost squinted shut. "Yeah, I drove Rashell home," I said. "I drove her home and I dropped her off. I did not get out of my truck. I did not go into her house. I did not have a lap dance, as much as I would have enjoyed it. And, I did not crawl into her bed, although that offer was on the table, too."

Mandy gasped. Squaring her shoulders, she stuck her nose in the air. "As if I give a damn who you screw."

"You should give a damn," I snarled. Grabbing her, I pulled Mandy to me and brutally jammed my mouth on hers. My impulsive action shocked me as much as it did the woman in my arms. Then, surprisingly, she responded. Her hands gripped my waist, fingers digging in. Her lips parted, and then her tongue tangoed with mine. She sighed the sweetest sound. I drew her closer, wrapped her in my arms.

Vaguely, somewhere on the edge of awareness, a tapping sounded.

"Nate, are you still here?" Nicole called through the closed door.

The knob rattled. Mandy pushed me away as the door swung open.

"Oh!" Nicole exclaimed. "I didn't know you were having a meeting."

"We'll pick this up where we left off another time," I told Mandy.

"I don't think this topic deserves further discussion," she countered, with eyes flashing blue fire once more. "Just remember, you tell her tonight or I will tomorrow."

Mandy left, blowing past Nicole as briskly as a winter wind.

"What was that all about?" the tax technician asked, walking into my office.

"That," I said curtly, waving my arm in the direction of Mandy's wake, "is your fault."

Nicole's mouth dropped open but no sound came out.

"If I had known Rashell was your cousin, I never would have hired her. It's obvious neither one of you can keep your mouth shut."

"I'm sorry," Nicole said. "I had no idea Mandy would get upset. Frankly, I don't know why she did. I won't say anything else—I promise."

"It's a little late for that, isn't it?"

"I didn't mean anything by it," she pouted with a hurt expression on her face. "I'm sorry."

"Hell," I said, relenting. "I'm sorry for snapping at you. It's just that Mandy feels honor bound to tell Britney."

"Why?"

"Who knows why women do the things they do? Maybe they made a pact with each other or something. All I know is, if I don't tell my future sister-in-law everything, Mandy will. Either way, my ass is grass."

Laying her hand on my arm, Nicole gently squeezed. "You know I wouldn't say or do anything to hurt you." Her voice contrite, she again said, "I'm sorry, Nate."

I blew out a breath. "Yeah, so am I. More than you can imagine."

WALKING TO MY TRUCK, I SPEED DIALED JUSTIN'S CELL. VOICEMAIL picked up. "Hey, bro, Nate here. It's ten after five. Call me as soon as you get this message. It's important."

On the drive home, I contemplated various types of torture Justin might employ to deliver exquisite pain without leaving any marks. After all, I doubted my brother wanted wedding pictures showing his best man bruised and bloodied. Then, parking in front of his condominium unit and seeing Britney's cream colored PT Cruiser, I remembered that any idiot with a half-assed knowledge of Photoshop could do a decent job of doctoring digital pictures. Bruised and bloodied immediately ratcheted up from possibility to probability.

Britney greeted me with a smile that was not nearly as warm as before the fateful bachelor bash. She was cutting vegetable for dinner and I had to duck to buss her cheek, which had not been cheerfully presented.

Not readily seeing my brother, I asked, "Where's Justin?"

"He ran to the store for some chicken thighs," she replied, not looking up from her task. "He should be back in a few minutes."

"Okay. Well . . . I guess I'll, ah, go change clothes."

Britney looked up then with a curious cast to her cobalt eyes. "Do you feel okay?" You're not coming down with something, not right before the wedding, I hope."

"No," I assured her. "I'm fine. I'll just go change." I fled the room before she could ask any more questions.

Once in my bedroom, I had second thoughts. Maybe it would be better to spill the beans before Justin came back. If I told Britney about the lap dancing in front of my brother, he might throttle me in front of his fiancée. I didn't want to take the chance of that happening. Hurriedly, I pulled on my sweats and reached for the door knob.

Justin's laughter drifted back from the kitchen. He was home.

Sluggishly, like a condemned man walking the long mile, I moved to join my brother and his girl.

Justin's arms encircled her waist from behind as he nibbled on her neck. She leaned back into him and a humming purr emitted from between her closed lips.

I cleared my throat to announce my presence. As they broke apart, I apologized, "Sorry to interrupt."

"You're not interrupting anything," Justin said, but the sharp edge to his eyes belied his words.

Feeling like the proverbial third wheel, I jammed my hands into my pockets.

"I don't suppose you'd like to go do something for a couple hours, would you?" he asked me.

Britney's elbow shot back and caught him in the gut. He woofed but held his ground.

I let out a long suffering sigh. "Sorry I can't oblige you, bro. I need to talk to Britney."

"About what?" he wanted to know.

For a moment, I thought it might be best to keep the counter that divided the kitchen from the dining area between us, until I remembered how fast Justin was on his feet. "Why don't we all sit at the table?" I suggested.

"We'd better humor him," Britney said, taking her betrothed's arm and guiding him out of the kitchen. "He looks serious about something."

"This better be good," Justin growled as he sat in the chair closest to the door leading to the garage.

I sat opposite him while Britney sat between us. I hoped when my brother exploded, which he would, she'd be able to keep him off me. Taking a deep breath, I plunged in. "It's about Saturday night."

Justin tensed. Britney glanced his way and then looked back at me.

"Sunday morning, we—meaning Dad, Mike, Justin, and me —we didn't tell everything that happened Saturday night." Neither of them moved.

"Go on," Britney urged.

Swallowing audibly, I continued, "After the movies, there was some dancing."

"Dancing? You mean you guys danced with each other?" she asked incredulously.

Unable to control himself, my brother coughed to disguise a snort.

"Ah, no . . ."

"Just spit it out," Justin ordered.

A quick glance at him, prepared me to jump up and run. "It's like this, Britney, some of the guys—not Justin," I was fast to explain, "talked the bartender into dancing."

"The topless bartender?" she clarified.

"Yeah. And, um, a few of them paid her for lap dances." The words raced out of my mouth.

"Is that all?"

"Well . . . yeah."

Britney took Justin's hand, pulled it to her lips, and kiss his knuckles. "He told me about it last night."

"He did?"

"Yes. Your brother and I know how important trust is in a relationship. Without honesty, there is no trust. He had no choice but to tell me." She smiled warmly at me. "I had no choice but to accept the truth and love him for it."

"Do Mom and Becky know?"

"No," Justin said. "I asked Britney not to tell them and she agreed."

Britney chuckled, "He said they'd already negotiated a trip to Paris and wouldn't be able to improve upon it, so there was no point in telling them."

"Knowing Mom and Becky, I'm not so sure." Then another thought crossed my mind. "Did you tell Mandy?"

"No," Britney said, shaking her head. "I'm not going to tell Mandy because she can get righteously upset about things sometimes."

"Well, I have news for you. She knows."

⮾ Chapter 34 ⮿

THURSDAY AFTERNOON, MANDY AND BRITNEY HAD A FINAL consultation with the florist, and then met with the hotel manager to review the proposed set up for the ceremony and catering for the reception. The rehearsal was scheduled for five-thirty that evening. Justin and his parents showed up a few minutes after five. Phil and Karen Carey, along with the minister and his organist wife, followed on their heels. Only Nathan was late. As he shrugged out of his overcoat, he dismissed his tardiness with the curt explanation that a problem at work cropped up and required his attention.

The hotel manager pointed out the taped markings on the floor, which indicated where everything—the registry stand, guest seating, and ceremonial arch—would be located. The organ was already in place. A few chairs were brought in for the evening's use. Everyone took their positions, and then walked through the motions of the upcoming event. After doing this three times, each participant confirmed they knew their parts, and they adjourned to a private dining room downstairs for the rehearsal dinner.

Gifts were offered to the matron of honor, the best man, and to Phil for his role as substitute father-of-the-bride. The minister and his wife, virtual strangers to everyone, excused themselves after Bob Peters presented the first toast. The celebration continued for another hour.

When the party broke up, Nate made a point of helping Mandy with her coat. As she slipped her arms into the sleeves, he spoke in her ear. "We need to talk."

Over her shoulder, she asked, "About the wedding?"

"No, about work."

She turned to face him and started to button her coat. "Nate, I have a zillion things on my mind and work is not one of them."

"It's about your timber revenue calculations."

"Oh, please," Mandy huffed, annoyed with his implied criticism. "Don't tell me, you disagree with my figures."

Nate shrugged an acknowledgement.

Irritated, Mandy ripped her gloves from her pockets and proceeded to yank them on. "Do me a favor. Don't bring up work again until after the wedding. Whatever the problem is, we can discuss it Monday."

"Fine. First thing Monday morning. Your office," he agreed, and walked away.

Early Friday, Mandy went to the Portland airport to pick up Britney's mother. During the drive back to Seaside, Brenda Thompson expounded on her displeasures, one after another, regarding the inconveniences of the trip. After two aggravating hours of listening to complaints, and past caring about the woman's tribulations, Mandy delivered her disgruntled passenger directly to the hotel. When Britney and June Peters made their entrance, allowing the matron of honor to escape, Brenda was in the middle of a diatribe concerning the rehearsal, which had not been delayed until her arrival. She renewed her complaint to Britney, who quickly put an end to the matter of the rehearsal by reminding her mother it had been her own decision to fly in on the eve of the wedding.

Undeterred, Brenda expressed her dissatisfaction with her accommodations, claiming the room overlooking the ocean was inadequate, as if she was accustomed to living at the Hilton. June took umbrage, knowing her son was paying the bill, and suggested Brenda ask for another room—at her own expense.

The next grievance came as Britney removed her mother's new gown from the garment bag. It was, in Brenda's words, of inferior design. All through the fitting, she criticized her daughter with cutting remarks, just as she had throughout Britney's childhood. Ignoring the goads, she held her tongue, refusing to utter the words of conciliation she knew her mother desired.

June Peters, known for her tolerance of others, uncharacteristically spoke her mind. "In my opinion, Britney created a lovely gown for you. It disguises the most obvious flaws in your physique."

"I don't have flaws," the svelte southerner claimed, and turning back to the full length mirror, smoothed her hands down the front of the form-fitting gown. "The flaw is in the design, I tell you. It needs more flare below the knees."

June disagreed. "The godets provide adequate flare. Any more would look tacky." Receiving a bad-tempered glare, she added, "In my opinion."

"It makes no difference one way or the other," Britney stated. "It's too late to make changes."

"In that case, I suppose I have to live with it the way it is," Brenda grudgingly conceded.

"Let me help you out of it," Britney suggested, and leaned in to undo the temporary fastenings.

"Don't rush me, damn it. From as far back as I can remember you were always in a hurry."

"It's after five, Mother. June needs to get started on the final stitching." Removing the last pin, Britney eased the garment from her mother's shoulders.

"June?" Brenda sniffed, stepping out of the gown. "You said you would sew my dress."

"I said I'd design a gown for you. I didn't say I'd sew every last stitch. Besides, I'm running late."

"Late for what?" the older woman's tone was peevish.

"I have appointments for a massage and facial."

With an airy wave of her hand, Brenda said, "Cancel them and finish this dress."

"Mother, June agreed to complete the final stitching."

"How do you know she won't ruin the whole thing?" Britney's mother demanded, as if June wasn't in the room with them.

Galled by the irksome woman's treatment of her future daughter-in-law and the denigration of her own abilities, June threw herself once more into the conversation. "Brenda, I'll have you know, I started sewing as a child, making clothes for my Barbie dolls."

"Dressing dolls," the southern harridan disparaged, with her chin tilted at a belligerent angle, "hardly qualifies you to set a decent stitch in this wretched garment."

Britney had heard enough. Carelessly tossing the dress onto the king-sized bed, she turned back to face her mother. "If you don't like the gown and refuse to accept the generosity of my future mother-in-law, I'm sure June will gladly drive you to the outlet mall where you can choose something off the rack."

June bared her teeth in the semblance of a smile, and said, "It's not far from here."

Realizing she'd lost her little battle of wills, Brenda huffed, "It makes no difference to me who sews the damn thing. I won't be caught dead in it after the wedding."

WHITE FROST DRAPED THE LANDSCAPE, LIKE A GOSSAMER WEDDING veil, and sparkled in the morning sun, as if overlaid by brilliant diamonds.

Turning from the window, Nate asked, "Do you think the weather will keep people from coming to the wedding?"

"Nope," Justin responded, and calmly took the last bite of his breakfast cereal. "This type of frost doesn't last. It'll be gone by mid morning."

"If you say so." Nate paced into the kitchen and refilled his coffee mug.

"Bro, you're as jumpy as a room full of sand fleas," Justin said. "Eat some breakfast before you drink any more java."

"Not hungry."

"I don't care if you're hungry or not. I don't want the ceremony held up because you're in the head taking a leak."

"Speaking of which," the younger man said, before setting down his mug and making a beeline to the bathroom. When he returned, a spoon and bowl of snap, crackle, pop had replaced his coffee. "What's this?"

"Your breakfast. Now eat."

Obediently, Nathan dug in. "Why are you so calm? You're the groom. You're supposed to be asking me to get you out of this."

Justin crossed his arms and casually leaned backed against the counter. "Got news for you, bro," he said, with a grin on his face. "When you know you're marrying the right one, you don't want to get out of it."

"You're a lucky bastard," Nate commented, taking another bite. "How about some raisin toast to go with this?"

"I'm your brother, not your slave." Justin moved toward the refrigerator where he kept the bread. "But since I'm in a magnanimous mood, I'll get it for you."

"Thanks."

"Let's go over everything one last time."

"We've been over everything a half dozen times already."

"Once more won't hurt.

Taking the toast his brother held out, Nate sighed. "Your suitcases and wedding gift are in the trunk of your car. By the way, what did you get Britney?"

"I'm giving her the gift of time—a diamond studded watch with a Florentine finish to match our rings."

A low whistle escaped from between Nate's pursed lips. "Nice."

"Okay, what else?"

"Your plane tickets are in the side pocket of your carry-on bag. After we change into our monkey suits, we go to your office and pick up the rings, then drive directly to the hotel. We do not pass Go. We do not collect two hundred dollars."

"You forgot about putting the rings in the special zippered pocket Britney sewed into your cummerbund," Justin reminded his brother.

"Into the zippered pocket," Nate dutifully repeated.

"And when we get to the hotel?" Justin prompted.

"First, I hook up with Mandy to transfer Britney's suitcases to your car," Nate said. "Then I hunt down Brit's mom and escort her to the ballroom."

"There shouldn't be any hunting. She should be in her room, number six-nineteen."

"Six-nineteen, got it." Nate finished his toast and drank the last of the milk from his cereal bowl. "Anything else?"

"No," Justin said with a sigh. "I think that's got it."

***

"I NEVER REALIZED HOW MUCH EFFORT GOES INTO ORGANIZING A wedding, even a small one," Mandy grumbled as she placed an overnight bag and carry-on into the trunk of her car. "This town needs a wedding planner."

Britney nudged her friend aside and hefted her big suitcase in beside the other two. Turning toward Mandy, she pulled her into a warm hug. "I couldn't have managed without you. Thank you for everything."

"Don't thank me until after the honeymoon. All your stuff still needs to be moved over to Justin's. I'm not sure I'll have time to help with any of that."

"I wish you wouldn't worry about it. Justin and I will take care of it when we get home."

"You'll only have a weekend before you both go back to work. You can't possibly get moved in that amount of time."

"We don't plan to move much of anything right away. There's probably not even room for my stuff until Nate moves out. That's why I told you I'd pay half of next month's rent."

"You don't have to."

"Yes, I do. Now don't argue." Britney reached up and placed her hand on the trunk lid. "Do we have everything?"

"I think so, but let me check again." Bending over, Mandy stuck her head inside the compartment and rummaged through the boxes and bags. "Makeup, underclothes, shoes, suitcases. The garment bag with our dresses is in the back seat, right?"

"Yes."

Mandy stood up. "And June took your mom's dress back over to the hotel after she finished it?"

"Yes, again." Britney closed the truck. "While you were in the shower, June called. Said that when she delivered the dress this morning, she offered to help with my mother's makeup and hair. Got an old fashioned southern tongue lashing for her efforts."

"Too bad Justin didn't agree with the idea of sending your mom an announcement instead of inviting her."

Heaving out a deep sigh, Britney gave a determined smile. "It doesn't make any difference. Nothing's going to spoil my wedding day. Not even my mother."

***

Mandy's Toyota was parked two cars down from Justin's Camaro. Nate lugged the large suitcase from one trunk to the other, while Mandy carried the two smaller bags.

"What the hell did she pack?" he asked. "The kitchen sink?"

"I'm sworn to secrecy," Mandy said, with all seriousness. Then she chuckled. "But I will say there's not a chance of the newlyweds getting bored on their honeymoon."

"Toys, huh?"

"I'm not telling, although in Britney's defense, I'll remind you she needed to pack two weeks' worth of clothing."

"Not if she's honeymooning with Justin," Nate muttered.

Mandy gave him a bland look. "They have to come up for air sometime, to eat, if nothing else."

"That's what room service is for," Nate quipped, closing the trunk.

"Let's hope your brother doesn't see it that way. I saw Britney stuff a fat pile of tourist brochures in her suitcase."

"Poor Justin."

"That's what I thought," Mandy laughed. Looking at her watch, she said, "It's getting late. Britney and I need to get dressed and you need to escort the mother-of-the-bride from her room."

"How long can it possibly take an elevator to descend three floors?" Nate scoffed.

"Probably a lot less time than it will take you to get Britney's mom from her room to the elevator. Brenda Thompson is the original drama queen. I'd suggest an early start if you expect to get her to the wedding on time."

Entering the hotel lobby, Nate guided Mandy to the elevators. Once inside, he pushed buttons for the third and sixth floors. Arriving at the third floor, she stepped out, and then turned back, holding the doors open.

"In case I don't get a chance to tell you later, I want you to know you're very handsome in a tux." She released the doors, and as they started to close, waggled her fingers in a bye-bye gesture.

The wedding wouldn't begin for an hour, and the moment the door to room six-nineteen opened, it was obvious Mrs. Thompson hadn't expected him to arrive this early. He stood, staring like a gauche teenager. Brenda Thompson was a knockout, and she delivered a mind numbing one-two punch by greeting him wearing nothing but a sheer pink peignoir over her lacy push-up bra and thong panties. A sensuous smile slowly tilted her lips, reminding him of a cat about to lick up a bowl of cream.

Feeling a little fearful under her predatory gaze, Nate silently cursed Mandy for suggesting he come up here so soon. "Ah . . . you're not ready yet." Was that squeaky voice his? "I'll come back later."

"Don't be shy," Brenda said. Reaching out a hand, she pulled him into the room. "After all, two hours from now we'll be family."

"But you're not dressed."

Brenda shut the door. "How convenient."

"Really, Mrs. Thompson—"

"The name's Brenda." She came to stand in front of Nate. Her hands swept aside the front of her peignoir as they came to rest on her hips. She looked him up and down and smiled again. "It's nice to know my daughter has a good eye for men."

Once in the past, Nate had been attracted to an older woman; a sweet, motherly type—not a barracuda.

"Let's see how good an eye." Without warning, Brenda stepped forward and slipped her hands inside his jacket, skimming it off his shoulders.

Nate hurriedly moved away from her. "I suggest you get dressed," he ordered, as he grabbed his lapels and worked his shoulders to straighten the coat back into place. "It's almost time for the wedding."

Annoyance marred the face that resembled Britney's. "There's no need to hurry—to the wedding, that is. You can consider this a little appetizer before the main course of your wedding night."

Shock dropped Nate's jaw. "My wed—I'm not the groom. I'm the best man."

A challenging smile returned to Brenda's face. "Prove it."

Disgusted, Nate felt like running—fast and far. Instead, he calmly turned and reached for the doorknob. "You can find your own damn way downstairs."

"Wait!" she commanded. "If you're not interested in a little fun and games, I'll get dressed. It shouldn't take me more than half an hour."

Nate didn't release the handle until he heard the door separating the two rooms of the suite close behind the mother-of-the-bride.

✧ Chapter 35 ✧

THIRTY MINUTES BECAME FORTY, BUT NATE REFUSED TO KNOCK ON Brenda Thompson's bedroom door—not after surviving his first encounter with her. He'd wait another five minutes, and then with or without Britney's mother, he'd go downstairs to perform his duty as best man.

The door opened. Brenda emerged. She'd transformed herself from barracuda to soft, southern magnolia. "I'm ready, Mr. Peters."

If she expected him to offer his arm, Nate thought, she was sorely mistaken. Exiting her suite, he indicated the direction to the elevator. "This way, Mrs. Thompson."

She deliberately took his arm in a two-handed death grip and smiled sweetly to a couple coming toward them from a room down the hall. "You needn't shy away from me," Brenda said, for his ears only as the elevators doors slid open. "Your disinterest is obvious and it bothers me not in the least. I'm quite sure I'll find other entertainment easily enough."

The descent in the shared cubical was silent. Nate and Brenda disembarked on the ballroom floor; the other couple continued down.

Taking Brenda by the arm to keep her from walking away from him, Nate growled, "Personally, I don't care if you habitually seduce men half your age. But I won't stand by and let you embarrass my brother and his bride."

"Britney learned a long time ago to look the other way. For the one night I'm here, you and your brother can, too."

"My brother paid for your plane tickets, plus he's paying for your hotel room and meals. You owe him."

"I owe nothing to nobody, young man."

"The only reason you're here is because Justin insisted it would be improper to exclude you. He was wrong. He should have listened to Britney."

"Why, what did she say?"

"That she preferred to send you an announcement rather than an invitation. Now I understand why and I'll keep a close eye on you. You're not spoiling their day." Nate's grip on Brenda's arm tightened. To anyone watching, he was solicitously guiding the mother-of-the-bride to her place. In reality, his grip was too firm.

Another tuxedo-clad man walked up. Seeing the family resemblance to her escort, Brenda presumed he was the groom.

"Mrs. Thompson, I'm Justin Peters," he said. "Thank you for coming. I hope you enjoy your stay, even though it's too brief."

"Thank you," she simpered, allowing him to press her fingers. "I'm pleased to meet you."

Before she could say more, organ music cued everyone to take their places. After escorting Brenda Thompson to her chair the groom and best man went to stand next to the minister under the flowered arch. Within moments the melody changed; the first notes of the wedding march announced the arrival of the bride.

Watching as the matron of honor paced slowly down the carpeted aisle, Nate was unable to drag his eyes away from her. Her form-fitting gown was of the sheerest royal blue chiffon over matching silk. It draped artistically from one shoulder, leaving the other bare. Her fiery hair, swept up in an elegant coif, exposed the smooth kissability of her graceful neck.

A moment later, the assemblage rose to greet the bride. Britney glowed with happiness beneath yards of white tulle and shimmering satin as she glided on the arm of her boss, Phil Carey. Her braid wound around her head like a crown. The diaphanous veil trailed three feet behind the long train of her elegant gown. Coming to a stop beside her betrothed, she accepted his offered hand. Together they faced the minister.

As words of fidelity and faith in the future were spoken, Nate gazed at Mandy. In a fancifully romantic vision, he imagined the two of them standing beside each other under the flowered arch, of vows exchanged, of love filled nights and happy days, of babies . . . the dream dispersed like wheat seed on the wind when Justin nudged him. Inattentively, Nate saw Britney hand her bouquet to the matron of honor.

"Give me the rings," Justin grumbled, out of the side of his mouth.

Dazed, Nate fumbled them out of the special pocket of his cummerbund and handed them over.

"With this ring, I thee wed . . ."

What on earth was he thinking? He might as well imagine throwing a lighted match onto the floor of a tinder dry forest as to consider spending the rest of his life with the firebrand. Either would be explosive.

"You may kiss the bride."

Nate and Mandy's eyes caught—held—and then slid away when Britney turned to reclaim her bouquet.

Grinning broadly, the bride and groom faced their guests, accepted their applause, and led the way back up the carpeted aisle to the connecting banquet room. The receiving line formed, Britney and Justin, Mandy and Nate, Brenda, June and Bob. Kisses from the bride were sought and received.

After dinner was served, good wishes were toasted with champagne, cake was cut, and presents were opened. The bride and groom waltzed. Throughout the reception, under the alert vigilance of the best man, the mother-of-the-bride fumed about having to behave in an appropriately chaste manner.

No ONE WAS SURPRISED, EXCEPT THE MATRON OF HONOR, WHEN the bride's bouquet flew in her direction. Instinctively, she threw her hands up . . . and caught the flowers. Immediately, June Peters hugged Mandy and kissed her cheek, as if she was already a member of the family.

She avoided looking in Nate's direction, and wished her eyes had not constantly strayed to his during the ceremony. Looking at him looking at her had felt intimate, like sharing the most privately held secrets; such as the secret of their time together—their one night of passion. The night she dared not remember. The night she couldn't forget. The night Mandy discovered she'd fallen hopelessly in love with Nathan Peters.

He'd never know. No one would ever know. She'd promised herself that. It was one thing to love a man; quite another to let him break her heart. Two men already had—she wouldn't allow a third.

Later, Mandy watched Nate talk to the band leader. As they shook hands, she saw some bills pass from one to the other. Then Nate turned and walked in her direction.

"Last song before the band packs up and goes home. Come dance with me." For the first time that evening, he held out his hand to her. Mandy took it.

The song was an old favorite made popular by Roberta Flack back in the seventies, a tale of love, romantically told, of the sun and the moon and the stars, and an earth that trembled like the heart of a captive bird, and a joy to last until the end of time.

Holding her close, Nate breathed in the sultry promise of her perfume. "This song reminds me of you," he murmured into her hair.

His breath was warm—the words seductive. Mandy's heart trembled. Unable to stop herself, she closed her eyes and laid her head on his shoulder. Dreamily, they glided over the floor in each other's arms, as if they had a hundred times before.

Smoothly, softly, almost sadly, the song ended.

Bob Peters took to the stage and was handed a microphone. "Thank you, everyone, for joining my son and his new wife for their knot-tying ceremony. Your presence here today meant a lot to Justin and Britney. They'd tell you so themselves, but in case some of you didn't notice, the two of them snuck out of here during that last song. I guess they were impatient to start their honeymoon."

Whistles and catcalls interrupted his speech. He put up his hands. When the noise subsided, he quickly finished, "If you're of a mind to stick around, the hotel management said there's a piano bar off the lobby. So, folks, thanks again for coming. Have a good night." The microphone squealed as he handed it back to the lead singer.

"I guess that's our cue," Nate commented to Mandy, referring to their job of transporting the wedding gifts to Justin's condo. "How do you want to work this?"

"Britney arranged for a luggage cart to haul this stuff to my car. It should be just outside the door."

"I'll get it after the crowd thins out," Nate decided.

"I need to make sure the top layer of the cake is boxed up," Mandy said. "Britney was adamant that I put it in the freezer so she and Justin can eat it on their first anniversary."

"Won't it get freezer burned by then?" Nate asked, making a face.

"I don't know. My marriage didn't last that long," Mandy stated, and without another word, walked away.

As the guests were leaving, Nate's relatives offered to help. The only help he needed, he told them all, was in keeping an eye on Britney's mother. Assured of their cooperation, he concentrated on the job at hand. Soon, the gifts were stowed in the trunk and back seat of Mandy's Toyota; the boxed cake sat on the floor behind the driver's seat. A final check of the ballroom and they were satisfied their duties as wedding attendants were fulfilled.

"There's a lot more here than I expected," Mandy said as she turned the key in the ignition. "Did Justin give you any idea where we're supposed to put all this stuff?"

From the passenger seat, Nate shook his head and shrugged. "In his bedroom, I guess."

"They'll be tired when they come home, plus it'll be late. I doubt they'll want to crawl over their wedding gifts to get into bed." Mandy tapped her fingers on the steering wheel.

"You have a point. Why don't we take everything over to your place? Let them sort it out when they get back."

Mandy started shaking her head before Nate finished speaking. She backed out of the parking space. "They don't get back until February fourth. I'll be moved by then."

"What?"

"Yeah, I found a one bedroom apartment in Astoria. It's closer to work and costs less than renting a house."

"Why didn't I know about this?

Frowning, Mandy pulled onto the street and headed toward Justin's condo. "Since when do I need to run anything by you?"

"You don't," Nate admitted. "I'm just surprised that Britney didn't mention the two of you giving your thirty days notice."

"She doesn't know," Mandy informed him huffily. "She's had so much on her mind I didn't want to worry her about the house. I'll put her stuff in storage and she can decide what to do with it when she gets back."

"That's kind of presumptuous, isn't it?"

"Not as presumptuous as moving in with your brother and not moving out before he brings his bride home," Mandy countered.

"I offered to move," Nate said, in self defense. "Justin and I agreed it didn't make sense to go to the expense of renting a place when the escrow on my house is due to close any day."

"Did either of you think to ask Britney?" She turned into the condominium complex.

Nate dug Justin's garage door opener out of his pocket and pushed the button. The door rolled up and Mandy drove forward. Pushing the button a second time, the door lowered, closing them in.

Feeling chagrined, he said, "In answer to your question, no, neither of us asked Britney. At least, not at the time. I don't know if Justin talked to her about it later."

"I don't know either, and it's none of my business," Mandy said, unbuckling her seatbelt and opening the car door. "Forget I mentioned it."

For the time being, Nate was happy to let the subject drop.

Still dressed in their wedding attire, they emptied the car, placing the smaller boxes on the dining room table and stacking the bigger ones in the living room. While Mandy rearranged things in the refrigerator's freezer to make room for the cake, Nate popped the cork on a bottle of champagne.

At the sound, Mandy turned. "What are you doing?"

"Pouring a glass of bubbly for a beautiful woman," he replied, and handed her a flute. Reaching across her shoulder, he closed the freezer door.

"Where did you get this?" He was close enough for her to smell the woodsy scent of his aftershave. Mandy's heart fluttered.

"Pilfered it from the reception. I figured we'd be thirsty after toting in all their loot."

"You're horrible," she laughed, her blue eyes sparkling like faceted gemstones as she took a sip. "In a nice kind of way."

"I'd rather you think of me as nice in a masculine sort of way," he said, and without taking his eyes from hers, sipped from his glass.

"I do." The softly spoken words sounded like a vow.

Nate set his flute of champagne on the counter, stepped closer, and ran a fingertip up her bare arm. "Stay with me tonight," he suggested quietly.

Mesmerized by the seductive fire in his eyes, Mandy's mind went blank. She was unable to move or speak, unable to deny her desire.

"You'll be glad if you do," he murmured. One hand caressed the sensitive skin at the juncture of her neck and exposed shoulder; the other took her wineglass and placed it next to his on the counter. "I promise."

Then Nate cupped Mandy's face in his hands. Her eyes drifted closed. His lips touched hers. Their mouths opened. Their tongues met and danced a leisurely waltz.

Then, he kissed a trail along her jaw. "I want you." His breath whispered warmly in her ear, fanning the embers of her desire. His teeth gently nipped her lobe. The embers burst into flame.

"Yes," she breathed, tilting her head back, allowing him to brush warm kisses down her neck. Molten fire raced up Mandy's spine, shimmered and sparkled along her arms, all the way to her fingertips. She leaned into him and savored the feel of his warm, hard body against hers.

When Nate's fingers toyed with the rhinestone broach that held the front and back strap of the dress together, Mandy shivered and grew weak in the knees.

"From the first moment I saw you walking down the aisle today, I've wanted to open this clasp. He pressed the center of the imitation jewel between his thumb and finger, unwittingly releasing the mechanism. The bodice of the dress fell away. Taking a half step back, Nate gazed upon the flesh of her breasts that peeked above the light blue cups of her strapless bra. Almost forgetting to breath, he tenderly stroked the back of his knuckles along the satiny smoothness of her skin before dipping his head to kiss her fragrant softness.

A moan escaped from between Mandy's lips.

Arms encircling her, Nate's adept fingers undid the hooks of her bra and discarded it. Then he found her pouting crests with his mouth, his tongue, and his teeth.

As heat pooled low in her belly, Mandy groaned deep in her throat. She slipped her fingers into his tawny hair, unconsciously pulling him closer.

Nate tried to slide the gown from her hips, but the dress stubbornly retained its hold. "How do you get out of this thing?" He voiced the query with husky impatience.

"A zipper, here at the side," Mandy told him, indicating a barely noticeable tab at the top of the seam-like closure. She pulled it down and the gown whispered to the floor. Her remaining undergarments consisted of only a baby blue thong and thigh-hugging stockings.

The leap of Nate's manhood throbbed with aching need.

Still wearing her electric blue high heels, Mandy emerged from the lake of blue silk and chiffon at her feet. Softly as a breeze, she murmured, "You're overdressed."

With more calm than he felt, Nate stripped off the jacket of his rented tuxedo, carefully folded it, and set it on the counter next to their half consumed flutes of champagne. He unsnapped the strap of the pre-tied bow encircling his neck and dropped it on top of the jacket.

Mandy flicked open the buttons of his shirt as Nate reached behind his back to unhook the fastening of the cummerbund. In haste, his fingers fumbled with the unfamiliar contraption. It came loose with a small ripping sound and he flung it away.

Both he and Mandy eagerly tugged his shirt tails from the waistband of his trousers, but when she reached for his belt buckle, Nate stilled her hands.

"If we don't slow down, I'll hike you onto the counter and take you right here."

"What are you waiting for?" Her demand was breathless as she resumed her efforts.

Releasing her hands, Nate reached around, grabbed her buttocks, and lifted Mandy onto an empty section of the counter. He spread her thighs and stepped between them. His mouth claimed hers in a greedy, nipping kiss.

She continued groping at his waist, until finally, the buckle came loose and Mandy whipped the belt from the loops.

Past impatient, Nate pulled the front tabs apart and unzipped his pants. With one strong arm surrounding Mandy's waist, he lifted her off the counter, and with his free hand, ripped the thong down her legs, tossing it behind him.

In one fluid motion he imbedded himself in Mandy's silky warm sheath, hitching her closer to more firmly seat himself inside her. She wrapped her arms around his neck and her legs around his waist, crossing her ankles to secure her hold.

Without moving, Nate throbbed inside her, felt her pulse in return. He gritted his teeth and breathed in slow breaths to maintain his control. But Mandy wiggled her hips, and he was lost. Crushing her in a tight embrace, he moved with deep, pounding thrusts. His mouth came down at the apex of her neck and shoulder in a warm, wet kiss. She groaned. Unable to restrain himself, Nate bit down, and felt Mandy climax as she threw back her head and screamed incoherently. Elated by her inarticulate words, Nate followed with a pounding orgasm of his own.

✥ Chapter 36 ✥

MY BREATH STILL RASPED IN MANDY'S EAR WHEN SHE UNCROSSED her ankles and slid her luscious legs down my flanks. Her high heels caught on the trousers that encased my calves. She flailed her feet but couldn't get loose.

"I'm tangled up."

"Kick off your shoes," I suggested.

"I'm not sure I can," she said, trying to raise her legs to wrap around my hips again, and failing. My arms holding her quivered. "Don't drop me."

"I'm trying not to, but I can't stand here holding you forever with my pants down around my ankles."

The ridiculousness of the situation struck us both at the same time. Mandy giggled.

"Don't laugh," I commanded.

"I can't help it," she chortled.

I snorted, unable to refrain from being amused by my humiliation. "Don't make me laugh. I might drop you."

"Don't you dare," Mandy cried. At last she freed herself from her shoes and dropped her feet to the floor. Pulling away from me, she looked down—and snickered, not once but twice—before giving in to a fit of laughter at the ludicrous picture I made.

I tried to feel offended but the absurdity of it all got the better of me. Helpless to do otherwise, I threw my head back and guffawed. My hilarity fed Mandy's humor. She grabbed her midsection, and bending at the waist, cackled resoundingly.

As my laughter began to ebb, I toed off my dress shoes, kicked the pants off my legs, and stripped the sox from my feet. Noting that Mandy's laughter was also subsiding, I grabbed her around the waist and dragged her into an amorous embrace, kissing her long and possessively before letting her go.

Her clear lake blue eyes had heated and looked as cloudy as steam rising from a hot spring. Now was not the time to ask if she'd meant the words of love she'd shouted during coitus. Instead, I silently took her hand and led her from the kitchen to the living room.

"Kneel down facing the couch."

She did as instructed without question, unmindful of her stockings.

"You might want to hold on," I said, kneeling behind her.

She leaned forward and braced her elbows on the seat cushion, giving me a delicious view of her perfect backside. I stroked the smooth silkiness of her gluteus maximus. Leaning over her, I whispered in her ear, "You have the most beautiful ass I've ever seen."

She looked over her shoulder at me and deliberately pressed her sweet lushness against my rising manhood.

Finding the entrance to her femininity, I buried myself deep, as deep as she had insinuated herself into the pores and sinews of my flesh, into the very fiber of my being. She tilted her hips to better accept my hard thrusts. A shout formed in my chest, stumbled up my throat, and emerged as a groan. "God, you feel good."

Dropping her head to rest on her forearms, Mandy whimpered and gave her ass an erotic waggle.

Teeth clenched to keep from losing it; I reached around and fondled her clitoris. Wanting again to hear Mandy say she loved me, I rasped, "Say it again."

The only sounds were her cries of pleasure as she came apart in my arms. Disappointment, sharp and sad, was cut short by my own climax.

A snuffling noise brought me back to my senses. Not moving, I stopped breathing in an effort to identify the sound, and felt the woman kneeling beneath me take in a shuddering little breath.

It is moments like these that every man fears. At any time, a woman's tears are difficult to endure, but after sex, especially great sex—the best sex a guy's ever had—tears are justifiable cause for complete panic.

Removing myself from Mandy's body, I shifted to kneel beside her. Gently, I stroked the hair from her face and kissed her temple. "Shh."

With her eyes squeezed tightly closed, Mandy sniffled again. "Shh."

"I don't," she mumbled.

"You don't what?" I whispered, continuing to stroke her hair.

Mandy sat back on her heels and stared at me with what looked like defiance in her moist blue eyes.

My hand dropped to her shoulder in a soothing caress. "You don't what?" I repeated, as gently as possible.

"I don't love you."

Knife sharp, the words sliced into my gut. Then a sick kind of relief washed over me. Her denial of love released me from an obligation to express my own soft, and very surprising, emotions. I stood, holding out my hand. Mandy took it and I help her to her feet. "Let's go to bed."

She looked ready to object, but all it took was a little tug on her hand and she followed me down the hall to my room.

SUNDAY MORNING, AFTER SHARING SLOW, SLEEPY SEX WITH THE firebrand, I impressed her with my culinary expertise by preparing a vegetable and cheese frittata, a technique I'd learned from a long ago girlfriend after serving her scrambled eggs due to my inability to successfully turn a promised omelet.

Unfortunately, neither the sex nor the breakfast was enough to entice Mandy to accompany me in chauffeuring Britney's mother to PDX. In fact, Mandy laughed over my concerns about being alone with the woman and accused me of fabricating the story of her pre-wedding seduction attempt.

In the end, I was spared the drive altogether. My mother, ever protective of her children, insisted she and Dad make a small detour on their way home to deliver Brenda Thompson to the Portland airport.

Mike and Becky, having promised Robbie and Ruth a half day at the arcade before starting the trek home, invited me along. Not having spent much time with my niece and nephew since moving to the coast, I gladly accepted. While the kids attacked the first available arcade machines, I asked Mike and Becky their opinions of me continuing to live at Justin's after the newlyweds returned from their honeymoon. Their answers made me wish I hadn't asked. Mike called me an idiot. Becky backed him up by saying I could be obtuse and stay, or considerate and move.

Later, needing no additional opinion, I called my realtor and asked again if the bank might consider renting to me until the escrow closed. Kimberly doubted they would but agreed to call them with my request.

In anticipation of a first thing Monday morning conference about the timber revenue calculations, I arrived at work an hour early. Seeing Mandy's tan Toyota in the parking lot led me to believe the Deputy Assessor/Tax Collector was hard at work double checking her figures.

After divesting myself of gloves and overcoat in my office, I headed downstairs. As expected, Mandy was at her desk. Printout pages cluttered the top. She was completely absorbed in making line-by-line comparisons to information displayed on her computer screen. Unaware of me watching, she ticked off items on the printout with a red pencil while highlighting corresponding numbers on her monitor.

To alert her to my presence, I tapped on the open door as I walked through.

Her head snapping up, Mandy said, "I'm not through checking these calculations. Give me a little more time."

"I'm in no hurry," I informed her, and lowered myself into one of the chairs across from her desk.

She turned backed to the computer and continued to work.

Silently, so as not to break her concentration, I contemplated her profile. Soon, a rosy glow colored her face, revealing her awareness of my appreciative perusal.

After a while, she set down her red pencil and turned to face me. "I've been here since five-thirty this morning going over these figures."

Nodding my head in acknowledgement, I said, "You wouldn't have to do that if you were more careful to not make errors."

Her soft peaches and cream cheeks fired to an angry red. "There are no errors," she ground out.

"What do you mean?"

Mandy stood, and placing her palms flat on her desk, leaned forward. "I mean, there were no errors!" she shouted.

"There had to be," I insisted.

"What makes you think so," she seethed.

One of the property appraisers walked past the open door and curiously looked inside, which made me conscious of the other employees arriving at work. Standing, I crossed to the door and closed it.

Turning around, I said, "Mandy, I compared the figures you submitted to last quarter's disbursements. The numbers were way off, so I asked Nicole about it."

"You what?" Mandy shrieked, her color heightening even more.

"You weren't here," I yelled, shutting her up. In a more reasonable voice, I said, "I'm unfamiliar with timber revenue disbursements and didn't want to screw it up. You weren't here. What choice did I have?"

Mandy dropped down into her chair and sighed heavily. "What did Nicole say?"

"That it didn't look right. She thought there were too many discrepancies from last quarter."

"That happens sometimes. Logging operations shift around. The money we receive goes to the taxing districts from where the logs were harvested."

"So, what you're saying," I asked, to get clarification, "is that if a large part of the logging moves from north county to south, or from east to west . . ."

"Exactly."

"Too bad your Tax Technician doesn't know that," I said, unable to keep the sarcasm from my voice.

Mandy raised an eyebrow. "She knows. Don't think for one minute that she doesn't."

Giving a skeptical shake of the head, I opened the door and left.

FROM THE BEGINNING, THE RELATIONSHIP BETWEEN THE DEPUTY Assessor/Tax Collector and the Tax Technician had been rough. At first, Mandy thought it was caused by a personality clash, an unfortunate situation that could be worked through using skills she'd learned in her college business management classes. A friendly get-to-know-each-other lunch didn't help; neither did a number of closed door conferences. The first formal and very negative employee review of Nicole's performance landed back on Mandy's desk with instructions to tone down the most derogatory portions. Afterward, the tax technician had been smug about receiving a raise not recommended by her immediate supervisor. When it came to this subordinate, Mandy oftentimes felt locked in a power struggle—one she might lose. Today was one of those times.

Nicole's manipulations had always been aggravating but over the past few months, since about the time Nathan Peters arrived on the scene, they had become more disturbing.

Ever conscious of her managerial responsibilities to both her employer and employees, Mandy kept meticulous notes about her subordinates' activities and performance. She gave praise when due and took appropriate corrective action when necessary—except where the Tax Technician was concerned. As sister of the county's head honcho, Nicole was a force unto herself. For this one staff member, Mandy's hands were tied.

She updated her notes with details of this most recent incident and then reviewed the entire file for objectivity, if such a thing still existed in relation to this problematical employee. Satisfied she had not exaggerated any incident, Mandy called her boss for an appointment. He reluctantly agreed to meet her that afternoon. With a course of action set in motion, Mandy printed out the numerous pages of Nicole's file and proceeded to prepare for what would undoubtedly be a difficult conference.

Ernie Gunderson, boss to both Nate and Mandy, was a man she liked and respected. His open minded and fair support applied to everything—except Nicole. To date, he hadn't felt it necessary to address the woman's unsatisfactory performance. Mandy hoped she had documentation enough to change his mind.

Anticipation, with a good dose of anxiety, gave her a nervous stomach. She skipped lunch, which she regretted as soon as she showed up at Ernie's door. They exchanged brief pleasantries as they settled on either side of his desk, then immediately got down to business when Mandy handed over a sheaf of papers.

Quickly, Ernie glanced over the sheets. Halfway through, his mouth turned down at the edges and he looked up with unreadable eyes. "I presume you prepared this with the intention of taking disciplinary action."

To prevent from twisting her hands in her lap, Mandy held herself rigidly still. "Yes."

Sighing, Ernie set the inciting papers on his desk and rubbed his eyes. "Let me give this some thought."

His words gave Mandy hope that the issues with Nicole would finally get resolved.

Her boss referred to his computerized calendar and sighed again. "Damn busy week. We'll take care of this on Monday."

"That's a week away."

"Earliest I can do." After clicking his mouse a couple time, Ernie typed a few words on the keyboard. "This shouldn't take more than about twenty minutes."

"What time?" Mandy asked.

The phone on Ernie's desk buzzed. As he reached for it, he said, "I'll call when I have a few minutes."

❧ Chapter 37 ❧

THE CALL FROM KIMBERLY CAME IN LATE AFTERNOON. THE BANK was no more willing to rent the house now than they had been when I'd first offered on it. I could move in the day after closing and no sooner. Period. End of discussion.

The escrow on the house wouldn't close until February ninth, putting it out of my reach for almost a week after Justin and Britney were due back. It was impractical to consider renting an apartment for that amount of time, which left me the choice of moving into a motel or bed and breakfast.

Tuesday I asked around the office for recommendations, checked out the business websites for the ones I received, made a few phone calls, and ended up with a reservation at a quaint, old Victorian B and B on the east side of town.

As soon as I hung up the phone it rang. Ernie Gunderson said that if I wasn't too busy he'd like me to stop by his office sometime today. Figuring if I had time to see about my living arrangements I had time for my boss, I went right over.

With two months on the job under my belt, only one remained of the probationary period specified in my employment contract. This meeting turned out to be somewhat similar to the sit down we'd had following my thirty day anniversary. Then, Ernie's questions pertained mostly to how well I felt I'd settled into my position. This month, he seemed more concerned about my relations with the other department managers. He went right down the list of their names, not missing a one. Particular attention was paid to my interactions with the Assessment and Taxation Department, to the point I silently questioned whether or not Mandy had voiced a complaint. Fishing for an answer, I asked my boss how he viewed my job performance and interdepartmental relations. After all, turn about was fair play. Assuring me he was well satisfied, Ernie ushered me out of his office with a firm handshake and smile.

Normally, I'm well focused on the job and there was plenty of work on my desk to keep me busy. Today, however, my concentration was marred. Something about my interview with Ernie felt off but there was nothing I could put my finger on. It just felt a bit out of whack. It crossed my mind to pick up the phone and talk to Mandy about it, but then I decided to do fifty pushups instead.

The next afternoon, right after lunch, Nicole plunked herself into a chair on the other side of my desk, grinning from ear to ear. "I hear you're looking for a place to stay for a few days."

"I was but not anymore."

The friendly smile slid from her face. "Oh, then I guess you don't need my help." She stood.

"I made a reservation at a B and B."

"In that case," she said, and sat back down, "maybe I can help after all."

Hoping to quickly dispense with the interruption, I set my pen down and gave her my full attention. "In what way?"

"You need a room. I have a huge house. Save yourself some money and stay with me."

"Thanks for the thought but—"

"What's it cost to stay a week at a decent place this time of year? Five, six hundred?"

"Including tax, about five-fifty."

"Plus meals," she reminded me. "Restaurants aren't cheap."

I crossed my forearms on the desktop. "What's your point?"

"My house has six bedrooms and four baths. Tyler and I use one of each. We have more than enough room for a week long guest."

"Again, thank you—"

"I'm stuck making breakfast and dinner for the rug rat every day, so I can include meals."

"I can't take advantage, Nicole."

"You won't be taking advantage if you pay me two or three hundred for room and board. You come out ahead and so do I." As I started to shake my head, she rushed on, "Please, Nate. I can use the extra cash."

We stared at each other, both a little embarrassed by her admission.

"At least think about it," she muttered, lowering her eyes and picking at some non-existent lint on her slacks. "Maybe stop by after work and have a look."

Here was a vulnerability I hadn't suspected Nicole of possessing. She hid it well behind a tough façade. "I suppose it wouldn't hurt to look."

"I'm a really good cook," she threw in earnestly. "I learned as a kid. It was either that or starve because my mother was not the domestic type."

"I'm busy tonight," I lied, buying time to think of a reason to reject her offer. "Let's make it tomorrow, right after work."

"Sounds good." Her face beamed as she stood and hurried to the door. "It'll be great having another adult in the house for a few days."

She was gone before I could say 'no promises' and I let the issue slide rather than running after her.

I'd seen the outside of Nicole's house once before, in the dark. At the time, its size hadn't impressed me. That changed when I parked in the driveway after work Thursday night. The place was huge, two stories, reminiscent of an old Victorian. It bragged a daylight basement and a steep roof, which probably accommodated a walk-in attic. The southwest corner flaunted an octagonal turret room full of windows.

Getting out of the truck, I ducked my head against the heavy evening mist, ran up the steps to the front door, and pressed the doorbell. Big Ben chimes sounded from within. I heard the stomp of little feet before the door was opened by a diminutively short butler.

"Hi, I'm Tyler," the child shouted in greeting. "Who are you?"

The door opened wider and Nicole placed a hand on the little guy's shoulder. "That'll be enough out of you, young man. Now, go wash up."

Reluctantly, the urchin turned and disappeared inside.

"Come on in, Nate." As inviting as her words, a rich and delectable aroma drifted out of the house.

"It smells like I'm interrupting your dinner hour. I can come back tomorrow."

She wrapped her fingers around my wrist and talked me inside by saying, "I thought if I fed you dinner it would help convince you to accept my offer."

Never one to turn down food, especially a home cooked meal; I shed my overcoat and handed it to Nicole.

While hanging up my coat, she asked, "Would you like to see the house before or after dinner?"

"Whatever works for you is fine with me."

"Tyler gets cranky if he doesn't eat."

As if to prove her point, the little boy cried out from another room, "Mom, I'm starving."

She led me through an elegantly formal dining room into a massive, commercial grade kitchen. Three places were set at a butcher block table. Nicole retrieved small plates of green salad from the walk-in refrigerator and handed them, one by one, to Tyler to set on the table. After sliding her hands into hot mitts, she pulled a tray of warm, dinner rolls from the top of her double ovens. These she placed on a hot pad in the middle of the table, and said, "Go ahead and sit down. I'll bring over bowls of stew."

It was rich, thick, and fragrant. One bite melted my resistance. "Hmm, this is delicious." I took another enthusiastic bite."

"Thank you." She picked up a whole wheat roll and buttered it for Tyler. "Help yourself, Nate, and don't be shy about seconds."

I wasn't. By the time she suggested dessert, I was stuffed, so I had only one scoop of rocky road.

The little guy was fading fast but begged his mom to show me his room. With Tyler chattering all the way, we trooped up an impressive curving staircase that looked as though it belonged on the set of a Civil War movie.

Tyler's was a typical little boy's room, except for the size—it was bigger than Justin's master bedroom. Two sets of bunk beds took up one corner, with matching chests of drawers on the wall at each foot. In an alcove, next to long, sliding closet doors, a school desk faced a chalkboard wall. The room seemed entirely too large and lonely for its one little boy occupant.

The kid perked up enough to show me his most prized possessions, all hidden away in a pirate's toy chest and buried in the back corner of his closet. He was cute until his mother tried to coax him into a pair of Peter Pan pajamas, then he pouted.

Once ready for bed, Tyler hopped onto his bottom bunk and beckoned to me. I crouched beside him and was surprised when he threw his arms around my neck in a good night hug. In manly camaraderie, I hugged him back, and then beat a fast retreat to the hall.

Nicole tucked her son under the covers before turning out his light and closing his door. "I'll show you the guest suite I had in mind," she said, leading me two doors farther along the wide hallway.

This smaller room was still more than adequate in size. The furnishings, heavy and slightly masculine, consisted of a queen size bed, a hunter's green leather upholstered dressing bench at its foot, bedside cabinets with matching brass lamps, a mirrored bureau, and in one corner beneath a window, a small round table with two chairs.

"There's plenty of closet space," she said, indicating a set of louvered doors next to the table and chairs. She pushed open a door on the opposite side of the room. "And a full bath, which is shared with another guest room, but of course, it's not occupied. You can lock the connecting door if you want."

"With all the space you have, I'm surprised you haven't turned this place into a B and B," I remarked. "You'd probably make a fortune."

"I would hate sharing my home with strangers," she said. Then, seeing the look on my face, added, "You're not a stranger. You're a friend and friends help each other out."

A subtle way of reminding me she was short on cash.

"Have you considered taking in a boarder, someone you know?"

She shrugged and led the way back downstairs.

"This place is huge, Nicole. It's hard to wrap my head around the fact that you and Tyler live here alone."

"I was married when we had the place built."

"Still."

"My ex is a doctor," she said, testily. "He had more money than time. Let's help each other out. One week, breakfast and dinner included, three-fifty."

It was more than she'd mentioned yesterday but a lot less than what I'd pay to stay at the B and B. There was also a week's worth of restaurant or fast food dinners, neither of which I minded on an occasional basis but tired of within a day or two. "Sounds like an offer I'd be an idiot to refuse."

Nicole smiled. "I'm glad to hear that. When do you want to move in?"

"A week from tonight. The lovebirds return from their honeymoon February fourth. That's next Friday. I'll move my stuff over after work the night before. If everything goes as planned, the escrow on my house closes the following Wednesday and I can move in any time after that."

"Okay." She looked sheepish. "Do you mind paying me before the end of this month?"

I felt sorry for her. "I'll pay you tomorrow, it that helps."

"It would help a lot," she said, with another smile.

That night, when I got home, I canceled my reservation at the B and B.

⊰ Chapter 38 ⊱

LIKE THE CHICKEN OR THE EGG, IT WAS DEBATABLE WHICH preceded which, office politics or office gossip. Not that it mattered to Mandy. She found each distracting, annoying, and totally unavoidable.

Today, Monday, the last day of January, she should be focused on clearing her backlog of work so she could spend the rest of the week concentrating on the department's budget. Instead, as she made her way through the tax office bullpen, she was trying to decide if she had enough energy to climb the flight of stairs to the third floor or if she'd wimp out and take the elevator. Normally, the stairs were a bit of stimulating exercise she enjoyed, but Mandy had spent long hours over the weekend moving to and partially unpacking in her new apartment. With barely sixteen hours of sleep since awakening last Friday and the ache of sore muscles, the elevator seemed a slower but smarter choice.

Since the day following the wedding, Mandy had devoted every spare minute to packing up everything in the Gearhart cottage, a chore that had given her not only a legitimate excuse to avoid seeing Nathan Peters away from work, but also the time to emotionally distance herself from him.

The elevator doors slid open. Mandy stepped out, turned the corner, and slammed into the brick wall of Nate's chest. His hands gripped her shoulders, and as her heart leaped, she realized she had accomplished her first goal, but failed miserably at her second.

The image of him pulling her into an embrace flashed through her mind before his hands fell away and he stepped back.

"Christ, slow down. You came barreling around—"

"Is it true?"

Not needing to ask, he did anyway. "Is what true?"

"That you're moving in with Nicole."

"Would it bother you if I did?" Nate could kick himself for asking.

Of course it bothers me. I can't stand the thought of you with another woman—especially Nicole. "That's not the point."

Suddenly, they both became aware of the nonchalant alertness of Nate's employees.

"Let's talk in my office," he said, and turning, led the way. He closed the door behind Mandy, waved her to a chair, and attacked before she was settled. "You've avoided me for over a week. I want to know why."

"I've been moving." Mandy almost flinched at the defensiveness in her voice.

"I would have helped."

Her chin dropped. "I didn't want to impose," she muttered.

"Impose!" Nate exploded, and then lowered his voice so it wouldn't carry through the door. "Asking for my help isn't imposing. We're lovers, for Christ's sake."

"No, we're not!" Mandy shouted, jumping out of the chair in alarm.

Nate's eyes narrowed to thin slits. He crossed his arms to keep from reaching out for her. His next words came out ominously soft. "My hands and my lips have touched every inch of your body. I've been inside you and I've heard you scream in ecstasy. How can you say we're not lovers?"

At his words, an unwanted flutter of desire stirred low in her belly. Mandy planted her feet in a belligerent stance. Her fisted hands came to her hips. "This isn't about you and me," she declared.

"Than what is it about?"

"It's about you moving in with Nicole." Too late Mandy recognized how jealous she must appear. She raised her chin a notch. "Not that it matters to me."

Nate uncrossed his arms and took a step closer. "Liar."

Mandy blinked. Warily, she backed up, her hands clasping her elbows, as though to get a grip on herself.

"If you ask me to move in with you instead of Nicole," he took another step forward, "I would, you know."

"I can't," she murmured.

"Why not?"

"Because . . ." *A week isn't long enough.*

"We'd make love every night." His voice was enticingly soft as he came closer still. "All night, every night."

His promise whipped the flutter of desire into a whirlwind of need. Pulse pounding, Mandy's chest rose and fell with the rush of air in and out of her lungs. She felt on the edge of a precipice. He brushed his knuckles across her cheek. Her eyes closed against the longing she felt. His breath was warm on her face. She awaited his kiss.

"Ask me." The whispered words seemed more thought than sound.

Without volition her lips moved to form the question.

The phone buzzed, causing them both to jump. Nate saw movement through his window. Across the courtyard, one floor down, Nicole stood at the large bay window, phone to her ear, gesturing in his direction.

"Shit," he muttered, realizing he and Mandy were visible to anyone looking up from the tax office. He grabbed the receiver and growled, "What's up?"

"Ernie wants to see Mandy in his office right away."

"I'll tell her." He hung up the phone. "Ernie's looking for you."

Relief washed over Mandy. Whether from anticipation of resolving the issues with Nicole or escaping from Nate, she wasn't sure. At the moment, she didn't care. "Good, I've been waiting to hear from him."

On the phone when Mandy arrived, Ernie waved a hand to indicate she should enter and take a seat, so she did.

Within a minute, he concluded his conversation, rose and closed his office door. Returning to his desk, he tapped his fingers on the papers Mandy had left with him a week ago, scowling in her direction. "Why can't you and Nicole get along?" he asked.

Sudden anxiety churned in Mandy's stomach.

"You've been here four years. That's more than enough time to resolve your personality conflict."

"My—" Mandy's mouth snapped shut. She breathed deeply through her nose and started fresh. "Nicole's job performance has been, and continues to be, a detriment to my department."

Ernie's head wagged slowly side to side.

Flicking her hand in the direction of the papers on his desk, Mandy said, "I've documented everything."

"So has she," he stated, shocking Mandy. Ernie touched a folder on his desk. "Her evidence is as compelling as yours."

"I don't believe that." Mandy reached for the file but Ernie flattened his hand on it.

"I've reviewed Nicole's personnel records. Her annual reviews aren't glowing but they don't reflect the unacceptable performance indicated in your notes." He picked up Mandy's papers. "Little of what I see written here appear in her reviews or in her personnel file.

With a bite of sarcasm, Mandy stated, "Of course not. You rejected the first unsatisfactory review with instructions to delete the most damaging sections. I understood perfectly what you wanted, what was expected."

"I don't know what you're talking about."

Unable to hold her tongue, she lashed out. "Damn it, Ernie. You molly coddle Nicole because of who she's related to, but it can be God, for all I care."

With his face reddening, Ernie demanded, "What are you saying?"

"I'm fed up with the situation. Nicole is incompetent and manipulative."

Sitting back in his chair, he eyed his subordinate coldly. "She says the same thing about you."

Mandy felt her insides convulse. She swallowed to keep the bile down. "You can't believe that."

"I believe what is in here," he said, tapping Nicole's personnel file.

"That's not fair," Mandy cried. "Following your instructions prevented me from writing accurate reviews."

Ernie's face flushed again. "I have never returned a completed review for revisions. Not to you or anyone else. I respect my department managers' abilities to know their subordinates well enough to provide fair and accurate employee evaluations."

"But—"

"The only time I intervene," he continued, "is if an employee complains of unfair treatment from a supervisor. I now have such a complaint from Nicole."

Shocked beyond words, Mandy stared at her boss open mouthed.

"As substantiated from another source, her complaints appear to have some merit."

"What?!" No one in her department openly complained about the tax technician, but Mandy was aware of occasional grousing. She didn't believe her other subordinates would side with the Nicole.

"The issues between the two of you aren't confined to your department, as I'm sure you know."

The bottom fell out of her stomach. A sick, cold sweat dampened her palms. Mandy knew the source of substantiation. "Nathan Peters."

"I refuse to name names."

"You don't have to."

"The truth is, Mandy, I polled all the managers who have direct interaction with your department."

"There's no point in trying to cover up for him," Mandy seethed, thrusting herself to her feet in agitation. "He always takes her side. But you might think twice before taking everything he says at face value. He's moving in with her, you know."

Slapping the flat of his hands on his desktop, Ernie rose. "Now you're fabricating stories out of thin air. I happen to know for a fact that Nate's buying a house. He's already arranged time off in order to move."

"Ask him."

"I've had enough of this. First, unfounded accusations against a subordinate and now malicious gossip about another manager. You leave me no choice, Mandy, but to levy a formal reprimand."

"You can't," she cried, as unexpected tears burned her eyes. Throat closing, she choked out the next words. "It's true. Everything I'm saying is true."

✥ Chapter 39 ✥

SHE WAS AVOIDING ME AGAIN. TAKING A STEP BACK WAS FINE WITH me, if that's what she wanted. After all, it was one thing to pay room and board to Nicole for a week and quite another to live with Mandy. I've never lived with a woman, in the true sense of the word, for a very good reason—it implies commitment. I'm not into commitment. At least, I never have been.

Lovers are fun—for a while. But inevitably, commitment rears its ugly head. I preferred to ease out of a relationship before that happened. To part as friends before continued friendship was an impossibility.

Occasionally, in the past, a woman wanted out before I did. And that was okay, too. I never lost any sleep over it.

This time was different.

This time, I needed constant reminders that it was for the best—for a couple of reasons. First and foremost, we work together. Mingling professional and personal relationships is like trying to mix oil and water. You can shake all you want but the two always separate.

Second was my brother's marriage to Mandy's best friend. Away from the office our paths would continue cross for years to come. She and I needed to live on friendly terms for Justin and Britney's sake, if nothing else.

Who the hell was I kidding?

Standing and staring out my office window, jingling the coins in my pants pocket, I admitted I wasn't ready for Mandy's decision to move on. But I would respect it.

After getting called away from my office Monday afternoon, she had remained barricaded in her own all week, ostensibly to work on her department's budget. She neglected to return my phone calls. She refused to make time to see me. She left me no choice. Last night, I moved my few belongings into one of Nicole's spare bedrooms.

I blew out a breath of dissatisfaction. Acknowledging Mandy's decision was easier than accepting it.

Turning from the window, I saw Justin. He stood in the doorway with his brows knit.

"Hey, bro," I said. "What brings you here?"

"I wasn't paying attention leaving the airport and got headed in the wrong direction," he told me, coming into the office. "Figured by the time I could get turned around, it'd be just as fast to drive home through Astoria."

Grabbing him in a rough bear hug, I asked, "So, where's your bride?"

"Brit's with Mandy giving her a severely edited play by play of the honeymoon."

"Yeah, right," I laughed. "If she leaves out the good parts, there's probably not much left to tell."

"More than you'd think, bro. When you're on your honeymoon, the better part of two weeks is a pretty long time," he said, settling into one of the chairs in front of my desk. "They'll be awhile."

"Don't get too comfortable," I countered. "I've got five that says Britney shows up any second."

"You're on." Justin looked a little too smug.

"I happen to know Mandy's kept her door locked all week and has been too busy to return any but the most urgent phone calls," I informed him.

Justin grinned. "And I happen to know they went out for a cup of tea." Holding out his hand, palm up, he waggled his fingers. "Fork over, bro."

Cursing under my breath, I dug my wallet out of my back pocket. So, the little snit had all the time in the world for her friend, but couldn't—or wouldn't—take two minutes to return any of the messages left by her lover. Her ex-lover, I reminded myself. Disgruntled, I slapped a five dollar bill into Justin's hand.

"One of these days, you'll learn," he said, pocketing the money. "Now, why don't you tell me what's bothering you?"

"What makes you think anything's bothering me?" I asked, guardedly.

"You were rattling the coins in your pocket. You only do that when you're troubled."

"You think you know so much."

"I do."

After closing the office door, I flopped down in the chair next to my brother and dropped my head in my hands. "I am so screwed," I said.

"Job or woman?"

I turned my head and looked at him. The knowledge of a lifelong familiarity passed between us. Where to begin?

Justin was my brother. I trusted him. He was my attorney. Legal issues were held in strictest confidence. He was also married—to Mandy's best friend. That complicated matters.

I sat back and sighed, deep and long. "A little of both, I guess."

Silence took a good, long stretch. Maybe gave a yawn or two as it settled between us. I waited it out, curious to see if my brother or my attorney would ask the next question.

"Is sexual harassment involved?"

"God, no!"

"Are the two issues even related?"

The answer to that was a little murky. "In a manner of speaking, but not really."

"What the hell is that supposed to mean?" he demanded, combing the fingers of one hand through his hair. Not a good sign.

Agitated, I stood and paced the small chamber. My fingers worked the coins in my pocket. I didn't want to mention Mandy's name. "There is a woman here at work—another manager," I hastened to add, seeing the expression on his face. "We kind of became involved."

"Meaning, you had sex."

Huffing out an impatient breath, I conceded his point. "Yes. We had sex. But it was more than that. It was great. *She* is great."

"I take it this mysterious, paragon of a woman doesn't feel the same way."

"Who knows?" I shrugged. "I think she does, but she's skittish."

Justin knew I wasn't finished and kept his mouth shut.

"The thing is, more than one person pointed out that it would be gauche for me to remain at your place once you and your bride returned from your honeymoon."

"Let Brit and me be the judge of that."

"Too late. I already moved."

His brows dipped toward his nose. "Since when?"

"Last night."

He sat back. "Go on."

"To make a long story short, I'm paying room and board to one of the woman's subordinates until the escrow closes on the house."

"Refresh my memory, how long is that?"

"Less than a week. It closes Wednesday afternoon before we leave for Goldendale. I can move in as soon as we get back."

The piercing gleam in my brother's eyes convinced me he should have been a prosecuting attorney. Not only did it make me feel guilty, it demanded I confess all. "There are issues with the subordinate. Man—ak." I coughed to keep her name from slipping out. "Man, she was pissed when she found out. She came storming in here demanding to know if it was true."

"Why should she care?"

I stopped my pacing. "Well, ah . . . as I said, she has issues with the subordinate. She's kind of paranoid about her."

"Her?"

"Yeah. The subordinate is a female."

Justin barked out a laugh. "Let me get this straight. You're romancing one woman and living with another."

"That's about right." The truth didn't set me free. It made me want to vomit.

A pitying smirk replaced Justin's prosecutorial expression of a moment ago. "You're right," he said. "You are so screwed."

❧ Chapter 40 ❧

THE RESTAURANT WAS QUIET. MIDWAY BETWEEN THE LATE LUNCH crowd leaving and the early dinner patrons arriving was the perfect time for a cozy chat of honeymoon reminisces.

"So, that's about it," Britney concluded, and took her last sip of tea.

"I'm glad the two of you had such a great time," Mandy said, feeling a pang of envy. "To tell the truth, I was skeptical when I saw all the tourist brochures you packed in your suitcase."

"So was Justin when he saw them," Britney laughed and changed the subject. "Now that we're home, I need to get serious about moving out of the Gearhart house. The thing is, I just don't know where we'll put it all."

Relieved her friend had broached the issue, the redhead said, "I have a surprise for you. You're already moved, in a manner of speaking."

Britney, who had been rummaging in her purse for her wallet, stopped and looked at her friend.

"Your furniture and everything is in storage," Mandy informed her. "I hope you don't mind."

Slowly, Britney shook her head. "No, I guess not. But why did you—." Her eyes lit up. "Did you find another roommate?"

"No, I moved."

"You did what?"

"I wanted a place closer to work and found a cute little apartment over by the old Youngs Bay Bridge. It's brand new. I'm the unit's first tenant."

"Tell me—"

"I will, I promise, but not right now. I'm under a deadline and need to get back to the office."

After paying, they dashed through the rain to Mandy's car.

"I want to hear everything," the newlywed said, buckling her seatbelt. "Come to dinner tomorrow."

"Will Nate be there?"

"I should imagine so. After all, he lives with us."

"Not anymore, he doesn't," Mandy muttered, pulling away from the curb.

Turning in her seat, Britney stared in surprise.

Her companion pushed out a breath. "I suggested that as newlyweds, you and Justin needed some space. Apparently, he agreed." Her voice turned sour. "He's rooming with a woman from work."

"Oh, Mandy, I'm sorry. I thought for sure you and Nate had the beginning of something going on between you."

Driving into the county lot, Mandy found a space, and parked the car before answering. "No, there's nothing going on between Nate and me."

SATURDAY AFTERNOON JUSTIN AND I REVIEWED ALL THE FACTS OF my case against Klickitat County. As far as I could tell, everything looked good.

Afterward, we relaxed with a beer at the counter that separated his kitchen from his dining room, watching Britney put the finishing touches on a salad she planned to serve with Irish stew. I'd been salivating for an hour from the savory aroma. Now my stomach growled.

"The stew smells so good, I'm ready to arm wrestle the two of you for the whole pot."

"You'd lose," my brother grunted.

Ignoring him, I addressed my sister-in-law. "Your friend better get here pretty soon, otherwise, she's likely to miss out." It was foolish but I couldn't help wanting to see the firebrand.

"Mandy's not coming. She's been living out of boxes this past week," Britney informed us and passed the salad bowl across the counter for Justin to put on the table. Bustling around the kitchen getting dishes and utensils, she continued, "She needed to finish unpacking."

If I wanted to give her the benefit of the doubt that, along with her work on the budget, might explain why she was too busy to return my calls.

The table was set. A basket of warm rolls was added. The pot of hearty stew went in the center on a hot pad. We sat and dug in.

"The last couple of years have been hard on Mandy," Britney said.

Resisting the urge to satisfy my curiosity, I allowed the comment to lie undisturbed.

"In what way?" Justin asked, unintentionally helping me out.

"I shouldn't tell tales out of school, but I'm worried about her. I think she's run into a rough patch at work."

That perked my ears up. "She tell you that?" Thankfully, the question came out sounding casual.

"No, but I don't know what else it could be. She'd tell me if it was man problems." Britney shook her head and shrugged. "She hasn't said a word. Besides, I don't think she's dated anyone seriously since that horrible man last year."

"It's always the man," I mumbled.

"In her case, it was the *men*," Britney clarified. "Her marriage lasted less than a year. The s.o.b. wanted an open marriage."

"I don't get it," Justin tossed in disgustedly. "Why do some men want to share their women?"

"Beats me," I said.

"After Mandy divorced the creep, she was *so* off men. She hadn't dated in over a year," Britney resumed. "Then, this banker, Sam Samuelson, of all the ridiculous names, pursued her relentlessly."

Dishing up a second helping of stew, Justin nodded. "Yeah, I remember him. Didn't like him from the get-go."

"You were more perceptive then me. I made the mistake of encouraging her in the relationship. I think she was half way to falling in love." Her sympathetic voice hardened. "He said some ugly things to her. Emotionally knocked her off her feet.

Since then, Mandy's job is all that's kept her going. It's everything to her."

The picture Britney painted didn't resemble the woman I knew. At Mt. Hood, Mandy had blithely picked up a man, intending to have sex with him. Then, learning he was married, she'd had no qualms in shifting her intentions to me. When it came to sex, the woman had no hang-ups.

A person devoted to the job would be very conscientious and not likely to make a lot of errors. That didn't sound like Mandy, either. In the short time I'd worked at Clatsop County, there had been numerous errors in her work as it applied to mine. Plus, her on-the-job avoidance of me was unprofessional.

Britney stood to clear the table. "Anyway, tomorrow I plan to find out what the problem is." She looked at me. "If it's job related, I hope you can help."

❧ Chapter 41 ❧

Football—sweaty, competitive, brutal. A testosterone dominated game, of men, for men.

Super Bowl Sunday—the pinnacle of football season—a day for kicking back with like minded men, a day for arm chair quarterbacking past games with the TV sports announcers, a day and evening of over indulging in nachos, beer, and locker room humor.

"I wish you had told me you planned to have dinner at your brother's last night," Nicole complained to me Sunday morning. Her voice had a brittle quality. "I went to a lot of trouble to fix you a nice meal."

We were eating a breakfast of oatmeal and raisins, not my favorite, with a sausage patty on the side.

"Sorry," I mumbled around a mouthful. Trying to be funny, I added, "I'm not used to checking in with the chef."

The tightening of her lips told me my witticism fell flat.

"Look, Nicole, I'm truly sorry. It never crossed my mind that you'd put out extra effort just because I'm staying here."

"Of course, I would. You're my guest."

I could see her point about the meals. "It won't happen again. I promise."

"All right," she said, grudgingly.

We went back to eating—in silence. Tyler was at his father's for the weekend so we didn't have his childish chatter to fill the void. I hurried to finish.

Sipping her coffee, Nicole watched me. Somehow, I knew she had more on her mind.

"By the way," she purred. I'd noticed she did that when she wanted something. "I need your help this morning."

I wanted to cut loose of Nicole as soon as possible, but to placate her, I said, "Sure. Anything."

"I've invited some of my friends over to watch the Super Bowl. We need to decorate the media room with the teams' colors."

Some people had a TV room, a family room, or a den. Nicole had a media room, complete with a sixty-four inch plasma HDTV, surround sound, a U shaped unit of recliner couches, and a center coffee table with a top that rose on scissor hinges to dining room table height for "civilized" eating while watching TV.

"I bought rolls of crepe paper for the ceiling and NFL plastic plates and beer cups.

It seemed she was waiting for a response. Swallowing, I said, "Great," for lack of anything better.

"We'll have a betting pool. It'll be twenty dollars to enter each of ten categories. They include the first team to score, the scores at the end of each quarter, the number of turnovers in each quarter, and . . ." She paused as she mentally reviewed her list, "Oh, yeah, and the winning team, of course."

"Of course." It sounded more complicated than the Super Bowl pools I was familiar with.

"When people start arriving, I'll be busy getting them settled with food and beverages." As she handed me a sheet of paper, she laid a bomb on me. "Here are the rules. You'll need to oversee the betting pool."

"Wait a minute," I objected, tossing the paper on the table. "I'll help you decorate your TV room, but I have other plans for watching the game."

Nicole's face turned as crimson as the color of the favored team's football jerseys. "But you can't," she spewed angrily. "You're my guest and I planned this whole party for you."

"Wait a minute," I said. "As I recall, you were paid three hundred fifty dollars. That makes me a boarder, not a guest."

"That's beside the point."

"No, Nicole. That *is* the point. I'm rooming here temporarily, very short term. Our lives are completely separate. It's presumptuous to expect me to participate in your life's activities."

"But what about my friends?"

"They're your friends, not mine. I'll help you decorate, but that's all."

"But—"

"Nicole. Watch the game. Enjoy your friends. Have fun. And leave me out of it."

She slammed her coffee mug on the table. "You're going to your brother's, aren't you? I suppose Mandy will be there."

"Where and with whom I watch the game is my business."

"I'd be careful about hitching my wagon to a falling star, if I were you," Nicole said, spitefully. "She might take you down with her."

"What are you talking about?"

Sitting back in her chair, a sneer contorted her face. "A formal reprimand was put in Mandy's personnel file last week."

"How do you know?"

The smirk slipped. "I, ah, heard it through the grapevine. It's common knowledge around the office," she added.

Nicole was lying. Her eyes gave her away. Personnel records were as confidential as Top Secret documents. The only way information contained in them would be "common knowledge" was if the employee personally spread the word. It was conceivable someone would brag about an accolade, I doubted anyone would talk openly about being reprimanded— especially Mandy. Nicole knew something she shouldn't and I wanted to know how she came by her information.

"Where do you suggest I 'hitch my wagon,' as you so quaintly put it?" I asked.

She shrugged. "To a rising star, of course."

"Of course," I agreed. "However, today I have no choice. I promised my brother I'd watch the game with him."

Smiling brightly, Nicole prompted, "So, invite him to join us. I don't mind."

But I do. "I'm sorry, I can't."

"Why not?"

Her nosy persistence irritated me. But a snippet of truth was probably the fastest means of escape. Everything about the forthcoming arbitration meeting had been hashed out last night, but sighing, I said, "He's handling a legal issue for me. Today's the only time we have to discuss it before . . . well, before."

"Damn it, Nate."

"Come on, Nicole. Don't get upset."

"Come on, yourself," she shouted. "I planned everything for you and now you're leaving. I have every right to be furious."

"Fine. Have it your way." Standing and carrying my dishes to the sink, I rinsed and placed them in the dishwasher, then turned. "I can be packed and out of here within fifteen minutes, if that's what you want. If so, I'll require a refund."

"No! Don't go."

"I'm not staying for your party."

"All right," she pouted, crossing her arms. She looked a lot like Tyler at bedtime.

"Let's decorate your TV room."

Down in the mouth, she corrected me. "It's a media room."

"Okay, your 'media room'." I walked out of the kitchen, and thankfully, she followed without further argument.

❧ Chapter 42 ❧

"WHERE THE HELL HAVE YOU BEEN?" JUSTIN ASKED, AS HE OPENED his front door. "I expected you two hours ago."

"I got stuck helping Nicole get ready for a Super Bowl party." Grimacing, I made quotation marks with my fingers. "She wanted her 'media room' decorated in both teams' colors."

"Why?"

"Beats me," I said, shedding my raincoat. "Neither team is from west of the Rockies."

"My point exactly."

A program of football bloopers, with the sound muted, was playing on Justin's big screen TV. Watching the action, I asked, "Is it too early for a beer?"

"Not for me 'cause I don't have to drive home. You wouldn't have to either if you still lived here."

Justin had given me shit about moving. "Up yours," I ribbed him, in a friendly rebuff, and headed toward the kitchen and a cold beer. "Where's Britney?"

"She and Mandy went over to the storage unit to sort out what Brit wants to keep and what she wants to donate to Goodwill. I told her not to bother. We need to sell this place and buy a house."

I cracked a brew and passed it to Justin then opened another for myself. "If you buy a house, you'll have to mow a lawn. As I recall, you hate mowing."

"I do, but this place is too small to raise a family."

"True," I commented. Making a rounding motion with my free hand in the region of my abdomen, I asked, "So, is Britney . . . ?"

"Too soon to tell, but we're working on it every chance we get," he said, grinning from ear to ear. "With any luck, this time next year, I'll be a proud papa."

Unexpectedly, a surge of envy rippled through my veins as I envisioned my brother holding a squalling infant. But the baby I saw had spiky red hair and chubby cheeks with the blush of a ripe peach—a little girl to grow up looking like Mandy.

"Unless you have a preference, I'll flip you for red or green."

It took a moment to realize he was referring to the jersey colors of the opposing football teams. I dug a quarter from my pocket, looked at Justin's sly face, and then tucked the coin back where it belonged. "You flip, I'll call."

"Whatever."

As his coin turned end over end, I called heads. He snatched the quarter out of the air and slapped it onto his wrist. When he lifted his hand, tails was showing.

"Damn it, Justin. How do you do it? Statistically, that should be heads."

"Just lucky, I guess." He gave me a shit eating grin. "I'll take red."

"I knew you would."

"Want to bet our first baby's a boy?"

"Not particularly," I said, and we wandered into his living room.

On the silent TV, a giddy group of ex-football players—turned sports commentators—were laughing at someone's good natured ribbing. A moment later, the programmer cut to a beer commercial.

"Will your wife be home soon?"

"Hard to say."

"Is Mandy coming back with her?"

Justin took a sip from his beer bottle, eyeing me the whole time. "Brit will probably invite her to dinner. What's it to you?

"I heard something work related and wanted to verify it," I said with a shrug.

***

THE RAIN STOPPED AROUND THE TIME LATE AFTERNOON SLID INTO early evening. The two women continued rummaging through boxes. Overhead, the single, naked light bulb glared, casting wavering shadows in the narrow confines of the storage unit as they worked.

It was fully dark when Britney closed up the last box and set it aside. "We didn't accomplish very much."

"What did you expect?" Mandy asked. "We both had to pare down quite a bit before moving to Gearhart. That was less than six months ago."

Britney made a face. "You're right. I don't know what I was thinking." She sank onto her coffee table. It was the only available place to sit. Pointing to a number of boxes they'd stacked by the entrance door, Britney said, "That stuff will get me by for a while. It's too much to take home tonight so I'll ask Justin to get it tomorrow after work. I don't know what to do with everything else. Leave it here, I guess, at least for the time being."

Chilled to the bone in spite of her winter coat, Mandy shivered. "It's freezing in here."

"Yeah," Britney agreed. "I didn't notice it while we were working. It's a good thing I started a pot of split pea soup in the slow cooker this morning. It'll warm us up in no time."

"Mmm. That sounds good."

"Until the game is over, Justin and Nate will be glued to the TV."

"Nate's there?"

"Sure, where else would he watch the Super Bowl?"

In the harsh light, it was impossible for Mandy to hide the flush rising to her face. "I thought he'd watch the game with Nicole."

Scrutinizing her friend, Britney asked, "Why would you think that?"

Easing herself down onto the table, Mandy said, "At work last week Nicole carried on and on about the Super Bowl party she was planning for Nate. I assumed he knew about it."

Britney bumped their shoulders. "I can assure you, he's watching the game with my husband."

"In that case," Mandy said, her posture slumping, "I think I'll skip dinner and just go home."

"Don't be ridiculous!" Britney objected. "You've worked all afternoon. You deserve a hot meal without having to cook it. What kind of friend would I be if I didn't feed you?"

"You don't understand," the redhead mumbled.

"Then maybe you'd better explain it to me."

Mandy hung her head. "He's living with Nicole now," she whispered.

"What difference does that make?"

"Oh, God," she cried, raising her face to the ceiling. Tears glistened on her cheeks. "He moved in with her after making love with me."

The admission left Britney speechless. Gathering her thoughts, she put her arm around her friend's shoulders. "You said there was nothing going on between you."

"There isn't."

"But you just said—"

"It just sort of happened after the wedding. The time at Mt. Hood doesn't count."

"You had sex with Nate at Mt. Hood?" Britney blurted. "*And* after the wedding?"

Jumping to her feet, Mandy bawled, "What difference does it make? He's with Nicole now."

Britney stood, took her friend by the shoulders, and looked her in the eyes. "Do you want Nate to know how much that hurts?"

Sulkily, Mandy shook her head. "No."

"That's all the more reason for you to come to dinner. Let him think it doesn't make any difference to you."

❦ Chapter 43 ❧

IT WAS HALF TIME. THE SCORE WAS TIED. JUSTIN WAS PUTTING together a salad to go with the soup. Nate was toasting some whole wheat bagels, a food item he'd never seen in Justin's kitchen before.

The front door opened and Britney called out a greeting.

"We're in the kitchen," Justin called back. In an aside to his brother, he said, "Better toast up a couple more bagels."

But Nate had something else in mind. Dashing out of the kitchen, he intercepted Mandy in the entrance way. "We need to talk."

"No, we don't," she said, slipping out of her coat.

"It's about work."

She looked at him with ice in her clear blue eyes. "It's Sunday. If you want to rag on me about the budget wait until tomorrow."

"It's not about the budget," he said, grabbing her wrist to pull her along behind him.

She dug in her heels. "Let me go."

"Not until we talk." He tugged.

She didn't budge. "I have nothing to say to you."

Deciding he'd carry her if he had to, Nate picked her up.

"Put me down," Mandy hollered, struggling in his arms.

She was stronger than she looked. "Quit wiggling," he growled as he carried her through the living room, passed the shocked faces of his brother and sister-in-law. Entering the spare bedroom, Nate dumped her on the bed.

Mandy bounced once. This was the bed she'd shared with him. The bed in which they'd made love the night of the wedding—and the morning after. Remembering, she felt her backside burn with the knowledge. She jumped up and made for the door.

Nate beat her to it. Slammed it shut. His big hand, flat against the panel, held it closed.

Frustrated, Mandy tugged at the knob and ground out from between clenched teeth. "Let me out!"

"Not until you tell me what transpired in Ernie's office last week."

Her struggles stopped. She crossed her arms around her midriff. The flash of daggers flying from her eyes belied her defensive posture. "What do you want to know?" Mandy asked, with deadly calm.

"Is it true you were reprimanded?"

She snorted. "You should know. You had a hand in it. Nicole and you are two of a kind. You're together in this, aren't you?"

"I'm not together with anyone in anything. I go to work to do my job. I presume everyone else does, too."

"You're not naïve, so don't pretend you're oblivious to office politics."

"I'm not, but I don't go out of my way to manipulate circumstances or people."

"In that case, it must come natural. May I go now?"

"You haven't answered my question."

"Yes, I received a reprimand. As if you didn't know," she snarled. "Now, get out of my way."

He moved aside. She jerked the door open.

"I didn't know," Nate professed, as she moved passed him. "Will it help if I talk to Ernie?"

She spun around with fire in her eyes. "You've done enough already. I don't need any more of your type of help. Stay out of my business at work and stay away from me." Mandy stomped away.

A few seconds later, Nate heard the front door slam. He walked back to the living room.

"Where did Mandy go?" Britney asked, from behind the kitchen counter.

"What difference does it make?" he replied, slumping into a chair in front of the TV.

"It makes a difference to me." Hurrying to the front door, Britney opened it and saw her friend drive away. Turning, she glared at Nate. "She left."

Coming into the living room, Justin stood in front of his brother. "What did you say to her?"

"Nothing. It's more like what she said to me."

Half time was over. Nate's team kicked the ball. The opposing team ran it back for a touchdown.

ANGRY OVER MANDY'S ABRUPT DEPARTURE, BRITNEY MADE SURE I knew it.

An interception was thrown by my team. It resulted in another seven points chalked up against them.

Justin was irate over me disturbing his wife's peace of mind. He was forceful in telling me so.

My team fumbled the ball. The opposition recovered it. A minute later, they scored seven more points.

I'd had enough and didn't stick around for more.

Going back to Nicole's before the game was over was out of the question. So was going to a sports bar to witness more of the Super Bowl debacle. I thought about stopping at the topless bar to lift my spirits; then remembered Rashell was Nicole's cousin.

I found myself driving around, going no place in particular. My thoughts, however, were aimed in one direction only—the situation with Mandy. It was untenable. As things stood, we weren't lovers or friends. Something needed to change. Unfortunately, nothing came to mind.

It was after ten when I let myself into Nicole's house. Sconces lit my way to the stairs. All the doors in the upper hallway were closed—except mine. It stood ajar. Before leaving the house I distinctly remember closing it.

Entering, I flipped the wall switch. Light flooded the room. Nicole, sitting on the near side of the bed, threw a hand up to shade her eyes. Simultaneously, she reached over and turned on a bedside lamp. The hem of her lime green baby doll night gown rode up to expose the backs of her thighs.

"Turn off the overhead light," she instructed. "It's too bright."

"I like it bright." Then, conscience it was her house, I politely asked, "What are you doing here?"

She leaned back onto her elbows, draping herself invitingly across the bed. "I thought if your team won, you'd want to celebrate. Or, if your team lost, you'd want to commiserate."

Stepping farther into the room, I shed my coat. "I only had twenty bucks riding on the game. That's not enough to deserve either celebration or commiseration."

"I won five hundred. That's deserving of something," she purred.

"Sure it is, sweetheart," I said. "Unfortunately, I can't oblige you tonight."

Coldness hardened her eyes. Raising one foot to the mattress, and all but splaying herself before me, she asked, "Why not, *sweetheart*?"

Without a word, I crossed to the bed and sat next to her. My eyes ran over the length of her body. I reached out and placed a hand on her knee. Slowly, my eyes and my hand slid up her thigh.

Nicole's head dropped back. She hummed deep in her throat.

"You make it damn difficult to say no," I murmured.

Her eyes flew open. "What?"

"I won't get involved with a subordinate co-worker."

"You're kidding, right?"

I shrugged. "I'm serious."

"Then let's pretend I'm not a subordinate co-worker," she suggested in a throaty voice.

Squeezing the soft flesh of her thigh, I rejected her offer. "Sorry, but that could leave me open to a sexual harassment suit."

Forcefully brushing my hand from her thigh, she sliced me a scathing look and stood "That's a pathetic excuse," she snarled. A moment later she was across the room, slamming the door closed behind her as she left.

Rising from the bed, I yanked my pullover off over my head. That's when I noticed the closet door wasn't shut tight.

There was a reason neither of my brothers liked rooming with me as kids. I'm a neat freak. I like organization. Habitually, I close dresser drawers and closet doors.

Also, there is a place for everything and I like everything in its place, such as my locked briefcase. It should have been flush against the wall where I wouldn't trip over it. Instead, it sat a good three inches out from where I'd left it.

There was only one conclusion I could make. Nicole hadn't been in my room for the sole purpose of seducing me.

∽ Chapter 44 ∾

THE THOUGHT WAS IN MY MIND WHEN I AWAKENED. WHETHER IT woke me up or just popped to the forefront in that brief instance between sleep and wakefulness I wasn't sure. Whichever it was didn't matter. It was the idea that was important.

While I showered and dressed, the concept took shape. It was a full flesh and bones plan by the time I arrived at work.

The first thing I did after hanging up my overcoat was pick up the phone and dial Mandy's extension. It went directly to voicemail. When prompted, I left a reminder that her department's budget was due today. I suggested she turn it in to me by noon. That part of the message was intended to raise her hackles enough, I hoped, for her to defy me.

When I returned to my office after a mid morning break, I had a voicemail from my realtor asking me to call. She answered on the first ring.

"We've hit a snag," she said. "The close of escrow will be delayed."

"No way," I said. "I'm ready. The bank's ready. The—"

"The bank's not ready," she interrupted.

"Why the hell not?" I wanted things wrapped up so I could move this weekend.

"They said it was because of an unsettled arbitration you disclosed in the application package."

The bottom fell out of my stomach. "They've had almost a month to address that but haven't said a thing." Anger built with every word I spoke. "Why is it an issue now?"

"I'm sorry. I guess it got overlooked. The loan officer was doing a final review of your file when she saw you had a pending legal issue. It sent up a red flag," Kimberly explained. "But don't worry, if you can provide them with a copy of the settlement agreement by tomorrow we can still close before the weekend."

"I don't have a copy of the damned settlement agreement," I ground out in a harsh voice.

There was a short pause before she asked, "How long will it take for you to get a copy?"

"I don't know. The arbitration meeting isn't until Thursday."

"You haven't even gone to arbitration, yet?" I heard the concern in her voice. "Oh, Nate, that might present a problem."

"The only problem I see is if I can't move in this weekend."

"You have a bigger problem than that," she informed me. "The bank said they want the escrow closed before month end or they'll cancel the deal."

"They can't do that," I almost yelled into the phone.

"Yes, they can. The first buyers, the ones you bumped, came back with another offer," Kimberly said. "It's identical to yours and meets the requirements of their government lender. The bank wants to get the property off their books by month end."

"Can't you do something?" I demanded.

"I did do something. They were going to give you seventy-two hours to produce the settlement document. I had quite a time convincing them that their oversight was not your problem. I bought you time."

"Shit!"

"Make that *shit happens*," she said curtly, and hung up the phone.

I called my brother. He was in a client meeting. His assistant said she had instructions to hold all calls. My plea to interrupt him fell on unfertile ground. She promised to give him the message as soon as he was available. To my mind, that wasn't soon enough.

Thirty-five floor-pacing minutes later, he called. In one huge, breath-expending sentence, the entire conversation with

Kimberly Long spewed out of my mouth. Unperturbed, my
brother told me to calm down.

As if. . . .

Slowly, I took and released three deep breaths. It helped.
Logically, and somewhat calmly, I related the details to Justin.

Instead of easing my worries, all he said was, "We'll see what
we can do."

"What's that supposed to mean?"

"It means, I still think the arbitration will go in your favor.
I'll explain that you have extenuating circumstances that
require an immediate determination."

"And then what?"

"And then, we hope for the best." Before I had time to
process his words, Justin's subdued voice continued, "Nate, I
know you want me to say you have nothing to worry about, but
I can't. This is an unfortunate development. I'll do the best I
can. That's all I can promise."

He knew I trusted him to do that.

By one-fifteen Mandy still had not provided me with her
department's budget. When I called her extension it again
went to voicemail. I disconnected without leaving a message.
Instead, I called Nicole.

This morning she'd given me the cold shoulder at breakfast.
I hoped that by now she was over her pique about last night.

When she answered, I said, "I need your help."

"Why should I help you?" she pouted.

"Don't friends help friends?"

The sound of a long-suffering sigh came over the phone. "I
suppose so," she huffed. "What do you want?"

"Department budgets were due early last week. I have one
from every administrative manager except Mandy."

"What's that got to do with me?" Nicole's tone of voice
indicated her interest.

"I thought maybe you could help the process along."

There was a long pause before she said, "I'll see what I can
do."

About four o'clock I received an email from Mandy with the
budget attached. I saved the spreadsheet to a password

protected flash drive and locked it in my briefcase before leaving for the night.

"You didn't do me any favors by asking for my help this afternoon," Nicole informed me during dinner.

"How's that?"

"I stuck my head in Mandy's office to let her know you called. Something needs to be done about that bitch."

"What happened?"

"I told her you needed the budget ASAP. She about bit my head off, said she'd get the budget to you when she was damned good and ready."

Taking another bite of chicken casserole, I chewed, swallowed, and lied. "She's taking her sweet time about it, too. I still don't have it. This really screws things up."

"Why?"

"I'm in the middle of another project that I need to wrap up by tomorrow. Then I'll be out of town for the rest of the week."

Nicole set her fork down and looked at me intently. "That's outrageous. There must be something you can do about that woman."

"Like what?"

"Maybe you should talk to Ernie about the situation," she suggested.

"Yeah, maybe. I'll think about it while I'm gone."

"When you get back, you need to do more than think about it. Something's got to change, Nate."

Forking up another bite, I nodded. "You're right about that, Nicole. Something's got to change."

❧ Chapter 45 ❧

WEDNESDAY AFTERNOON, JUSTIN AND I DROVE TO GOLDENDALE IN his Chevy Camaro. We rented a U-Haul truck and loaded everything from my storage unit into it. I'd need to put the furniture and most of my other personal possessions back into storage in Astoria, but at least they'd be close at hand for when I moved into my house—assuming, of course, I was able to buy the house.

We spent the night with our parents. They knew all the circumstances that had led up to my job change. After dinner, Justin gave them a point-by-point explanation of how he planned to handle my side of the dispute.

The next morning I was ready to leave the farmhouse by seven-thirty, but my brother drove me crazy while he dawdled over breakfast and leisurely related the highlights of his honeymoon to our parents.

We arrived at the nine o'clock meeting with only minutes to spare. I had anticipated an unpleasant confrontation with the Klickitat County Manager, who had pressed the issue against me, and the Finance Director, who had been my direct supervisor. Neither was present. Klickitat was represented by the county attorney and the Human Resources Administrator. I wasn't sure if I should feel insulted or relieved. Whispering my thoughts to Justin, he replied with a shrug.

The meeting commenced with the gaunt-faced mediator briefly summarizing her understanding of the issues under discussion. Justin and the county attorney each expressed agreement with the summary. The arbiter then declared her intention of reconciling the matter before the end of the day. With the mediator, the county attorney, and the Human Resources Administrator all being female, I felt an unreasonable gender-oriented prejudice against me.

Since county actions instigated the dispute, they presented first. Their attorney spent the first half hour outlining Klickitat County's policy regarding the use of compensatory time. During the next hour she nearly put me to sleep expounding on the federal Family Medical Leave Act in excruciating detail. She then explained the particulars of the county's policy of compliance, which required the use of paid sick and vacation time, when available. After a short break, in the final hour before noon, I perked up a little when accused by the attorney of intentionally and inappropriately using comp time in a manner unauthorized by established policy and to the county's financial detriment.

She argued the case against me rationally, and judging by the condemning looks the vinegary mediator aimed at me, rather successfully. All through the morning as she talked, the optimism I'd felt going into the meeting slowly dissipated.

The afternoon session began with Justin presenting a thorough history of my employment with Klickitat County, including mention of the seven hundred hours of comp time I'd accumulated in five years of perfect attendance. He praised my diligence in representing the county through extracurricular community involvement and extolled the exceptionally favorable reviews I'd received in the course of my tenure as Assistant Finance Director. Justin also conceded the need for deep budget cuts due to the sharp decline of tax revenue caused by the recent recession. And then, my attorney elaborated on the hardship caused by our father's heart attack during the height of the harvest season.

We were now at a sticky point.

My brother's contention was my oversight in formally applying for paid leave under FMLA was inadvertent. His reasoning was that I fulfilled my obligation to the county by telling my direct supervisor of the need to take one day a week off from work due to my father's illness. Justin went on to assert it had been the Finance Director's responsibility to either inform Human Resources or instruct his subordinate to do so. As a result of the department head's failure, Justin said I was not notified of my rights and obligations under the Act, therefore, the fault in the matter before us lay at the doorstep of the county.

He went on to present a recently dated letter from our father's physician detailing the illness, the imposition of physical restrictions, and the need for assistance during the recovery period. No mention was made of the type of assistance required and we were not obliged to reveal the specific assistance I rendered.

Pointedly, the arbitrator turned accusatory eyes toward the county representatives and asked if the Finance Director had been informed of my need for family medical leave. Neither the attorney nor the Human Resources Administrator could confirm or deny my ex-boss' knowledge.

The iron haired mediator then wanted to know why the Finance Director was not in attendance, since it appeared he was in sole possession of information germane to the issue under discussion. The county attorney stated she did not know the specific reason for his absence and suggested they attempt to contact him by phone.

Justin immediately voiced his opposition to questioning a person in absentia for reasons of verifiable identification.

Agreeing, the arbiter proceeded to remind the county representatives that today's meeting had been scheduled for two months. She sternly chastised them for their unpreparedness.

Then, in a fair and unbiased, although long winded dissertation, she recapped the facts as presented. Not once during the forty-odd minutes did she indicate a preference for one side or the other. I was on the knife edge of agony by the time she asked for, and received from each of us—one by one—confirmation that she restated the case accurately.

In the cool room, I sweated. Not knowing which way old sourpuss' decision would go, my gut twisted with apprehension.

Surprisingly, the severe-faced adjudicator turned my way and graced me with a girlish smile as she rendered judgment in my favor.

Grinning so wide my jaw cracked, I wanted to jump up and kiss the sweet, old bat. I didn't think she'd mind. Justin's hand on my forearm reined in my enthusiasm.

As part of the ruling, Klickitat County was instructed to pay not only my back wages, but also one hundred percent of the arbitration expense. Counsel for the county angrily crammed papers into her briefcase while shushing the objections of the Human Resources Administrator.

After they left the room, Justin briefly stated a pending escrow required written substantiation of today's resolution at the earliest possible date.

The ball breaking iron maiden was back. Frosty hazel eyes that only a moment ago had smiled warmly into mine communicated the imposition of the request. We would receive the documentation when we received it, she informed us dismissively.

With my elation all but subdued, I expressed my thanks for her time and impartiality. In return, I received a short lecture reminding me her time was paid for and impartiality was a requirement of the job.

Sliding a glance at my brother, I saw he was silently amused at my obvious ploy to win her favor in producing the necessary document in record time.

⋖ Chapter 46 ⋗

No one at work knew about the delayed escrow closing on the house I was buying. Not my boss, not Mandy, and *especially* not Nicole. They thought I took time off work to transport my belongings from Goldendale and move into my new home. I did nothing to alter that belief.

For one thing, other than Justin and my realtor, no one knew about the arbitration situation. I intended to keep it that way.

For another, I hadn't been comfortable living with Nicole. It was something done to help her out financially but not an arrangement I was inclined to continue. The few possessions I'd originally brought to Clatsop County with me had been moved back to Justin's last Wednesday before we drove to Goldendale. I planned to stay with my brother and his bride until my house was available, assuming it ever was. I had my doubts.

Kimberly Long congratulated me when I called to tell her about the favorable outcome of the legal issue. "Closing documents for escrow can be prepared as soon as the bank receives confirmation of the settlement," she said. "We are under a time constraint, don't forget."

As if I could.

"Under no condition," she continued, "is the bank willing to extend the close of escrow past month end."

"I know. My attorney will fax the document over as soon as it arrives."

"You might have to stay on him," she suggested.

My response was a dry bark of humor. "Believe me, he wants this concluded as much as me, maybe more."

Over breakfast this morning the newlyweds exchanged Valentine cards with sweet, sentimental sayings inside. Britney gave her husband a pair of baby blue silk boxers with bright red lips all over. They could only be described as cute. I don't know any man who likes to wear cute, but one look from my brother and I withheld my laughter.

Justin excused himself from the table, went out to the garage, and came back a moment later with a smallish box wrapped in a shiny, candy-apple red foil paper with a pure white bow on top. "I was going to wait until this evening," he said. Glancing my way, he added, "But there isn't any point."

His gift, I presumed, was a sexy, little seduction she'd wear only briefly before Justin peeled her out of it. I didn't care to stick around to find out for sure. "Time for me to head out," I said, getting up from the table, even though it was only seven o'clock. "By the way, I need to work late tonight. Don't hold dinner. I'll grab something in town."

"Are you sure?" Britney asked.

She didn't notice that her question caused Justin's brows to tip toward his nose.

"Yeah, positive." Kissing her on the cheek, I whispered, "Enjoy your Valentine's Day."

A tinge of pink colored her cheeks. "I will," she promised.

Shortly after arriving at work half an hour early, I dialed Nicole's extension and left a message for her to call me. She did about an hour later.

"Get everything moved okay?" she asked as soon as I answered.

Holding the phone to my ear, I scooted around my desk to the window. "Everything I own is now in Astoria," I replied, evasively. Across the courtyard, I could see her sitting at her desk.

"When are you going to invite me over for a sauna?"

Ignoring her question and referring to the budget Mandy had supposedly withheld from me, I asked, "How are you doing on that project we discussed last week?"

Through the window, I saw Nicole look over her shoulder furtively.

Her response came over the phone in a whisper. "I transferred the information you wanted to a CD. I can give it to you at lunch."

"No, that won't do," I said quietly, mimicking her tone. "I needed it last week."

At her desk, she again looked around the bullpen. "You'll have to wait. I can't get away right now."

"Email it to me."

"You'll have to wait—"

"I need it *now*. Just email it," I insisted, and rounding my desk, hung up the phone.

Quickly moving back to the window, I carefully sidled up next to it and peered across the courtyard.

Nicole was no longer at her station. I waited, and before long, she returned with a CD in her hand. From her movements, I presumed she was copying files from the CD to her computer, which she would then email to me. Sure enough, within a minute I heard the ding of an arriving electronic communication. Continuing to watch, I saw Nicole leave her desk, taking the CD with her.

Once she was out of sight, I locked my office door, retrieved the flash drive with Mandy's budget from my briefcase, and plugged it into my computer. Then, I opened the file attachment from Nicole's email. Aligning the two spreadsheets side by side on the monitor, I proceeded to compare them line item by line item.

It was interesting to see how Nicole had massaged the figures. Nothing was blatantly out of whack, but over the course of a year the budget, as submitted by Nicole, would fail in a number of significant categories at varying intervals. Somehow, she was able to tap into Mandy's password protected files and alter them to suit her whim.

I called my boss and requested a meeting. One thing I'd learned about Ernie Gunderson in the three months I'd worked at Clatsop County was that he marched to the beat of a slow drum. He wanted to put me off for a week but I pressed for a more immediate time. Three-thirty tomorrow was the earliest he would fit me in.

Next, I called Mandy. "Happy Valentine's Day," I greeted her.

"Same to you," she replied, in a manner that suggested where I could put it.

"Ooh, that sounds sour. Let me sweeten your day by taking you to lunch."

"As if eating with you—." Changing to a honeyed tone, she asked, "What can I do for you, Nate?"

"A wide open question like that—"

"Stop!"

"As I said," letting go of the tease, "let's have lunch."

"Why?"

"So we can discuss your budget."

"And that's supposed to sweeten my day?" Her sarcasm was back. "I have a better idea. Forget lunch. Accept the budget as submitted."

Putting all banter aside, I asked seriously, "Which budget?"

For ten simmering seconds I heard only silence. Then, cautiously, Mandy said, "Explain yourself."

"Over lunch."

Resigned, she sighed. "Fine. Stop by my office when you're ready."

"That won't do. No one from your department, or mine for that matter, should see us together."

Mandy barked out a sound of disbelief. "What's the matter, Nate? Is Nicole the jealous type? Afraid word will get back to her if you're seen having lunch with me on Valentine's Day?"

"Something like that." It humored me that Mandy thought Nicole was jealous when it was obviously the other way around.

"Well, forget it. I'm not that curious about your cryptic little comment."

"Maybe you should be."

Without a word, she hung up.

"Damn it!" She needed a heads up before the shit it the fan, which it most assuredly would.

❧ Chapter 47 ❧

FROM BEGINNING TO END, THE PHONE CONVERSATION WITH NATE rattled Mandy. His initial greeting of Happy Valentine's Day, delivered in his deep, smooth voice, sounded far too intimate. Her heart danced at his words. She squelched it with a discordant response. Then, surprised, and admittedly flattered, by Nate's invitation, Mandy snapped at him to hide her pleasure.

At his playful teasing she felt a weakening of her resolve to maintain a cool, reserved, and strictly professional demeanor toward him. Maybe she even felt a small niggle of hope that he cared—until he mentioned the budget.

She should have known it was only coincidental his invitation to lunch came on Valentine's Day. It was Monday and the first opportunity to discuss the budget since she'd given it to him. He probably wanted their meeting to take place in a neutral location to prevent a shouting match between them. He obviously didn't want word of their luncheon getting back to Nicole; otherwise, he wouldn't suggest a clandestine meeting. Undoubtedly, Mandy thought, if Nate took her to lunch and his new heart throb found out, he'd have a difficult time tonight.

Briefly, Mandy considered enjoying a meal at Nate's expense, in more ways than one. Nicole had a vindictive streak as wide as the Columbia River. If Mandy let a misleading comment about a Valentine lunch slip out in front of her subordinate, it would definitely cook the gander's goose.

But that wouldn't do. First, there would be nothing pleasurable about eating while arguing about the budget. Her stomach gave an uncomfortable twitch at just the thought. Second, when it came to the job, a lack of pettiness was a point of pride for Mandy. Lowering herself to Nicole's level of spitefulness simply was not an option.

The best course of action was to beard the lion in his den. Mandy stamped out of her office, determined to settle the budget issue with Nate.

The four employees whose desks comprised the bullpen were all clustered around Nicole's stall. They appeared to be engrossed in a taste treat, their eyes rolling as they all hummed appreciation.

An elderly couple, smiles on their faces, stood in the customer area, watching. They didn't seem to mind being ignored by their public servants. Hurrying past the grouping, Mandy slapped a pleasant expression on her face, and asked, "Have you been helped?"

"That sweet girl was waiting on us until the flowers and candy arrived," the white haired woman said, in a whispery voice. She looked adoringly toward the stout man at her side. "I remember the first time Eldon sent me flowers."

With a twinkle in his faded brown eyes, he said, "Made you my Valentine."

Girlish spots of pink bloomed on intricately wrinkled cheeks. "Swept me off my feet, you did," she acknowledged.

The impromptu employee party broke up. Flinging her boss a glance of barely concealed enmity, Nicole returned to the counter with a red, heart-shaped candy box in hand. "Sorry for the interruption." She removed the bow-topped lid from the red box. "Have a piece of chocolate. They're filled with the most delicious creamy fudge."

Eldon started to reach out but his wife slapped at his hand. "No you don't, mister," she scolded from habit, then flushed in embarrassment. Looking wistfully at the candy, she explained, "We shouldn't eat sugary sweets. Thank you, anyway."

Tipping a quick smirk toward Mandy, Nicole replaced the lid without offering any. "Then, we'll get rid of the temptation," she cajoled, in a stage whisper and sauntered back to her desk to set the box down.

With the area now clear of other employees, Mandy noticed the bouquet of flowers at the work station. She'd never seen anything of the kind outside of a hotel lobby—or a church. It was a magnificent arrangement of white lilies and red roses, a dozen of each. It was the type of bouquet that professed the sweetness of newfound love.

An arrow of bitter sorrow pierced Mandy's heart. An unconscious sound of mortal pain escaped her throat.

Smiling triumphantly, Nicole sashayed back toward the counter.

In her rush to run away, Mandy turned and tripped awkwardly over her own feet. She fled the building, entirely forgetful of her mission to confront the Assistant Finance Director about her department's budget. She stumbled to her car, but without keys was unable to crawl inside. Oblivious to the icy temperature, she crossed her arms on the roof of her vehicle and buried her face in the crook of one elbow. Hot tears of indignation and disillusionment burned her cold skin.

Nathan Peters, standing at his window, silently witnessed Mandy's distress. Unable to comfort her, his heart ached more than it should. Hoping to brighten her day, he picked up the phone and ordered a cheery bouquet of yellow daisies. When asked about a card, he instructed the florist to write "Be mine."

"IT'S DARLING. SO BRIGHT AND CHEERFUL," MANDY, TALKING TO her best friend on the phone, referred to the enchanting bouquet sitting on her desk. At the customer counter a few minutes ago, she'd accepted it directly from the hands of the florist.

Burnished red and orange floral accents popped amid the dazzling yellow flowers. The arrangement, although of average size, was diminutive compared to the elegant monstrosity that graced Nicole's desk. Mandy didn't care. The sassy bouquet was exactly what she'd needed to lift her dispirited mood.

"Who sent them?" Britney asked.

"I have no idea," was Mandy's contented reply.

"Wasn't there a card?"

"Yes. It said, 'Be Mine,' but it wasn't signed."

"The florist probably got interrupted in the middle of writing it. You need to call her before she closes to find out who sent them."

"No," Mandy refused. "I'm not sure I'd like them near as well if I knew." Actually, she was afraid she wouldn't like them at all.

"Don't be ridiculous. Hang up the phone and call her," Britney instructed. "Then call me right back. I'm dying to know."

"Not going to happen," Mandy declared in a sing song. "I just wanted to share my surprise with you. Now that I have, I'm satisfied."

"Mandy!"

"Go enjoy a candlelit dinner with your sexy husband, and when you're through, work on making that baby you both want."

"Oh, my gosh. It's almost five," Britney realized. "I've got to go. Call the florist," she urged, before hanging up.

Happy in her ignorance, Mandy picked up her briefcase and the bouquet then left for home.

❧ Chapter 48 ❧

I DIDN'T HAVE MANDY'S ADDRESS. BRITNEY WOULD GIVE IT TO ME, if I was inclined to call her. I wasn't so inclined.

Another option was to get it from the Human Resources Department. As a rule, employee records were confidential. That was as it should be. Getting Mandy's new address, however, wasn't too difficult.

At one minute to five I called and identified myself as the Assistant Finance Director, and then asked for the address, as if entitled to it. The clerk balked, of course, so I asked for Perry Martins, the Director of Human Resources.

Perry and I had met a few times, most notably on my first day of work, and then again two weeks ago when he supplied me with his department's budget. We were scheduled to meet next week to discuss it.

Fortunately, Perry was still in his office.

"What can I do for you, Nate?"

"I need Mandy Kearney's home address."

"Personal employee information is confidential."

"I have to talk to Mandy tonight. She's already left the office. I tried calling her cell," I fibbed, "but it went to voice mail. I don't know if she turned it off or what, but it's important I talk to her. If she's not at home I can leave a note on her door to call me."

There was a pause on the other end of the line. I held my breath, hoping I hadn't over sold my case.

"Is it business or personal?" he finally asked, a revealing question in itself. "Because—"

"It's strictly business," I hastened to say, curious as to how much gossip surrounded the firebrand and me. Then added, "Mandy's the best friend of my brother's wife. I can call her, but they're newlyweds and planned a special evening. I hate to interrupt them." Again, I was concerned I'd said more than necessary.

"No, don't bother the lovebirds on Valentine's Day." I heard the click of computer keys. "She lives in the new apartment complex by the old Youngs Bay Bridge. Apartment one twenty-six."

"Thanks, I owe you."

"I'll remind you of that when we go over my budget," he chuckled.

"You do that, Perry. Talk to you later." I hung up, grabbed my coat, and headed out the door.

The apartments were squeezed into a narrow strip of land between West Marine Drive and Youngs Bay. A cruise through the lot showed me Mandy's car, an indication she was home. After parking, I sat in my truck, and in the fading light, stared at the cold waters of the bay for a couple of minutes.

When I knocked on Mandy's door, would she let me in? Or, would she slam it in my face? With the firebrand, there was no telling.

From the start, I'd played a game of catch-up ball where she was concerned. For every forward pass completed, I'd fumbled the ball a half dozen times. I felt as though it was the last few minutes of the fourth quarter, and with two touchdowns to my credit, I was losing the game. Only this wasn't a game. It was my life—mine and Mandy's. The two of us together. A team. A winning team. Winning—together—it was the only option.

Opening the door, I swung out of the cab. To hell with the budget. Mandy and I had more important things to talk about than the damn budget.

Large picture windows in the three story building provided the occupants with a view of the bay. As I strode toward apartment one twenty-six, I prayed Mandy wouldn't observe my approach and bar the door against me.

While I was still five yards away, it opened. Relief flowed over me like a cresting wave. It receded when the firebrand crossed her arms and leaned against the jam.

Slowing my pace, I advanced more cautiously.

"Go away, Nate." Her voice had a hard, flat, uncompromising quality to it.

"We need to talk," I countered, drawing closer.

"You're stalking me."

That statement stopped me in my tracks.

"Get back in your truck and leave, or I'll call the cops."

My heart stuttered. My breath caught in my throat. Had she tossed a bucket of icy water in my face, I couldn't have been more shocked.

Satisfied with my stupefaction, Mandy straightened and moved to close the door.

My momentary paralysis fell away. Without thought, I raced forward and wedged my body into the narrowing slit.

Crying out in surprise, Mandy stumbled back.

I slid inside and closed the door at my back. Without thought, I flipped the deadbolt.

Mandy ran to her purse and extracted her phone.

Quickly, I crossed the room and easily wrested the instrument from her hands before she could make good on her threat. "Damn it," I growled. "Will you just listen to me for a minute?"

Defiantly, her chin came up. As quick as lightning, her arm flew out and her hand smacked my face, sounding like a clap of thunder. My head snapped to the side from the force of the blow. I felt the imprint of her hand burn in the flesh of my cheek.

She drew in a breath. I thought she'd scream but her hands covered her mouth. Tears glistened in her sapphire blue eyes. First one drop of liquid crystal and then another spilled over her lashes.

"Don't cry," I begged breathlessly—desperately. Wanting to gather Mandy into my arms and comfort her, I refrained for fear it would worsen her tears. "Please, don't cry."

"I've never hit anyone in my life," she murmured from behind her fingers.

"I probably deserved it," I offered, not knowing if I had.

For whatever reason, my statement distressed Mandy even more. Closing her eyes, she wrapped her arms around her waist, and tipped her head back. A sharp, agonizing keen escaped her throat.

Instantly, my arms were around her, my hand pressing her head to my chest. I buried my face in her hair and inhaled the sweet fragrance of coconut. "Shh. Shh."

Hard, wet, wracking sobs replaced the wordless mewling.

I kissed her hair, murmured comforting sounds between the press of my lips. Her arms came around my waist and held through the fury of her emotions. After a while the storm blew out, and the moment awareness returned, she released me. As Mandy's body stiffened, my arms reluctantly fell away.

Mascara smudged the hollows beneath her eyes. Red blotches ravaged her face. She'd never been more beautiful.

"I love you, Mandy." There was a quiet desperation in my voice. I wondered if she heard it.

Eyes that a moment before held an embarrassed self-awareness, now flashed steel blue with razor sharp anger. "Don't lie to me," she commanded in a hard voice.

My heart cringed at her accusation. "I'm not!" Grabbing her hand, I dropped to one knee. "Mandy, I love you. Please marry me."

She blinked rapidly. In shock, I think. But she couldn't have been more shocked than me.

❦ Chapter 49 ❧

SNATCHING HER HAND AWAY, MANDY LAUGHED. SHE SOUNDED A little hysterical at first. Then, with the cold blue steel of her beautiful eyes, she cut me in two. "You *love* me—as if," she spat.

Still stunned by my gesture, I slowly rose.

"You wouldn't know love if it bit you on the butt," she said derisively.

"I'm afraid it has," I muttered under my breath.

"I don't know what you hoped to accomplish with your theatrics, but I'm not buying your song and dance."

Mandy didn't take my impulsive proposal seriously, but elated by the rightness of my spontaneous declaration, I settled into a new equilibrium. Sounding too earnest, I implored, "Listen to me, Mandy. We're perfect for each other."

She wrapped her arms around her waist again, a defensive move, however, her eyes were still hard. "You're not mistaking sex for love, are you, Nate? You can't possibly be that naïve."

I flushed at her disparaging words, feeling my face heat, as if exposed to too much sun. "It's more than just sex, and you know it."

Mandy's left eyebrow rose questioningly. "Really?" With false sympathy, she added, "Poor Nate."

Without warning, the burn of irritation flashed into flames of red-hot anger. "If I remember correctly, it was you," I said, jabbing a finger in her direction, "not me, who cried out love words during sex. Is that naivety on my part or manipulation on yours?"

Jamming my hands into my pockets, my fingers rattled around the keys and coins. As my choler rose, so did the volume of my voice. "I'm beginning to think the whole seduction scene with Karl Williams was designed to manipulate me. And after the wedding, was that just frosting on the cake to you?"

No. Her mouth formed the word soundlessly as she shook her head from side to side.

"Then what was it?" I ground out, reaching for her and gripping her shoulders. She flinched from the force of my fingers pressing into the softness of her flesh. Reminded of Mandy's shorter stature and delicate build, I released her, appalled by my brutish conduct. I stepped back, and for one speechless moment, we stared at each other.

And then, in a soft voice, barely moving her lips, Mandy said, "It wasn't anything. It was only sex."

Disappointment, and something that felt like wounded pride, lanced through me. "All right, have it your way," I snapped, and with an abrupt about face, walked out, slamming the door behind me.

Too late, Mandy thought of all the things she could have said to him—screamed at him—had not pride reached out, snagged the words, and held them captive on her tongue.

The man's arrogance was as boundless as the Pacific Ocean. How dare he toss out a marriage proposal to her on the same day he romanced Nicole French with candy and flowers! How dare Mandy's foolish heart somersault with joy at his words?

Agitated, she paced the room. "Yes" had come so close to spilling off her lips. She'd come so close to yelling it at the top of her lungs and throwing herself into Nate's arms.

But Tom, her ex-husband, had impetuously proposed on bended knee, and then six months after the wedding, had spent the night in another woman's bed. Following a night of shared passion at Mt. Hood, it had taken even less time for Nathan Peters.

Before, with Tom, Mandy knew she'd been a naïve, starry-eyed fool. What would she be if she let a similar thing happen a second time around? A damned stupid fool, Mandy thought. And then, foolishly, she sat down and cried.

DAMN THE WOMAN. AND DAMN HER FIERY RED HAIR. IT MATCHED her temper and was the reason I called her firebrand.

She was obstinate, stubborn as a mule, and bull-headed to boot. Mandy was everything I wanted—in a lover and in a wife. Now all I had to do was convince her to want me in return.

Oh, she wanted me, wanted sex with me. At least, she had. And she'd exulted in her body's response to mine. How could she turn away from me without a backward glance?

Unwilling to return to my brother's place and interrupt their romantic Valentine evening, I aimed my truck in a meandering drive around Astoria. Before long my headlights illuminated the house by the river and I realized my wandering hadn't been aimless.

That December afternoon not so long ago, when I'd parked my truck in this exact spot, Mandy had been with me. We both liked the house at first sight. Walking through it together, we fell in love with it—together. Somewhere along the way, maybe that day, maybe another, I fell in love with Mandy.

Damn, I wanted her—all of her. Not just the lovemaking, although I wanted that as well. I wanted the temper, the tears, and the tranquil turmoil of a lifetime together.

Without Mandy the house in front of me would always be just that—a house—never a home.

That thought brought the chill of the night seeping through my coat and into my bones. The dash clock read ten thirty-eight; late enough to head back to Seaside. Turning the key in the ignition, the engine roared to life. So did my resolve and determination to marry Mandy.

❦ Chapter 50 ❧

PRINTOUTS OF THE TWO ASSESSMENT AND TAXATION DEPARTMENT budgets lay side by side on Ernie's desk. After I'd walked him through the discrepancies I'd found in key line items, he'd gathered the pages of each into the two neat stacks. His right index finger unconsciously tapped the perfectly aligned pages of the fake budget as he contemplated my allegations against the tax technician. The minutes ticked by without a sound. Uncomfortable with the prolonged silence, I shifted in my chair.

As if coming out of a trance, Ernie drew in a long breath and blew out a heavy sigh, frowning as he did so. "Mandy gave you this budget last week," he said, placing his left hand on one set of papers. "Is that correct?"

"Yes. Late Monday afternoon."

"And when did Nicole give you this budget?" He tapped his right index finger again.

"Yesterday, but I asked her to get it for me last Monday, shortly after lunch."

"Before Mandy emailed her budget to you?" he asked.

"Yes."

Slowly, Ernie's head bobbed up and down, as if waiting for my clarification to settle the muddy waters of the issue. Apparently, it didn't. "Do I have this right? Mandy gave you one budget last Monday and Nicole gave you another yesterday?"

"Yes. That's right," I said, holding my impatience in check.

Ernie sat back in his chair and rubbed the knuckles of his right hand across his cheek, making a rasping sound on the day's growth of gray whiskers. Having always considered his tendency to move at a snail's pace as an indication of a meticulous nature, I began to doubt that assessment.

"Have you talked to Mandy about the differences between these two budgets?" he asked.

I hesitated before answering. "No."

"Well, it's obvious the second one is superfluous. I don't know why you wasted your time and the taxpayer's money looking at it."

His obtuseness irritated me. "I told you, Nicole might have unauthorized access to Mandy's files."

Leaning forward and tapping the fake budget again, Ernie stated vehemently, "The truth is, you don't know where these figures came from. For all you know, Mandy may have given Nicole access to this file. Did it ever occur to you that Nicole might have given you an earlier, working draft by mistake?"

Ernie's blind argument raised my hackles. "I suspect Nicole has unauthorized access to a number of Mandy's password protected files. If she does, it could explain the errors I've accused Mandy of making."

Emphatically jumping to his feet, Ernie raised his voice. "That is a damned serious allegation."

"Damn right, it's serious," I responded, furiously coming out of my chair. "And it needs a closer look. Either you do it, or I will."

"Are you threatening me?" he yelled.

"Yes, damn it," I bellowed right back.

At an impasse, we stared at each other across his desk. Ernie rolled his shoulders and resumed his seat, but didn't back down. His pale eyes were cold and a bloodless smile twitched his lips.

"What are you going to do, go to the County Manager?" he asked. "A lot of luck you'll have with that. Nicole is his sister, don't forget."

Nepotism, it reeked as bad as a pile of fresh manure. At his smooth, unconcerned words my fingers curled into fists.

"I suggest you cool off a little, Nate, before you do something you'll regret. For now, this conversation is between just the two of us. It's in your best interests to leave it that way."

Drawing one long, slow breath, I relaxed my fingers one by one and flexed them until my hands were no longer knotted. I watched as he shredded each page of Nicole's budget.

When he was through, Ernie looked up at me. "I have a few things to finish up before calling it a day. I'm sure you do, too."

YES, I HAD SOMETHING TO DO BEFORE DAY'S END. MAYBE ERNIE'S conscience allowed him to overlook the possibility of subterfuge by Nicole, but mine didn't. Resenting my boss's expectation of silence, I refused to sacrifice my integrity for this job or any other.

Leaving his office, I returned to mine. After printing out another set of both budgets, I marched toward the lair of the County Manager. Seeing his door was open, I nodded to his middle aged secretary as I walked passed. Once inside the lion's den, I closed the heavy, wooden panel behind me, ensuring our privacy.

George Fulton was young, not yet forty. My understanding was he'd grown up here, had left the area to attend college, and then had worked in the State's capitol for a number of years. Taking this job had returned him to the bosom of his extended family.

"Afternoon, Nate," he said, standing and reaching across his desk. We shook hands. His eyes shifted toward the door. Perhaps he thought closing it presumptuous of me, but he nodded toward a chair. We both sat, and he asked, "What brings you here so late in the day?"

Wondering if Ernie had alerted him to my suspicions, I said, "Something came to my attention that I can't ignore. To do so would be a dereliction of duty."

His bland expression remained unchanged. "Go on."

"A situation exists that compromises not only the performance of my job as Assistant Finance Director, but also that of the Deputy Assessor/Tax collector."

George rose and said, "Take your complaint to Ernie. He's fair and open minded. Quite capable of smoothing out interdepartmental differences."

"This goes far beyond petty differences between two departments. Besides, I did speak to Ernie and he blew me off."

A frown marred George Fulton's brow. "Obviously Ernie doesn't think the issue merits attention. And personally, Nate, I don't adhere to employees going over their supervisor's head."

"The issue involves the possible unauthorized access and alteration of password protected files by a subordinate employee." Continuing, I laid my job on the line. "I believe the subordinate's actions were maliciously deliberate."

Sitting again, the man before me asked, "And Ernie refused to look into your allegation?"

I nodded.

"That doesn't sound like him," George said, rubbing his forehead. "Not one bit. Tell me about your conversation with him."

I leaned forward, handed over the two budgets, briefly recapped the situation leaving out the identity of the subordinate, and ended my narrative without repeating Ernie's comment of implied nepotism.

"Okay, cut to the chase," the County Manager instructed from between tight lips. "Who's the subordinate?"

The urge to squirm in my chair was strong. I resisted it, and after blowing out a deep breath, said, "Nicole French."

George Fulton's face flushed, hot and bright. "Son of a bitch!" he bit out.

I waited for the sharp and swift axe to fall. Surprisingly, my only regret was knowing I couldn't buy the riverside house without a job.

George heaved himself out of his chair. He crossed to the door and yanked it open. Prepared to leave before getting thrown out, I started to rise.

With a spiked look, George nailed me to the chair. "Where the hell do you think you're going?" he demanded.

A shrug and shake of my head indicated nowhere.

"Cassie," he called to his secretary. "Get a hold of Ernie Gunderson. Tell him I want to see him in my office. Pronto." He started to close the door but turned back. "And call Mandy Kearney. Tell her not to leave the office."

❧ Chapter 51 ❧

WHEN ERNIE WALKED INTO THE COUNTY MANAGER'S OFFICE AND saw me, his jaw dropped. He was obviously stunned that I ignored his warning. Or, maybe, it was that George hadn't summarily fired me. Whichever, Ernie's recovery was quick.

"If you spent more time tending to your assigned tasks and less time—"

"Sit down, Ernie," George instructed wearily. He kept us both waiting as he calmly stood, walked to the door, and closed it. "I presume you know why you're here, so we won't waste time having Nate reiterate his view of the issue. Just give us yours."

"He's accused your sister—"

"Nate is concerned over a possible security breach by a county employee. Apparently, you aren't. I'd like to know why."

"Of course, I'm concerned." Ernie sliced me a cutting glance. "However, I prefer to handle the situation with discretion."

"Meaning what, exactly?"

"You know what I mean."

"Spell it out."

"She's your sister—"

"Nicole is a county employee, over whom I have no direct supervision. As with any other employee, I expect my department managers to provide fair and objective supervision, which includes appropriate disciplinary action when needed," George stated in a sharp tone of voice. "Are we clear on that?"

To give Ernie credit, he sat up straighter in his chair and threw his chin out. But his next words heated my blood. "Nate has it in for Nicole."

"That's a damn lie," I asserted.

Glaring at me, he ignored my interruption. "She told me so herself. Right after she kicked you out of her house."

"Kicked me out?!"

"Hold it right there," the County Manager commanded. "You had your say, Nate. Now it's Ernie's turn."

"But this is bullshit!"

George held up his hand. "You'll have an opportunity to refute anything he says, but for now, I want to hear from Ernie."

I felt like knocking the smug look off my boss' face; instead, I fixed him with a withering stare.

"Nicole told me Nate asked to rent a room—"

"That's a lie."

"Nate," George Fulton pinned me with a finger pointed in my direction. "If you interrupt one more time, I'll fire your ass faster than you can fart."

My jaw was clenched so hard, no doubt they both heard my teeth grind.

Ernie continued, "Nate asked to rent a room until the escrow on his house closed. Nicole agreed to help him out, but she told me she had reservations about the arrangement." He shifted uneasily in his chair. "If she'd said anything to me about it before the fact, I would have advised her against it."

"And why is that?" George asked.

With a self-deprecating shrug, Ernie admitted, "Because of Nicole's previous complaint. I didn't take it seriously but probably should have."

This was too much. Unable to sit still, I slumped down in the chair and jammed my hands in my pockets. Flexing my fingers, I jingled the coins and keys. That earned me a glance from the County Manager but he nodded toward Ernie to proceed.

"Back in December, Nate asked Nicole out on a date. In and of itself, there's nothing wrong with that. But Nicole told me she had to fend off his advances. She wanted to file for sexual harassment."

Unable to speak, I jumped up, hands fisted in my pockets now, and paced around my chair. Seeing George's stern frown directed toward me, I plunked myself down again without a sound.

Ernie resumed his story. "I talked Nicole out of it. Told her it was her fault for agreeing to the date. Hell, what red-blooded American man wouldn't make a pass at Nicole? Out on a date, she should have expected it. The way I see it, away from the office doesn't count unless it carries over into work. It didn't appear to, so I let it drop."

George glanced at his watch. Reflexively, Ernie and I looked at ours. "You have five minutes to wrap this up, Ernie. I want to hear from Nate again and don't want to be late for a dinner engagement at six."

"Not much left to tell. Nicole agreed to rent a room to Nate. I guess everything went smoothly until Super Bowl Sunday. Nicole said she'd planned a party and had asked Nate to make himself scare. He obliged but when he returned later that night, half drunk, he wouldn't take no for an answer. She had to threaten him with calling the police before he left her alone."

Ernie glared at me. "The way I see it, Nate's covering his tracks by trying to get Nicole fired."

Those last words soured my stomach.

"Well, Nate?" George asked.

"First off, it wasn't a date," I said, glaring at Ernie. "Nicole tried to call it that, but it wasn't."

Shifting my gaze, I told the County Manager about Mandy Kearney's and my involvement in my brother's wedding. I explained that a celebration had been planned for after Justin and Britney obtained their marriage license. When Mandy declined to attend due to a prior commitment, I didn't want to feel like a third wheel during dinner and invited Nicole along.

"You made a pass at her," Ernie claimed.

Looking at him, I shook my head. "Wrong. *She* made a pass at *me*." Then, remembering the relationships involved, felt the hot blood of embarrassment rush to my face.

"Is that all?" This was from George.

My eyes swung in his direction. "No."

Briefly, I recounted Nicole's request that I help her out financially by renting from her rather than staying at a bed and breakfast, stating I had a cancelled reservation to prove it.

At a nod from the man behind the desk, I continued with an explanation of Nicole's Super Bowl party plans. I hesitated only when getting to the incident in the bedroom, but somehow got through that, too.

To wrap things up, I gave an account of my run-ins with Mandy over what I had presumed were her errors and now considered attempts of sabotage by Nicole.

By this time, I didn't think my chances of continued employment were worth shit. "You can fire me if you want, Mr. Fulton," I said formally. "But the truth is, Nicole French is a county employee whom I believe—"

"I know what you think, Nate. You laid it out quite clearly an hour ago."

He picked up the receiver of his phone and spoke into it. "Cassie, ask Mandy Kearney to come to my office. And then call my wife and tell her I'll be late."

Replacing the instrument in its cradle, George gave us each a hard look. "It shouldn't need saying, however, I'll remind both of you. When it comes to county business, Nicole is an employee first and my sister second. Any questions?"

This last was directed at Ernie but both of us shook our heads in acknowledgement.

"All right, we'll hear what Mandy has to say about Nate's allegations, and then we'll call it a night. I'm not making any snap decisions about this but I will get to the bottom of it. Is that clear?"

We both nodded our understanding.

❧ Chapter 52 ❧

THE LATE AFTERNOON CALL FROM GEORGE FULTON'S SECRETARY instructing, more like demanding, Mandy to remain in her office disturbed her. A lot of things about her job and the people she worked with disturbed her. She preferred to think most of it started after Nathan Peters accepted the position of Assistant Finance Director, but knew that wasn't true. The problems with Nicole French had been ongoing from the beginning. They had only escalated since Nate's arrival.

Instinctively, Mandy knew the forthcoming summons to the County Manager's office pertained to the boiling issues with Nate and Nicole. What she didn't know was which of the two would blow the lid off the pot.

Unable to work for the worry, Mandy paced her small office.

If it was Nicole, it would cost Mandy her job. That would infuriate her, but she'd move on and find other work.

With Nate the price was higher. Not only her job, but also her heart was involved. It had been broken before but never fractured beyond repair. If Nate betrayed her, Mandy's heart would shatter into a million pieces. How she'd survive that, she didn't know.

Standing at the window, Mandy watched a freighter move slowly up the Columbia River. It was odd that she never saw them head back out to sea.

Turning away, she glanced around her office. When the call came, who would she find with George Fulton? Nate or Nicole? Which of the two would deliver the Judas kiss?

Her phone buzzed. Mandy was about to find out.

SHE WOULDN'T GO DOWN WITHOUT A FIGHT, MANDY TOLD HERSELF. Intuition and a sense of self-preservation had prompted her to keep a private and detailed file on Nicole. It was stored on an encrypted flash drive and kept in her purse, never leaving her possession.

Sometimes she'd felt a little paranoid locking her office door and updating her notes, but it was her only shield against the poison darts Nicole so accurately fired in her direction. With no one to guard Mandy's backside, she doubted it was sufficient to save her job, though it might be enough to convince the county to provide a decent severance package in exchange for her silence.

She clasped the encrypted thumb drive tightly in her fist as she walked, head held high, to the County Manager's office. An encouraging smile and a nod of Cassie's head toward the closed door indicated Mandy should enter. Pausing with her hand on the knob, she took a deep, fortifying breath before pushing open the heavy wood panel.

Ernie and George sat on opposite sides of the desk. For a fraction of one second Mandy thought it was just the two of them. And then a movement to her left caught her eye and she turned her head in that direction.

It felt as if an iron fist plowed into her midsection. Mandy's breath rushed out with an audible whoosh. Her vision faded, momentarily replaced with pinpoints of light on a black background. God, don't let me faint, she thought. Painfully, her lungs convulsed and Mandy gulped in a breath of air.

"Sit down before you fall down," Nate murmured quietly in her ear as he cupped her elbows in his hands. Gently, it seemed, he eased her into a chair.

"Thank you for staying late on short notice, Mandy." George's voice came to her as though through a long tunnel.

Her reply, whatever it was, apparently satisfied the man because his head bobbed up and down in an understanding nod. As the cloudy sensation in her head began to clear, his next words sent her mind reeling again.

"This afternoon, after discussing the situation with Ernie, Nate came to me with a serious allegation—"

"You bastard!" Mandy cried, flying out of the chair and straight at her accuser.

Nate grabbed her wrists before she could rake his face with her nails. "Damn it, you little firebrand, will you listen for a minute?"

"No. You're a liar."

He gave her forearms one quick shake. "Just listen, damn it. I'm on your side," he growled.

The fire in his eyes, more than his words, snagged her attention. She stopped struggling and he released her.

"As I was saying," George continued cautiously, the way a man would when suddenly confronted by a wild beast. "Nate made a serious allegation against Nicole French." George slid a thin stack of papers across his desk toward Mandy. "Take a look at this and tell me what you think."

Gingerly, she gathered the papers and resumed her seat. Before long, a furrow of confusion drew her brows together. "This isn't right." Her eyes darted toward Nate before shifting to George. "Where did you get this?"

"From Nate. He said Nicole gave it to him."

Slanting a look at Nate towering above her, Mandy said, "I don't understand."

He crouched next to her chair. "Remember last week when I left you a phone message to get your budget to me by noon?"

She nodded.

"It was deliberate. I hoped your stubborn streak would cause you to dig your heels in to spite me. It worked." He gave a little shrug. "You see, with just cause, which I've already explained to George and Ernie, I'd begun to suspect Nicole of tampering with your password protected files."

"But how?"

Nate stood and unconsciously leaned on the County Manager's desk. "We don't know. The point is, last Monday, right after lunch, I told Nicole I needed a copy of your budget. This is what she gave me." He flicked his finger against the papers Mandy held.

She looked at the stack and then back at Nate. "It's like the mistakes on the tax receipt spreadsheets. Wrong enough to cause problems but not enough to be obvious."

"Exactly."

Mandy looked at George. "I came here prepared to defend myself against false accusations." She held up the flash drive. "I guess I didn't need this."

"What is it?"

"Documentation of issues I've had with Nicole since I started working here. Most of this you won't find in her personnel file," Mandy said, sliding a glance toward Ernie.

George held out his hand for the diminutive electronic drive. When Mandy hesitated to give it to him, he wiggled his fingers.

Warily, Mandy placed it in his palm. "It's encrypted and accessible only to me."

"Give me the password." He slid a pen and notepad across to her. Again, she hesitated. "You're going to have to trust me on this, Mandy."

"Ernie and I are witnesses," Nate assured her. Pinning the other man with a hard look, he added, "We'll back you up if it comes to that."

"And I'm supposed to believe you?" Mandy scoffed.

Abashed, Nate felt his face redden, but calmly replied. "Yes, you are."

"Tell me, Nate, doesn't this bother your conscience?" Seeing his confusion, she added, "Just yesterday you sent Nicole flowers and candy."

Affronted, Nate objected, "No, I didn't."

"I saw them. White lilies and roses—"

"I sent the flowers and candy," George stated. "It was Nicole's birthday and she is my sister, after all."

⊸ Chapter 53 ⊱

Mandy couldn't get back to her office fast enough. She almost ran through the empty building. But close on her heels she heard another set of footsteps—angry footsteps.

Gaining the sanctuary of her room, Mandy turned to close the door. A large hand slapped against the panel and pushed it open. Nate entered.

The usual friendliness in his dark brown eyes was edged out by anger. The door snapped shut at his back. Wrath was evident in his quietly suppressed voice. "Until last night, I have never in my life told a woman I loved her. Do you really think me capable of proposing marriage to you a few short hours after sending another woman flowers and candy?" Mandy opened her mouth, but Nate cut her off. "I suppose you think I slept with her, too."

Raising her chin defiantly, Mandy said, "I really don't care one way or the other."

"Liar."

"Get out."

In one aggressive step, Nate closed the distance between them. Roughly, he gripped her shoulders as he pulled her firmly against his body. Fury sparked in his eyes. "I'll leave when I'm damn good and ready." Then his mouth came down on hers.

His determined assault weakened Mandy's knees. Without thought or intent, she clung to the sleeves of his suit coat for support. Before she recovered from her momentary vulnerability, Nate breached the barrier of her softening lips. His tongue swept in and tangled with hers.

His arms came around her. His hands squeezed her buttocks. A quick lift and Mandy found herself sitting on the edge of her desk. Nate nudged her knees apart and stepped between her thighs. She felt the hard bulge of his arousal nuzzle the soft, moist heart of her femininity.

She moaned when his mouth left hers and found that special place at the juncture of her neck and shoulder. Involuntarily, her hips thrust forward, seating his manhood more firmly against her pleasure spot.

And then, abruptly, Nate stepped away.

Without his support, Mandy almost fell off the edge of the desk. But, somehow, she managed to catch herself.

"Still want me to leave?" Nate asked with knowing satisfaction in his husky voice. His heated eyes dropped down to her parted thighs.

Quickly, Mandy jerked her skirt to her knees. Sliding off the desk, she leaned against it, doubtful she could stand unassisted. Her breath came hard and fast as indignation overrode frustrated arousal. "Yes." The word tripped off her stiff lips.

Nate's eyes and jaw hardened. "All right, Mandy, I'll go. But don't expect me to come chasing after you again. When you wake up and decide to acknowledge what's between us, you'll have to come to me." In two paces he was at the door. Yanking it open, he gave one last furious glance over his shoulder and then strode out.

Mandy rushed after him and grabbed either side of the door frame. "Hell will freeze over first," she yelled to his retreating back.

Wednesday morning Nate conducted two budget interviews and was preparing for a third when Justin sauntered through the open office door.

"Are you lost?" Nate sniffed, not wanting the interruption. "The courthouse is down and over one block."

Shrugging out of his wet trench coat, Justin said, "Already been there and done that. I only had one court case today, and it was a slam dunk." He settled himself into a chair. "Last night and this morning you seemed to have your panties in a twist—"

"Bite me."

"—so I decided to stop by and deliver the good news in person." He paused for effect. Since he was representing his brother on only one legal issue, Justin expected Nate to bounce up and down with excitement. He didn't.

Instead, he stood and jammed his hands into his pockets. "I don't know. I'm beginning to think I've rushed into everything a little too precipitously." Coins and keys jingled. "I'm not sure I want to stick around this area."

"What?"

"Hell, it rains all the time."

"What do you expect? The entire Pacific Northwest is a rain forest. Besides, it doesn't rain all the time, just more than you're used to."

"That's the whole point." Now, in addition to the pocket jingle, Nate paced to the door of his small office, and with his elbow, swung the panel shut. "I was raised in high desert country."

"We both were, Nate."

"I don't belong here."

Becoming as disturbed as his brother, the lawyer shoved his fingers through his hair. "What the hell are you talking about?"

"I never should have come here."

"Come off it. I don't know what your problem is, but it sure as hell is not the rain."

"It doesn't make any difference what it is," the younger man argued. "I don't think I want to stay here."

"Don't tell me you're having job problems again."

"No, it's nothing like that," Nate said in an offhand manner as he continued to pace. "I can handle anything they throw at me."

"If it's not the job, wha—? Ah, shit. It's a woman, isn't it?"

Nate stopped in his tracks and faced his brother. "Yeah," he admitted, and then snidely added, "I guess I figured that if love could bite an over-the-hill playboy like you on the ass and have it work out okay, it would be a piece of cake for a young stud like me."

Justin didn't rise to the bait the way Nate expected.

"Is it the bartender from my bachelor party?"

"Rashell? No. She's nice enough, but not my type."

Justin's eyebrows rose in astonished disbelief. The bartender was exactly the type that used to catch his brother's eye. A scowl descended on Justin's face. "It's not that woman you were living with, is it?"

"God, no. Although, she's part of the problem."

"Why doesn't that surprise me?"

"The first time in my life a woman matters, *really matters*," Nate said as if his brother hadn't spoken. "And she doesn't want to have a damn thing to do with me."

The two men stared at each other, and then Justin said, "You know, Britney took some convincing before she came around to my way of thinking. Maybe yours will, too."

Nate snorted.

"Listen, bro," Justin coaxed, bringing the conversation back on track. "You have a very narrow window of opportunity to buy the house you're so wild about. Are you sure you want to throw it away?"

"I couldn't live there without her," Nate intoned, as he slumped into his chair. "It's not just the house. It's the way her eyes lit up the moment she saw it. She imbued every room with her enthusiasm. She fell in love with it the same time I did. I think that's when I fell in love with *her*."

"Holy shit," Justin cried. "You're talking about Mandy."

With a long, drawn out sigh, Nate nodded. "Yep, I fell in love with the firebrand."

A grin spread over the attorney's face and he rubbed his hands together. "Hot damn. Britney's going to love this."

⚜ Chapter 54 ⚜

THE NEWS ABOUT NATE AND MANDY'S AFFAIR WAS TOO JUICY FOR Justin to share with Britney over the phone. He wanted to see the expression on his bride's face when he told her. But, unfortunately, that delectable little tidbit would have to wait until the evening.

On their honeymoon, Britney had confided high hopes for a match between her roommate and his brother. Justin had scoffed at the idea of those two falling in love. But fallen they had. At least his brother had. Apparently, Mandy had not.

Nate said he didn't want the riverside house without Mandy in it and Justin didn't waste time trying to convince him otherwise. Beneath his lovelorn brother's easygoing façade was titanium stubbornness. After spending ten miserable minutes commiserating, the attorney left.

Aiming his silver convertible south, Justin set Nate's romantic troubles from his mind and concentrated on his own. Britney was miffed about something. But he didn't know what? In addition to the sexy red teddy he gave her at breakfast Monday, he sent his wife flowers at work and took her out for a romantic Valentine dinner. Justin lost his appetite, and almost his temper, when Britney declined a flute of Dom Pérignon after the bottle was opened. Then, at home she rebuffed his amorous advances, claiming exhaustion, as she had the previous two nights.

When it came to making love, Justin believed all women, even wives, owned the right to say no. At the same time, he felt withholding sex as a means of manipulation was just plain wrong. He'd never expected it from Britney. And he wouldn't put up with it, not if he could figure out how to prevent it.

Parking his Camaro behind the office, Justin went inside. Maryann, his administrative assistant, handed over a fistful of phone messages and reminded him of an appointment scheduled toward the end of the day.

The late afternoon meeting concerned the final settlement of a substantial estate. Heretofore congenially agreeable, the five heirs blew into his office squabbling about a few pieces of antique furniture. Valued at thirty-two thousand, the items represented less than one percent of the multi-million dollar estate.

The oldest sister, prizing the furniture, wanted it. The other sister and three brothers, preferred to sell it and divide the proceeds. A monetary adjustment to the estate disbursements could easily resolve the issue, except the woman objected, saying that was like "buying" a portion of her inheritance. Before long, the value of every piece of personal property previously distributed amongst them was brought into question and argued about. At one point, the youngest, a man in his fifties, preposterously demanded an accounting of all the cash their parents had given every one of them from the time each sibling had attained the age of majority. This only heightened the argument as he was more prosperous than others.

Soon every prior agreement of the all-but-settled estate disintegrated into discord. Finally, acknowledging a complete loss of control and shouting to be heard over five angry voices, Justin suggested they each retain separate lawyers and squander their millions on attorneys' fees. Affronted, the five ceased their bickering. After another quarter hour they and agreed to another meeting the following week.

At some point during the fiasco, Maryann had packed it in for the day. Since it was nearing five-thirty, Justin cleared his desk and left.

A foul mood sailed along with him like a seagull riding the wind. The morning's blustery rain had calmed to a drenching, foggy mist. Another strong gale was forecast for Friday, but Justin expected an angry squall to hit the Peter's household long before then—probably when he confronted his bride about her sudden disinterest in sex.

He parked on the street in front of his condo, having relinquished possession of the one car garage to Britney. It was the type of gallantry he believed his wife deserved. Ill humor made him reconsider the courtesy.

Entering his home, Justin slammed the door and shrugged out of his trench coat. He tossed the damp garment over a coat tree Britney had recently placed in the entry. Making a beeline toward the kitchen, he wanted the fortitude a beer could provide. He drew up short when he saw his wife standing in the dining room, her hair falling unrestrained about her.

The first time he'd seen Britney, it was braided into a thick rope and draped over one shoulder. The length hadn't registered until the next time they met. Then, she'd left it loose, like a dark haired Godiva, and the mahogany veil flowed to her knees. Today, instead of almost five feet of lush tresses, her mane stopped short at her hipline.

Stunned, Justin blurted, "What happened to your hair?"

Britney gave him an uncertain smile. "I had it cut," she said. "About fifteen inches worth. Three was to even it up and twelve was needed to make a wig."

"Why do you need a wig?"

"I don't, but some unfortunate child with cancer does. Chemotherapy causes a kid's hair to fall out," she explained, as if he didn't know.

"Do we know someone whose child has cancer?" he asked.

"No, but that doesn't matter. Someone somewhere needs it." She walked closer until she stood in front of her husband. "I was going to shorten it a little at a time, but this makes more sense. I'll let them take another thirteen inches in a couple of months."

"Why?" Justin demanded. "I love your hair."

"A couple of months after that I'll let them whack the rest off . . ." her voice faltered and she started to cry.

A sudden thought occurred. Was Britney's recent exhaustion the result of some horrendous disease? Terror clutched his heart. He groped behind him for a chair. Finding one, he dropped heavily into it. Then he took his wife's hand and pulled her onto his lap. "Britney, honey, what's the matter? Whatever it is, we'll fight it. We'll get the best doctors. We'll do whatever—"

She placed her fingers on his lips. "It's okay, Justin. I'm not sick. I'm pregnant."

"Pregnant?" The relief felt heady.

"Yeah, I thought I should have short hair by the time the baby's born." She started crying again.

Hugging his wife so close she squeaked, Justin exclaimed, "My God, we're going to have a baby!" Then he drew her away. "Brit, this is wonderful. I had no idea it would happen so soon."

Her sob, hidden behind the veil of her hair, was a small keening sound.

He tipped her chin up to look into her face. "Brit, baby," Justin murmured. "I thought you'd be happy. Why are you crying?"

"Because," she sniffled. "Other than trimming off split ends, I've never cut my hair before." She fell on his shoulder and cried her heart out.

❧ Chapter 55 ❧

IN DEFERENCE TO HIS WIFE'S DELICATE EMOTIONAL STATE, JUSTIN offered to prepare dinner while she rested. Britney immediately acquiesced and went to lie down in the bedroom. A half hour later, with the meal ready to serve, Justin found her sound asleep.

Unsure whether or not to wake her, Nathan answered that question by slamming the front door as he arrived home.

Britney's eyes opened. Seeing her husband perched on the edge of their bed, she smiled.

When the door across the hall banged closed, Justin frowned in that direction.

"It's okay," Britney said. "I shouldn't sleep anymore or I'll be awake all night."

Looking back to examine her face, he asked, "Are you sure?"

"Positive," she said, sitting up. "What's for dinner?"

"Tuna salad and chicken noodle soup. It's out of a can but it's all I could think of on short notice."

He stood up and Britney swung her feet to the floor. "Sounds good to me, I'm starving."

They heard Nate leave his bedroom. A moment later, he called out their names.

"We have a problem," Justin whispered. Then corrected himself, "Rather, Nate has a problem. Unfortunately, since he's living here, it's our problem, too."

"He's moving soon, isn't he?" Britney whispered back.

"Hey, you two lovebirds," Nate said from the open doorway. "The soup was about to boil over. Are you ready to eat or should I close the door and give you some privacy?"

"We're coming out," Britney said, coloring slightly at his innuendo.

Slinging an arm across her shoulders, Justin asked, "Should we tell him now or later?"

"You can't very well not tell me, now," Nate quipped.

"Go ahead," Justin prodded.

"No, you tell him. He's your brother."

"When you two figure out who's going to tell me your big secret," Nate said, turning to go, "I'll be in the dining room eating dinner."

"Britney's pregnant," Justin blurted, with a prideful grin on his face.

"Wow," Nate murmured, turning back. "That didn't take long. I guess congratulations are in order." He smiled, but his eyes held the hint of sadness. "When's the baby due?"

"In about eight and a half months," Britney tittered, and with a sidelong glance at her husband, added, "I bought a home pregnancy test a couple days ago but was afraid of jinxing everything by using it. That's stupid, I know. Anyway, I finally worked up the nerve to do it today on my lunch hour."

"And presto, the rabbit died," Justin teased as they all herded toward the kitchen and dining room. "Tell me, how do they fit a full grown rabbit into that little box?"

DINNER, A RATHER SHORT EPISODE, WAS DOMINATED BY TALK OF the baby. For his brother's sake, Nate forced a demeanor of good cheer, but he excused himself as soon as he finished eating and left for parts unknown. He said it was to give the newlyweds a quiet evening alone; they all knew it was because their happiness magnified Nate's discontent.

"Why is he so miserable?" Britney asked as they washed up after dinner.

"You won't believe it when I tell you," her husband said with male glee over his brother's wretchedness, a condition Justin believed most men brought on themselves. "He's been having an affair. And you'll never guess with whom."

"Mandy," Britney said, taking the wind out of his sails. "She told me about it when we got back from our honeymoon."

"You didn't tell me." Justin sounded offended.

"She told me in confidence."

"But I'm your husband."

"And she's my friend," Britney said, drying her hands, adding as she turned on the dishwasher, "What she told me didn't concern you."

Justin followed his wife into the living room, and argued, "It concerned my brother. What concerns him, concerns me."

Not understanding his pique, Britney picked up the TV remote, "Mandy said it wasn't serious. Kind of a one night stand, except it happened twice."

"Oh, it's serious," Justin insisted, removing the control from her hand. "Nate wouldn't have proposed over a one night stand."

"Marriage?"

"Yes." He hissed the word angrily. "He proposed Monday night and Mandy turned him down flat."

Britney stood staring at her husband, speechless with disbelief.

Fingers raking his hair, Justin said, "Nate's refusing to go through with the purchase of the house. Says he can't stand to stick around here without her."

"My God, I don't believe this."

"It's true."

"I mean, I can't believe she turned him down. Mandy loves Nate. She told me so herself."

"Your friend sure has a strange way of showing it," Justin scoffed.

"We have to do something."

"Like what?"

"I don't know," Britney said, picking up her purse and rummaging through it for her phone. "I need to talk some sense into her head."

"Good luck with that."

After speed dialing her friend, Britney said, "Hi, let's have dinner tomorrow night." A moment later, looking at Justin, she said into the phone, "No, just the two of us. I'll drive to Astoria after work. You name the place."

They agreed on Britney picking up a roasted chicken from the grocery on her drive over and Mandy tossing together a salad. Nothing was said about wine, for which Britney was grateful because she was off alcohol for the duration of her pregnancy.

Mandy was setting the table when Britney arrived, and other than a greeting and hug, they both limited their conversation to inconsequentials until the food was served.

"How's married life treating you?" Mandy asked, hoping to get this part of the conversation out of the way as quickly as possible.

Grinning, Britney sidestepped subtlety, "Fabulous, you should give it a try again sometime soon."

"Been there, done that," Mandy clipped out. She glared at her friend. "And don't see any point in doing it again."

"You know, not all men are like Tom," Britney said gently, referring to Mandy's ex-husband. Then she took a bite of chicken.

"No, others are like Sam," Mandy replied with a lemony twist to her mouth. "No sooner do I trust a man than he walks all over me. Never again, thank you very much." She set her fork on her plate, having lost her appetite. Most food didn't agree with her anymore.

"Is that what happened between you and Nate?" Britney asked after swallowing. "Did he give you the doormat treatment?"

"Nate and I don't get along. And I'd rather not talk about him." Mandy got up from the table and took her half empty plate to the sink. Keeping her back turned, she was unable to keep from asking, "Has he moved yet or is he still living with you and Justin?"

"Still with us, but not for much longer, I hope. We need time to convert his bedroom into a nursery."

Mandy whipped around. "Are you—?"

"Yeah, I'm going to have a baby," Britney all but sang, glowing with happiness.

A pinched look came into Mandy's stricken eyes moments before crumbling into tears.

The smile fled Britney's face as she rose and quickly crossed the small area. Gathering her friend into her arms, she rocked as Mandy cried.

When her sobs abated, Britney cooed, "Come on, girl, let's sit you down on the davenport and I'll brew us a pot of tea. Then I want you to tell me what's troubling you."

"I can't."

"Of course, you can, Mandy. You're the sister I never had. If you can't tell me, who can you tell?"

She sniffled. "If I tell you, you'll tell Justin and he'll tell Nate."

Britney led Mandy into the living room and they both sank onto the couch. "I won't, I promise. What's said between us stays between us."

Raising red-rimmed eyes, Mandy sniffled again. "You promise?"

"I swear it," Britney said emphatically.

In a small, sniffling voice, Mandy said, "I think I might be pregnant."

❧ Chapter 56 ❧

ALL THE SIGNS POINTED TOWARD PREGNANCY. HER PERIOD WAS almost two weeks late. Food didn't sit well on her stomach— lately just the thought of it was enough to nauseate. But Mandy wasn't *sure* she was pregnant, and she wasn't sure if she wanted to be sure. Uncertainty left room for denial. If she took a home pregnancy test, and the stick turned blue, it would remove all doubt. The slim hope of failing the test was small motivation compared to the possibility of passing.

Insisting such thinking was foolish, Britney left to go buy a kit. When she returned, the first words out of her mouth were, "What precautions have you taken?"

"To keep from getting pregnant?"

Britney gave Mandy a look. "Among other things."

The redhead blushed as only redheads can. "Not much of anything," she admitted. "At Mt. Hood I used a spermicidal, but the night of your wedding I wasn't prepared. Things just kind of happened . . . unexpectedly, you know," Mandy said, shrugging like a carelessly naughty teenager.

"That would explain an accidental pregnancy. Did you talk to Nate about the possibility of anything else?"

A quick shake of her head indicated Mandy had not.

"Let's hope he's exercised more caution with his previous partners," Britney said on a long sigh. She held out the package containing the kit. "Regardless of this test result, you need to have a conversation with Nate. Tomorrow, if not sooner."

With a trembling hand, Mandy took the package and headed toward the bathroom. Ten minutes later, face pale and feeling hollow inside, she came back out. The stick had a bright blue stripe in the window. "You won't tell, will you? You promised you wouldn't."

"Time's running out," Kimberly Long told me over the phone. "Either you provide a copy of the arbitration determination letter before the bank closes at six o'clock tonight or they'll cancel the sale."

"They can't do that," I objected, not knowing why. I didn't intend to stay in Clatsop County without Mandy by my side. Seeing her, day in and day out, loving her, and knowing she'd played me for a fool, would be unbearable. I refused to do it. Contrarily, I argued, "You told me I had until the end of the month."

"No, I said the bank wants the house off their books by the end of the month," she corrected me. "That means the escrow needs to close no later than February twenty-eighth. If you can't produce proof the arbitration is settled, the bank needs time to move forward with the backup buyers."

Why don't I just tell her the deal is off?

"The arbitration is settled, isn't it, Nate? In your favor, I mean."

"Yes," I replied with angry discontent.

"If you're having second thoughts," Kimberly said, uncannily, "maybe it will help to look at the house again."

"It won't."

She waited, but I didn't elaborate.

"Six o'clock tonight," she repeated. "I can't buy you anymore time."

When I didn't respond, she disconnected. No sooner did I replace the receiver than the phone rang again.

"Are you willing to listen to reason, yet?" my brother asked in his best lawyerly voice. It was the same tone he'd used the previous evening to harangue me about my decision to find a new job and move out of the area. "You're a fool to let Mandy and that house slip through your fingers," Justin said again, as he had last night.

"No, a fool is someone who recognizes an impossible situation but plows ahead anyway," I countered. "How many times do I have to tell you? Mandy doesn't want anything to do with me."

"You love her, don't you?" It was a rhetorical question, the answer to which we'd been over a number of times. "You don't walk out on love at the first sign of trouble," he said, beating a familiar drum.

Last night, while my newest sister-in-law, the traitor, had gone to Mandy's for a girl's only dinner, leaving Justin and me to fend for ourselves, he'd made the same assertion. He said I was giving up without a fight and called me cowardly. My swinging fist proved the lack of a yellow stripe on my back. Fortunately, Justin sidestepped. The punch landed rather harmlessly on the meaty part of his shoulder, eliminating the need for retaliation and a full blown fist fight.

We both knew of Mandy's experience with men walking out on her. "It's what she expects," I reminded him now.

"So show her you're here for the long haul," he argued. "Buy the house, dig in your heels, and take your time bringing her around to your way of thinking."

"If I thought for one minute the firebrand might change her mind about marrying me," I said, feeling bitter, "I'd go that route. But, believe me, Justin, that ain't gonna happen. I don't stand a chance of Mandy changing her mind."

"Britney thinks otherwise. That's why she went over there last night," my brother informed me. "To talk some sense into her."

"Fat chance that."

"Britney thinks Mandy will come around."

"On what basis?" I sneered.

"I don't know." He sighed in frustration. "Those two women have a Las Vegas-soul-sister pact or something. What's said between them stays between them."

"So, you don't really know."

Again, a heavy breath came over the line. "Give me the word and I'll fax the determination letter to your realtor."

Once the bank received the needed document, I'd lose the earnest money if I backed out of the deal. If they cancelled the transaction my money would be refunded. Justin knew that as well as I.

Hesitating to answer, I waited for my brother to badger me some more. He didn't. As always, as he knew it would, slacking off after giving it his best shot was more effective than further argument. "I don't know. I'll think about it."

"Maybe you'll think more clearly looking at the river through the big picture window you told me about," the sly devil suggested.

"Maybe you need to back off some more," I retorted, and hung up.

A wavering stirred in my gut. I tried to ignore it but half an hour later I picked up the phone.

"Kimberly, Nate Peters here. I got to thinking about it and decided I should look at the house again."

"I can meet you there in half an hour," she said.

"No, I don't get off work 'til five. Let's make it five-fifteen."

"That doesn't leave much time to get the documentation to me, unless you plan to bring it with you."

"The truth is, Kimberly, you were right about me having second thoughts. Five minutes is probably all I need to put this thing to rest in my mind." I didn't say it was all I needed for the final requiem, however much I believed just that.

❧ Chapter 57 ❧

GEORGE FULTON'S SECRETARY CALLED NICOLE LATE FRIDAY afternoon. "Ms. French, Mr. Fulton would like to see you in his office at your earliest convenience."

It rankled that George wouldn't call her himself. No-o, she thought snidely, her brother believed in going through channels—doing everything by the book.

The one and only time, years ago, Nicole had called him to complain about a situation at work, George had unequivocally informed her that he would not undermine his department managers by interceding on her behalf. From that day forward, between the hours of eight in the morning and five at night, her own brother, damn him, refused to take her calls.

Nicole felt turnabout was fair play—and long overdue.

"Ms. French?" Carrie inquired politely, put off by the extended silence. "Are you still there?"

"Yes."

"Mr. Fulton would like to see you in his office," the secretary repeated.

"Please tell George I'm working. If he wishes to see me, he can stop by my home this evening," Nicole said with the insincere sweetness of stevia. He'd always coveted her house and she liked flaunting it at him.

"Perhaps I wasn't clear, Ms. French," Carrie said, determined to fulfill her duties. "The County Manager wants to see you immediately."

Nicole dropped all pretense of cordiality. "You can tell my brother if he wants to talk with me, he can damn well pick up his phone and call me himself." Hammering the instrument back into its cradle, she noticed the attention of her coworkers. Slipping a smile onto her face and addressing no one in particular, she joked, "Brothers, you can't live with 'em . . . thank God."

It took less than a minute for her phone to ring again. She considered ignoring it, but answered on the fourth ring.

"Ye-es?" The word came out in two syllables.

Exasperated, George growled, "Everything is a game to you, isn't it?"

"Why George, how nice of you to call. We haven't spoken in ages."

"Cut the crap, Nicole. This isn't a social call, and you know it. I want you in my office and I want you in here NOW!"

Nicole jerked the phone away from her ear with a frown. She felt as if every eye was on her as she gingerly replaced the receiver. Tossing her head, she huffed out a breath, and stood. "Well, it appears my brother can't run the county without my assistance. I'll be back as soon as I fix his little problem."

She hid her angst behind a nonchalant sashay out the door of the bullpen. By the time she strode into her brother's office fury had pushed her steps into a militant march. Standing with her hands firmly gripping her hips, she snapped, "Here I am, brother dear."

Used to his sister's tantrums, and knowing how to push her buttons, George sat back in his chair and calmly steepled his fingers. "Please close the door and sit down."

Deliberately, she reached out and slammed the heavy wooden panel into its frame. "What's this about?" she demanded, turning back to face him.

"Sit."

Doing so, she growled, "Fine, I'm sitting. Now get on with it."

The case against his sister was as much conjecture on George's part as it was evidence against her. Maybe more conjecture than hard evidence, when he got right down to it, he acknowledged. But George knew Nicole. He'd grown up with her subterfuge, and had, too many times to count, been punished because of her games. Over time, he'd learned how to out fox Nicole, as he planned to do now, because without hard evidence, he needed an admission.

Leaning forward, George placed his forearms on his desk, hands clasped. "The game's over, Nicole. You've been found out and there's nothing I can do to help you."

"What do you mean?" The first bit of wariness was in her voice.

"I know that you forged a note from Ernie Gunderson instructing Mandy Kearney to alter the first performance review she conducted on you."

"Oh, that," Nicole dismissed it with a flick of her hand. "She expects the impossible."

George let it drop, having confirmed the allegation. "I know about the budget you gave Nate Peters. How did you manage to get into Mandy's files?"

Nicole's mouth fell open, again confirming George's suspicions, but no sound emerged.

"I know you altered tax receipt figures on more than one occasion. And that, dear sister, could have resulted in serious financial consequences for the county."

"So what? You can't prove anything," she claimed, jumping out of her chair.

"Sit down," he barked, knowing that was as much admission as he'd get from his sister. "The county attorney agrees the evidence is sufficient to defend against a wrongful termination accusation."

Her breath caught in her throat and Nicole's knees gave way. "You wouldn't."

"I have no choice. My first responsibility is to the citizens of Clatsop County." He slid an envelope across his desk toward her. "I'm sorry, Nicole, this is your final paycheck."

"You can't," she choked out, tears filling her eyes. "What about my house? How am I supposed to make the payments?"

Familiar with the way his sister turned the faucet on and off at will, George's lip curled in disgust. "That place is an ostentatious white elephant. You'd be better off without it."

"You bastard. You've always envied me that house."

"Get real, Nicole. That house is a monstrosity. I never understood why Allen put up with your grandiose plans for the place."

"Because I'm a good fuck," Nicole screamed.

"Keep your voice down!"

"He couldn't get enough of me," she taunted, the satisfaction on her face loathsome to see.

"That's enough."

"That pregnancy ruined everything. My boobs droop. My belly has stretch marks." She coughed out a humorless laugh and continued her bitter tirade. "And if that's not bad enough, I'm saddled with the brat for the next umpteen years."

His sister's attitude appalled George, who loved his nephew. He also liked and respected Allen French—a hell of a lot more than his sister at the moment. "If you don't want to raise your own child, give Allen custody of Tyler."

"Oh, he'd like that," she admitted caustically. "Think of the thousands he'd save every year in child support. But what about me? I'm barely scraping by. What am I going to do now?" Nicole turned on the water works again.

"Listen," George said, sinking into the chair beside his sister. Awkwardly, he patted her shoulder. "You dropped out of college to get married. You need to go back to school and finish your degree. It's the only way you'll ever get a job that pays well enough."

"How am I supposed to do that?" she demanded, nearly biting his head off. "Thanks to you, I can't even afford a night out."

"Make Allen pay."

She snorted.

"He will," George insisted, hoping his sister's ex-husband would forgive him. "He will if you give him custody of Tyler while you're away at college."

Nicole's tears dried up as fast as they'd started flowing. She stared at her brother, a smile slowly sliding into place. "Gee, Georgie, you're pretty smart, aren't you?"

With an effort, he smiled back at his sister. "Sometimes."

⋞ Chapter 58 ⋟

THE PHONE ON BRITNEY'S DESK RANG. SHE ANSWERED.

"I talked to Nate again," Justin said. "If I know my brother, which I do, he'll have to look at that house one last time before giving it up. How are things on your end?"

"Fine. I'm leaving work early and plan to walk into Mandy's office at ten minutes to five. I'm not giving her a choice but to leave with me."

"Good. You have the address?"

"It's in my purse."

"Okay, see you tonight."

"MANDY, MR. FULTON WOULD LIKE TO SEE YOU IN HIS OFFICE AT your earliest convenience," Carrie, his secretary, said over the phone.

Which meant Mandy needed to drop everything and hightail it over there immediately. Walking through the bullpen, she noticed Nicole wasn't at her desk.

So, this it is, Mandy thought, fully expecting to find brother and sister united against her. The only question in her mind was whether or not Nate would be in on this, too. She wouldn't put it past him after their last confrontation.

When Mandy arrived Carrie smiled and gave a thumbs-up, a rare giveaway from the woman who held the county's secrets with tight-lipped ferocity. The gesture inspired a spark of hope that Mandy quickly doused.

"Come in," George Fulton said, rising from behind his desk as she stopped in his doorway. He waved toward a chair. "Please sit down."

Moving forward, Mandy was vaguely aware of the door closing at her back, leaving her alone with the County Manager.

He held out a flash drive. "I believe this belongs to you."

She was afraid to take it, but did.

"I copied the contents into Nicole's personnel file along with my termination recommendation," he intoned solemnly as he resumed his place behind the desk.

Mandy swallowed loudly. "Recommendation?" Her voice squeaked and she cleared her throat. "For whose termination?"

George sat back in his chair with a fleeting twitch of his lips. "Nicole's, of course."

As a tidal wave of relief flooded over Mandy, she felt lightheaded. Unaccountably, she said, "I'm sorry."

"It was her own fault, although, I wish it hadn't come to this," he replied. "You can thank Nathan Peters for bringing it to my attention."

Mandy's breath caught but the County Manager didn't seem to notice.

"It should have been Ernie," he continued. "His oversight earned him a formal reprimand."

This time her gasp was audible.

"Normally, I wouldn't share that information, especially with his subordinate, but Ernie and I agreed the integrity of your future working relationship was more important than confidentiality in this matter."

"I see," she murmured.

"All right, then," George said, rising.

"Is Nicole gone?" Mandy asked, somewhat confused since managers were usually in charge of hiring and firing for their own departments.

"Yes. To save her from embarrassment, I suggested she leave quietly. Nicole and I will clear out her desk over the weekend."

"I see."

"I'd appreciate it if you'd help squelch the rumor mill."

"Of course," Mandy replied, not bothering to tell the County Manager that his sister had been the hub of said mill.

"Get the vacant position posted as soon as possible," George instructed as he escorted Mandy to the door.

"Yes, I will," she said, wanting to skip back to her office to complete that task right away.

Elated over the removal of her nemesis, Mandy knew she should stop by Nate's office and express her gratitude for his intervention. After all, in helping to preserve her job, he had put his own at risk. Her footsteps faltered. That acknowledgement made her feel small because she felt it was more, much more, than she'd have done for him.

Nate had put it all on the line, she thought. His heart and his job—for her. She had risked nothing for him. Even now, when so much was as stake, Mandy cowered from the thought of revealing the truth to Nate.

The truth was, in addition to the pregnancy, she loved him. Maybe she had from the very beginning, back when she first met him during the summer. His midnight eyes had sparkled roguishly with the kind of playful naughtiness that enticed a woman into forgetting that men couldn't be trusted. Some men, anyway, maybe others could. Could Nate be trusted? Yes, Mandy realized, yes, she could trust Nate, not only with her job but also with her heart.

But once she told him about the pregnancy, would *he* trust *her*? Would he believe a sudden profession of love from her? Or, would he think she was willing to marry him only because of the baby? And, in doubting her love, would Nate grow to resent her?

Breaking into Mandy's thoughts, a voice said, "There you are."

Britney was standing on the customer side of the counter, next to the door that opened into the bullpen. "No one knew where you were and I thought I'd missed you."

Surprised and glad to see her friend, Mandy asked, "What are you doing here?"

Linking arms, Britney said, "I've come to spirit you away. Let's get your purse and whatever else you need, then get out of here."

"WHERE ARE WE GOING?" MANDY WANTED TO KNOW.

"You'll see." Britney clicked open the doors to her cream colored PT Cruiser. They ducked inside and fastened their seatbelts. Starting the engine, she said, "Did I tell you Justin wants to trade in his snazzy convertible for a minivan?"

"You're kidding, right?"

"Nope," Britney said, driving out of the county parking lot onto Ninth Street. She crossed Duane, and then turned right onto Commercial. "I think it makes more sense to trade in this car, since it's older, and keep his for date night."

"I agree completely." As they turned into the Alderbrook neighborhood, Mandy again asked, "Where are we going?"

"You'll see," Britney repeated.

Nate's truck and another vehicle were parked in the driveway of the house at the end of the block. Britney drove up in front and parked at the curb.

"Why are you stopping here?" Mandy demanded, sounding alarmed.

"Because you need to have a conversation with Nate."

"No! Take me back to my car—right this minute."

"Mandy, listen to me," Britney said, turning in her seat and clasping her friend's hands. "You're going to have his baby. You need to tell him."

"Why?"

"You know why. Besides, he wants to marry you, a significant fact you didn't bother telling me."

"When he finds out I'm pregnant, he'll change his mind fast enough."

"No, he won't," Britney objected, in defense of her brother-in-law. "Nate loves you."

"But he won't believe *I* love *him*. Don't you see? He'll think my only reason for marrying him is the baby. He'll resent that and end up hating me because of it."

Shaking her head, Britney snorted. "Don't be ridiculous. The man's head over heels for you. Now, go in there and tell him—before it's too late."

✎ Chapter 59 ❧

STANDING AT THE BIG BAY WINDOW IN THE LIVING ROOM, WATCHING a laden freighter riding low in the water as it made its way upriver in the twilight, disappointment weighted heavily on my heart. I could envision sharing this view with Mandy on stormy winter nights and clear summer days, if only she weren't so stubbornly set against me.

Kimberly Long unlocked the front door and said she'd stay in the kitchen while I looked through the house. She must be tired of waiting. In fifteen minutes, I hadn't made it past this window and knew I'd get no farther. The loss of this house, this room, this view, was symbolic of my greater loss. I couldn't let go.

I sensed movement behind me.

"Nate?"

Mandy's voice—conjured while I dreamed of a future that would never be. If I didn't turn, perhaps I wouldn't awaken.

My dream moved closer, repeated my name, and placed a hand on my arm.

Looking down, I saw Mandy's hand. It was real. She stood next to me. When I looked into her eyes my heart soared as high and free as an eagle sailing on the wind. "What are you doing here?" My voice sounded like the engine of an old river scow.

Quietly, with shy embarrassment it seemed, she replied, "You said you wouldn't chase after me again."

A last ray of winter sun burnished her fiery hair before the light faded to dusk.

"Please don't remind me. Only a fool would make such an idiotic statement."

"You meant it, though, didn't you?"

I'd heard once that a lie was both murder and suicide. I'd never comprehended the true meaning of that before this moment. If I lied, she'd know. Instead, I said, "Are you chasing me now?"

Mandy looked toward the window. There was no reflection, only the dark night. Her fingers twisted together, as if writhing in pain. "If you had lied, I could have walked out of here without a qualm."

"Do you want to?"

She shook her head, and then looked at me again, perhaps unsure if I could see the gesture. "No, Nate, I can't walk out." She hesitated. "Because I love you."

That small speck of hope that her hand on my arm had settled in my heart, now burst forth like the beautiful beginning of a new universe. I reached out to make my dream a reality, but it seemed as elusive as ever.

Stepping back, Mandy said, "There's something you need to know." She rushed on, all her words running together. "I'm pregnant, but that's not why I'm here. You probably won't believe that—"

"Wait, *wait*, WAIT." I grabbed her shoulders. "Did you say you're pregnant?"

Without looking at me, except to stare at my chest, Mandy nodded her head.

Quickly, I drew her into my arms and danced around with joy. "This is perfect. *We're* perfect—perfect together."

"No! No, we're not." She pushed away from me, an anguished expression on her face. "Nothing's perfect. I'm pregnant."

I took her hands in mine. "What can I say, Mandy? It's not a perfect world."

"No, it's not," she cried, obviously upset. "In a perfect world, it would only rain at night. There would be eternal springtime. We'd be young forever, and hearts would never be broken."

"You're wrong, Mandy," I countered, exasperated with the foolish firebrand. "In your perfect world we'd never see the beauty of a rainbow, or feel the heat of summer on our shoulders, or snowflakes on our eyelashes. We'd never have the pleasure of fond and distant memories.

"And worst of all, sweetheart," I said, taking her into my arms, "we'd never experience the joy of sharing the love in our hearts a second time around. I can't promise you a perfect world, my precious firebrand, but I can promise to love you for the rest of my life."

"But I'm pregnant," she reminded me—as if I could possibly forget.

With one hand, I cradled her head against my shoulder. The other, I pressed to her belly. "And I'll cherish both of you forever."

Mandy sobbed and then sniffled. "I love you, Nate."

I smiled against her hair. "I know you do. I've never doubted your love, even when you did."

From the shadows we heard Kimberly Long ask, "Does this mean you want to go ahead with the house purchase?"

"Do we?" I asked Mandy.

"Yes," she said, agreeing to that and so much more.

Holding hands, we turned from the window. "I'd better call Justin and get a copy of that determination letter."

"Oh, he brought it by already," the realtor informed us. "Since I needed to stay and lock up after you, he said he'd stop by the bank to drop it off before they closed."

In the darkening night I looked at Mandy, my own personal firebrand, the woman I loved.

She squeezed my hand. "Let's go home, Nate," she murmured.

Squeezing back, I said. "We already are."

###

Connect me on Facebook:
https://www.facebook.com/paulajudith.johnson

Website: http://www.paulajudithjohnson.com

Other books by Paula Judith Johnson
Sweetbriar:
(ebook editions) https://www.smashwords.com/books/view/78919
(print) http://www.createspace.com/3475235
Starting Over:
(ebook editions) https://www.smashwords.com/books/view/369309
(print) https://www.createspace.com/4452247

The Thought of You (print only)
https://www.createspace.com/3745844
by Teresa & Wayne Brown

Sweetbriar

by Paula Judith Johnson

In the turbulent years leading up to the War of 1812, American Bradley Anderson, strong-willed captain of the merchantman, *Angel Star*, foresworn to live life on his own terms and heedless of the feeling of others, lusts after the beautiful Beth Avery.

But Lady Beth, the pampered daughter of Milton Avery, 4th Earl of Rockwell, resists the longing in her heart. Choosing to remain in the safety of her homeland, Lady Beth is determined to marry a fellow Englishman.

While free-spirited Louise Jetter, desiring to cast aside the restrictions of her English Puritan upbringing, risks all for love as England and America clash in the rising tides of war.

Readers reviews of **Sweetbriar**

•   I love a book that I hate to put down. Sweetbriar held my imagination captive from cover to cover. Its characters are artfully realistic yet dashingly romantic. *Larae*

•   Great book, it stayed with me long after I finished it. Complicated plot, you don't what's going to happen next. *Bev*

•   Excellent plot, characters, bits of humor that gave it a light touch. I cared about the characters and got into the story. *Lorna*

•   Your love scenes gave me the vapors. *Donna*

•   Thoroughly enjoyed Sweetbriar. I liked the historical background and the depth of the characters, both good and bad. *Gene*

•   One of those things that make a good author is their ability to make an unreal character look real. This author is no exception. The story is entertaining and was well told. *Kim*

•   I loved the back and forth over the Atlantic during the early 1800's and getting a sense of the conflicts of the period. The romances pulled me in. I loved the characters and hope to see this as a movie. *Ann*

Prologue

Summer 1804, England

SO IT WAS WAR AGAIN. War with France was nothing new. Its wrath had been almost continuous for more than a hundred years. But the conflict was as inconvenient as the persistent ache of a rotting tooth, throbbing and pulsating, always there. Attaining power again, the younger William Pitt called for an Anglo-Austro-Russian coalition against France to stop Napoleon's insatiable thirst for conquering the continent. So war was as inevitable as the sun rising in the east. And that meant, sooner or later, merchant trade with other countries would be affected. And when trade was hampered, everyone suffered; the importers, the exporters and the multitudes of people who yearned for their merchandise. Yes, war was damned inconvenient.

Fall 1804, England

THIRTEEN YEAR OLD BETH AWAKENED slowly while a vague feeling of depression weighed heavily upon her mind. Listlessly she crawled out of bed, opened the heavy drapes, and encountered a thick misty fog that shrouded the landscape. The summer birds of the past few weeks had flown, for the only sound she heard was the mournful cawing of ravens in the distance.

Suddenly, the full realization of death flooded back upon her. Tears welled up from the hollow pit of her stomach and burned at the back of her eyes. The long awaited joy of a baby brother or sister had mutated into a soul wrenching ache. Her beloved mama was dead. Today they would bury her with the small body of the stillborn baby cradled in her arms.

"I AM THE RESURRECTION AND the life, saith the Lord: he that believeth in Me, though he were dead, yet shall he live: and whosoever liveth and believeth in Me shall never die," the Anglican priest solemnly intoned.

The early morning mist thickened until a cold, drizzling rain engulfed the countryside. Mourners slowly trailed behind the black clad priest and the coffin to the grave site. The bare oak trees were skeletal; the ancient tombstones, like ghostly sentinels, waited to welcome another into their midst. Beth shivered. She had always taken pleasure in coming to the family plot in the spring to place flowers on the graves. Reading the names and dates of long dead ancestors was an amusing pastime for a child. She would never enjoy that task again.

"Lord, Thou hast been our refuge: from one generation to another. Before the mountains were brought forth, or ever the earth and the world were made: Thou art God from everlasting, world without end." Small rivulets of mud from the heaped earth splattered on the coffin and, like the ticking of a clock, slowly tapped the time to eternity.

Chilled to the bone despite the thick black wool of her dress and cloak, Beth tightly clutched her father's hand and felt him quiver. A reserved man, he had no patience with emotional displays, deeming them signs of a weak character. Over the years, when childhood calamities befell, he had always advised Beth to be strong and keep a stiff upper lip. So she stood stoically beside her father. He quivered again. Beth looked up and was stunned to see him silently weeping.

"Forasmuch as it hath pleased almighty God in His great mercy to take unto Himself the soul of our dear sister here departed, we therefore commit her body to the ground." Heavy mud thudded hollowly on the coffin. "Earth to earth, ashes to ashes, dust to dust; in sure and certain hope of the resurrection to eternal life through our Lord Jesus Christ..." The deluge roared down in heavy sheets, drowning out the words of the priest.

Beth wanted him done and everyone gone so she could bury the hyacinth bulbs she'd brought in her pocket. She wanted the delicate beauty of the flowers to adorn her mother's grave each spring.

"The grace of our Lord Jesus Christ, and the love of God, and the fellowship of the Holy Ghost, be with us all evermore."

Mourners paused only briefly in the driving torrent to give condolences to the new widower, then hastened away, black capes billowing in the wind.

Beth quickly buried the bulbs and stood. Her father, staring at the grave, appeared rooted to the ground as solidly as the hundred year old oaks surrounding them. Gently tugging his hand to gain his attention she said, "Come father, we must go. Now that Mama's gone, I'll have to look after you. If we stay much longer, we'll both catch our death." The bleak words lingered in the cold air momentarily then were snatched away by the ghostly hand of the wind.

Fall 1804, America

THE SHIP'S CUTTER BUMPED ALONGSIDE the *Angel Star* and Bradley Anderson clambered aboard, the box that contained his sextant snuggled close to his chest. Exultantly his eyes swept over the decks. The *Angel Star* was a beauty and she was his. She was of a new design. The high rounded bilge and somewhat flared topsides gave a heart shaped look to her midsection. The stem and stern were considerably raked and low sided with a sharp ended hull. This made the deep draft greatest at the heel of the rudder. Forward the draft was half that of the ship's aft end. Being heavily sparred and canvassed put her in a speed class of her own and made her the desire of every merchant captain in America.

Few men received command of a merchant ship at twenty-two years of age and no one could say Bradley Anderson had not earned his place in his father's fleet. From earliest childhood the boy had seized every opportunity to accompany his father to the shipyard and the docks, avidly asking questions of the crewmen and officers. Impatient to embark upon a life at sea, Brad was twelve when he stole away from home and signed on board his first ship as cabin boy. That first voyage lasted eight grueling months, long enough to break a boy or make a man. The youngster who returned home was no longer a child but a young man who clearly knew his course in life. The ensuing years were demanding. Brad was shunned by the common sailors for being the owner's son and considered extra baggage by the officers, even though he labored twice as hard as any man to prove his worth. Captain O'Malley, in trying to break Brad, was ruthless in his demands only to find his young charge had the perseverance of few men O'Malley had encountered before. Slowly a grudging respect grew between the two and finally, over the years, a genuine friendship.

Now, after three arduous years of serving as Quinn O'Malley's first mate, Brad had earned the right to command a ship. He possessed the leadership needed to obtain instantaneous obedience from every man on board, had learned to make coolheaded decisions, and had acquired the hard bargaining skills needed to make a good profit. These were all important qualities for any merchant captain.

But Charles Anderson did not see eye to eye with his son's desire to work at sea and was appalled by his plea to command the new ship. Brad must learn to oversee the business from shore, the older man contended, and outright refused the request.

Flabbergasted by the idea of sailing a desk instead of a ship, Brad determinedly argued his case for hours. He was steadfastly rebuffed. In the end, exasperation flashed like lightning in Brad's stormy gray eyes and he thundered, "From the time I was just a boy I've dedicated my life to learning everything there is to know about commanding a merchant ship. I've worked every job on board and know as much as any gape-tooth old salt alive. Now you want me to throw it all overboard. But the sea is in my blood and by my word, if I don't receive command of a ship from you, I'll take my services elsewhere."

"I won't be threatened," Charles slammed his palms down on his desk, aggravated by his son's obstinate outburst.

Brad responded hotly, "It is not a threat. I mean what I say."

For ten long minutes Charles regarded his stubborn son, too livid to speak. Finally, in a tight voice he growled, "Quinn O'Malley is the best captain I employ and I see he taught you well. You drive a hard bargain because you know I'll not have you work elsewhere. You may have the new ship. But remember, this business will be yours someday and you have the responsibility to learn the administration. You can't pursue your present course forever."

"I know, Dad," Brad said quietly with a self-satisfied smile and crossed his arms over his chest. "But I'm still young. Just give me some time."

Fall 1804, American Frontier

GREED FOR LAND CAUSED ONGOING strife between native Indians and white settlers. Recently a young Sauk brave was imprisoned for murder and a Sauk council of war sent Quashquame and three other chieftains to St. Louis to meet with the American chief and buy their man's freedom.

Upon hearing of their mission, William Henry Harrison, Governor of the Northwest Territories, ordered kegs of whiskey sent out to the Indian faction.

"But sir, this delegation didn't come to negotiate a land treaty. They came to pay reparation to the murdered man's relatives. This is their custom for redeeming their Indian brethren and restoring him to his family," Colonel Michaels explained.

"Listen, Michaels," Harrison stated sharply, "we've desired western expansion since before our war for independence and that desire has escalated since the Louisiana Purchase. The President authorized me to negotiate land treaties with the Indians and that's what I intend to do. Some beads, cloth, blankets, knives, and whiskey are all it takes, especially if they drink plenty of whiskey before we negotiate the treaty."

"But, sir –"

"If they want their murdering red devil back, they must pay in land," barked the governor. "Just keep them whiskeyed up for a few days. That's all we need do to get them to give us the land in exchange for the man's life."

And so, a few days later, the Sauk chieftains agreed to give some land and made their marks on the Treaty of St. Louis. But they didn't realize they were ceding all of the country east of the Mississippi River and south of the waters of the Jeffreon to the American government. That realization came later. Much later.

And did they achieve their goal by relinquishing the land? When Quashquame and his party readied for their journey home, their Indian brother was released from prison, only to be shot dead in the street!

###

Why Do I Use a Pen Name?

Years ago, in 1948 to be exact, Phil and Joan Johnson were expecting the birth of their first baby. Joan wanted a girl she could name Paula Judith. Instead she bore a son and they named him Steven Walter.

Eighteen months later, expecting their second child, Mrs. Johnson was sure she would have a girl she could name Paula Judith. Again a son was born. He was named Paul Phillip.

After three years Joan was pregnant again. She recognized that all the children born to her husband's siblings were boys. She refused to tempt fate and resigned herself to bearing a house full of male children.

Amazingly a daughter was born. Not wanting the confusion of having children named Paul and Paula so close together, they named the girl (me) Teresa Marie.

A few years later, expecting a fourth baby, Joan hoped for a daughter to name Paula Judith. Instead, my brother, Martin Perry arrived.

Unexpectedly, fifteen years after this long saga began, another birth was anticipated. Mom said she had no doubt it would be a girl. She could tell, she said, by how the child was carried in her womb. The favored name, Paula Judith, was resurrected.

My parents didn't consider male names because it wasn't necessary—or so they thought. It took three days for Mom and Dad to decide on the name Kenneth Raymond for my youngest brother.

By writing under the name of Paula Judith Johnson, I gave my mother the daughter she always wanted.